Praise for Diana Pharaoh Francis

RT Magazine Top Pick! *Trace of Magic* (The Diamond City Magic series)

RT Magazine Top Pick! *Edge of Dreams* (The Diamond City Magic series)

"A heck of a ride!"

—Fantasy Literature.com on *Crimson Wind*

". . . Diana Pharaoh Francis has a talent for crafting an intricate world of magic and mobsters. The non-stop action kept me at the edge of my seat, and I absolutely loved the pure grittiness and violence of the story . . ."

—Stacey Brutger, Goodreads review on *Trace of Magic*

"Exciting and different . . . original."

—Curled Up with a Good Book on *Bitter Night*

"*Bitter Night* is not to be missed . . . unusual and ceaselessly entertaining series starter."

—My Bookish Ways

Bell Bridge Books titles from Diana Pharaoh Francis

The Diamond City Magic Novels

Trace of Magic

Edge of Dreams

Whisper of Shadows

Shades of Memory

The Crosspointe Chronicles

The Cipher

The Black Ship

The Turning Tide

The Hollow Crown (coming soon)

The Witchkin Murders

Magicfall
Book 1

by

Diana Pharaoh Francis

Bell Bridge Books

This is a work of fiction. Names, characters, places and incidents are either the products of the author's imagination or are used fictitiously. Any resemblance to actual persons (living or dead), events or locations is entirely coincidental.

Bell Bridge Books
PO BOX 300921
Memphis, TN 38130
Print ISBN: 978-1-61194-952-0

Bell Bridge Books is an Imprint of BelleBooks, Inc.

We at BelleBooks enjoy hearing from readers.
Visit our websites
BelleBooks.com
BellBridgeBooks.com
ImaJinnBooks.com

10 9 8 7 6 5 4 3 2 1

Cover design: Debra Dixon
Interior design: Hank Smith
Photo/Art credits:
Woman (manipulated) © Chaoss | Dreamstime.com
Background (manipulated) © Yuliia Lashyna | Dreamstime.com
Background (manipulated) © Unholyvault | Dreamstime.com

:Lwmj:01:

Dedication

For Viggo, whom I miss terribly, and for Dusty and Sierra. You are always in my heart.

Chapter 1

Kayla

THE SCAVENGE HAD proved more successful than Kayla had expected, and she'd expected a lot. She'd come away with a treasure trove of difficult-to-find foods and spices, prescription and over-the-counter medicines, tampons and pads which brought a premium price, and most important of all, two cartons of cigarettes, three jars of peanut butter, and a stockpile of Mountain Dew, the latter of which she'd have to get later. She was already practically bent double with the weight of the backpack without the soda. It was too bad about the Skittles, but this was a good haul.

Going up into The Deadwood offered the chance to mine houses that hadn't already been picked over by a hundred other scavengers. Mostly because the rest of them liked breathing and so stayed away. Kayla wasn't so burdened with common sense. That, and she carried a gun, several knives, and a couple of magical taser charms. Not to mention she was pretty decent at hand-to-hand. Leftover habits and skills from her life as a cop. She could more than take care of herself against people hiding in dark alleys.

Of course, The Deadwood was filled with a lot more dangerous beings than the ordinary street scum that preyed on pedestrians back before Magicfall. Before the Witchwar. Before the whole world had turned inside out and all the monsters in the closets and under the beds came crawling out of hiding. Back when Kayla was just an ordinary human.

The Witchwar exploded within days of Magicfall—a worldwide eruption of magic that birthed The Deadwood, changed Kayla, and set off an untold number of other bizarre transformations straight out of fairytales and hallucinogenic nightmares. The entire world had been engulfed.

Right smack in the middle of all the chaos, witches leading armies of supernatural warriors and creatures out of myth, legend, and nightmare marched against the human cities that had survived. Humans were like termites eating up the world. They needed to be eradicated like roaches.

The war had gone on for a year or so when the attacks on the cities stopped. It still wasn't clear why. Maybe they figured enough humans had died, or maybe they figured out humans aren't so easy to kill. Over the last couple of years, an uneasy truce had developed between humans and witchkin. Turns out, we needed each other.

Kayla hitched the backpack higher, bending forward to help balance it. Her lips twisted in self-ridicule. How the mighty had fallen. From cop to scavenger. Before the shit had hit the fan, she'd been a detective, a damned good one. Then she'd been infected with magic and game over. Bye bye career, friends, and, worst of all, Ray.

A familiar ache bloomed in her chest. She missed him every day, even after everything he'd said, everything he'd called her, when she quit.

Back then she'd had zero control over herself. Not that she'd improved much since. But quitting the department had been a no-brainer. With the Witchwar and hatred of the supernaturals, she'd have either been lynched when it got out, or else locked up in a zoo somewhere.

Leaving had been the right decision. The only decision. Regretting it didn't change that. And Kayla regretted it with all the fabric of her being.

She pulled her mind from the quagmire of memories and what-ifs that circled her like sharks, chomping down whenever she didn't keep her mind on task. *Focus*, she told herself. *Forget about who you were before. Staying alive today is all that counts.*

The Deadwood lay west of downtown Portland inside the neighborhood that used to be Goose Hollow and extending into the Southwest Hills and Washington Park. When the magic had struck, a sinister black forest had grown up in the blink of an eye. The twisted, gnarled trees grew taller than the houses, and were spaced far enough apart to allow a lot of the buildings to survive. Possessive nettles and vines swayed and wriggled from the trees, growing over most of the houses. The blowtorch hooked to Kayla's belt had convinced them to withdraw and allow her access.

Within the shadowed gloom of The Deadwood, hundreds of denizens lived and hunted. All too often, folks who wandered too close disappeared, never to be heard from again. So people—human and not—avoided the place, which suited Kayla just fine. The untouched houses made the forest a scavenger paradise. If you could stay alive long enough to get out with your haul.

Since Magicfall and then the Witchwar, so many of the comforts of everyday American life had stopped getting made. Sure, the metal infrastructure of the cities had protected them from complete transformation and given birth to the technomages who worked with all sorts of technology, which meant industry could still function. But shipping proved supremely expensive and dangerous, so anything the locals needed either had to be made in Portland, or it had to be scavenged.

Tampons were popular. And chocolate. A lot of foods, really. Jeans, too. And silk. Some enterprising entrepreneur had started a toilet paper factory on the east side, so that wasn't much in demand anymore, but pots and pans were. Medications, cosmetics, spices, CDs and DVDs, olive oil, guns, ammunition, bows, arrows, toys . . . anything that couldn't be obtained without a lot of money or magic.

Most people didn't like going to Spider Island—over where the Willamette had expanded into a giant lake covering West Linn and Oregon City—to buy magic. That's where witches and other supernaturals had set up a bazaar to sell their skills and wares. Humans called it Nuketown, since they'd have liked to nuke the place.

Humans had a love/hate relationship with magic. They liked the benefits, but feared the dangers, not to mention all the mythological creatures besides witches that had crawled out of the woodwork after Magicfall.

They counted the technomages as good guys since they'd fought on the human side in the war and because mages made most electronics work again. People still couldn't live without their cell phones and video games, and it was damned nice to still have working modern hospitals and refrigerators.

Unlike witches, technomages had hard limits to their powers. They worked with industrial magic and couldn't heal or make charms or anything separate from wire, steel, electricity, and computers—or what computers had turned in to, which was an amorphous semi-sentient cloud of information the technomages called The Oracle. Every big city had birthed one. The mages were working on getting them to talk to each other like the old internet.

That made Nuketown necessary and despised all at once. Most humans only went there when desperate, usually preferring to buy from middlemen, a service that Nessa—Kayla's usual buyer for salvage—often performed. A few went for the thrill.

Kayla hitched the pack higher again and dodged around a glass bush. It chimed in the light breeze. It marked the edge of The Deadwood and the return to civilization. She climbed up a bank to the road, using the thick, wiry grass to help pull herself up.

The asphalt had buckled and cracked apart, leaving knee-deep potholes and long trenches. Portland's ubiquitous blackberry vines crawled across the road and sprouted out of the crevices and holes. The city hadn't gotten around to repairing this road yet. Maybe they wouldn't, not with it so close to The Deadwood.

It took her a little over an hour to work her way back to downtown. After that, it got trickier. Fog had rolled in off the river again, smothering sound and sight. The breeze did nothing to dissipate it. Kayla could only see a few feet ahead of herself before the walls of gray nothingness closed in around her. She sighed and turned west.

The tule fogs rolled in once or twice a week. They didn't usually last more than a day. They'd started after Magicfall and didn't seem to coincide with any weather phenomena. It tended to settle maybe a mile wide on either side of the river. As annoying as it could be, Kayla couldn't hate it. It had given her cover more than a few times when the transformation had taken her and she'd no way to hide.

Tonight she had no need. Her shifter form wasn't threatening. She decided to head uphill until she was above the fog and go home for the night. She'd take her scavengings to Nessa in the morning.

A noise from the right sent the hair on the back of her neck prickling. A ring of metal, like a sword being unsheathed, and muffled movement. A loud sound and the tang of something in the air—hot, wet, stony, acrid. She recoiled as it coated the insides of her nose and mouth, feeling caustic.

Kayla's cop genes ignited. She jerked forward a step then made herself stop and retreat. Not her circus, not anymore. She'd walked away from all that. She should leave it alone, whatever was happening.

She took a couple more steps toward home and stopped. *Goddammit. Curiosity killed the cat*, she told herself, then slid the pack from her shoulders, setting it down against a fire hydrant. She glanced around, seeing only cottony fog. Odds were nobody would see her pack and take it. Even if they did . . . there were always more backpacks and more stuff to scavenge.

She drew her .357 semi-auto from her hip holster. All carry laws had been suspended after Magicfall. Mostly because everybody ignored them. The blow-torch bottle bounced against her thigh as she followed the noises.

She moved cautiously, placing each foot carefully to keep from tripping or worse. She nudged up against a curb at the side of the road and stepped up onto the sidewalk. It shuddered and rippled under her feet, and she began to sink. Kayla jumped back onto the solid asphalt. Her boots stuck to the ground. She smelled the acrid stench of her rubber soles melting. *Dammit*. She liked these boots.

Weird spots like this one popped up all the time. They all manifested different properties and none particularly pleasant. The worst part was they could appear anywhere at any time, with no warning. Once reported, technomages would get rid of them, but finding them was usually a matter of stepping into one. Sometimes that was fatal.

She jerked her boots free from where they'd cooled and stuck to the ground, and followed the curb, listening closely. More noise came from the left. Kayla tested the sidewalk and found it solid. For now, anyway.

Taking several quick steps, she scuttled across, finding herself at the top of a flight of steps at the edge of a small park. The muted sounds of running water made her stomach drop. She'd stumbled into Keller Fountain Park.

Taking up the entire block, the ziggurat-shaped fountain for which the park was named had been constructed into the side of a steep hill. On the high side, an angular maze of wading canals channeled water over a mashed-together collection of square-topped pyramids of various heights and sizes. The blocky juts and peaks had always reminded her of an Aztec temple. The different sizes created deep chimney insets in between, some fifteen feet wide and ten feet deep, others a scant five. Water cascaded down each of the flat planes. No little fountains of neatly contained water here.

She shuddered. Her worst nightmare. Now she *really* should leave.

She didn't move.

Kayla drew in a slow breath. Something was wrong here. She could feel it. Her instincts had never let her down before. She wouldn't forgive herself if something awful happened because she was too worried about herself to check it out.

She started down the steps, listening for telltale sounds, trying to hear through the splashing of the fountains.

Then—

Guttural words—not English—spoken in a gravel-filled voice that rumbled through the air like thunder. A cadence to the language, sort of chanting, but nothing musical about it. Weighted silence, heavy and breathless. Movement. A rippling and clutching in the fog. A red glow washing outward, turning the fog bloody.

Magic.

The wave of power hit Kayla like a club and sent her sprawling onto the shallow steps. The hard concrete cut into her back and legs.

She lay still a long moment, her head reeling from where she'd hit it on the cement. *Perfect.* Carefully she examined the sudden lump on the back of her skull with the fingers of her left hand. At least her ponytail had kept the blow from knocking her out. She still clutched her gun in her other hand. Old habits died hard.

She firmed her grip and sat up, glancing down at herself. A shiny white powder covered her clothing and the ground all around. Kayla stood, dusting herself off with one hand. The powder clung to her skin and clothing.

She licked her lips. Fine grit coated her tongue. It tasted like vinegar and something putrid. Worse than the air before the spell. She grimaced and spit. If her fall hadn't already alerted whoever had set that spell, a little spitting wouldn't give her away.

The sour grains clung to her mouth and then seemed to absorb into her skin. That couldn't be good. She resisted the urge to try dusting herself off again. She didn't need to give the stuff more opportunity to infect her, whatever it was. On the positive side, she hadn't broken out in boils and weeping sores. That was good.

She resumed her descent to the bottom of the fountains. Gray cement platforms layered over each other like giant slices of bread stacked ten or so feet back from the angular, red fountain walls. Between, a patchwork of rectangular pools collected water.

The splashing of the fountain covered any sounds there might have been. Holding her gun ready, Kayla walked closer, heading for the central platform, knowing instinctively that it was the best place in the park to cast a spell. Her feet found the first of the stacked cement sheets. Three others were layered on the sides and in front of the base platform. She stopped again to listen, breathing silently. Still nothing.

Adrenaline thrummed through her veins. She stepped up on the left platform and then to the highest central platform. She expected to find a spell circle like the kind used by witches, but as she stepped up, she found only cement coated in a sheet of silvery-white powder.

She circled the platform, angling inward until she came to the middle. Nothing. What was she missing?

Her brows furrowed. Maybe someone had used an amulet or charm? A hex? Kayla didn't know enough about magic to make a decent guess.

A thought struck her, and she gritted her teeth. Son of a bitch. Of course. Things couldn't just be simple, could they?

She crossed to the edge of the platform where it jutted several feet above the catch pools and squatted down. She could only see a foot or two out into the fog. A scum of white powder floated across the top of the otherwise clear water, disguising the mortared river rock bottom.

Kayla rubbed her hand over her mouth. Was she really considering jumping in? This wasn't her problem, and anyway, who knew what *this* even was? Nobody would thank her for getting involved. And if she went into the water—

She could only hold off a transformation for so long once she got wet. If she dried quickly, she could keep it from happening, but wading into water? Risky. Too fucking risky *and* stupid.

Kayla straightened and turned away from the water and then stopped. Instinct fought against instinct. The need to protect herself wrestled with the need to serve and protect the people of the city. Being a cop was in her DNA, and leaving the force hadn't changed that. God, could she be any more fucked up?

Don't tempt fate, she admonished herself. *The universe never refuses that kind of challenge.*

She pivoted back around. The water wasn't deep. Mid-calf, maybe to her knees. That wasn't so much. She could handle it, no problem.

In your dreams, came the mocking voice of reality in her head.

"No one will see with the fog," she said out loud, her voice paper thin, but steady with purpose. Her heart, her soul, had already decided. Time for her brain to get with the program.

She gave a little hop and splashed down into the pool.

Chapter 2

Kayla

COOL WATER SPLASHED up her thighs as Kayla landed in the water. It soaked through her pants and filled her boots, settling just above her knees. At only five foot four inches, she should have expected that. The moment the water kissed her skin, she felt the transformation trying to start. She clamped down on it, bending all her will to keeping the change from happening. She couldn't hold long. A minute. Maybe two.

Quickly she waded through the pool to the base of the waterfall. The spray from the water and fog beaded on her ball cap and bathed her face. Deep inside, she felt a quiver run through her. *Crap. Not yet.*

Putting all her strength of will into holding her shape, Kayla examined the waterfall in front of her. Nothing seemed out of the ordinary. But the sound seemed off. Uneven.

She moved through the fog inside the shallow alcove before her, only to stop cold when she came up against the wide vertical plane of the central fall, red planes of stone jutting out on either side. No water fell over it. Instead, three bodies hung pinned like specimens to the wall, the mutilated corpses arranged as part of a grisly ritual.

She'd seen everything she needed to. Now to get the hell out of the water.

Kayla backed away, flinging herself up onto one of the cement platforms. She scrabbled at her neck to draw out her necklace. On it hung an amulet. She invoked it, feeling it heat under her hand. Brilliant yellow light streamed out from between her fingers, and then desert heat washed over her. Instantly she was dry.

She waited. Sometimes the transformation was too far along and getting dry didn't matter. The ripples inside her increased, wriggling like panicked eels. She clenched her hand on the amulet, the edges of the brass sun disk digging into her palm. She made herself breathe slowly, gritting her teeth and clenching her entire body. *Please don't shift, please don't shift, please don't shift.*

The words tumbled over one another in her brain. She pressed down on the expanding ripples inside her. She felt the battle between what she was and what she wanted to be. But getting dry had robbed her transformation of its strength, and at last she felt a *give*, like shoving a car over a curb.

She lay still, panting as if she'd been running uphill in mud. Her heart slowed, and the adrenaline pounding in her veins drained away. She became aware that she was still clutching her gun and the amulet in her hands. She tucked the latter back beneath her shirt and then rolled over, rising into a crouch. Her ears strained to sort through the sounds of the rushing water.

Nothing.

Whoever had committed the murders she'd just discovered seemed to be gone. Her mind started rolling over her next steps to investigate, and she caught herself up short. Not her. Still not her circus.

Sighing, she stood. God but she missed the work. She'd been damned good at it, too. But if she'd stayed on the force—

Sooner or later her brothers and sisters in blue would have found out and then the shit would have hit the fan. Big time.

The brass would have kicked her out on her ass, and her fellow cops would either have despised her or felt sorry for her. That is, if they decided not to hunt her down and put a bullet in her head, all in the name of cleaning up the city.

At least she still had some dignity and self-respect, not to mention her life. She planned to keep it that way, come hell or high water. Her mouth twisted. Or any water at all. One of these days she'd get a handle on controlling the transformation and then maybe she could go back. Nobody needed to know about her little quirk, and they needed people. Word was the thin blue line was *very* thin these days.

But only if and when she wouldn't transform every time it started raining.

All the same, she couldn't help wondering—who had cast the spell? What was it for? And were they gone or lurking around?

The last question she should have asked herself before hightailing it out of the water, but she hadn't been thinking then. All she'd wanted to do then was stop her transformation at all costs.

She shook her head. She was nearly invulnerable in her other form—at least when it came to normal weapons like guns or knives or even explosives. It would have been smarter to let it happen, as much as she hated it. The fog would have hidden her from anyone more than a few steps away. Then again, it was hiding her from anybody wanting to use her for target practice now. Of course, a witch could just blow away the fog and incinerate her where she stood, which meant she was damned lucky to still be alive.

Not wanting to push her luck, she retraced her steps back to her backpack. She didn't need to get involved by reporting the murders. The fog would lift, someone would notice, and there'd be an investigation.

If the evidence wasn't destroyed by then.

"Shit."

She bent and pulled her phone out of the strap pocket of the backpack. It was an older model—a clamshell style she'd found while scavenging. Powered by technomagic, it worked fine and was sturdier than a touchscreen phone.

She flipped it open and tapped in a number from memory. She wasn't likely to ever forget it. Hopefully it hadn't changed.

Ray picked up on the second ring. "Garza here."

An ache of pain and regret flashed through Kayla. She'd missed his voice. His humor. His call-it-like-it-is attitude. Ray had been the best friend she'd ever had. She'd trusted him with her life, and he'd trusted her with his. Tears burned her eyes, and she blinked to clear them. Now was not the time. She set the pain aside to deal with later.

"Hey, Ray. Long time."

Seconds ticked past. "Reese?"

"It's me."

Another silence. "What the hell do you want?"

Kayla cringed at the animosity dripping from his voice. "I got a murder for you. Three murders, actually."

His voice shifted into cool professionalism. "Where? Who?"

"Keller Fountain, downtown. Don't know the victims, didn't see the perpetrator. Whoever it was seems to have fled the scene." She paused. "Someone cast a spell. I got hit in the wash. There's white dust everywhere. Absorbs right into the skin. No idea what it does."

Kayla could tell by his distracted voice that he was writing notes. "How long ago?"

"Maybe fifteen minutes."

A disgusted noise. "And it took you this long to call?"

She didn't answer since he wasn't really looking for one, and he wouldn't like the one he got if she did.

"All right. I'm sending a hazmat crew to clear the scene. Where are you?"

"A little ways up Southwest Third."

"Get back to the park. Hazmat will need to clear you, too. And Reese? Stay out of the scene, and don't even think about disappearing before I get there."

"I was already in the scene. Anyway, *I* called *you*," she said. "Why would I do that if I was just going to ditch?"

"Maybe because your calling card is leaving when the going gets tough."

He hung up before Kayla could respond. She glared at her phone. *Asshole.* What the hell did he know? He had no idea what it had done to her to quit the force, to quit their partnership. Being a cop had meant her entire life.

She tried to ignore the hurt that dug into her with sharp barbs, but tears burned in her eyes. To be fair, he didn't know because she hadn't told him, but he hadn't trusted that she'd had a good reason, either.

She grabbed her pack and carried it across the street to Keller Auditorium. The fog made it impossible to see more than a foot or two ahead of her, and she nearly ran into one of the slender white pillars holding up the high portico in front of the building. She dropped her pack against its base and found herself pacing around it as she waited for the hazmat team and Ray to show up.

Did she really want to do this? See Ray? Get in the middle of an investigation? Just talking to her old partner had opened a vault of painful memories and regrets. Seeing him face-to-face was going to be infinitely worse.

As the minutes passed, it was all she could do to not walk away. Only her unwillingness to fulfill Ray's bitter accusation kept her there.

Why do you even care? she asked herself. *You made your choice. Be a big girl and deal with it.*

Even with the stern pep talk, the siren signaling the arrival of the hazmat crew twisted her stomach into a knot. Then another thought occurred to her, sending chills running over her skin.

They'd want to wash her down. The longest she'd ever been able to stave off a transformation when totally submerged was just over a minute, which was why she no longer took showers and lived on sponge baths. Being tired, hungry, and seriously stressed would only speed the transformation if they hosed her down.

She grabbed her backpack. Not a chance. She was *not* gonna let that happen.

Chapter 3

Ray

RAY HUNG UP THE phone and stared, unseeing, down at his notes. Of all the people he'd imagined might be on the other end of the phone line, Kayla had been the last. Hell, she hadn't even been on the list. He hadn't expected to hear from her ever again, not after the way they'd ended things.

He ran his hands through his hair. He hadn't believed it when she said she was quitting the force. It was unthinkable. At first he'd laughed, but then she'd packed her stuff, and it got real.

He'd lost it. He'd said things he shouldn't have. He'd felt so betrayed. For himself and for the city. How could she walk away right when everything had gone to hell? Magic everywhere had turned the world inside out, and a lot of cops had been lost to attacks by monsters, or just caught in the middle of a magic catastrophe.

Kayla had known how badly they needed her. She'd always claimed to have been born to be a cop, and then she'd walked out when the force needed her most. When *he* needed her most. The one person he trusted. The one person he might have been able to tell he'd developed magical powers. She wouldn't have condemned him.

He snarled silently. *If* she'd stuck around.

Now four years later and he had a chance to see her face-to-face again. His hands clenched even as his pulse pounded.

After that last day, he'd waited for her to come to her senses. To call him. To come back. She never did.

Instead, she practically became a ghost. She'd moved out of her apartment and vanished. After a few months of licking his wounds, he'd looked for her, hoping to get some answers. Nothing. He'd started to be afraid she'd left the city, or worse, but then about a year later he'd seen her crossing the street in his rearview mirror. She'd been gone by the time he turned around. He'd begun to think he'd imagined her when he found her again, four months later. This time he'd followed her.

He'd kept his distance to keep her from noticing him.

Gone was the spit-and-shine woman he remembered. Instead of sharp, crisp creases in her shirt and pants, she wore ragged jeans, battered boots, an old army jacket, and a Blazers ball cap that looked as though it had been run

11

over. No makeup, and she'd scraped her dark hair up into a ponytail. The rest of her body was muscular, but the sharp cut of her cheekbones suggested she wasn't eating as much as she should. She carried a heavy backpack with an assortment of weapons attached to her belt.

She stopped at a taco cart, and her gaze roved warily as if she anticipated danger. Her body seemed tense, as though she was coiled to run or fight. After handing over her money, she'd taken her food and given the vendor a fleeting smile, saying something that made him laugh, before moving on.

After that, she stopped at a two-story brick building on the corner of SW 3rd and Salmon just catty corner to the old courthouse. A multitude of thorny vines hanging to the sidewalk in thick curtains shrouded the building. A sandwich board on the corner said "Nessa's." It was a shop for scavenged goods, magical objects, and locally produced items.

Kayla disappeared inside. Ray'd waited, ignoring calls on his cell until she emerged several hours later, her pack considerably lighter. He'd lost her shortly after that when one of the tule fogs rolled in and he could barely see more than a few feet in front of himself.

He'd seen her a few times since, and once even started to approach her before thinking better of it. He still felt raw when it came to Kayla. She should have come back, should have explained. As her partner, he had a right to at least to know why she'd left him high and dry right when the world was going to hell. Maybe tonight he'd get the answer.

Ray pulled himself back to the here and now. *Don't get your hopes up*, he warned himself. *She probably ran off as soon as she hung up. Probably a good thing, too. You're finally starting to get past that shit.* It was true. He'd begun going days and even weeks without thinking about her.

And if she hadn't run? Ray didn't let himself consider how his entire body clenched at the thought. He didn't know if it was hope, anticipation, or fury.

He picked up his phone to call for a hazmat crew and paused. He checked the caller I.D., copying the number into his notebook, and saving it into his contacts. If Kayla disappeared, at least he'd have a way to track her down. *For the case*, he told himself unconvincingly.

Ray made the call to hazmat, and then gathered his things, urgency biting his ass. How long would she wait?

"What's up, Garza?" Sharon Dix swiveled her chair to watch him.

He eyed her. She was a decent detective. Cold, calculated, and smart. She wasn't well-liked. She had the personality of a cheese grater and tended to focus on one trail and forget to look down the others.

"Got a murder call."

She perked up. "Who? Where?"

"Don't know who. Keller Fountain."

He'd kept walking, but now she stood, reaching for her suit jacket.

"I'll come with."

He scowled. "Don't bother. Hazmat has to clear the scene first. Magic was involved."

Instead of discouraging her, the information seemed to pique her interest. "What kind of spells?"

"No idea yet."

Sharon donned her jacket and reached for her purse. Ray frowned.

"I can handle this. Work your own cases."

She cast an assessing look at him. "My load is light right now."

"Something could come in." And likely would. The force was spread thin. Mostly detectives took uniforms or trainees with them to crime scenes these days. There weren't enough detectives available to waste one by partnering up.

"Something might, but it hasn't yet, and I don't feel like fucking with paperwork right now." She frowned at him. "Why don't you want me to come along?"

Ray's lips peeled back in a semblance of a smile. "Doesn't matter to me, so long as you remember whose case it is."

"I'm sure if I forget, you'll remind me," she said, sailing past him toward the stairs.

Ray followed, eyeing her balefully. Sharon Dix wasn't beautiful by any stretch. She had a nice enough body, if a little on the boney side, but her prominent front teeth made him think of a rabid beaver every time he looked at her. Add a weak chin, and she looked as though she couldn't be trusted, which she couldn't.

Dix didn't care what she had to do to get ahead. Loyalty meant nothing to her. If she needed or wanted something from someone, she'd suck up to them like a whore on her knees until she got what she wanted. Even if there had been enough detectives in the department to partner up, she'd still work solo. Nobody wanted to get stuck with her. Especially Ray, especially tonight.

They picked up their car in the parking garage. It was a pre-Magicfall blue-and-white, but the engine had been replaced with a magical construct. It still operated the same way, but was dead quiet and required no fuel.

Ray got behind the wheel and backed out. As they pulled onto the street, he flipped on the light bar on top of the roof. Sharon turned to face him.

"So, who called in the murder?"

"Someone stumbled on the scene."

"Hmmm."

Ray grimaced. "I know the witness. She didn't call in her own crime."

"Are you sure?"

He wasn't sure of much anymore, Kayla least of all. But she wouldn't commit murder and call it in. She knew protocols and investigations. She'd know reporting the crime made her a suspect. She wouldn't be that stupid.

"I'm sure," he said with finality.

Sharon nodded. After a moment she spoke again. "I'll take the case."

"I told you it's mine."

She waved dismissively. "You have a conflict of interest, knowing the discovery witness."

He cast her a sideways look. "Not a problem."

"Brass might not see it that way."

Was that a threat? If so, she didn't know shit about him because she'd only succeeded in pissing him off more than he already was.

"Shove off, Dix. It's my damned case, and I'll thank you to keep your hands to yourself."

"Touchy."

Ray gritted his teeth but didn't reply. His silence didn't deter his companion.

"What's the deal? I just offered you a gift. Why aren't you grabbing it with both hands?"

"Maybe I don't need or want your gifts." He lifted his hands and made air quotes around the last word.

"What's that supposed to mean?"

"It means you don't give gifts. Everything you do is with an eye toward what you can get out of it," Ray said baldly.

"Nothing wrong with ambition."

"You leave too many bodies in your wake. I'm not interested in being one of them."

"I'm a woman in a job that favors men. If I don't look after myself, who will?"

"So why do you want *this* case?"

She shrugged. "No particular reason."

Ray cast a sidelong look her. "Right."

Dix smiled in an entirely unfriendly way. "The way you came out of your office like your ass was on fire, I knew it had to be juicy. And juicy cases get a detective noticed by people who count. Word is they're thinking of opening a new division, and I plan to head it up. I've got a good record and I've passed all the tests, but a little attention on me would seal the deal."

Ray had heard the rumors of a new division, too. Whatever was in the works was top secret, but word was the mayor, city council, and the union were all a hundred percent behind it. Which meant it was going to be a serious clusterfuck. Dix was welcome to it. Thank God he wouldn't have to work under her.

"Sorry to disappoint, but you're wrong about the case. Far as I know, it's your basic run-of-the-mill homicide."

"All the same, I want to see for myself," she said with an arch tone that said she didn't believe a word he said.

"Suit yourself. Just stay the hell out my way."

RAY AND DIX WERE stationed out of the temporary headquarters building at the old Portland campus of Linfield College. It wasn't far from Keller Fountain Park. He shot over to Burnside and up to Southwest 3rd, passing Nellie's on the way.

They ran into the thick bank of fog a couple blocks past the defunct Highway 405. Ray slowed, biting back frustration. The thick soup would add a good ten minutes or more to his travel time. Ten minutes or more for Kayla to disappear.

He reached for the shield button on the dash, but Dix beat him to it. A wave of spiderwebbing lavender magic rippled across the exterior of the car and expanded, forming a cocoon about three feet away. It would protect them from attacks and accidents. Ray sped up. He felt Dix's eyes on him.

"Like I said . . . juicy," she said smugly.

He cast an annoyed look at her. Her eyes opened wider in feigned innocence.

"What? It's obvious you're in a hurry to get on scene. You don't have to be a detective to see that. So, what makes this case so special?"

"You've got something in your teeth," he told her.

She reached into her purse for a tissue, scrubbing at her teeth with it. "Is it gone?"

Since she'd never had anything in her teeth, the nonexistent bit of lettuce was gone.

"Sure," Ray said with barely a glance at her.

She made a sound and rubbed at her teeth again, using the tissue to polish each one individually. He shook his head. *Women.* At least she'd shut up.

He made himself slow down again when they deflected off something. He caught a glimpse of fur and gray skin as he veered up onto the sidewalk and bounced off the stump of a parking meter.

"Jesus Christ! Watch where you're going!" Dix shrieked as her head knocked against her window. She braced her hands on the dash. "What the hell is wrong with you?"

Ray didn't bother telling her about the creature he'd run into. Luckily the shield had been up. The damned things were beyond expensive and had to be recharged after eight hours of use, but damn, they were worth every penny the department had spent. He only wished the brass would budget in personal shields.

He backed up and then turned to get back onto the road. He slowed a little—but only to make sure he didn't miss the turn onto 3rd Street, then he sped up again.

He went back to the last time he'd talked to Kayla. *Talked.* He'd ranted and shouted like a madman. He wasn't proud of it. His shock and panic at her announcement had driven him to say unforgivable things. Loudly and with a lot of swearing. He'd beaten her with his words. It hadn't made him feel better then, and the memory disgusted him now. A man didn't lose himself like that. In the end he'd told her he never wanted to see her again, and until her call today, she'd given him exactly what he asked for.

Except he didn't want that. Did he? Just thinking about that day cut him to the bone, the betrayal and hurt just as potent now as then. He'd been lying to himself that he'd gotten past her. His teeth clenched, his jaw knotting. If he wanted answers, he'd have to control his anger. And once he got the answers, what then? Would he walk away? Put her in the rearview forever?

He didn't know. What he *did* know is that he wanted to see her now, which meant arriving before she ghosted away.

The hazmat team had already deployed by the time he pulled up. Ray shut off the car, leaving the red-and-blue emergency lights flashing. He stepped out, turning to look for Kayla, but the fog barely let him see Dix on the other side of the vehicle.

He walked to the back of the open hazmat van to see if they'd seen her. He found Zach Logan, a technomage.

"Hey, Logan. What do you have for me?" Ray offered his hand.

The other man turned. A couple inches taller than Ray, with broad shoulders and a narrow waist, he looked like a surfer. A clip held his long blond hair away from his face. He shook Ray's hand.

"Hey, Ray. Definitely got magic here. A decently powerful spell was cast. Left behind a hell of a residue." He pointed at the flecks of dust floating in the air. "That's everywhere. Seems benign, but I won't know for sure until I can examine the scene. Techs are putting up the fog-killers. Should be ready to go soon. One other thing. The casting wasn't technomagic. I can clean it up, but a witch would be able to tell us more."

Witches weren't allowed on the force. They were barely tolerated in the city. Ray had argued in the past for having one on staff for just this sort of event, but he was always shot down. Too risky. The unofficial motto in any copshop was: the only good witch was a dead witch. All the same, a murder that involved a major magic spell cast in downtown would certainly get brass approval to bring in a consulting witch.

"Let's see what the scene can tell us first," Ray said. "Have you seen the witness who called it in?"

Logan hadn't been around before Magicfall. He'd never met Kayla. The technomage shook his head, and at that moment, the fog-killers kicked on. In moments, the park cleared.

Ray quickly took in the scene. The white dust lay in a thin veil over everything, except where footsteps had scuffed it. The water from one of the broad fallways had somehow been diverted. In its place hung three bodies—three non-human bodies—surrounded by intricate ritual markings.

"Thought you said this was a homicide?" Dix demanded, hands on her hips as she looked over the park.

"That's right."

"Then where's the body? The *human* body," she added. "Because those things sure as hell aren't any of our business," she declared, hooking her thumb at the dead creatures.

"This crime isn't any of *your* business either way," Ray said caustically.

"It isn't any of your business either. We're wasting our time. Let Logan and his team figure out what happened."

"Go ahead and leave," Ray said. "Nobody wants you here."

She whipped around, shooting him a venomous look. "Fuck off, Garza."

"Sorry it's not juicy enough for you." He looked at Logan. "I'm going to find my witness. Let me know when I can go down there." He tipped his head toward the fountain.

The technomage's brow furrowed. He leaned forward, his voice dropping. "She's a bitch, but she's right. Animal control is supposed to handle this sort of thing."

"Not today."

Ray turned and crossed the street blindly, heading for Keller Auditorium. He'd start looking for Kayla there. He narrowly avoided running into one of the pillars out front. He stepped around it.

"Kayla?"

He heard a sound suspiciously like a sigh. "Here."

She stepped out of the fog, putting her within arm's reach. It was all he could do to not snatch her arm so she couldn't run off.

He drank her in. She looked much the same as she did when he'd followed her the first time. Jeans, tee shirt, a light jacket. She'd drawn her hair up in a messy ponytail. Dirt smudged her cheeks and forehead. A small scrape marred her chin. His gaze locked with hers. Shadows moved inside her eyes. Secrets.

Swallowing a wash of feeling he didn't want to examine too closely, Ray hooked his thumbs in his front pockets and thrust out his chin.

"You told me this was a murder," he said, his lip curling.

She blinked at him, scowling, then looked toward the fountain. "There were three bodies."

"Non-human."

Her head jerked back. Her eyes widened. "So what? They're still people."

He shook his head, falling back on department policy. "We don't have the manpower to watch out for witchkin. They can police themselves."

"You don't think they deserve justice?"

"I think this is a magical crime, and without a human involved, it falls out of my jurisdiction."

"That's bullshit."

The accusation and condemnation in her voice put his hackles up. "We don't have a choice. There are only so many of us to go around, and we can't spend time on cases that fall outside our mission."

"Your mission?"

"To protect and to serve. Humans."

"But the city is far more than humans now. You don't think they deserve to be protected? Or are they just disposable?" Color climbed into her cheeks, and her eyes snapped fire.

"They have to take care of themselves, unless and until they harm a human. Then we step in."

It was a cold, hard truth. It didn't sit well with Ray, either, but he understood it. After the Magicfall when beings called the Guardians unleashed a tsunami of wild magic on the world in order to stop human encroachment and give strength to the magical denizens of the world, the world had turned inside out. Life as everyone knew it ended.

Whatever the wild magic touched it changed. Enchanted forests, glass mountains, endless fields of tornados, fathomless depths, and more suddenly erupted. Worse were the mutations. Humans who'd been touched by magic had changed into creatures of myth and fairytale, some more bizarre than others. Ray had developed witch powers, turning him witchkin, a fact he'd sell his soul to change. Humans hated all witchkin—those tainted by magic—except for the technomages who protected the city. The resentment, suspicion, and hate ran deep. Even in Portland, the proud home of all things weird, witchkin weren't welcome.

Kayla shook her head and muttered something.

"What did you say?"

She leveled her gaze at him. "I said, good thing I got out when I did. How can you stomach that crap?"

Ray jerked like she'd struck him. Fury ignited. "Maybe if you hadn't left, things might be different, so you can take your holier-than-thou attitude and shove it up your ass sideways."

Her lips tightened, and her eyes narrowed, but she didn't reply. That only pissed him off more. Why couldn't she just speak her damned mind for once?

"Why did you even call me anyway?"

"Because there was a ritual murder, and I thought we used to be friends!" The angry words exploded.

"Friends? Are you kidding me? You walked out on me, and I haven't heard a word from you since? Does that sound like friendship?" He leaned in. "If that's you being my friend, then no thanks. Next time, call somebody else. We were *never* friends."

She recoiled, staring at him wide-eyed and wounded. Instantly he felt a pang of regret. Then an indifferent mask fell across her expression. Or maybe it wasn't a mask. Maybe that was the real her and her initial reaction had been the fake. He despised himself for wondering, for caring that he might have hurt her.

"I take it you don't want to hear what happened, then?" Her voice had turned distant and cold.

"Wrong." He fished a notebook out of his pocket. That magic spell would require investigation. "Walk me through what happened."

She glared, but then folded her arms and told her story. He took down notes, not asking any questions until the end. She had cop recall and gave him all the salient points.

"So, you didn't feel any ill effects from the powder?"

"No."

"And you didn't see who cast the spell?"

"No. Just that there wasn't a witch circle."

He nodded. "Did you see any signs of anybody else in the area?"

She shook her head. "Nobody. Human or otherwise," she added acidly.

His jaw hardened. "Did you find that odd? It's downtown Portland. It's never deserted."

She shrugged. "It's foggy. Could be a ton of people around for all I know."

"You didn't see any people at all?" He checked his watch. "It's barely two o'clock in the afternoon."

"People?" she echoed. "Are you referring to just humans or *all* people?"

He made a growling sound. "Dammit, Kayla. You know what I mean."

Her chin lifted. "I don't think I do. I mean, you don't even have a homicide here, what with three bodies that don't qualify under police policy."

"It's not police policy. It's guidance handed down by the mayor and the city council."

"How can you follow it? You know witchkin aren't animals. They are people, just like us."

"Not just like us," he said, though his heart wasn't in the argument. He might not like magic—in fact he hated it with every fiber of his being—but that didn't mean the witchkin weren't people. Their magic wasn't their fault. It wasn't anybody's fault. It was a damned curse.

The look Kayla turned on him dripped disgust. "I never thought I'd hear something as shitty as that from you."

"Yeah? Well I never thought you'd bail on the job. Or leave me high and dry without a partner. I guess we're both disappointed. Sucks, doesn't it?"

Satisfaction burned through him when he saw her flinch. At least it was *some* goddamned reaction.

"Are we done?" she asked coldly.

"I want hazmat to check you out," he said, snapping his notebook shut. "See if there's any evidence of the spell or its effects on you."

"This isn't mage magic. The hazmat technomage isn't going to be able to tell anything," she said in a flat voice that lacked any emotion.

She was right. His stomach tightened in unexpected concern. What was the powder she'd absorbed doing to her even now, standing here in front of him while he just watched? His concern irritated him.

God but he was mind-fucked when it came to Kayla. Partners on the force shared a deep relationship based on a level of trust that most marriages didn't achieve. Partners served as lifelines, confessors, moral supports, and they were always there to wade through the deep shit with you and make sure you got out alive.

Ray had depended on her. Trusted her with everything. He hadn't trusted anybody since. He doubted he ever would. If his partner of three years could abandon him so easily, then anybody could betray him. Never again. Especially now that he had a secret that, if exposed, would mean losing his job, his friends, his family, and everything else he cared about.

"We'll get you checked out by a witch," he said finally, deciding that was the logical next step in investigating the spell and had nothing to do with making sure she was safe.

She rolled her eyes in that infuriating way she had. "I can take care of myself."

"Can you?"

Her brow furrowed. "What's that supposed to mean?"

"It means you look like you're homeless and haven't eaten in a couple of days."

"Careful. I might start thinking you give a shit."

"Don't jump to conclusions. It's just an observation."

She nodded. "Don't worry. You made yourself clear four years ago. I'm not likely to forget."

"I shouldn't have said those things. Not that way," he admitted roughly.

Again the flush. She looked away. "Doesn't matter. That was then. This is now. After today, you won't have to see me again. Consider this a bad dream."

"Fucking nightmare," he agreed, then reached for her arm intending to drag her to the hazmat van if necessary. She deftly sidestepped, putting her hands up as if to push him away.

"What the hell, Garza? You know better. Do you want this stuff on you, too?"

Rookie stupid mistake. Damned fool. He was losing his mind. Why did she have that effect on him?

Ray just gestured for her to walk ahead of him. "Let's get you checked out."

"I said I'm fine."

"That powder is evidence. That means you're evidence, not to mention a public hazard if that stuff is dangerous. So get your ass across the street."

"You always were bossy. I guess some things never change."

Ray quickly fell in behind her as she started across the street.

Kayla was wrong. She'd changed. He'd changed. The world had gone batshit crazy, and everybody was fucked up. Leave it to him to be most fucked up of all.

Chapter 4

Ray

BACK AT THE HAZMAT van, Ray turned Kayla over to Logan. "Check her out. See what you can about the powder she absorbed. How long before you can clear the scene?"

"Techs are taking samples. I should be able to neutralize any lingering magic." As he spoke, Logan's gaze fixed on Kayla. He stretched out a hand, protected by spelled gloves. "Zach Logan."

She looked at his hand for a long moment, then took it. "Kayla Reese."

"So you're the witness," Logan said.

"So I am."

He smiled, teeth white against his tanned skin. Kayla smiled back. Ray had an inexplicable urge to punch Logan in the head.

"What can you tell me about the magic that happened here?" Logan asked.

"Not much. I heard some noises, some words I didn't understand, and then *Wham!* I got hit in the wash. Are you going to take my clothes?"

Logan eyed her up and down. "I don't think so. The techs have collected samples of the powder. Right now, I want to neutralize the dust, at least externally. I can do that much. You'll have to see a witch about what it does. But hey, at least it hasn't turned you into a frog. That's got to count for something, right?"

Kayla smiled ruefully. "I bet your cup is always half full."

He shook his head and grinned cheerfully. "Nah. My cup's always overflowing." He winked. "Give me a second to collect what I need."

The technomage climbed up inside the van, and Ray could hear rummaging. A moment later Logan returned carrying a mesh net made of gold wires.

"No need to be afraid. The mesh will cocoon you for a few seconds and then it will open. I'll run a spell through it to burn out any active magic. It shouldn't hurt."

A flash of unease ran across Kayla's face and then was gone. So—it appeared that as much as she defended the magical denizens of the city, she also feared them, or at least their magic. Good. At least she wasn't complaisant. She needed to have a healthy respect for the dangers of magic.

Logan shook the pliable metal blanket out onto the ground. "Step into the middle," he told Kayla.

She eyed it, and then sighed and went to stand where he directed.

"Now, I'm going to close it up around you and invoke the spell. Again, it shouldn't hurt, and I'll be able to free you in about a minute. Okay?"

"This your witness?"

Ray had forgotten Dix. She came up beside him and scrutinized Kayla. "That's right."

She flicked on the flashlight she carried and shined it on Kayla's face. "Wait a minute. I know you," Dix said, eyes narrowing as she examined Kayla, who squinted and lifted her hand to shade her eyes.

"What the hell is your damage?" she demanded. "Get that fucking light out of my face."

Dix didn't move. "You're Kayla Reese," she said slowly, then a smug, knowing smile spread over her face as she turned to Ray. "I get it now. *She's* why you were in such a rush to get out here."

He didn't bother to deny it. "You're a helluva detective, Dix. You deserve a commendation."

His sarcasm didn't faze her. "Maybe this case is juicier than I thought." She looked like the proverbial cat with the cream.

"Quiet now," Logan said, and then to Kayla, "Relax. You'll feel a little warmth, but that's about it."

"You're sure?" Ray asked before he could stop himself.

"What's the matter? Hoping I'd fry like a bug in a zapper?" Kayla asked.

He shrugged. "You did give me your statement. I guess it's true I don't have much use for you anymore."

Logan shot him a startled look and then turned back to Kayla. "I, however, would be devastated if any little part of you got damaged." He put a dramatic hand over his heart. "I would be forever distressed if I could not have the pleasure of knowing you better."

Kayla's lips twitched. "Do you plan to know me better?"

Logan grinned at her. "Most definitely."

"Whether I like it or not?"

"How could you not like it? I'm handsome, intelligent, charming, funny, and talented."

"You're full of yourself, anyway. Dare I ask what sorts of talents you have?"

He waggled his eyebrows up and down. "*That* is something for you to discover. I promise you will not regret the effort."

Dix rolled her eyes. "Why don't the two of you get a room, already."

Ray's teeth clamped together. He shoved his hands into his pockets. Logan was *flirting* with Kayla, and she was flirting back. The urge to punch the technomage came back, and it was all Ray could do to hold himself still.

"Can we get on with it?" he said brusquely. "We don't have all day to waste."

Logan tossed him a casual salute. "Yessir." He looked at Kayla. "Are you ready?"

"As I'll ever be."

"Don't worry. I'll be gentle."

Kayla didn't answer. She stood stiffly, her feet wide as if bracing herself against a hard wind.

Logan peeled off his gloves and tossed them into a decontamination canister. A puff of smoke, and the smell of summer roses wafted through the air. That was new. Last time it had been freshly baked chocolate chip cookies. Before that it had been an ocean breeze, and Ray remembered another time it was mowed grass. Logan liked to switch things up and didn't mind wasting his efforts on silly things.

The technomage stood back and closed his eyes. He held his hands out, palms down. Ray felt magic surge. The hairs on his body prickled, and ozone filled the air. Logan opened his eyes, and yellow sparks danced in his irises. Crackling power enveloped him, turning him nearly incandescent. The bastard was powerful. Why he'd taken a shit job on the police force with crap pay and bad hours, Ray didn't know, but they were damned lucky to have him.

Logan now directed the energy he'd gathered into the mesh. It crept through each wire and link, lighting the metal up like the morning sun. The mesh rippled, and then the edges rose over Kayla's head, sealing seamlessly into a cocoon. The brilliant yellow flashed a bloody orange, and then the mesh dropped to the ground around her feet with a musical metallic sound.

Ray couldn't stop himself from stepping forward and reaching out to steady her. "Hey, are you okay?"

She pushed away from him. "Sorry to disappoint, but it looks like I am." She looked at Logan. "Is that it? Are we done? I'm ready to get out of here."

He flung forward a handful of blue sparks that swirled around her and then vanished. He nodded. "All clear. Except for what got inside you. That's going to take a witch to sort out. My spell was just boots stomping out ants. You need someone who knows more about witch magic than I do."

"Thank you. I appreciate your help."

He flashed his grin again. "No problem. Now sit down. I want to check you out."

"I'm fine." Kayla folded her arms over chest. A clear refusal of any examination.

"You tell yourself that, honey, but we both know you're lying. Now come on, sit. I won't bite unless you ask me to." He took her by the shoulders and gently pushed her down onto the bumper of the truck.

Ray studied her, looking for signs of injury. He hadn't noticed anything before. What had he missed?

"You're pushy," she groused at Logan.

"Thanks for noticing."

"It wasn't a compliment."

"Sure it was. You like me. Don't try to deny it. Now, are you going to tell me where you're hurt or am I going to have to search?"

"You'd like that wouldn't you?" Her mouth hinted at a smile.

"Can you tuck your dick back into your pants so we can get on with this?" Dix asked. "We haven't got all day."

For once, Ray was in complete agreement with her.

"It appears the peanut gallery has an opinion and no manners," Logan said to Kayla. "Where are you hurt?"

Ray tensed as he waited for her reply. He hated feeling useless, like a third wheel, but he had nothing to do until the scene was clear, and that was Logan's show. In the meantime, he did not want to worry about Kayla. He folded his arms and began to pace impatiently.

"It's not worth mentioning," she said.

"I'll be the judge of that," Logan replied. "Well?"

She shook her head and gave a short sigh. "Fine. I got knocked on my ass on the steps. Got some bruises on my back and a lump on my head."

"Let's see." Logan didn't wait for permission but ran gentle fingers over the back of her head. Magic flared pink around his hand. "Good. No concussion."

"I could have told you that," Kayla said.

"I prefer to see for myself. Lean forward. I want to see the bruises."

"No thanks."

"It wasn't a request."

Her chin jutted in that mulish way she had that said she'd rather jump into a live volcano than do anything remotely reasonable. After being partners for four years, Ray was all too familiar with the look.

She stood up. "I'm entitled to say no to medical care."

Logan made a frustrated sound. "That's stupid, not to mention ridiculous."

"Welcome to my world," Ray muttered.

Kayla shot him an irritated look. "Mind your own business."

"Today you are my business, so suck it up, Buttercup."

She turned her back on him. "It's not like you can fix anything," Kayla pointed out to Logan.

"But you'd know if you needed to go to the hospital. You could have cracked a rib or a vertebra."

"Oh, please," Dix said. "If she wants to suffer, let her. Some people are just too stupid for their own good."

"If I'd broken something, I'd be in pain," Kayla argued. "I'm not. At least, not that much."

"Jesus, Kayla, shut up and let the man do his damned job," Ray growled.

She spun around, glaring at him. Her whole body radiated fury. "You can go to hell," she said. "I'm done here. If this isn't a murder, then you don't need me. I want to leave."

Ray shook his head. "You're going to walk through the scene with me, soon as hazmat clears it."

"That's pointless. You've got my statement. I've got nothing useful to add." She shoved at him to get out of her way.

Ray grabbed her arms. "Careful or I'll arrest you for assaulting a police officer," he said in a low voice. "Those bodies may not be my jurisdiction, but that spell that laid you out is. So, you *will* walk through the scene with me. Understand?"

She glared up at him, and then twisted out of his grip. Ray let her go. She rubbed her arms, and Ray felt a surge of unwanted guilt. As much as he wanted to shake her and demand answers to about a thousand questions, it made him nauseous to think he might have actually hurt her. His stepfather had been the kind to hurt women. Ray had sworn he was never going to be like him.

"Fine. Whatever you want," she said.

"Good. Glad we got that settled. Now let Logan have a look at you before he starts climbing walls." He gave her a little push.

Just then, his cell vibrated in his pants pocket. Captain Crice's number came up on the caller I.D. This couldn't be good. He walked back to the police cruiser to get a little privacy before he answered.

"Garza? Where the hell are you? What's your status?" Captain Crice shot the questions like bullets, not bothering to wait for answers. "Whatever it is, drop it. I've got a priority case. A kidnapping."

"Sir, I'm processing a scene of ritual magic. It involves blood sacrifice." Blood sacrifice nearly always meant black magic, which meant the potential danger here was also a high priority. "Hazmat is clearing the scene, now."

"I'll send another detective to take over."

"But sir—"

"Dammit, Garza, shut your pie hole. This isn't a request, and it sure as hell isn't a debate. You get your ass in gear and get going." He rattled off an address.

Ray glanced upward, closing his eyes and suppressing a sigh. "Yes, sir. Dix is on site. I'll leave her in charge."

"I expect you on scene in a half hour. I'll meet you there."

Ray's brow furrowed, tension tightening his gut. Whatever this case was, it was big to get the captain personally involved. "Who's the victim?"

"Theresa Runyon along with Margaret Valentine, her daughter. Kidnappers took them right out of their home."

Ray let out a low whistle. "Holy shit."

"Holy shit is right. The place is a fortress. I've already got the family and half the city council breathing down my neck."

"How long have they been missing?"

"Between twelve to eighteen hours."

"And we're only getting a call now? Shit." Not that Ray was all that surprised. The Runyons had more money than God and a lot of secrets. They probably called in lawyers and PIs and a private army before they even thought of calling in the proper authorities. Better to get all their ducks in a row to cover their asses first. In fact, it was more surprising at this point that they'd called in the cops at all instead of handling it quietly on their own. "Any ransom demands?"

"None. Now light a fire under your ass."

The line cut off. Ray rubbed a hand over his face, his thoughts racing. The lack of a ransom demand was ominous. Not a lot of point to kidnapping rich women if you weren't going to sell them back to their family. Which meant there had to be some other motivation for the kidnapping. Something personal. Undoubtedly the Runyons would stonewall him rather than air their dirty laundry.

This was the very definition of a juicy case. He almost smiled at the irony. Dix was going to be pissed she hadn't caught it. A case like this could catapult his career into the stratosphere if he succeeded in getting the two women back. On the other hand, if he didn't, he'd be walking a beat in no time, if he wasn't booted off the force altogether.

God but he hated politics.

Urgency gnawed on him. He was almost a day behind in the investigation, and he hadn't even started yet. He had to haul ass. Which meant leaving Kayla.

Tracking her down again would be simple enough, he told himself. He had her number.

Ray shoved his phone back into his pocket and walked back around the front of the cruiser.

"Dix! You get your wish. You're taking over here."

She stiffened, her hands on her hips. "I've changed my mind."

"Captain's orders. He's assigned me a priority case. Make sure you get pictures of everything on that fountain wall."

"I know how to do my damned job, Garza," she declared, her voice dripping with pure venom. Or maybe it was jealousy. She's been doing a lot of ass-kissing to make it to the top of the captain's best detective list. Maybe she should work harder on her detective skills.

Ray cast a look at Kayla, scrabbling for something to say, something that could fix things between them. His earlier outburst that they weren't friends had been true, but not what he wanted. He wanted her back in his life. Hell, if he was really honest with himself, he wanted her back as a partner, but that wouldn't happen, even if he could talk her into returning to the force. Not enough manpower to assign partners. Hadn't been since Magicfall.

That left friendship, if they could find a way to get back there. If she was even willing to open up and explain what had made her quit. He needed that more than he could say.

He let out a breath. Nothing he said right now would change anything. He needed time and a chance to think.

He had a kidnapping to solve, and he was wasting time. So Ray did the one thing he knew how to do: his job.

He left without another word.

Chapter 5

Kayla

KAYLA WATCHED Ray disappear into the fog, her stomach twisting. That had gone about as well as their last meeting four years ago, only with less yelling. And Ray hadn't broken his hand punching a wall. On second thought, this time had gone a lot better. Well, maybe except for the female detective who clearly didn't like getting this case dumped on her.

"I'm going to make that bastard regret this with every molecule of his being." The detective swore a blue streak, pacing back and forth as she expanded on all the things she planned to do to Ray once she got her hands on him.

"Is she always this . . . ?" Kayla asked the technomage.

"Volatile?" Zach supplied helpfully as he put away the mesh blanket.

"I was going to say unprofessional, but sure. Volatile works."

"Wouldn't know. I only see Detective Dix on the job. Maybe you can ask her cats."

Kayla snorted. "Cats?"

He grinned. "She's bound to have a dozen or so, don't you think? She fits the type. Anyhow, her bark isn't as bad as her bite."

"I'm sure Ray will take great comfort in that," Kayla said dryly.

"What's the story with you two, anyhow?" Zach propped his shoulder against the corner of the van, watching her intently.

"What do you mean?" Kayla asked, feigning innocence.

He grinned again, laugh lines creasing the corners of his mouth. "I may not be a detective, but I'm not an idiot either. You two have a history. I've never seen Ray so—" Zach's eyes narrowed as he considered his words. "Let's go with irritated, shall we?"

"Hell if I know. Maybe he's just an asshole."

"Now see, that's what I mean. You've taken quite a dislike to the man for someone who's never met him before. What gives?"

"She's his old partner," Detective Dix declared, having ended her tantrum and now presenting a no-nonsense demeanor. "Turned in her shield right after Magicfall." Her evident disgust echoed Ray's.

Zach whistled and eyed Kayla. "So that was you."

"Seems like," she said, since he expected a reply.

"Word is you were a hotshot detective. You and Ray were the superstars of the department."

"*I* heard you put your tail between your legs and ran like a deer after Magicfall," Detective Dix said, voice dripping contempt.

Kayla gave a syrupy smile, refusing to be needled. "Yes, I did. Fast as I could." She watched with glee as Dix's face turned red. Nothing like ruining someone's bitter attack to piss them off.

"I need to get your statement," the detective said, taking out a notebook wrapped in tooled leather. Her pen looked expensive, too.

Kayla wondered how many pens she had to replace in a month. Stupid to carry anything expensive. "Garza already took my statement. Get it from him."

"That's Detective Garza to you. And I want to hear your story for myself."

"But first, I want to check her out," Zach said, straightening up.

"I'm sure you do," Dix said with an acid twist of her lips. "How long before the scene is ready for you to sterilize?"

He turned to look over the fountain square where three techs had spooled wires around the outer edges and set up an array of spidery metal sculptures in various sizes. They now worked on making measurements and adjustments as they spaced everything apart.

"Looks like five or ten minutes."

"Then you'd better hurry up, because when they're ready, you're going to work." Dix glanced at Kayla. "*Real* work," she added.

"Come on then," Zach said to Kayla. "Show me your injuries."

"Are you asking me to strip for you? Because I'm not that kind of girl."

He shook his head. "I'm a professional. I just want to check out any wounds you may have."

"You may be a professional technomage, but you're not a doctor or an EMT, so what exactly do you think you're going to do if I am hurt? Give me a Band-Aid and a couple of aspirin?"

"I'll know whether to call an ambulance or the coroner."

"I'm not dying, and I don't need an ambulance. You're off the hook."

Impatience colored his voice. "I was a field medic before Magicfall, and I've kept up my training and certification. I'm qualified to check you out, so no more excuses. Let me look at you."

"Look all you want." Kayla took a step back and spread her arms, turning in a circle until she faced Zach again. "Tell me when you've seen enough."

He just skewered her on his gaze, not speaking.

Kayla sighed. He wasn't letting her go until he examined her. She'd have told him he could stick it where the sun didn't shine and just disappeared into the fog, but as the tech in charge of clearing the site he had the power to drag her back. "Fine."

"Did you black out when you hit your head?"

"No."

"Are you feeling dizzy or nauseous?" As he spoke, Zach took out a pen light and shined it in her eyes, tipping her head to get a better look. "Your pupils look all right. Do you have a headache?"

"Of course I have a headache. I bounced my head off a cement step. Isn't this pointless? You already said I didn't have a concussion." She pulled out of his grip.

"And a concussion is the only possible head injury you could have," he said, rolling his eyes. "You should get a scan. Check for swelling and contusions."

"I'll get right on that." Just as soon as she gave the devil a blowjob.

These days medical care was mostly free, but she had no intention of exposing herself to tests. Right now, nobody could tell she was a supernatural. Not even other supernaturals who had a radar for knowing when someone wasn't human. But who knew what hospital machines and technomagic would be able to see?

"I mean it. You could have a brain bleed or swelling. Either could cause you serious damage or even kill you."

"I get it. Are we done?"

He made an exasperated sound. "Turn around. Let me see your back."

"You're wasting your time."

"My time to waste. Turn around."

Kayla groaned and turned. He didn't wait for her permission or warn her before he lifted her pea coat and pushed up her sweatshirt and cami. The damp cold raised goosebumps on her skin. She shivered.

"You landed hard. Go ahead and take a deep breath."

Kayla yelped and jerked away when she felt the press of a cold metal disk on her back. "What the hell?"

"It's called a stethoscope." He held up the round end, the two earpieces inside his ears. "We medical types use them to listen to your heart and lungs. Nothing to be afraid of," he added, laughing at her.

"I know what they are. A little warning might have been nice, though. Do you keep that thing in a deep freeze?"

"Yep. Just to torture my patients. Get over it."

Kayla snorted, but allowed him to push her around so her back faced him and raised her clothing out of the way again. He pressed the stethoscope against her again. This time she didn't move.

"Deep breath. . . . Let it out. . . . Again. . . . Let it out. . . . Once more. . . . Let it out. . . . Last one. . . ." He straightened, pulling the headset out of his ears. "Doesn't sound like you've punctured anything. Does this hurt?"

His hands spanned her sides, his thumbs pressing into her skin along the curve of her ribs from her spine outward.

"Ow! Christ! You're hitting my brand-new bruises." Kayla twisted away, pulling down her clothing as she turned back around to face the technomage. "Do you get off on making people hurt or am I just special?"

Zach's brows arched, the corner of his mouth quirking. "Can't it be both?"

Now it was her turn to roll her eyes. "It's efficient anyhow. Can you chew bubblegum at the same time?"

"And juggle. I'm very accomplished."

"And modest."

"That too."

Kayla couldn't help the snicker of laughter that escaped her. He smiled. Sweet lord but he was handsome. No doubt about it. No doubt he knew it, too. Part of it was his supreme confidence, as though he knew himself well and liked who he was. No secrets chewing away inside him. No running away from his problems. If he had demons, he had confronted and befriended them. She envied that more than she could possibly say.

"Ready, boss?"

One of the techs had approached. She wore a silvery-white containment suit. A hard, clear shield provided a window for her to see through. Her voice came from a speaker on her shoulder and sounded tinny.

Zach nodded at her. "I'll be set up in a minute." His look gathered in Detective Dix and Kayla. "You two stay here by the truck. Wait until I give the all clear."

He strode away, striding up the hill to the street and stopping at what looked like a tangled sculpture of scrap metal. He turned so he faced the park. He closed his eyes and spread his arms wide.

"Man, I love to watch him work," said one of the four techs who came to stand beside Kayla. "He makes it look so easy."

"He's not too bad on the eyes either," said one of the female techs. She peeled the hood of her suit off her head. Her short dark hair was plastered to her head with sweat.

"He's a tomcat," said the other female tech as she also pulled off her hood, revealing blond hair fastened up in a bun. "But he doesn't play where he works, if you know what I mean."

"I'm available whenever he wants, though," said one of the male techs. He was shorter than Zach with pale blond hair and a bit of a baby face. Like the other techs, he'd been sweating heavily inside the suit.

Both of the women techs looked at him, and then each other, and then giggled and whispered together.

Kayla bit back a smile at the male tech's consternation.

Her attention veered back to Zach as a pulse of magic traveled around the outer edges of the square, following the pattern of wires laid down by the techs. Transparent golden flames rose up until they were as tall as the technomage. Kayla didn't feel any heat coming from them, but all the hair on her body stood on end like she stood in the middle of a staticky sock. Even her scalp prickled. She shifted in place to try to ease the pin-prick feeling, but it only increased as Zach added power to his spellwork.

Each of the metal sculptures began to turn colors. First blue, then red, then yellow, then ultra violet. Streamers of magic unfurled from each one, rippling like the aurora borealis, then winding and weaving together into a lattice above the square. Now the entire place was enclosed in a box of power, anchored by the sculptures and wire lines, and fed by Zach.

Kayla had seen technomages work. After Magicfall, they'd restored or created roads and bridges, then stabilized the hospitals. Next came electrical production using windmills and passive turbines in all the underground pipes. As those turbines spun, magic collected the electricity and channeled it to the electrical stations and then out to the city.

There hadn't been many who could master their newfound power at first. The new technomages were pioneers, produced by the marriage of magic and the technology and industry of the city and learning their craft on the fly. They'd saved Portland. They'd saved a lot of cities and a lot of people. With their help, Portland was thriving.

But watching Zach manipulate magic was very different than any other technomagic working she'd ever witnessed. For one, he was super strong. Sure, the other mages had put on a show, but only because they'd combined their strength. This demonstration was all Zach.

The ground gave a liquid heave beneath her feet. The magic of the power box surrounding the square brightened, the golden flames turning white, and then silver. As they did, they collapsed, sweeping inward and vanishing as they met in the middle. The lattice above slowly settled, like silk on a hot breeze. When it lay across the ground, fountains, steps, trees, and bushes, the violet mantle started to pulse, sending rippling light across itself. The pulses bounced back from the invisible barrier framing the square, and soon the pulses turned into a hypnotizing dance of light and shadow.

And then, before Kayla had gotten her fill of the beautiful display, the light faded, leaving behind a hush. A few seconds later, the techs squealed and whistled, then clapped to celebrate Zach's handiwork.

He turned from where he'd been standing and shook himself out, as though his muscles were cramped. He rolled his head on his shoulders and scrubbed his hands across his face. The techs continued to cheer. He tossed a little wave at them before starting back down the hill to the van.

"Can we go down and examine the scene now?" Detective Dix's voice cut through the happy hijinks of the techs.

"It's clear," one of the men said.

"Give me some booties and gloves," she demanded. "And shut off the damned water."

He climbed into the van and returned with a pair of light-blue over-the-shoe slipcovers for both Kayla and the detective, as well as two pairs of black nitrile gloves. The two women slipped them on, and Kayla followed the detective down the steps to the cement platforms. The floodlights that the techs had set up with the fog-lifting equipment shone bright on the fountain face with the displayed bodies. As they approached, the water ceased to flow.

The first body was clearly a shifter killed mid-transformation. It looked like a cat shifter, its face frozen in an agonized snarl, its body rigidly twisted. Sprouts of spotted fur on its face and body suggested it was a leopard shifter, or maybe a cheetah.

The second body was some kind of nymph or dryad or naiad. Something in that family. Kayla had been working on trying to figure out what sorts of species of creatures lived in Portland, but it wasn't easy. It wasn't like you could walk up to someone and ask them what they were. "Pissed off," was the general answer.

The nymph girl's skin was fishbelly white, her long dark hair matted and tangled with leaves and twigs. There were no signs of defensive wounds on her arms or hands, and her feet and legs showed no scrapes or bruises either. She hadn't tried to run to escape her killer.

The third body was nothing she recognized. Sort of a fox-looking creature with white fur and five black tails. It's legs were completely black with claws that looked more catlike than canine.

The fox creature and the shifter had been hung upside down and pinned in place like dissected frogs, their skin and chests pulled wide, their internal organs nowhere in sight. The nymph in the middle hung from a spike driven through the middle of her forehead and into the stone. Unlike the others, her chest and stomach remained intact, though the latter bulged oddly, almost like she'd swallowed a starfish-shaped soccer ball.

Kayla's gaze ran over the writing that seemed to have been burned into the red cement wall of the fountain. It was lovely, more like art than anything else. The writing was paired with pictures and surrounded in a kind of Egyptian cartouche.

A low whistle made Kayla turn.

"That is something," Zach said, coming to stand beside them.

He radiated energy like a walking bolt of lightning. Kayla rubbed down her arms to flatten the hair that prickled uneasily.

"Can't you calm that down?" Dix complained.

"'Fraid not. Hazard of the trade," Zach said with an easy smile. He looked back at the fountain wall. "What the hell is this about?"

"Nothing good," Dix said. "Anyhow snap some pictures, and we'll send the corpses to the crematorium."

Kayla sucked in a sharp breath, barely managing to hold her tongue.

"We'd better get someone to look over the bodies. See if they can tell what kind of spell was cast," Zach said.

"You sterilized the area," Dix said. "What's going to be left?"

"That's what we have to find out." He glanced at her. "I can shepherd the tech review if you'd like, send you anything interesting that pops up."

She wavered and then gave a slight nod. "Knock yourself out. There's no crime here unless it's illegal magic. No point wasting my time unless that's confirmed." Her nose wrinkled. "What is that godawful smell?"

Burned soap was what Kayla had thought when she'd first arrived. A kind of oily, cleansing odor wrapped up in a fireworks stink.

At the question, Zach just shrugged. "Maybe from the ingredients in the spell."

"Where are their intestines?" Kayla asked, leaning to look into the water basin.

"Good question," Zach said.

Dix was already halfway up the fountain steps. She held her cell phone to her ear.

"Doesn't look like they struggled, does it?" Kayla asked.

"Why do you say that?"

"No ligature marks or bruises or any signs of defensive wounds. The cuts are clean and straight."

"Could have been done postmortem."

"Could have been," Kayla echoed, but her gut told her that the victims had been alive when they were killed. Bodies usually meant blood magic, which meant living victims. Couldn't put the power of death in a spell if you didn't have the living as fuel for the spell.

Her gaze ran over the flowing script. It almost looked like calligraphy, but in no language she'd ever seen. The images were more crudely made—jagged, without the flowing curves of the script. Almost as if they were from two different languages.

"What happens now?" she asked Zach.

"My team and I will collect any evidence and send the bodies to the morgue."

"So, there will be an autopsy?"

He shook his head. "Not likely. Mostly we'll bring in a witch to check out how the bodies fit into the spell if they can. Then they'll go to the crematorium."

Kayla had to bite her tongue to keep from saying what she thought of the lack of care for the people who'd died. And they were people. Maybe not human, but definitely people. They could think and love and mourn and desire. Believing otherwise was wrong. Hateful.

Would she be so sure of that if she wasn't one of the hated? She hoped so. But then her conscience pricked. She *was* one of the hated, and she wasn't going to let these three victims get swept under the rug just because they might have weird blood or two shapes or look like an animal. Not when she could do something about it. At least she could track down their families and let them know what had happened.

Zach seemed to forget about her as he summoned his techs and gave them orders. In the meantime, Kayla surreptitiously fished her phone out of her pocket and snapped pictures of the bodies and the writing, hoping she'd be able to see the details later.

"I'd better get out of your way," she said as Zach's techs scurried off.

He cocked his head. "In a hurry?"

"I still have to drop off my salvage."

"I may need more information."

Uh huh. He was back to flirting with her, and Kayla had to admit it felt nice. She hadn't been exactly swimming in male attention since leaving the force. Not that she worked to get it. She looked homeless, and she hadn't shaved her legs or pits since she didn't know how long.

"So, you just expect me to sit around for hours until you get done?"

He gave a little shrug. "If afterward you let me take you to dinner, then I most definitely do want you to wait."

Kayla folded her arms. "And why would I want to sit around bored out of my gourd for hours just to spend time with you?"

"My scintillating company, of course."

She snorted. "That's all you've got to offer?"

"You wound me."

"I doubt it. Anyway, I still have to take care of my salvage."

"It can wait, can't it? You won't regret coming out with me."

She couldn't help her smile. "You certainly have a high opinion of yourself."

"What can I say? I'm the whole package: looks, brains, talent, and personality. And a sense of humor. You're going to love me."

Kayla bit her lips to keep from laughing out loud. "I regret to inform you that I'm a hard-hearted bitch, and I'm pretty sure I'm incapable of love except for good coffee, death-by-chocolate cake, and dark ale. I've been told"—by her family, by Ray— "that I cannot be trusted, and if you stupidly choose to do so, I will stab you in the back."

He gave her a long look, his eyes narrowing as he considered her. Kayla had a feeling her words had revealed more about her feelings than she'd wanted. Hurt. Bitterness. Anger. Things she kept locked up behind titanium bars and steel doors. Apparently, those safeguards were not enough to keep those emotions contained. Not after today anyway.

"I'm willing to take my chances," Zach said softly, almost like he thought she was fragile and could break apart at any second.

As if. She'd been through the grinders of hell, and she hadn't broken yet. And that was all *before* she'd joined the police department. She wasn't about to break down now over a little emotional turmoil.

"Your willingness to take risks is duly noted. I, however, am risk averse."

"If you were, you would never had checked out the crime scene. Plus, you were a cop. There's no such thing as a cop who doesn't like risks."

She'd have liked to argue, but he was right. *Dammit.*

He caught her hand, his grip warm and firm. "It's just dinner." He gave her puppy eyes, which made it impossible to refuse. Plus, the promise of food and fun company was hard to pass up. She didn't have many friends, or any friends, and she didn't feel like being alone. Then she'd have to think about Ray and the past. Putting that off seemed like a fine idea.

"Okay," she said with a sigh. "But you'd better go fast. I'm not good at waiting."

He grinned broadly. "We'll be quick," he promised. "In the meantime, you can park yourself in the van until we're done. It'll be more comfortable." He bent a little closer. "I promise the wait will be worth your while." His smile was wicked and far too sure of himself.

It was Kayla's turn to roll her eyes at his outrageousness, but even so, she couldn't suppress her smile. She couldn't remember the last time she'd actually gone out with anyone. Or the last time she'd even wanted to.

Maybe it was time to get her shit together and get back out there.

And maybe she was about to commit enormous stupidity. She sighed. Only time would tell, and like the man said, she liked risk. She just hoped she didn't come to regret it.

Chapter 6

Ray

RAY ARRIVED AT THE Runyon estate in just under twenty-five minutes. It stood on the crown of a broad hill west of the river. A brick wall topped with vicious spikes surrounded the place with a broad iron gate guarded by two men in black suits carrying military-grade automatic rifles.

He stopped to show his credentials. One of the beefy guards examined it carefully before turning away to speak into a microphone in the sleeve of his jacket. The other guard just watched grim-faced, finger on his trigger, his gun pointed at a polite angle just to the side of Ray. If the idiot sneezed and jerked his finger, at least Ray wouldn't get cut in half. He hoped.

"Go on in," the first guard said as the seam between the two gates split and they slid apart. "Follow the road up to the main house."

Ray nodded and rolled inside. A borealis of red, blue, and white flickering lights rose above the treetops ahead. He followed the zigzagging road up the hill until it flattened out into a long straight drive. The house looked like a modern version of an old French chateau, complete with gray stone walls and a slate tile roof. The façade was lit up like a Vegas casino, with a dozen cop cars parked out front, along with three CSU vans, a hazmat team, five fire-trucks, and two ambulances.

Ray drove slowly, passing between two swathes of manicured lawns pocked with decorative garden plots broken by an artfully aged tumbling stone wall covered in moss. The drive appeared to be the main route in, though Ray expected there was a service entrance in the back somewhere. He'd have to determine what the security protocols were for the back.

The tree line stopped at the crown of the hill, leaving precious few places for a kidnapper to hide his approach or escape. So, whoever had taken the women had either used some sort of spell to make himself invisible, or he'd had help. More than one perp would make this an even harder task. Taking two women out of a fortress without getting caught wasn't easy. It would have been almost impossible for a single person.

Unless they used magic.

He parked his cruiser and stepped out of the car, his gaze sweeping the grounds. From here, the Runyons had a clear view of what was left of Mt. Hood after the eruption of magic from its cone. To the south he could see

Lake Oswego, which now was miles bigger than it had been and could technically be called a wide spot in the Willamette River since the river flowed directly into it on one side and out on the other. Beyond, he could see Glass Mountain, shimmering brightly despite the overcast sky. To the west were the singing spires, a forest of faceted crystals that rose high into the sky and sounded like all the ghosts crying in hell when the wind blew.

"Garza! About time you got here." Crice came striding across the broad circular plaza in front of the house.

Ray didn't bother to tell the captain he'd made it to the scene in well under the half-hour time limit he'd been given. He could have arrived instantly and Crice would still have been pissed.

Ray glanced back as several other pairs of headlights crested the hill and came barreling up the drive. None of them were cops or emergency vehicles.

"Christ." Crice groaned. "More damned people to trample the crime scene." He fished in his coat pocket and drew out a pack of cigarettes. He lit one, drawing deeply and blowing out the smoke on a heavy sigh.

"It's not been kept clear?" Ray couldn't hide his surprise.

"There's been an army trooping in and out of the house all night. Any evidence we might have found outside was compromised before we were ever called to the scene. You don't tell Alistair Runyon what to do and keep your job."

Crice gave Ray a hard look. "Garza, I want this solved and fast. You're lead, and the department's entire resources are yours. Whatever you need, you get this done and fast. Find those women and get them home, or the best you'll be able to hope for is scraping for food in the gutters. Alistair Runyon will turn you into a pariah. He'll make your life a living hell."

The captain's mouth twisted. "And you'll be better off than I will be. So get to work and I want updates every two hours."

Ray's brows went up. Crice gave a rough bark of laughter that sounded more like gravel in a blender.

"Every two hours. Don't worry about waking me up. I'm not going to sleep until this over. Now get your ass inside."

Ray normally liked the chance to get a wide look at a crime scene, gradually telescoping his focus to the exact location of the event. Not tonight. He didn't have the luxury of time, and even if he did, the place was in an uproar. Too damned many people.

He threaded between the cars and ducked under the yellow-and-black crime-scene tape cutting across the front walk. He flashed his badge at the uniform guarding the taped-off area and proceeded up the fan of shallow, white stone steps spreading across three quarters of the imposing front. The house stood four stories tall, with the front steps taking him up to the imposing entrance on the second floor.

On the left, a pair of open French doors led inside. Within, he could hear raised voices. He paused to listen.

"I swear to God, if you don't call her, I will go find her myself!" The male voice was young. Probably late teens, early twenties.

"Don't think to push me, Landon. I'm in no mood for your stupidity. *I* will handle this. You keep your mouth shut. Do you understand?"

"I understand all right. You'd rather keep your secrets than get mother and grandmother back."

"Watch your mouth, boy. I make allowances for your fears, but remember your place."

Ray could hear the threat dripping from the man's stony voice. That was Alistair Runyon. The other must be a nephew, son of the missing Margaret Valentine, Runyon's sister. Ray wondered what secrets the man was keeping that would help find his mother and sister. And who was the *she* the kid wanted his uncle to call? Ray'd have to question the nephew without Runyon present.

"Sir?"

The voices in the house went silent, and then the glass doors closed with a firm *thunk*. Ray kept the irritation from his expression as he glanced at the uniformed officer who waited for him and quickly checked her brass name bar: "L. Gilisi."

"Detective Frasier said he's ready to update you."

Ray glanced once more at the glass doors before following Gilisi into the house. He stopped outside to don gloves and pull booties over his shoes, though from what the captain had said, too many people had tromped through already for it to matter what he tracked in.

Once inside the spacious entry hall, he ran into a hushed crowd. Quickly, he cataloged them. Several servants wept and comforted one another. A half-dozen burly bodyguards stood by the walls looking vigilant and angry. They kept their hands close to their weapons as they watched the gathered people. Thirteen civilians confronted three uniforms who stood on the bottom step of the massive staircase, jackhammering them with questions and not giving them time to answer. Not that they'd have said anything. They knew better.

Techs dressed in blue coveralls bustled back and forth carrying bulky cases containing tools for collecting evidence, along with sacks full of evidence they'd already collected.

Tim Frasier, a short, wiry detective who'd been in the job for less than two years, approached. "Ray, good to see you."

"What have we got?"

Tim motioned for Ray to follow him down a hallway where they couldn't be overheard.

"Some time last night, Theresa Runyon, age sixty-seven, and her daughter Margaret Valentine, age forty-one, disappeared. Notification came in at—" he checked his watch "—at two thirty-eight. Witnesses say the women went to bed shortly after ten o'clock and weren't seen again. No signs of breaking and entering, or a struggle. They just vanished."

Frasier looked at Ray. "The kidnappers had to have a key, or someone let them in, or they used magic. CSU is doing their thing, but—"

"But?"

Frasier shook his head, frowning. "It doesn't add up."

Ray snorted inwardly. *Tell me something I didn't know.* He was interested in the other man's thinking, though. Frasier didn't have a lot of experience, but he had good instincts. "What doesn't add up?"

"Their rooms are too clean, for one. The beds don't look like they've been slept in. There's no sign of dirty clothes, nothing out of place. Practically sterile."

"What do the maids say? Did they clean?"

"They say no."

"You don't believe them."

Frasier shook his head and shrugged. "If they didn't clean, then those rooms are just for show and the women live elsewhere."

"What else?" Ray asked.

"Everybody is real careful about what they say, and too many stories are too pat, too identical. They've been coached."

"Do you like someone for the kidnapping?"

Frasier grimaced and shook his head. "I don't know. It seems like there had to be someone inside. That or the kidnappers used magic, but I'd bet my teeth this place is warded against magical incursion. One thing I do know is that nobody is telling us the whole truth."

Ray nodded, unsurprised. He'd expected as much, especially after over-hearing the conversation between Runyon and his nephew. "Anything else?"

"Seems like Theresa Runyon held a lot of the purse strings. That gives Alistair Runyon a motive. She wasn't a particularly nice woman, and I get the impression she ruled the roost with an iron fist. He and his sister are the only heirs. They don't come back, he gets it all. So long as they're out of the way, he's in charge."

"But he has an unimpeachable alibi," Ray guessed.

"He says he had a playdate with a couple of lady friends. Got home around dawn. He noticed his mother and sister missing when they didn't show up for breakfast—I guess the old lady is a stickler for everybody attending meals. When he realized they weren't home and hadn't taken a car or a chauffeur, he had his secretary reach out in case they'd gone shopping or visiting friends, but no go. It's unheard of for either of them to disappear without a word, so he decided he'd better call us in."

"You don't believe him."

"He's definitely holding something back."

"Everybody lies to the cops," Ray muttered. "All right, let me know when the techs are done with the scene. I'm going to talk to Runyon. Did you get the names and contact information for his companions last night?"

Frasier shook his head with a wry smile. "Above my pay grade to ask him a question like that. I like my job."

In his place, Ray wouldn't have asked either. The Runyons had the money and power to do just about anything they wanted, and few would try to get in their way. Word was Alistair was a vindictive son of a bitch, too.

"After I'm done with Runyon, I want to talk to the nephew and the staff. Set up an interview room for me."

"On it."

Frasier hurried away, and Ray headed for his collision with Runyon.

"Oh, one more thing," Frasier said, stopping.

"What's that?"

"Runyon's got his attorneys with him. All three of them." He grinned and walked away again.

Ray swore. Lawyers were boils on the ass of the universe.

Chapter 7

Ray

AFTER ASKING A maid to take him to Runyon, Ray found himself facing off against a pair of polished walnut doors with square inset panels. He knocked and let himself in.

He scanned the room, quickly taking in the people and the furniture. An ornate desk sat on the right side of the room with bookcases behind. Two barrel chairs sat facing it. Behind sat a couch and several easy chairs, all arranged around a massive wet bar. A TV hung beside it. Three older men sat drinking from rock glasses, while another poured a new one. A fifth man—more a boy—paced in front of the now-closed glass French doors. He froze in place when he saw Ray, his hands clenching and unclenching with angry energy. Ray pegged him as Landon Valentine.

"Alistair Runyon? I'm Detective Garza. I'd like to speak with you about your mother and sister."

The man in question sat with his legs crossed, one arm on the couch, the other swirling his drink. He eyed Ray with sharp dislike, his mouth thinning.

"Detective," he drawled with obvious contempt. He didn't stand up or offer his hand. He gestured instead to the man on his left. "This is Calvin Buchanan, my attorney. And these are William Moller and Bennet Kimball, also my attorneys."

Ray nodded a greeting to each of them. His gaze skipped to the young man who still wore a look of fury, though now his attention had shifted to Runyon.

"That's my nephew, Landon. He was just leaving."

"I'll need to speak to him, too." He didn't make it a request.

"I don't think that will be necessary," Runyon said dismissively. "He's been away and just returned today. Go now, Landon."

The kid's face reddened, his jaw clenching so hard Ray thought his teeth might crack to pieces. He gave a jerky nod and strode out, slamming the doors behind him.

Ray drew his notebook out of his coat along with his pencil. He flipped open the cover. This interview wouldn't go well. He'd be lucky to get anything useful out of Runyon. Landon Valentine, however. . . . He'd find a way to interview the boy without Runyon around.

"Can you tell me what happened, sir?"

Runyon's lip curled. "I already gave a statement. Surely you're not so incompetent you haven't read it."

Ray's eyes narrowed, but he didn't lose his temper. He'd dealt with a lot of assholes in his career, and he had a job to do. He kept both his face and voice blandly earnest. His lack of reaction would piss the other man off. "Yes, sir, but I'd like to hear it from you. You may remember more details."

"You're wasting my time. Get out there and find my damned mother and sister!" Runyon's thick face turned red as he gestured violently with his hand, then slugged down half his drink.

"I will, sir, but I could do that more quickly if you'd just go over the events and timeline of last night and today with me." Ray offered a placating smile.

"Alistair, let the detective do his work," Bennet Kimball said, brushing invisible lint off his crossed knee. "You know how this works."

Runyon glared at Ray but spoke to his companions. "I should demand a different detective. This one is next to useless."

Ray didn't let himself react, but Runyon's pronouncement sounded personal. What was his problem? Ray had never met the man in his life, nor had he worked on any cases related to Runyon, at least that he knew of. So, what was the man's beef with him?

A question to tuck away for later.

"All right, ask your damned questions," Runyon said grudgingly, pointedly not asking Ray to sit.

"When was the last time you saw your sister and mother?"

"Yesterday evening."

"What time was that?"

"Around six. We had early cocktails, and then I left to attend a dinner party. I stayed the night with friends and returned early this morning. When my mother and Margaret failed to come down for breakfast, I found it odd. When we couldn't track them down, we called the police."

"At what time was breakfast scheduled?"

"Eight o'clock. Sharp."

That left a whole lot of real estate on the clock before Runyon logged a call to the police. Looking for the women would have taken a matter of an hour at most, with the army of people the Runyons employed.

"They didn't answer calls to their cell phones?"

"Everything went to voice mail." The way Runyon's eyes flicked downward told Ray he was lying. The question was why? Because the man was involved in the disappearances of the women? Or because of some secret he wanted to cover up?

"No one has contacted you for a ransom?"

"Don't you think I would have told you that?" Runyon demanded. "God knows I'd pay whatever necessary."

He guzzled the rest of his drink and slammed the glass down on a side table before springing to his feet. "I have precious little family left, and I'm not about to lose any more." He jabbed his finger in Ray's direction. "I'm holding you personally responsible if anything happens to them, do you understand? If you don't bring them back safely, I will make sure you regret ever being born. Now get the hell out of my sight!"

"I appreciate your feelings and I can assure you the PPD will do everything in our power to find your mother and sister," Ray said, ignoring the blustered order. Runyon's emotions seemed genuine enough, but still something seemed off.

"I don't give a shit whether you appreciate my feelings," Runyon sneered. "Just do your damned job and do it quick."

"I think that's quite enough for now," William Moller announced as he rested a hand on Runyon's shoulder. "Alistair is understandably upset, and I'm sure you have leads you must pursue. Time is of the essence in these cases, as you know. If you have more questions, we'll arrange a time for you to ask them later."

And by later, he meant never.

Ray resisted the urge to snort at Moller's admonition that time was of the essence. If they really believed that, they wouldn't have waited six and a half hours before calling the police. He merely nodded, knowing he'd get nothing more at the moment. "If you can think of anything else, please call me." He drew out his card and handed it to Moller before exiting the room.

Now to find Landon Valentine and find out what he knew. This wasn't a simple case of abduction, and until Ray figured out what the hell it was, he wasn't going to find the two women. At least not alive.

OVER THE NEXT few hours, Ray spoke to the staff and every single friend and acquaintance who milled about like hyenas waiting to rip up their kill. Aside from Runyon and his three lawyers who remained cloistered in his office, the only person Ray hadn't managed to interview was Landon Valentine. He'd vanished after storming out of his uncle's office, though guards at the gates assured Ray that he hadn't departed the premises.

Two gates. He'd been right about a service road up to the manor. Its gate was more industrial than ornate, since the visitors through there had little importance. The guards posted there also claimed they had not allowed anyone in or out during the window when Theresa Runyon and Margaret Valentine had gone missing or after. That meant Landon Valentine was most likely still inside the fence.

Ray resisted the urge to rub his gritty eyes, ignoring the growling of his stomach. He'd managed to grab a cup of coffee but hadn't eaten since breakfast. He'd have to scrounge something. He vaguely remembered leaving a bag of pretzels in his squad car a day or so ago. It wasn't much, but he'd take it in a heartbeat. He checked his watch. Six o'clock and he'd not made any progress. He didn't expect to get sleep again until he found the women, hopefully soon. Hopefully alive. If he didn't, Alistair Runyon would be using Ray's nutsack for a coin purse.

To find them, he needed a lead. For that, he needed to get answers, and those started with finding Landon.

Ray didn't like magic. Sure, it could be useful, but it was damned unnatural and a whole lot like cheating. Instead of working for something, people just did a bibbity-bobbity-boo, and voila! Done. No effort, no sweat, no earning your accomplishment. Magic made people soft. Complacent. They didn't have to solve their own problems; they could just pay someone to do it for them.

Even after the nightmare of the Witchwar, even though nobody trusted a witch, people still swarmed Nuketown looking to buy spells. Some witches had even gone so far as to open up shops in the city, despite the continuing distrust and anger for their kind.

Ray didn't like that some invisible force could come out of nowhere and create havoc or save the world. He didn't like that you couldn't see it coming and had no idea when it might show up. It was like relying on God. Send up your prayers and maybe you'd get a miracle or maybe you'd be damned, or more likely the bastard would just ignore you. Except magic came around a lot more often than any god or devil, and it fucked things up. It fucked people up.

And yet—

Ray scraped his teeth over his lower lip. He needed a lead and now. He needed to find Landon. He delayed a moment in considering his nonexistent options. He didn't have any. Which meant he was going to have to do the one thing he hated above all things.

After glancing around to make sure no one saw him, he slipped out of the main foyer and ducked into a side passage. He hurried, turning a corner before finding a small sitting room.

He examined the feminine room and floral upholstery wrapping the chairs and sofa and white sheer curtains blousing around the windows. A blue, patterned rug covered most of the white carpet. Several antique glass cabinets lined the walls containing delicate porcelain dishes. A huge vase of pink and white roses scented the air.

Ray slipped a reluctant hand in his pocket and drew out his knife. He turned it in his fingers. The handle was made of antler, the ridges smoothed by years of use. It had been his grandfather's. He was fairly certain this would work. The Runyons probably hadn't installed any hard-core magic suppressors inside the house. The wealthy prided themselves on having magical amenities in their homes, whether to keep the bathrooms clean or change the wallpaper on a whim.

Closing his fingers around the knife, Ray focused his attention on what he needed to do. Easier said than done. His mind kept skipping away to anything else, and he had to drag it back. Finally, a reddish glow formed around his fist, like flame over wood coals. Magic rippled and crawled inside him, nosing through his body like a not-quite-angry ghost.

He shuddered and flinched from himself, his gorge rising. The flame around his hand flared and shredded apart into uneven blobs and splatters. Ray clenched his teeth and bent his will to his magic. As he tried to mold it into what he wanted—a spell that would lead him to Landon—sudden zaps of power popped all over his body. What the hell?

Ray cut off the flow of magic, heart thundering against his ribs. He looked down at himself. He appeared no different from before he'd started formulating his spell, but his body was alive with pulsing power. It swirled around him in an almost-visible cloud. It scraped over his skin, hot and gritty. He broke out in a cold sweat, his chest tightening.

He had no idea what to do or if this was normal or not. After Magicfall, he'd developed witchy powers. He'd avoided working magic until it began to leak out when he least expected it. He discovered a witch had to practice witchcraft or face a backlash from dammed-up power. That had led to secret experiments based on the lore he could glean from whatever scraps of gossip and news that he ran across.

He'd decided that if he had to release the magic, at least he could make it useful. He'd worked out what he called a bloodhound spell. It worked more reliably if he had something like hair or fingernails from the person he was looking for, but if he focused enough, he could craft a spell that would track his target. His experience as a cop gave him the skills and attention to detail that helped him form the precise mental image needed.

But in the four years since he'd developed witch powers, he'd never experienced anything like this. In crafting his spell, he'd somehow summoned a cloud of magic that now collected around him, waiting to be used. Ray had no idea how to tap it or dispel it. Ray stood still as seconds dribbled past, waiting for the cloud to dissipate. Several minutes later it still hadn't. Urgency gnawed at him. Margaret Valentine and Theresa Runyon didn't have time for him to waste.

Suck it up, Garza, he told himself.

He decided to just bull through his spell and hope nothing exploded. Focusing again on the jackknife in his hand, he built an image of Landon in his mind, remembering his voice, his anger, and his fear. He gave as much detail to the portrait as he could, and then he fed his desire to find the young man into the knife, binding it with filaments of pure determination.

All around him, the cloud of magic thickened, pushing against him with smothering weight. He tied off his spell, and he released the power he held. Grasping the knife tightly, he backed toward the door. Instead of dissipating, the cloud clung to him.

Fuck. Now what?

Ray knew there were ways to siphon up that magic and either hold on to it or feed it into an object like his knife. Both were beyond his expertise. In fact, most magic fell into that territory, and he was just as happy to keep it that way. Still, he had to admit it would have been handy to know what to do to disarm the situation. Maybe he should get over himself enough to find out. It would be the smart thing to do. But the thought of consulting another witch—of admitting out loud that he was one himself—*No.* He'd managed this long without help. He could manage awhile longer. A long while.

As he racked his brain for a solution to the cloud, he realized that it had begun to thin and fade. Because he'd quit using his magic? It seemed logical. Would it accumulate again when he activated the spell tied to his knife? Hopefully not.

He opened his hand and looked down at his knife. It looked no different from before.

"Lead me to Landon," he said softly, invoking his spell. He'd heard that witches didn't need words to trigger a spell. Maybe that was true for some, but not for him.

Immediately the knife pushed forward in his hand. He caught it before it could shoot away. If he let it go, it would fly through the air to its goal. Unfortunately, it didn't care about walls or other obstacles. Finding Landon was going to be a little tougher than following a straight line.

In fact, running his target to ground took almost a whole frustrating hour. The delays included updating Captain Crice on his nonexistent progress and having to listen to the captain's threatening encouragement.

He ducked out the front door and walked around the house, trying to triangulate Landon's general location in the giant house. Surprisingly, the knife didn't point him back to the house, but instead guided him behind it.

The two-story, ten-car garage looked more like a small fortress curving around the outer edge of a broad, gray stone-cobbled courtyard just behind the house. An expansive rose garden the size of a small pasture spread out on the left side, and a barn with an attached arena stood off to the left. The service road slithered away just beyond the barn and disappeared into the march of trees surrounding the main grounds.

An unlocked side door on the west end of the garage allowed Ray entrance into the garage. Inky darkness filled the space, along with stifling silence. He pulled out his flashlight and switched it on, sweeping the beam across the first bay. It held a variety of tools, workbenches, cabinets, and toolboxes. A doorway in the back led into a small office space with a bathroom and refrigerator. He checked the other bays, finding a variety of vehicles, including snowmobiles and a dune buggy, but no Landon.

His pocketknife kept pulling him along until the second to the last bay, where it went quiescent in his palm. Ray frowned, turning in a circle, waiting for the tug of the knife to pull him along. Nothing. No sign of Landon. Had someone activated magic dampeners? Or maybe his spell had given up the ghost.

He leaned toward the latter. He was like a kid with a gun: able to pull the trigger but no idea how it worked. For the most part, the spells he'd tried since developing witch powers tended to turn out half-assed at best. He wasn't sure whether it was because he didn't know what he was doing, or whether he was just a minor power.

What did it mean that he wanted it to be the former?

Nothing good. Dammit, he didn't want to be a witch. His lip curled with self-disgust. But if he was one, he damned well didn't want to be a weak one.

Ray turned in a slow circle again. An almost inaudible sound came from above. He aimed his light at the ceiling as understanding hit. His spell hadn't failed. It had found Landon, except that the kid was upstairs, and Ray hadn't equipped his spell with a sense of dimension.

He slid the knife into his pocket before locating a set of stairs inside a round turret on the back corner of the garage. Ray jogged up the spiraling steps, then quietly opened the door to the second floor and glanced through. A long hallway stretched away following the curve of the garage. A bank of windows overlooked the grassy pastures behind the garage on the right, while a couple of doors broke the pale-yellow expanse on the left.

Taking the knife from his pocket, Ray let it guide him to the correct door. Instead of knocking, he twisted the knob and pushed the door open. Inside contained a broad game room with a TV, a long shuffleboard table, a pool table, a felt-covered poker table, a kitchenette, and shelves of board games and books, plus a few comfortable chairs scattered throughout.

Landon stood beyond the pool table chalking a pool cue as he scowled down at the table. Tense energy curled around him.

Ray knocked on the open door. Landon started, his head jerking up. "What are you doing here?"

"I'd like to talk to you," Ray said, adopting the soothing voice he reserved for scared dogs and kids. "I need to ask you a few questions."

Landon's fingers flexed on the cue, his lips thin with hard-held emotion. "No," he said finally, biting the word off with an audible click of his teeth.

"No?" Ray repeated, brows rising. "I need your help to find your mother and grandmother. You want me to find them, right?"

Not the right tack to take. The kid's body went rigid, and he started to shake.

"Fuck you," he said. "Fuck you, and fuck Uncle Alistair, and fuck the fucking kidnappers."

"Who did you want him to call?" Ray asked. Asking the unexpected might just win him a truthful response.

Landon gave Ray a considering look. Finally, he gave a little curl of his lip as he answered.

"My cousin. She used to be a cop. Uncle Alistair hates her, but she knows her shit and she'll know—"

"She'll know?" Ray prompted, holding his distance, not wanting to push the young man into clamming up.

Landon tipped his head back, eyes closing as he grimaced. He straightened. "What to do. My uncle's got enemies. And then there's—" He broke off again.

"There's what?"

Landon's expression closed. "I'd better not say anything else until she's here."

Several more attempts at questioning resulted in head shakes and dead-eye stares.

Dammit. It would be faster to get the cousin here than try to talk the kid out of his stubbornness.

Ray took out his notebook. "All right. What's her name? How do I contact her?"

Landon's teeth bared in a bitter smile. "That's the joke. I don't know. I haven't seen her since before Magicfall. She and my uncle had a big fight. She wanted to be a cop, and he was pissed. Called her all kinds of names and said he'd cut her off. Said she disgraced the Runyon name and if she left, she was no longer part of the family."

"But she left anyway?"

"Oh, yeah," he said with obvious hurt colored with reluctant admiration. "Nothing going to stop *her*. She told him all the ways he could stick his ultimatum up his ass, so he had security escort her out. She didn't get to take anything with her, just the clothes she had on. She didn't even get to take her car. That was years before Magicfall."

"And you haven't heard from her since?"

Landon's jaw knotted. "I saw her name in the papers some. She quit using Runyon and went with her mom's name. I thought maybe she'd come find me at school or practice, but—" He gave a bitter little shrug. "Guess she got busy."

Ray felt for the kid. Obviously, he'd cared about his cousin more than she'd cared about him. He thought of Kayla. That's what you get for putting your heart and faith in a woman. They shit all over you.

"You said she was a cop. Where did she serve? Metropolitan police? County Sheriff's office?" If Landon had seen her name in the papers, then she was local. If she'd survived Magicfall and the Witchwar, he'd be able to track her down pretty easily. A big if. A whole lot of people hadn't survived.

"Metropolitan. She was a homicide detective."

Better and better. One or two phone calls and he should be able to find her if she was still on the job. If not, he could at least get her last-known address.

"Give me her name and I'll send someone to pick her up. In the meantime, you can give me some details on what happened today. It may really help us find your mother and grandmother."

Landon hesitated. "I'll talk when she gets here."

"Every second we waste, the kidnappers get farther away."

"I'll talk when she's here. That's it," Landon said flatly, and something moved in his eyes, something like fear.

Whatever was going on, he was afraid. Hopefully his cousin would be able to reassure him. Ray hoped to hell he could find her and quick.

"What's your cousin's name?"

And then Landon cut Ray's knees out from under him.

"Kayla. Kayla Reese."

Chapter 8

Kayla

KAYLA CURLED UP on the passenger seat in the hazmat van and let herself fall asleep. She dreamed of bodies writhing in pain, dripping blood, and begging for death. Then her dreams turned to Ray. Guilt and sorrow clamped her chest, and in her dream, she longed to confess, to explain what she'd become so he would know she'd done the right thing. He wouldn't have wanted her around if he'd known. She'd saved them both a lot of heartache.

She startled awake when Zach knocked on her window. Kayla straightened up, blinking groggily. Zach opened the door.

"Almost done here. We'll drop the van off with the evidence and grab my car. Just give me ten more minutes." He paused, cocking his head. "You're not going to back out, are you?"

Kayla's immediate impulse was to change her mind, grab up her pack, and disappear into the fog. It was the smartest thing to do. But seeing Ray had reminded her of all she'd lost. She didn't have any friends left, except Nessa, who didn't really count, since she only half lived in reality, and maybe not even that much. Zach had already proven he was good company, and he didn't come with the baggage of having known her before Magicfall.

"I'm not sure it's a great idea."

He folded his arms and considered her. "How about this? If you come, I'll get you the results of the coroner's exam on the three bodies."

"What makes you think I want to see that?"

He grinned. "Once a cop, always a cop. Am I wrong?"

"I admit I *am* curious."

In fact, Kayla had planned to call an old friend down at the morgue to see if she could finagle the information. This was a sure thing.

"Then it's a deal," Zach said, correctly translating her comment as agreement.

He shut the door, and in less than the promised ten minutes, the techs clambered into the back of the van while Zach slid in behind the wheel. He fastened his seat belt before waving his palm over a row of copper sigils inset into the top of the dashboard. A green light lit on the steering column, and he slid the gearshift into drive.

The fog had already closed back around them like a cottony fist. If anything, it seemed to have thickened. Zach touched another set of sigils on the center of the steering wheel, and suddenly Kayla could see through the fog. Or rather, she could see a kind of digital stick-figure construct of an area in front of them, probably fifty feet long and thirty feet wide. It reminded her of radar or sonar or some kind of *-ar* that pinged off their immediate surroundings and showed a constructed electromagical image of the area. It was enough to keep them on the road and off unsuspecting pedestrians.

"Nice trick," she said.

Zach glanced at her. "You haven't seen this before? It's pretty standard in taxis and busses."

She shrugged. "I mostly walk."

"Seriously?"

"I don't have the money to hire a technomage to retrofit a car for me. A lot of us don't."

And a lot of people—not human—just preferred using their own feet or paws or whatever they walked on. Kayla would have liked a car. That way she wouldn't risk getting wet when it rained. But taking a car into a salvage zone wouldn't be healthy for it. The Deadwood would either shred it into metal confetti or crush it flat. The forest didn't like steel intruding on its demesnes, and it really didn't like technomagic.

"But you used to be a cop."

"So?"

He looked uncomfortable. "They look after their own. I've fixed up hundreds of vehicles for former city workers from cops to janitors."

"I left the force right after Magicfall," she said. "They figured I'd abandoned them in their hour of need." Once she'd realized how deeply Ray hated her, she'd gone to great lengths to avoid the rest of her previous colleagues. If her own partner despised her that much, the others had to be rabid. Not that she'd put them to the test.

"Why did you leave?"

"Personal reasons," she said, turning to look out the window. "Are you always this nosey?"

"I'm interested, not nosey. You never wanted to come back?"

Every day. "Nope."

"So you decided scavenging was a better career choice? What did you do during the Witchwar?"

She'd fought it in the only way she could. Alone, with tooth and claw.

A shudder ran through her. She'd killed a lot of people—human and not. She couldn't allow herself to regret it, but she didn't take pride in it either. She'd been a soldier in a war nobody wanted, and she'd fought to protect her city and the people she'd once sworn to protect. Now that the war was over, many of her former enemies had turned into citizens. The whole thing had been so futile and pointless.

"I mostly stayed out of it," she lied, aware that he waited for an answer.

"Oh," was his only reply, but to Kayla's sensitive ears, the word held a wealth of disappointment and disapproval.

"Don't feel bad about canceling dinner," Kayla said into the silence that followed. "Not that you would. Just pull over and drop me off."

"Why would I do that?"

"Because I abandoned the job and the city. Because I sat out the war. Because I'm a selfish coward and you'd have to be batshit crazy to spend time with me on purpose."

Kayla clamped her teeth, bitter self-disgust flooding her veins. The damned fact was that the truth hurt. She *was* a selfish coward, if not the kind Ray and Zach thought she was. Maybe she should tell them the truth. Which was worse? Being a selfish coward or being a monster? Lucky her, she'd accomplished both.

"I must be batshit crazy, then," Zach said, interrupting her thoughts. "I've no intention of canceling."

"So why should I want to go to dinner with a self-confessed mental patient?" The urge to get out and go home to lick her wounds in peace swallowed her. She wanted nothing more than to hop into a hole and pull the dirt over her. She'd been wrong to call Ray, wrong to agree to dinner with Zach. Wrong to get near her old life. Better they all forgot she existed.

"Just give it a chance, okay? I swear I'm not judging you."

"Right."

"I admit I'm curious why you left when you did, but it's not really my business, is it? I'm sure you had good reasons."

Necessary, anyway. Good? Not so much. But the lack of judgement in his response eased the knot of guilt in her gut. Still, she couldn't let it go.

"What makes you think I had good reasons?"

The technomage turned into the entrance of the police lab without answering. The industrial gray cement building stood two stories and was shaped like an X, with the morgue taking up one arm, the forensic labs and offices taking up two more, and a parking lot and storage area in the last.

Zach drove down under the building into an underground loading dock. He turned around and backed up to the dock before putting the van into park and deactivating its magic. Instead of reaching for the door, he turned to look at Kayla.

"You cared enough about the killings to not only call the police, but also stick around and give a report. You got pissed as hell at the injustice of non-humans getting shafted as far as an investigation into their murders. Somebody who cares for strangers like that, non-human strangers to boot, doesn't just walk away when people need her. She doesn't walk away when war shows up on the doorstep of her city, not without a damned good reason."

Her heart warmed, and tears burned in her eyes. She swallowed them.

What did it say about Ray—once her partner and friend—that Zach, a stranger, could see her better than Ray did?

Feeling suddenly raw and exposed, she felt an urge to run. "There's a reason you're a technomage and not a detective," she drawled, pretending he hadn't hit the nail right on the head. "Your deduction skills suck."

He smiled smugly. "Do they? Or does the lady protest too much?"

Kayla shrugged. "I'm not protesting. I'm just amused. Now you should probably get back to work, and I should hit the road."

She reached for the door handle.

"You said you'd have dinner with me."

"I was hoping you'd forgotten about that."

"I have a very good memory. And I want to know you better. I want to know why you are lying about who you are."

God but the man was too insightful for her own good. He said all the right things, and every word made her want to open up and tell him her secrets. She craved the relief of finally coming out of the dark, craved understanding and acceptance. But it wasn't going to happen. Because if she told him that when she got wet she turned into a nightmare from a horror flick, it would be game over.

She sighed. "Look. I don't know what ideas you've got lurking in your brain when it comes to me, but let me set you straight: what you see is what you get. It's *all* you get. I am exactly what you see."

"Don't you get tired of walking through the world all alone?"

The question punched her in the gut like a fist and the air went out of her. Tears burned in the backs of her eyes. She hadn't chosen to be alone. Her father had chosen it for her when he'd attacked her and then disowned her. Her mother had chosen to leave her when she'd decided it was easier to abandon Kayla than stay and deal with her bastard of a husband. Her grandmother and aunt had chosen to look away and hadn't lifted a finger to stop her father's abuse. Ray had chosen to hate her when she'd quit the force rather than believe there had to be a good reason. The world had chosen to abandon her when they'd decided every magical creature and person except technomages were evil. Kayla hated being alone, but she hadn't chosen isolation, and she couldn't change it any more than she could become a pure human again.

She opened her mouth to give a scathing reply, but the words clumped in her throat. She felt her chin starting to crumple and the tears that burned her eyes. She twisted and grappled for the door handle.

"Hey," Zach said, grasping her arm. "Wait."

Kayla tried to shake him off, but he wouldn't let her. She'd have slugged him, but she didn't want him to see the way she was breaking down. She kept her face averted.

"Kayla, I'm sorry. I didn't mean to hurt you."

She wanted to crawl back into her tough shell, jeer at him, tell him she wasn't hurt, but if she tried to talk, she was pretty sure she'd start sobbing like a baby. It wasn't just him. It wasn't even mostly him. It was Ray and leaving the job she'd loved more than anything else in the world. It was remembering her family, and it was knowing how very alone she was and always would be. It was knowing that on wet days, she turned into a monster. A killing machine.

"Kayla, please."

A knock on his window caught his attention. He kept his hold on Kayla as he rolled down his window. An older man in dark-blue coveralls waited outside.

"Hey, boss. They need you up in the bio lab ASAP. Got a problem with one of the machines."

"Have Finch take care of it," Zach said, twisting his head to look back at Kayla.

"She's tried. Couldn't get it working. Says you created the spells to make it work, so you'll be able to fix it." When Zach didn't respond immediately, the older man added, "They're pretty wild about it. Saying the sky's gonna fall."

"Tell them I'm on my way," Zach said, still watching her.

The other man hesitated, and then walked away, clearly curious about what was happening between Zach and Kayla.

"I've got to get to work," Zach said, and his thumb swept back and forth over her forearm in a gentle motion. "But I can't go if you aren't going to stay."

"Yes, you can," she said, her voice thick with the tears she continued to swallow. "They need you, and I shouldn't have come. I don't belong here."

"I *want* you here."

She snorted and shook her head. "No, you don't, and if you do, you shouldn't."

"Look. I may be a pushy bastard, but I want you to stay. I want to know you. There's a room where you can nap while I'm getting squared away, and then I'll take you to the best restaurant in Portland. I promise I'll be charming and funny, and no rude questions."

Kayla wanted nothing more than to run, and that made her want to stay, to defy her fears and embarrassment and guilt. Dinner with Zach had gone from a potential enjoyable distraction to a painful punishment, but she'd be a coward if she ran off. Or rather, more of a coward.

"I guess," she said finally.

"You'll wait?"

She nodded. "But I wouldn't take over long if I were you."

The corner of his mouth kicked up, even though his gaze remained sober. "You don't cut a man a lot of slack, do you?"

"There are a lot of fish in the sea. It's not my fault you decided you wanted to mess with a lionfish. You can always go looking for someone easier."

"I don't need easy. I just need a chance," he said.

"You want a chance, you should play the lottery," she said, deliberately misunderstanding him.

"The lottery doesn't exist anymore."

"Then go find a back-alley game of craps."

He shook his head "Can't win the prize I want at playing craps. Now c'mon. Let's get you tucked in. You could definitely use another nap. You're kind of crabby." He got out and quickly strode around the front of the van to Kayla's door and opened it, standing in the doorway so she couldn't get out. "Though I may be persuaded to cut you some slack," he added suggestively.

Then he winked. Like, actually *winked*.

Kayla tilted her head to look up at him. "Please tell me you are *not* flirting with me."

He grinned. "Of course I am. Don't feel special, though. I flirt with everything that moves. It's my super power."

Kayla snorted. "Sounds more like a creeper power."

His grin widened. "Tomato, tomahto. Anyhow, let's get going. Sooner I fix the problem in the bio lab, sooner we can eat. I'm starved."

"I'm so going to regret this," she groused as she climbed out.

Zach grabbed her heavy pack before she could pick it up. He winced. "What have you got in here? It weighs a ton."

"That's my grocery money for the month."

"Find anything good?"

"Lots. Peanut butter, cinnamon, chocolate chips, olive oil, bunch of spices, some other stuff."

"I would give my left arm for the peanut butter and chocolate chips," he practically moaned.

"You're drooling."

"Damned right I am."

"I'd be willing to trade."

His expression lit up like a kid on Christmas morning. "Anything!"

"You suck at negotiating," Kayla pointed out. "You're supposed to play a little hard to get."

He shrugged. "What can I say? When it comes to peanut butter and chocolate, I'd grovel. On the ground. With bootlicking."

Kayla smiled despite herself. "As delightful as that sounds, I'd rather have something a little more concrete."

"I do great massages, and I'm an amazing cook."

"I was thinking more along the lines of a spell. You can have all four jars of peanut butter *and* the giant Costco bag of dark chocolate chips, and in exchange I get any kind of spell I want, whenever I want. No questions asked."

He rubbed his thumb over his lips as he considered her through narrowed eyes. Something had shifted in him. A predatory tension sharpened his gaze. The easygoing man was gone. In his place stood someone dangerous. Violence wrapped him like a second skin, and suspicion chilled his eyes.

"I don't do blank checks," he said in a flat voice. "People get hurt that way."

"Then I'll think of you whenever I'm dipping a spoonful of peanut butter into a bowl of chocolate chips and binging myself into a coma."

He looked up at the ceiling as if the patience fairy would sprinkle some magic dust on him. "Shit, Kayla, you hit low."

She shrugged. "I am what I am."

His gaze narrowed on her. "What would you use a carte blanche spell for, anyway?"

"No idea. But it's like buying insurance. When an emergency hits, maybe I won't be completely fucked."

He relaxed fractionally, but wary violence still clung to him. He eyed her as if she were a snake and couldn't decide if she was venomous or not. "I can't do 'no questions asked,' and I won't do anything that hurts the city or the innocent."

"Fair enough." She hadn't figured her gambit would work, but nothing ventured, nothing gained. But to her surprise, he continued.

"So to be clear, for the peanut butter and chocolate chips, I will owe you a spell—with safety conditions." A smirk spread across his lips. "Which means you'll *have* to call me at some point. In fact, let's make that a condition. To keep the deal from expiring, you have to have coffee with me once a month."

Kayla scowled. "That's not the deal."

"It is now."

She rolled her eyes. "Two months."

"Fine, but then it's a full meal."

She sighed. "So long as you're buying."

"Then it's a deal."

He held out his hand. She eyed it and then reluctantly slipped hers into his grasp to shake. As elated as she was to have the promise of the spell in her back pocket, she wasn't looking forward to regular dates with him. Or rather, she *was* looking forward to them, and *that* was definitely a problem.

Chapter 9

Kayla

THE NAP DID A lot to restore Kayla's equilibrium. Her scavenge journeys into The Deadwood always came with a hard crash afterward. It took every ounce of adrenaline, concentration, and mental energy she could scrape up just to get in and out alive. The trip, though exhilarating in its way, always left her feeling flat as a pancake. Stir in discovering a murder, emotional whiplash from seeing Ray, and fighting her transformation, and she'd been running on fumes.

Zach loaded her into his Land Rover and drove her to an Italian restaurant out by the old train station. It was a little hole-in-the wall family place with a rustic atmosphere. Not all the patrons were human, a fact that Kayla appreciated. Zach wasn't cryptophobic like so many humans. Not that he was human. But technomages had been the protectors and defenders of humanity in the Witchwar. Kayla expected most of them didn't like witchkin much.

The food was fresh and so good Kayla stuffed herself with lamb ravioli. Magicfall had left a good chunk of the rich farm fields of the Willamette valley mostly alone and flattened out a giant valley around Hagg Lake. That meant a lot of good food was readily available. Farmers had to contend with a growing population of feral pigs and giant carnivorous rodents, but nobody had to worry about starving.

Kayla and Zach drank wine and ate while he regaled Kayla with funny stories of learning magic and some of the bizarre jobs he'd had to do since Magicfall. He flirted outrageously, which confirmed he probably did flirt with anyone, including light poles and fenceposts. It was in his DNA.

Kayla's phone chimed. She started and stared down at her pocket. It chimed again.

"What's wrong?" Zach asked.

She shook her head, her brow furrowing. Only one person had her telephone number, and Nessa wouldn't pick up a phone to save her own life. Taking her cell out, she checked the number. Shock spiraled up her spine. *Ray.*

She put the phone to her ear. "Hello?"

"Kayla?" His voice was textured with gravel, as if he'd drunk half a bottle of whiskey.

"Yes." When he didn't say anything right away, she prompted him. "Ray?"

"I'm here. I've got something going on. I need you to come to my scene."

Her frown deepened, and a maelstrom of emotion spun through her. That he called, that he wanted her to weigh in on a case, that she might have to step back onto the stage of a life she loved and had fled. Her hand clenched around her napkin in her lap.

"Why?"

He made a sound as though he was sucking his teeth. He did that when he was distracted or worrying about something. "I've got a kidnapping."

"Okay."

"I think you know the victims."

Dread woke inside her and she braced herself. "Who?"

"Theresa Runyon and Margaret Valentine."

She felt the blood drain from her face. "Who—" She broke off before she could ask who'd taken them. Ray wouldn't have called her if he knew.

"What do you need me for?" The words came out sharper than she intended.

"Landon wants you here. He won't talk to me otherwise." He used his calm-the-witness voice. He paused and then said, "He's pretty shook up. He could use someone."

And doubtless her father was only making Landon feel worse. Alistair had a knack for that. He also wouldn't have told Ray the truth about the two women, and if their kidnapping had anything to do with their explosive secret, then Ray would need to know.

"Okay. I'll come."

"I'll call Logan. I need him here, too. I'll have him pick you up. Where are you?"

Kayla glanced at Zach. "He's here with me. Hold on. I'll let you talk to him."

She passed her phone to Zach. He listened and then nodded. "Got it. We'll get a van and be there asap."

He hung up the phone and handed it to her. "I guess we're off, then." He stood, holding a warm hand out to her.

"What about the check? We need to pay for dinner."

He shook his head. "I come in and help out pretty regularly. I try not to charge Antonio for it, but he refuses to take money when I eat."

"Are you okay to drive?" Kayla wasn't a big drinker, and though she'd only had a couple of glasses of wine, her head felt a little floaty.

"I'm good. Being a technomage changes my metabolism. I can't really get drunk anymore."

Kayla babbled all the way back to the lab. She didn't want to give Zach an opening to ask her unpleasant questions. Like why had Ray called her? And what did she have to do with the Runyons?

Unfortunately, Zach had the patience of a sniper and didn't give up easily.

"So where exactly are we going?" he asked as they pulled out of the garage.

Kayla eyed him. "Ray didn't tell you?"

"He said you'd know the way. He said to come in the back service entrance."

Oh. "Theresa Runyon and her daughter Margaret Valentine were kidnapped. We're going to their estate."

He let out a low whistle. "That's serious. No wonder he lit out like his ass was on fire." He thought for a moment and then drilled down to the questions Kayla didn't want him to ask. "Why does he need you there? How do you know where to go?"

She looked out the window, not seeing anything. Zach didn't prod her. She didn't owe him an answer, but he was bound to find out, and anyway, what did it really matter? Finally, she heaved a quiet sigh.

"Alistair Runyon is my father." That's it. One quiet declaration.

He gave a low whistle. "Holy shit."

She snorted.

"Did Ray know?"

"Nobody knew."

"How come?"

Kayla grimaced. "I despise my father with all my soul." She paused. "He disowned me. When I joined the academy."

"Ouch."

"You have no idea." And he never would. Nobody would.

"What about the two kidnap victims—Theresa Runyon and Margaret Valentine? Those are your grandmother and aunt?"

"Yes, on my father's side."

"I take it you're not close to them either?"

Kayla fell back into memory. As a child, her grandmother had fascinated her. Theresa always smelled of rich perfume. She let Kayla play with any of the expensive knickknacks that decorated the mansion. Though she wasn't the sort for a lot of physical affection, she'd been kind and loving in a distant sort of way.

Margaret and Landon hadn't moved to the estate until her husband died in a plane crash. Later Kayla had overheard her father lecturing her aunt on her poor choices and learned that Margaret's husband had been fleeing the country with most of their money and his mistress.

From the way he talked, Kayla had been certain her father had arranged the accident. Then he'd proceeded to dictate what her Aunt Margaret would do with her life and all of it was to be under his direction. Not that he could have said or done anything if Grandmother hadn't permitted it. She was the iron fist in the household.

That overheard conversation had taught Kayla how dangerous he could be, even to his family, and that if she wanted her own life, she was going to have to find a way to keep him in his place. It had taken her some time, but eventually she'd discovered the family's deepest, darkest secret and she'd had her key to freedom.

She made arrangements, and then she'd run like hell.

"Kayla?" Zach's voice brought her back to the present.

"I was closer to my Aunt Margaret than my grandmother. Mostly because of Landon, my cousin. We spent a lot of time together, even though he's younger than me by close to ten years. My aunt had lost her husband and was grieving, so I took care of Landon. She was nice to me."

"Not a ringing endorsement," Zach observed dryly.

"My family isn't generally close." Understatement of the century. The ties that bound the Runyons together were fear and greed, not love or loyalty.

"How long has it been since you've been home?"

"That place isn't home. It's never been home. I haven't been back there in a little more than nine years. Since I joined the academy."

"You rose up the police ladder quick. You must have been a real hotshot."

It had only taken her two years after graduating from the academy to earn her detective's badge. She'd been the youngest ever to qualify. She'd sometimes wondered if, even though her father had despised her career and had disowned her, he'd put pressure on the brass to promote her. It made sense. If it got out who she really was, he could brag on her brilliant rise and her outstanding record. If she was going to be a cop, at least she was a superstar, thanks to her Runyon genes. Just imagine if her real identity leaked out and she was mediocre at best. Oh, the humiliation! Her father would never accept that.

The possibility he'd caused her career to skyrocket the way it had drove her to make sure she more than earned everything she'd got. She'd worked double and triple shifts, taken extra classes, and attended lectures and seminars. She'd read everything she could get her hands on focusing on criminology, forensics, psychology, poisons, weapons—anything and everything that would help her solve crimes. She was a pit bull on every case she worked. She never gave up, and she never let go. That passion and drive were what had made Ray and her click so well as partners.

"I'm not sure I didn't have help," she confessed in a low voice. She'd never told anyone that before. Not even Ray. Especially not Ray.

"You think your family boosted your career?"

Zach's question reflected only curiosity and no condemnation.

"Maybe."

"You were a good cop."

She glanced at him. "How would you know?"

He lifted a shoulder in a little shrug. "I may have checked your record at the lab when you were asleep."

"How very stalkery of you."

"It's not like you were going to tell me anything."

"Ever heard of privacy?"

He chuckled. "Tell you what. Tit for tat. I'll give you access to my record and you can read all about me."

"Not the same thing. You *want* me to read about you. You're an attention whore."

"Sticks and stones," he said. "But you earned your career, if the stuff in the file is accurate."

She shifted uncomfortably in her seat. The conversation was hitting far too close to home. "It's not fiction, but lots of cops were as good as me and didn't get a rocket ride up the ladder."

"You solved more crimes, arrested more criminals, and put more convictable cases in front of the D.A. than any other cop. Ray got so pissed about losing you for a reason. Partners like you don't come along very often."

"He's pissed because I didn't stay on the force after Magicfall or come back during the Witchwar."

"He *is* a little high strung."

THE CLOSER THEY got to the estate, the more tense Kayla grew. She dreaded seeing Alistair again. Aside from letting people find out she was a shifter, it was the last thing on earth she wanted to do.

"How long have you known Ray?" she asked to distract herself.

"Met him about six months after Magicfall. I'd been trying to master my magic and was having more luck learning than some others. There was an attack—you remember the big fire across the river?"

Kayla nodded. Who didn't remember that? Most of everything between Highway 84 and the airport had been incinerated, including stones, cement, asphalt—everything. The fire had been mystical and had swept across the quarter like a punishment from God. Nobody caught up in it had survived.

"You helped stop it?"

"It flamed up just after sunset. Clearest night we'd had in weeks," Zach said. "We were training out in Beaverton—all of us technomages. We were trying to teach ourselves and each other, experimenting a lot. We didn't know shit about using our magic. All of a sudden, the sky lights on fire. The flames had to have been well over a hundred feet tall for us to see them all the way from there. They burned green and yellow. It was beautiful and terrifying.

"We were watching, not sure what we were seeing or what we should do, when this cop car comes flying up with sirens wailing. Ray jumps out and says the fire's an attack and we have to stop it before the city burns to the ground.

We all piled into whatever car we could find. I caught a ride with Ray. But when we got there, we were like a bunch of headless chickens. I put together a Hail Mary plan, but it turned into an argument. Meanwhile the fire was eating the city. The damned thing was so hot that even a hundred yards away, the heat could melt your hair."

"So how did you stop it?"

"Ray. He went drill sergeant on our asses. He'd had enough of listening to us argue. He came up with a pretty simple and elegant idea and asked if it could be done. Once we had the idea, it didn't take us but a few minutes to figure out how to make it work, and then another hour to get us all into place. After that, it was a piece of cake." He shook his head. "Not soon enough. A lot of people died that night. We should have worked faster. Shouldn't have wasted time arguing.

"Anyway, after that I got on board with the police department and helped out with the war whenever they needed me. We formed an association to network with technomages from other cities to share what we've learned. It's helped. I wouldn't be half as good as I am now if not for the stuff I learned through the TMA. That was Ray's idea, too."

The fact that Ray had pulled the technomages together and helped them network across cities didn't surprise Kayla. He was a take-charge guy and a problem solver. Nothing frustrated him more than running up against something he couldn't fix.

Kayla pissed him off a lot. A reluctant smile curved her lips. Poor guy. But some problems just couldn't be solved.

"He's a good cop. Good man. Good friend to have in your corner."

"Have you got a point?" Her look was challenging.

"Just saying. Word is you two used to be tight as a key and a lock. Shame to lose a friend like that."

"It is."

He darted a glance at her. "You going to do something about it?"

"You know how it is. All the king's horses and all the king's men couldn't put Humpty Dumpty back together." With that, she turned to look out the window again.

Zach let the conversation lapse until they drew closer to the estate, and Kayla gave him directions to the service entrance.

They trundled over the rippled and unrepaired asphalt, skirting several large potholes. Apparently, Alistair hadn't bothered to maintain the road. Zach swore as the tires slid off the road on Kayla's side and the top-heavy van tipped ominously. He twisted the wheel and gunned the gas. For a moment, the wheels spun on the muddy clay shoulder, and then the van lurched back onto the road.

"Remind me to equip the van with a levitation spell," he said as they jolted through another pothole.

"If you're going to go that far, why not just make it a flying car?"

"Can you imagine the chaos? No lights, no speed limits, and no roads. You'd have people crashing and dropping out of the sky like metal meteors. *Not* a good idea."

"But levitation is different?"

"If it's only a few inches or a foot and you keep your speeds down, follow the road, and obey the traffic laws, then yes, it's a whole lot different. Anyway, as rich as your family is, you'd think they'd take better care of the road."

"Why would they? It's not like they have to use it. Just the hired help."

They turned sharply around a jut of low-sweeping cedars and pulled up to the gate. A tiny white guard shack sat on the other side of a chain-link fence topped with razor wire. Four trucks and a half dozen guards with AR 15s and wearing body armor eyed the van. Three of them stepped through the door-sized gate. Two came to stand in front, guns raised and aimed at the windshield. The third approached the driver's side, gun at eye level.

"Roll your window down!"

Slowly lifting his hand from the wheel, Zach depressed the button. The window slid down into the door.

"Who are you and what is your business here?"

"Portland Metro Police," Zach said, hooking his thumb at the logo on the van. "I'm a technomage. Detective Ray Garza sent for me."

"I.D."

Zach pushed up his sleeve to reveal a metal band fastened around his wrist. He touched the design on the top and an image of his face along with other identifying information popped up in the air above it.

Kayla was pretty sure she'd seen something like it in a sci-fi flick a long time ago.

The guard examined the identification hologram and then nodded to Zach whose touch powered it off again.

"Who's she?" The guard jerked his chin at Kayla.

Zach didn't miss a beat. "Consultant. I'm to escort her to Detective Garza."

The guard gave them both a long searching look, then turned away, talking into a microphone attached to his collar. They waited as he conferred with someone, and then he nodded. "Follow your escort. Stay on the road and don't leave your vehicle until you're cleared to do so."

He waved and the gate rolled open. Two guards hopped into one of the four parked trucks and pulled out. Zach fell in behind.

"Tough crowd," Zach murmured. "Is it always like this?"

"My father probably called them in after the kidnapping. Locking the barn door is so helpful after the horses escape."

"What's your father going to do when he sees you?"

"Probably have me shot."

"I'm serious."

"So am I."

Unexpectedly, Zach reached out and wrapped warm fingers around her hand, squeezing gently. "I've got your back. So does Ray."

Kayla had her doubts about Ray but appreciated the sentiment.

Their escort led them up through trees and pulled up behind the imposing garage at the back of the house. Zach parked and hopped out, circling around to meet Kayla. He put a hand on her back as he guided her toward Ray who stepped out of a doorway on the side of the building.

Ray waved off the guards. When they'd disappeared back the way they'd come, he turned to Zach. "Something's weird with the house. I need you to check it out."

"Weird how?"

"I don't think there are any active magic suppression wards."

Zach looked startled. "Really? You'd think this place would be tiled with them. They can certainly afford it."

Kayla bit down on the tip of her tongue. She knew why, but much as she liked Zach, she should tell Ray first.

"Take a look around," Ray told the technomage. "Keep a low profile. I don't want Runyon crawling up my ass, and something tells me he won't be excited to see you."

Zach lifted his hand to his forehead in a mock salute. "Aye, aye Captain." He looked at Kayla. "You going to be all right?"

"Why wouldn't she be?" Ray growled.

"This place doesn't hold good memories for her," Zach said to the other man without looking away from Kayla. "Remember what I said," he told her. "You're not alone."

She nodded but didn't answer. She'd taken to carrying a water amulet with her. It functioned just the opposite of the one she'd used to dry herself after jumping into the fountain. This one would soak her to the skin in an instant, allowing her a swift transformation. If it came down to it, she'd activate it. Her father had no idea what she'd become, but Kayla was willing to give him an up-close-and-personal demonstration of her other half if necessary.

"You should get on it," Ray told Zach, who nodded and walked off in the direction of the house.

"You two are awfully cozy," Ray observed when the other man had vanished from site.

"He's nice," Kayla said.

"Nice enough to have dinner with."

She cocked her head and folded her arms over her chest. "Have you got a problem with that?"

"I didn't think he was your type."

"And what *is* my type?" It took all she had to keep the anger out of her voice. Did he think she didn't deserve a man like Zach?

She waited for his acid response, trying to convince herself that she didn't care what Ray thought.

"Your type is—" He stopped and looked away.

"Is what exactly?" She pushed, a sadomasochistic part of her wanting to hear his disparaging opinion.

"None of my fucking business," he said finally, his mouth tightening. "Come on. We're wasting time, and Landon's waiting."

He turned to go inside, and she followed him, curiosity gnawing at her. What had he been about to say? Not that she'd like the answer. Kayla was pretty sure Ray thought she ought to be with a slack-jawed, booger-eating lowlife. Unfortunately, she thought he might be right.

Chapter 10

Ray

WHAT WAS HIS fucking problem? He didn't need to antagonize Kayla, not when he needed her to get Landon talking. Yet after learning she'd been to dinner with Logan, he'd wanted to punch a wall. And when Logan put his hand on her back as if she belonged to him, Ray'd had to use every ounce of self-control he had not to punch his friend in the side of the head.

Why should he even care if they went out? Kayla was free to do anything she wanted with anybody she wanted.

Unbidden, his brain conjured an image of her and Logan wrapped in each other's arms. He recoiled, a jolt of hot emotion thrusting through his gut. The image looped through his brain again. And again. What in the holy fuck? He was reacting like he was jealous. But he wasn't. He couldn't be. It wasn't possible.

No, if she wanted Logan in her bed, more power to her. No skin off his ass.

So why did the thought of them together make him want to hurl Logan off a cliff? Why, when he'd started to tell her what he thought her type was, had his own name been the only one to pop into his head? And, God Almighty, why did the thought of her naked make his dick hard as cement?

"Ray?"

Kayla's voice jerked him out of his absorption, and he realized he'd stopped halfway up the stairs. Mechanically he started climbing again, his mind reeling at the stunning realization that he wanted Kayla.

He shook himself. He couldn't think about this now. He couldn't let himself be distracted because he had a literal hard-on for his old partner, the same partner who'd walked off and left him like trash in a dumpster.

Violent emotion flared again, and he ruthlessly smothered it. He didn't have time for this shit, and more importantly, he didn't want to care about Kayla, not even on a superficial level. She'd evaporated out of his life four years ago, and she'd leave again just as fast when this was over. Ray wasn't going to let his dick run his brain. If Logan wanted her, he could have her.

He told himself he believed that as he marched down the corridor to where Landon waited.

RAY HAD LEFT TO door to the game room open. When he went inside, he found Landon sitting in a blocky leather chair, his pool cue across his knees, his gaze fixed on the ceiling. When Ray appeared, the kid tensed, his hands white-knuckling around the wooden cue. His expression when he saw Kayla morphed into a mix of gratitude, hope, desperation, and then anger. A whole lot of anger. Ray could sympathize.

"Kay!" Landon rose jerkily to his feet as if pulled up on strings.

Kayla hesitated just inside the doorway. Ray turned to watch the reunion. Looking at Kayla, it was like seeing her for the first time. He scowled. He hadn't given it any thought back at Keller Fountain, but she seemed smaller than before. She appeared thin—almost gaunt. Dark circles rimmed her eyes, and tension lines bracketed her eyes and mouth. Though clean, she was ragged around the edges, almost as if she lived on the streets. Her jeans were frayed at the hems, and her boots barely had anything resembling a sole.

Four years ago, she'd been a ball of fire. She'd radiated energy and reckless confidence. He'd always been the one to talk her down from the wild risks she was willing to take to get a criminal off the street. But now?

She'd shrunk into herself, giving off a furtive vibe, as if she spent a lot of time looking over her shoulder and hiding in the shadows.

More startling was the vulnerability that colored her features as she stared at Landon. Raw emotion molded her expression. Her dark eyes had grown shiny. Were those unshed tears? Ray's stomach twisted, and the unwanted urge to get between her and anything that might hurt her clawed through him, especially when he realized the dominant expression was pain.

The knowledge felt invasive, like rifling through her underwear drawer. She was more naked now than she would be without clothes. It shamed him to intrude in such an intimate way.

Ray stuffed the feeling down. Being a cop brought him face-to-face with people at their lowest moments. The fact that he knew Kayla couldn't be allowed to stop him from properly executing his job. Two lives hung in the balance. Families of victims and witnesses all too often held back or hid vital information that might embarrass or implicate someone. Alistair Runyon was one of those. So far, so was Landon. As for Kayla—once upon a time he'd have said she was the most honest and blunt person he knew. Now she was just another question mark. Make that a bagful of question marks.

If he hoped to find Theresa Runyon and her daughter, he needed all the facts and fast. Without a ransom demand, the likelihood of their remaining alive—if they still lived—diminished with every passing minute. That meant he couldn't be squeamish about doing whatever was necessary to find them before the kidnapper got rid of them.

Landon had been so adamant about finding Kayla that Ray half expected the kid to fly into her arms and cry on her shoulder. Instead the stare-off went on. Kayla finally took a half step forward.

"I'm sorry this happened, Landon. I'll help any way I can to get them back for you."

At her words, the kid broke. All the anger and resentment that had been holding him together dissolved. The cue fell from his hands, and he covered his face and spun around, his chest jerking with harsh sobs.

Kayla wrapped him in her arms and pulled his head to her shoulder. She murmured things in Landon's ear that Ray couldn't hear. He shoved away from her, and she let him go, her expression rippling with guilt and pain.

"Don't touch me!"

Kayla flinched, and her shoulders wilted. She blinked as if trying not to cry.

Cry? Kayla? Ray stuffed his hands in his pockets to keep himself from trying to comfort her. She wouldn't welcome it, and for all he knew she was putting on an act. A really good act.

"You wanted me to come," she reminded Landon in a dead voice.

Landon scrubbed his hands over his face. He looked far younger than his twenty-two years. "You need to find my mom and Grandmother."

Kayla nodded. "I know." She licked her lips and wrapped her arms around her stomach. "What happened?"

He flicked a suspicious glance at Ray.

"He's okay," she said. "You can trust him."

Landon's jaw knotted, and his chin trembled. His lips pinched together, and he gave a microscopic head shake.

"My father won't touch you, I promise," she assured him in a steely voice. "Anyway, he's not going to be looking at you. You aren't the one who's going to let the cat out of the bag. I will. You just have to tell us what you know about the kidnapping."

"If you tell, he'll kill you."

Ray stiffened and jerked his hands from his pockets, eyes narrowing. The kid didn't mean it metaphorically.

Kayla only shrugged. "He can try. I'd bet on me, if I were you."

Landon stared at her a long moment. "*Now* you want to get in his face?" Red suffused his cheeks. "For Grandmother and my mother," he said bitterly.

Not for me.

Ray could almost hear the unspoken words.

A tear slid down Kayla's cheek. "I'm sorry."

"Fat lot of good that does."

"I should have taken you with me."

"You shouldn't have *left!*"

He kicked a small table. It flipped over, the glass shattering. Kayla flinched, her face paling. Ray could totally sympathize with Landon's frustration. He'd broken a lot of things over her, too, including most of his knuckles on his right hand. But punching that wall had felt good at the time.

"I'm sorry," she said again.

"Yeah, you *are* sorry," Landon declared bitterly. "You pretended pretty good, but you're just as much a selfish lying bastard as Uncle Alistair. But whatever. I'm over it. Now I just want you to get my mom and Grandmother back. Then you can do your disappearing act again. We won't miss you."

Seeing the flare of hurt in Kayla's eyes, it took all Ray had not to slug the kid, even though she'd made her bed and should have to lie in it.

She stepped back and seemed to draw into herself even tighter.

That's it. This little family reunion had gone on long enough. "Someone going to tell me what the fuck is going on?"

Landon startled as if he'd forgotten Ray was even there. "Nothing. Water under the bridge."

"The hell it is."

"It's fine," Kayla said, finding her voice again. "Landon's right. Old news."

"What did he mean that Runyon would kill you?"

Kayla gave a dismissive shrug. "Just a figure of speech. Alistair and I don't get along real well. That's all."

"You're lying," he declared flatly.

She just looked at him. His fingers curled into his palms. He wanted to strangle her. No, he wanted to shake some goddamned answers out of her. Instead he looked at Landon.

"Tell me what happened."

Ray didn't like the nervous slide of Landon's gaze away from his, and he definitely didn't like the way Kayla and the kid locked eyes as if they were having a silent conversation.

"I didn't actually see anything," Landon muttered.

Ray didn't know why or what about, but he knew Landon lied. And he knew he had to figure out the why and the what fast or his investigation was going nowhere. "What *can* you tell me?" he asked in a quiet voice.

The silent communication between Kayla and Landon went on for another few seconds.

"I found where it happened," Landon said finally. "Where they broke in."

"They got in *there*? Christ," Kayla muttered, wiping her hand over her mouth. "Seriously?"

The kid nodded.

"Of course. Why wouldn't that be at the heart of it?" She sighed. "Shit. Alistair must be shitting bricks."

Ray's temper simmered. Too many damned secrets, and he didn't know any of them. "Mind letting me on things? I'm not a damned mushroom. Quit keeping me in the dark and feeding me shit. We don't exactly have a lot of time here."

Kayla ignored him. "You should stay here. Plausible deniability," she said to Landon.

He shook his head. "Fuck him."

"Be sure. You get on his radar, and he'll target you more than he already has. It will be ugly. He already hates me, and there's not much worse he can do to me now."

The "now" caught Ray's attention. He was sure she was talking about her father, Alistair Runyon. What had he done to her before?

"I can handle him," Landon said, but Ray heard the tremble in the kid's voice.

"If that's what you want."

Kayla finally gave Ray her attention. She looked more bruised around the eyes than she had when they'd arrived. It annoyed the fuck out of him that he not only noticed, but that he cared.

"I should probably start with show and tell."

With that cryptic statement, she strode toward the door. Landon followed with Ray bringing up the rear.

She returned to the stairwell and went downstairs and outside into the balmy night. Clouds obscured the stars. It was going to rain soon.

"Text Zach," she told Ray. "You'll want him for this."

He frowned but did as told. Asking why would only waste time.

"Where exactly are we going?" he asked.

Kayla shook her head. "I don't want to color your perceptions. You should see it cold. After that I'll tell you everything you want to know."

He lifted on brow. "Everything?"

Her flush indicated she took his meaning. "There's no point. I left and talking about it won't change anything."

"No? It will tell me why my partner left me high and dry. Why she left a job she loved more than anything else in the world. Why she's never talked to me since until tonight."

Dammit! He hadn't meant to say anything, but the scene with Landon had cut too close to home, and his emotions were already running too close to the surface.

She flinched from the bitterness in his voice. "I haven't talked to you because you made it clear you didn't want anything to do with me," she said tautly. "I distinctly remember. You said, and I quote: 'If you go, then you're dead to me. I don't ever want to hear from you or see you again.'"

Ray grimaced. He didn't doubt he'd said something of the sort. He didn't remember it, but he'd been spewing all kinds of things in an effort to hurt her when he'd realized that she wasn't going to change her mind. He'd been so pissed off, so confused. He'd hit back at her with every weapon in his arsenal, blasting her with a verbal barrage of hatefulness and spite. Anything to not have to feel the awful sense of betrayal.

"We're talking now. Why don't you tell me why you left?"

He hadn't realized how much the not knowing had continued to fester inside him, growing like an untreated ulcer. How could it hurt more now than it had then? But back then, there was still hope she'd change her mind; hope that she'd care enough about him, about the job, to return. Now he knew better. Whatever ties they'd shared hadn't mattered to her at all.

She slashed a look at him. "It doesn't matter. All that does matter is I had my reasons, and those reasons haven't changed."

Ray swore and spit into the bushes, jamming his hands into his pants pockets. If he didn't keep them bound in some fashion, he'd strangle her.

A few minutes of tense silence later, Logan came out one of the back entrances of the house and joined them in the circular courtyard.

He frowned at Kayla. "Everything okay?"

"Fine," she replied, averting her gaze.

"Find anything?" Ray asked. Logan didn't answer for a moment, his gaze lingering on Kayla.

Ray ground his teeth, his inner King Kong starting to pound his chest.

"You're right. There's no active magic suppression. In fact, the place throbs with magical energy."

"Security spells? Maybe convenience spells?" Ray asked.

Logan shrugged. "Could be either, could be both, could be something else altogether. All I know is the magic here is powerful, and it's definitely witch magic."

"I'll show you why," Kayla said and took off again. Landon overtook her. He whispered rapidly to her.

She shook her head, speaking in a normal voice. "Not my secret to keep. I'm going to bet Grandmother and Aunt Margaret will forgive me if it helps to find them. Alistair would rather see them die than let the cat out of the bag. I've got news for him: the tabby's going free."

Instead of entering the house, she strode out through the rose garden. The center held one those meditation labyrinths, the path outlined with river rock and paved with white sand, all leading to a teak gazebo in the center. Clematis and roses climbed over the structure, turning it into a fragrant bower.

Kayla went to the entrance of the labyrinth and stopped. She broke a twig from the gnarled tree growing beside the opening and drew a set of marks into the sand with it. She stripped the leaves off the wood and sprinkled them over the marks she'd drawn. An amber glow lit the symbols, and then traveled to the rocks lining the path and outlined them in golden light.

Ray stared, startled by the flashy show of magic. "What's this?"

"You'll see," Kayla said. "Follow me and stay on the path."

With that, she walked the maze, winding back and forth. Landon trailed her, and then Ray followed by Logan.

They all climbed the three steps into the gazebo. The interior stood empty without a stick of furniture. A round wood panel polished to a warm sheen had been inlaid into the center of the floor. Kayla stepped into the middle of it, and the panel sank down. As she dropped, steps made of iron coiled down from the lip of the hole, until a spiral stairway offered them all a path to whatever lay below.

They descended into a small room with walls constructed of gray cinder block and solid steel doors on facing walls. Kayla waited tightlipped and shoulders hunched. Landon stood a few feet away, watching her. He gave Ray a wary look as Ray came to join them.

"Impressive bit of magic," Logan said as he stepped off the round wood panel. A few seconds later the stairs retracted and the panel rose into the air, fitting itself tightly back into its bezel.

"What is this place?" Ray asked.

"You'll see."

With that, she pressed a hand against the center of the left side door. It had no handle, Ray realized. More amber light outlined Kayla's fingers. She pushed and the door swung open, revealing a corridor made of the same industrial cinder block.

They followed it for about fifty feet. Back under the house, if Ray had to guess. At that point, the corridor turned and they faced another steel door. Kayla opened it and stepped back to let the others go inside.

The floor lit with pearl light as Ray stepped across the threshold. Ahead, he saw an arched opening about twenty feet wide. The top rose into a sharp point. The black shadows beyond gave no hint at what lay beyond.

Two slender columns of dark green rose on either side. As he drew closer, he realized that the columns were actually carved to look like trees with winter-bare limbs.

"That's petrified wood," Landon said. "From Hampton Butte near Bend. The only complete trees that have ever been found there."

"What's inside?" Ray asked.

"The scene of the crime," Kayla said. She gave Ray a thin smile. "Go in. It should be safe enough."

"There's a lot of magic here," Logan said, stepping closer to the opening. "Witch magic. Something else, too. Don't recognize it, though."

"Is it active?"

"Hard to say. Doesn't feel like it, but since I haven't encountered it before, I'm just talking out my ass. I could try clearing it, but without some idea of what it is, I could easily end up blowing us to smithereens."

Ray wasn't willing to bet their lives on Kayla's feeble assurance that they should be safe. "Can you shield us?"

Logan nodded and stepped back. He held his hands out to the sides, palms down. Blue sparks danced across the walls, ceiling, and floor, gathering around him and piling up around his legs. Soon he stood waist deep in the flecks of magic. More gathered until the glowing mound was about six feet in diameter and a good four feet deep.

Logan swept his hands down into the pile of magic, turning his palms up and keeping them submerged. The air shuddered and shook in Ray's lungs. He held his breath, making himself stand still though every instinct told him to run like hell.

His own magic danced eagerly just under his skin, answering not to the build of Logan's magic, but the siren song of whatever lay beyond the archway. He clamped down on the restless power. The last thing he needed was to lose what little control he had over it. He knew from experience it could be bad—devastating even.

A little over two years ago, he'd come down with a very bad case of the flu. As if that wasn't bad enough, it had quickly morphed into full-blown pneumonia. Luckily he lived alone, because as he sank into fever-induced delirium, he'd drawn on his power to fight demons that existed only in his crazed mind.

When he'd eventually come back to reality, he'd destroyed his house. Not by tearing it down, but by cutting through walls with whips of magic, or filling one bedroom with boiling mud. He'd managed to install a forest of eight-inch razor-edged spikes on the floor of his kitchen and on the walls of both showers. He couldn't begin to account for some of what he'd found. In the end, he'd packed up everything he could salvage and had moved into an abandoned place miles away, then returned and torched the place, once again using his magic to keep the fire from traveling anywhere else.

Logan had been murmuring and now thrust his hands up in the air as if he was throwing confetti. It looked like it. Blue flecks erupted upward and swirled near the ceiling in a widening spiral. After a moment, the flecks fell like snow, gathering around each of them and smoothing out into a thin blue shield.

"Pretty," Ray said.

Landon held out his arm and studied it. Kayla shuddered, her elbows clamped tight against her body, her hands knotted together across her stomach. She radiated tension. Ray frowned. Why? Was she afraid of magic? Was that why she'd left the department?

Priorities, Ray, he reminded himself. *You've been beating yourself over the head with the mystery of Kayla since the moment she quit. Now is not the time to play the mental masturbation game. Focus on doing your job. She's back in your life. You can tackle all those questions later.*

She was back in his life. The phrase echoed through his skull, and he realized that no matter how angry at her he was, no matter how much he resented her leaving, no matter how betrayed he still felt, the relief of seeing her again had loosened a noose around his throat he hadn't even realized was there. He felt as though he could really breathe again for the first time in four years.

He looked at her again. *Later*, he promised himself. *I'll get to the bottom of it later.*

Nodding at Logan, he stepped between the two trees and into the room on the other side. Instantly the floor lit. He stopped dead. A giant circle of opal or abalone had been inlaid into the dark stone floor. Within its circumference, each point of a five-rayed star touched the slope of the circle. Inside that was a triangle, and at the center of that, a small solid circle the size of a silver dollar.

"Jesus," Logan said, having stopped beside him.

Ray glanced over his shoulder at Kayla and Landon who stood braced as if against a coming storm.

Dozens of questions cascaded through his mind. He settled for: "Why do the Runyons keep a secret casting floor?"

The answer seemed obvious, but he wanted to hear it from Kayla.

"Witchcraft runs in the family," she said, her gaze dropping.

"Your grandmother?"

"And my aunt," she confirmed.

"What about your father?"

"No. He's completely human." She grimaced. "Or as human as any psychopath can be."

Ray wondered how Runyon felt about that. Theresa Runyon held the family purse strings, and she and her daughter were witches to boot. Could Alistair have wanted to get rid of them to take control of the family coffers? It was a definite possibility.

That's when his brain finally pieced together the puzzle.

Kayla had to be a witch.

It was the only thing that made sense. Ray couldn't imagine anything else that would make her leave the job. Not the way she loved it. Magicfall must have transformed her the same way it had Ray. But instead of trying to hide her disability like he had, she'd chosen to leave before anybody found out.

It fit.

Ray's anger and resentment flared wildly as it occurred to him what a waste the last four years had been. Kayla had never needed to walk away. He'd have helped her; they'd have helped each other. If only she'd just fucking *talked* to him!

Then reason asserted itself. Would he have voluntarily told her about becoming a witch? He didn't know. He might not have taken the risk. But she hadn't even tried to stay, to hide what she was and do the job. She'd chosen to leave and give up everything. To leave him.

It had probably been hard on her, and his bitter words at the end hadn't made her trust him. Even though she *should* have trusted him already. Still, he could see where she'd been coming from. He still couldn't entirely forgive her for just walking out, but at least now he knew why.

Now to figure out what to do about it. Did he tell her he was okay with her being a witch? Reveal that he was too? If he wanted to keep her in his life, then he had no choice; he had to tell her. But that was for later. Now was for tracking down the kidnappers.

Ray walked around the casting floor. He could feel magic pulsing like a heartbeat through the room. Many spells had been cast here, soaking into the walls and saturating the air.

Colorful tapestries hung at intervals, with shelves of various arcane implements and supplies spaced between. He saw a rainbow of candles, several hundred kinds of crystals in every color under the sun, plastic tubs neatly labeled and stacked on shelves. Sheaves of twigs and branches from all sorts of trees and bushes filled the small army of tall ceramic jars running down the wall on his right. Glass containers and canisters of herbs, dried flowers, seeds, nuts, and fruits lined the long shelves just above the branches.

Something caught his attention. He wasn't quite sure what. It was more something he sensed than anything concrete, like a breath of cold air in a hot room, or a flicker of shadow in the corner of his eye.

"What level could your grandmother and aunt craft? Do you know?" he asked Kayla as he continued to scan the room, looking for what was setting off his radar.

"Grandmother is the center—powerful enough to hold her own coven. My aunt was in the star. She might have reached the triangle by now, I don't know. The time I had anything to do with this"—her gesture encompassed the room—"I was seventeen. Things probably have changed a lot since then."

Ray did the math. Kayla was almost twenty-nine, so twelve years.

"Your grandmother had a coven?"

Kayla shrugged. "Other witches came to the house. I don't know if they just worked together or if they formed an actual coven."

"They weren't," Landon said, breaking his tense silence. "My mother complained about it. She would tell Grandmother that they should perform a coven ceremony. All Grandmother would say was that they couldn't afford it, and there was no room anyway."

Ray nodded, noting down the information, adding question marks to "no room" and "couldn't afford it."

"Did they take part in the Witchwar?"

"I don't know," Kayla said. "Landon?"

He opened his mouth and then closed it.

"It'll be okay," Kayla said, turning to face him. "We have to know. The kidnapper could have taken them for revenge."

He looked past her at Ray and then back to Kayla, clearly torn.

"If you want to find them, you need to tell us the whole truth," Ray said.

That seemed to break the dam.

"They didn't have a choice," he said abruptly. "Someone came to see Grandmother back then. I was helping her with her roses." He stopped.

"Who came to see her?" Kayla prompted.

"It was an angel. An honest-to-God angel. He had white wings edged in blue. He came down out of the sky and handed Grandmother a rolled-up piece of paper. Then he just flew away. Never said a word. Grandmother read the message, and her hands started shaking. She looked like she was going to pass out.

"I asked her what was wrong, and all she said was that sometimes a person has to make a hard choice. Then she went in the house. After that, she and mom packed up and left without saying anything to anybody. They didn't come back until the war ended."

He looked at Kayla. "I was stuck alone with Uncle Alistair. I thought they were dead, and then they came home. Now they're gone again." He swallowed, and his tough-guy exterior cracked. His chin trembled. "We had a fight. I told her I hate her. I told my mother I wished she was dead, leaving me alone with Uncle Alistair. Now—" His voice cracked.

Kayla pulled him into a tight hug, and to Ray's surprise, the kid let her.

"She knows that you love her," she said. "Kids and parents fight all the time, but parents know you don't really mean the things you say."

He pulled back. "You did. You hate Uncle Alistair. Everybody knows it."

"I'm a special case, and he deserves it. Aunt Margaret is nothing like my father, and she *does* know you love her," Kayla said stoutly.

"Ray."

Logan had been prowling around the other side of the spell circle and now beckoned for Ray to join him.

"Look," he said. The technomage pointed to a mark on the floor. It was coarse and angular and appeared to be written in blood.

"Do you recognize it?"

Logan shook his head. "It's not the only one, either." He pointed to several marks, all different, but with the same rough-hewn quality. "I don't think the witches made these."

"Why not?" Ray asked, examining each of them and snapping pictures on his phone.

"A witch would have used the spell circle. Plus, I'm no expert, but I don't recognize any of the symbols."

"Who would?" Ray asked.

"Not a clue. Maybe check Nuketown. See if any of the witches there will talk to you. They'd at least be able to say whether the symbols are witchy or not."

Ray backed up to get a better picture of one and bumped into Kayla who'd come to get a closer look.

"Have you seen anything like them before?" he asked, stepping aside.
She shook her head.

"Could your grandmother or aunt have put these here?"

"Anything is possible, but like Zach said, if these belonged to them, they'd have used the witch circle. It both protects them and concentrates their power."

"You think the kidnapper made them?" Landon asked Ray.

"It's possible," Ray said, tucking his phone back into his pocket. "What's curious is there's no obvious signs of a struggle. You'd think two witches would have fought back. Who else has access to this place? Maids? Your uncle?" he asked Landon.

"No maids. I don't know about my uncle. I don't think Grandmother would want him down here."

That hooked Ray's attention. "Did they not get along? Argue?"

"Not really. Mostly they did their own thing and left each other alone. They had a lot of parties and dinner parties, but mostly they only had meals together because Grandmother insisted."

"Does he know that they are witches?"

It was Kayla who answered. "Yes."

When she didn't elaborate, Ray prompted her. "How do you know? How does he feel about it?"

"He's known as long as I can remember. I don't think Grandmother hid it from him. He hardly ever talks about it, and it's rare that she mentions anything, but I remember a couple times when he asked if she'd succeeded in her spellcasting."

Ray noted that in his notebook. If Theresa Runyon had performed spells for her son's benefit, then he had a weaker motive to kidnap her. His mother and sister were valuable assets, unless they'd threatened him somehow. Maybe he planned to force them to perform spells they refused to cast. A definite possibility. He couldn't rule the bastard out.

"Is there any other way into this place?"

Kayla nodded. "Two, but both funnel through the same room. I'll show you."

With Landon, Ray, and Logan trailing after her, Kayla walked to a colorful batik tapestry depicting a woman at three different stages of life—young, middle-aged, and old. Arcane symbols had been embroidered on it in gold thread.

Kayla pushed the tapestry to one side and set her palm against what seemed to Ray a perfectly arbitrary spot in the whitewashed paneling. It didn't surprise him when once again, magic outlined her hand. She pushed, and a door swung silently open, revealing a kind of preparation room.

Along the walls hung silk robes in a variety of jewel-toned colors. Empty cubbies waited to be filled. Participating witches would clothe here before entering the casting room. Ray counted the robes, finding nineteen. Twenty-one made a complete witch circle, which meant that there was a good chance Valentine and Runyon had been wearing their robes when they were taken. He hadn't seen robes in their bedrooms.

Opposite the cubbies was a row of shower stalls. Blue tile swathed the walls and the floor, with glass-and-steel folding doors framing each stall.

Something continued to niggle at him. But what? Nothing seemed out of place, and there were no signs of a struggle or any more of the symbols Logan had discovered in the other room.

A wide flight of steps ran a third of the way up the far wall, then split in two, each set of stairs going in opposite directions.

"Where do these lead?" he asked.

"That one leads to one of the reception salons," Landon said, pointing. "The other goes to Grandmother's meditation room. The left is where the kidnappers came in."

"Show me."

Landon led the way up the steps, turning up the left side. At the top, the corridor made a right-hand turn. Landon took the corner with Ray close behind.

"Jesus." He stopped. What had been a steel door now lay crumpled and shredded in ribbons, like discarded tin foil.

"What the hell did that?" Ray glanced at Logan. "Can you tell if it was magic or something physical?"

The technomage squatted down, trailing his fingers over the crumpled metal. He shook his head as he straightened. "I can't feel any magical resonance."

"It looks like someone punched a hole in it and ripped it down with pure muscle," Kayla said.

Something in her voice made Ray look at her. She had her arms wrapped around her waist, and she swallowed as if she was about to puke. Why?

Ray examined the door again, but he found no clues to Kayla's unexpected reaction.

"What are you thinking?" Logan murmured.

"I don't know yet. I don't have a good sense of what went down. If the women were in the casting room as those symbols suggest, then how come that door didn't end up like this one? Whoever broke in here must have made a racket, and I'm willing to bet there were active wards. Surely the women knew something was coming. Why didn't they escape the way we came in? Why aren't there any signs of a struggle? What were those symbols for? And how the hell did the kidnapper get on and off the estate without anybody seeing him?"

Logan patted Ray's shoulder. "That, my friend, is why you are the detective and I am a mere technomage."

Ray grimaced. "Because I ask questions I don't have answers to?"

"Because you'll find the answers and make sense of all this."

Ray rubbed a hand over his mouth. "Maybe." At least now he had some leads, even if he didn't know what to make of them.

"I want to look downstairs again," he said.

He took a harder look at the preparation room. He examined every square inch, searching for whatever he'd missed the first time. He had to have overlooked something.

"He'd have had to take them by surprise," he muttered. "Except tearing that door would have given the women a hell of a lot of warning. So why didn't they defend themselves?" That bothered him the most. He was missing a key part of the mystery.

Ray tried to visualize what might have happened in the context of what he knew. He eyed the closed door into the casting room. Was it sound-proofed? If so and if they were inside the casting room at the time, they wouldn't have heard the door come down. But by that logic, how had the intruder broken through to the casting room without them noticing, and without leaving a mark on the entry door?

It wasn't until Kayla spoke that Ray realized he'd been speaking aloud.

"What if the kidnapper was already inside?"

He frowned. "Where would he hide? And even if he could have hidden, he'd have had to subdue both women without them fighting back. Even if he'd cleaned up, we'd see some evidence of a fight, and there's nothing. They didn't struggle."

She chewed her bottom lip, nodding. "Okay. He's inside and he's lying in wait. Maybe he's glamoured. Grandmother and Aunt Margaret aren't expecting anyone—this is a super safe space for them—so they don't pay much attention to what could be out of place."

She went to the stairs and turned as if she was making an entrance.

"So, I come down and put on my robe. I already showered upstairs."

"What about the ripped-up door? Why didn't they see it?"

Kayla looked over her shoulder. "It's not visible from the right side of the stairs. They must have come in that way."

"But they *might* have come the other way. As well-planned as this abduction obviously was, the kidnapper wouldn't have taken the chance that they'd use the wrong entrance. "

"They only came down that way when other witches were here. When it was just Grandmother and mom, they came down through Grandmother's meditation room," Landon said.

"You're sure?" Ray asked.

Landon nodded.

That meant insider information. "Okay," Ray said, looking at Kayla. "You come down and put on your robes. Then what? The attacker has to subdue you both quickly."

"If they couldn't see him, he could sneak up and grab one and knock her out, then put a gun to her head so the other cooperates," Kayla suggested.

It was feasible. "Okay, then what? Why does he go into the other room? What's the point of those symbols?"

"Maybe a spell to help him get out? Or possibly the spell immobilized my grandmother and aunt."

Without knowing what the symbols meant, it was impossible to say. Too many damned questions and not enough answers.

"This guy had to be pretty sure of himself to take out two witches in their own workroom," Logan said. "You wouldn't do that if you didn't have a solid plan to neutralize them and get them out."

Ray tapped his fingers on his thigh. "What if the spell he casts lets him control them? Then they'd cooperate and leave with him. Maybe they tell him exactly how to get out and cover their tracks. Maybe he'd make them use their magic to help. Is that possible?" Ray asked Logan.

"Sure."

"It sounds right," Kayla said.

Ray nodded agreement. Fuck but he'd missed this give-and-take as the two of them sorted out a scene together. It had always felt like their own special brand of magic. "It fits what we know."

"It also means he targeted them. He knew what they were and how to find them. He wanted witches. There had to be easier ones to get to, so why Grandmother and Aunt Margaret? How did he even know they were witches?" Kayla asked.

"Good questions. Here's another: what does he want them for? If he's not asked for ransom by now, he's got something in mind, and chances are it's not a pretty fate."

Kayla tossed a quick glance at Landon and then gave Ray a speaking look. She didn't want to raise the more likely and more frightening options in front of the kid. Ray tipped his head in a miniscule nod of understanding.

"Can you get samples of whatever the kidnapper used to make those symbols?" Ray asked Logan.

The technomage nodded, pulling a pair of nitrile gloves from his pocket, along with a small zipper case. Ray gave a little smile of approval. That's one thing he could count of Logan for—he was always prepared.

It took Logan twenty minutes to collect samples, take pictures, and document the location of the symbols. He also took pictures of both rooms and the crumpled steel door. Meanwhile, Kayla took Landon aside, speaking to him softly.

Though Ray wanted nothing more than to eavesdrop, she'd get more out of the kid if he didn't lurk. He had to trust her to relay what information she got from her cousin. Once upon a time that wouldn't have bothered him.

Now he didn't know if he could trust her.

He gave them space and wandered the casting room. He squatted beside the witch circle, careful not to touch it. Ray felt the tug of it calling him. Not for the first time, he wondered where his power would fit in a spell circle. The further out from the center point, the lower the power of the witch. He'd heard some witches couldn't scrape up enough magic power to participate in the circle at all.

Ray ran the tip of his tongue around the edges of his teeth and straightened to his feet. He didn't need to know where he'd fit in a witch circle. He didn't want to know.

He noticed Logan putting away his kit and small camera. Time to get going. He wasn't looking forward to the next step: interviewing Alistair Runyon again. But first, he'd send Logan back to the lab. Kayla he'd take home himself. He wanted to know where to find her if she stopped taking his calls. Plus, they had a few things to clear up, and this time, neither of them was escaping until everything was said.

Chapter 11

Kayla

SEISMIC QUAKES continued to run through Kayla as she pulled Landon to the side to speak with him. Seeing the wreck of the steel door hit her in the gut. Her other form could have easily torn it down in just that way. As soon as she saw it she knew that the kidnapper wasn't human. And it was smart.

The thought of Ray pursuing it alone made her stomach churn. He had no idea what something like that could do. He had no real defenses. Whether he knew it or not, he needed her with him on this case. Or rather, he needed her other self, the one with teeth and claws and armor.

Dear God, was she actually considering letting him see what she was? The entire concept made her want to sink into the ground. He'd made his opinion of non-humans very clear—they weren't worth his time or attention. They were vermin. *She* was vermin.

"What do you think took them?" Landon asked, having arrived at the same conclusion she had. The anger had drained from his voice, and he gazed at Kayla with desperate hope.

Kayla took a close look at him. He'd grown into a man since she last saw him. *Duh.* He hadn't even been in his teens when she left. He stood over six feet tall, with a lanky, muscular frame. He wore the expensive button-up attire that Grandmother and her father required of "proper" Runyons.

"I will find them. I promise."

He shook his head. "Don't. You can't promise that. And anyway, your promises aren't worth a lot, are they?"

Kayla put her hands on his shoulders, waiting until he met her serious gaze. "I'm sorry I left you. I'm sorry I let you down. I'm not going to do it again. I *will* find them." She didn't say that she'd find them alive. That she couldn't promise.

"You're not even a cop anymore."

"That doesn't mean I can't investigate."

"With him?" He tipped his chin toward Ray.

"Maybe."

"Why did you quit the force? That was all you ever talked about. You left us because you wanted to be a cop so bad and then you quit and you still didn't come back."

Kayla bit her lip. She owed him an answer. She owed him the truth.

"I had to," she said. "I didn't have a choice."

His dark brows furrowed. "Why?"

"Because of Magicfall." She didn't look away as she said it. She regretted so much staying away. She should have at least called him. She'd missed Landon more than she could possibly say. As far as she was concerned, he was her little brother, not just her cousin.

She waited for him to understand what she was saying. She knew he'd made the connection when his eyes widened. She waited for him to back away. She wouldn't blame him.

"You got your powers?" he asked.

Witch powers. Grandmother and Aunt Margaret had been so hopeful she'd carry on the family tradition. She shook her head. "I'm not a witch."

"But then . . ."

She could see him landing on the right conclusion. The only conclusion. "What are you?"

She gave a weak smile. "Scary. Really, fucking scary." She took a breath, her chest tight. This was the closest she'd come to telling anybody what had happened to her, and it felt awful.

"How about you? Have you developed powers?"

He shrugged. "Not yet."

Nobody could say for sure if being a witch was hereditary, though witches had popped up in their family tree for generations. It had infuriated her father to no end that he was barren and both his sister and mother overflowed with it.

"They've kept testing me. Grandmother says they could still manifest. Yours, too."

"I doubt it. Grandmother says it's rare to develop power after you turn twenty-five. You're the one still on the hot seat."

His lips tightened in a humorless smile. "Would piss off Uncle Alistair. He'd shit kittens."

"I'd pay to be there when he found out," she said with a vindictive smile. "Please send me an invitation."

"I would but it's not like I know where to find you."

"I'm not disappearing again," she said. "Give me your phone."

He drew it out of his pants pocket.

"Just what the hell do you think you're doing here?"

Kayla flinched as her father's icy voice cut through the silence. Landon got a panicked look, which quickly morphed into a mask of anger. She knew that trick. Better to look angry than afraid; better to show strength than weakness. Give her father an opening, and he'd slice you to the bone.

She stiffened her shoulders and raised her chin. She had nothing to fear from the man. He couldn't touch her. Not now, not after Magicfall. She just had to keep him from fucking with her head. He was a master of head games, but she had no intention of falling into any of his traps.

Kayla turned. Her father strode across the spellcasting floor. Just seeing him reminded her of all the things she hated about him. He was arrogant to the point of suicide, controlling, narcissistic as hell, and completely confident in his ability to manipulate and cow others into doing whatever he wanted.

Ray came to stand beside her and a half step ahead, as if he intended to shield her from anything her father might do. Funny, she'd done the same thing with Landon. Zach had stopped a few feet away. His posture made him look relaxed and curious, but she could see the flickers of power dancing around the tips of his fingers as he dangled his arm by his side.

Interesting. Not the reaction she'd expected. Did he know something about her father? Or maybe he just read Ray's and her reactions.

Zach hadn't dropped the shields he'd placed on each of them before entering the casting room. Then again, that might not be enough. Her father's motto was always 'go big or go home,' so anything was possible. He might not be a witch, but he didn't have to be one to activate a spell. Who knew what sort of arsenal he kept?

Kayla surreptitiously touched the silver band circling her wrist containing the spell that would soak her down and allow her to swiftly transform. She was as vulnerable as any other human in this shape, but her father wouldn't have much luck against her other self. Not that she wanted him to know her secret. Not that she wanted any of them to know, especially Ray. Zach and Landon might get over the shock and accept it, but Ray? Not a snowball's chance in hell.

One thing for sure: if she had to transform in front of Ray to fight her father, the bastard wouldn't survive the fight. She'd snap his head off and use it for a beach ball.

Alastair came to a halt a few feet away. His entire attention fixed on Kayla. The others might as well have not existed.

"I thought I told you to stay the hell off this property and out of our lives." His lip curled. "You pissed all over your name and for what? To become a *salvager?*"

The disgust with which he said the last word slapped Kayla in the face, though it didn't surprise her that he knew what she did. Before she could respond, Landon spoke up.

"I wanted her to come."

Her father slowly shifted his gaze to Landon. "Looks like we'll be having a talk soon. This is *my* house, and *my* rule is law."

"And here I thought Grandmother was the rightful owner," Kayla drawled.

"I'm the head of the household."

As if that meant anything.

"When were you going to tell me your mother and sister are witches?" Ray asked in that quiet way he had that sounded both curious and insulting.

Her father bristled. "It's got nothing to do with the case."

"Ah." Ray nodded sagely. "Then perhaps you can explain what happened to the steel door leading into the other room."

"Rats," her father said. "Giant rats."

"How unfortunate for you."

A tight, unfriendly smile pulled on her father's lips. "I'm taking care of them. I'll make them regret they ever heard the name Runyon."

"Are you saying you know who took Grandmother and Aunt Margaret?" Kayla demanded.

"I'm saying that nobody comes into my house without my permission and gets away with it." He eyed her up and down, his malice evident. "Especially you."

"And yet it looks like that's exactly what I'm going to do."

Alistair looked at Ray. "I want this woman arrested for breaking and entering and trespassing. If you don't, I will call Police Chief Harmon and you'll be out of a job. I have his personal cell number on speed dial."

Ray scratched at his jaw. "You could do that, sir. In fact, maybe you should. Of course, there's no telling what the press will think about it all. It would make a good story though. A rich man having his only child arrested for the crime of helping to find her kidnapped grandmother and aunt. Bet the papers would get a lot of mileage out of a story like that."

Her father's lips pinched together, his chin jutting. Ray had just made an enemy, and a vindictive one at that. All the same, Kayla's inner eleven-year-old was jumping up and down and sticking out her tongue triumphantly at her father.

"Understand this, Detective Garza. If the press gets wind of any of this, I will hold you personally responsible. If you fail to solve this case and return my mother and sister alive, I will make sure you regret it in ways you can't begin to imagine." He leaned in, threat emanating from his every pore. "But one way or another, you will pay for your insolence."

"While I'm being insolent, maybe you can tell me why you're obstructing my investigation. Someone might think you didn't want them found."

"You are mistaken." He glanced at Kayla. "Or duped. Finding them is my priority."

Ray's brows rose. He cocked his head. "You didn't think that them being witches was relevant? And the location of the crime scene—you lied about it."

Her father flushed, his lip curling. "That sounds perilously like an accusation." He jabbed a finger in Ray's direction. "I said they were taken from this house. A good detective would have located this place without help. But please, do go down this road. I look forward to crushing you into the ground. Now get the hell off my property."

Kayla didn't see any reason to argue. Being in the same vicinity as her father, poisoned the air and made it hard not to commit murder. Plus, they'd discovered all they were going to.

She shrugged and started for the door. Landon fell in beside her, followed by Zach.

"Always a pleasure, Mister Runyon," Ray said with a derisive salute before bringing up the rear.

"Not you, boy," her father said to Landon. "It's high time we discussed your place in this household."

Kayla glanced at her cousin. "You don't have to. You can stay with me."

He hesitated, then shook his head. "I'd better not. Just in case."

She knew what he meant. Just in case a ransom call came in. Just in case he learned something useful from her father or someone else. Just in case more evidence turned up. She gave a little nod of understanding, then pulled him into a hug, speaking quietly against his ear.

"If you need anything, get in touch with Ray. He has my number. And trust me. I *will* find them. I won't let you or them down."

As she loosened her grip and stepped back, Ray stepped forward, his notebook ready. "How do I contact you if I have questions or news?"

"You talk to me," her father said. "You don't need to bother my nephew."

But Landon was already offering Ray his number and email address. The internet wasn't what it used to be before Magicfall, but email was still fairly reliable and the regular postal service was not.

Ray wrote the contact information down, then handed Landon his card, which her cousin pocketed. None of that would matter if—or rather when—her father took away the card and Landon's cell phone. The house still had a working landline, but Kayla was willing to bet her father wouldn't give Landon a chance to use it. Nor would he get access to a computer or tablet. He was going to get locked up somewhere and let out only for meals and to be put on display.

She ought to drag him off and the hell with Alistair and his secrets. She swallowed her fury. Landon was entitled to make his own choices. He knew as well as she did what her father was capable of. If Landon wanted to stay, she couldn't interfere.

She fingered the phone in her pocket. With the bastard watching her like a hawk, she couldn't possibly slip it to Landon unseen.

Gritting her teeth at her helplessness, she strode toward the exit. She could feel her father's malevolent gaze boring through her as she went.

She stopped. She couldn't go like this. She couldn't let him think he could bully Landon without any consequence.

Spinning around, she stalked across the witch floor until she stood barely an inch from her father. She kept her voice low so the others couldn't hear what she said.

"Remember this, old man. There is nothing—and I mean *nothing*—I won't do if you hurt Landon or Ray or if you had anything to do with this kidnapping. I didn't quit the force because I couldn't hack it; I quit because *they* couldn't handle *me*. I am not the same as I used to be, and given half the chance, the thing I am now will gleefully tear you limb from limb. Hand to heaven. And after I've eaten my fill, I will drink every drop of your blood before I shit on your corpse."

She stood on tiptoe and bent a little closer so that her lips were close to his ear. "Please understand I am *not at all* speaking metaphorically, nor am I exaggerating. Having people find out witches run in your family will be the least of your problems if you fuck with anybody I care about."

She didn't wait to see his reaction. Her heart pounded as she stormed away. She'd told her father—*her fucking fascist father*—her secret, or as much as anyone in the world knew. She didn't know how, but she knew he'd use the information against her if he could.

Her lips tightened into a flat line. If it came down to it, she'd do exactly as she promised, and she'd enjoy every minute of it. For the first time since seeing the damage to the steel door, she was happy to be a monster. Monsters were scary, and she planned to be very terrifying.

Chapter 12

Ray

"RIDE WITH ME," Ray said to Kayla as they exited the rose garden. "I'll take you home."

It was an order more than a request, and he half expected her to blow him off.

She only hesitated a moment, and then nodded. "I'll get my pack out of the van and say goodbye to Zach."

Ray watched her walk away, anticipatory tension building in his gut. Finally, he was going to get answers. One way or another.

She went to the passenger door of the van and pulled out her pack. It was almost as big as she was and stuffed fat as a Christmas turkey. It clinked when she set it down. She unfastened the top flap and pulled out a giant bag of chocolate chips and four peanut butter jars, setting them all on the seat. Ray scowled as Logan approached her. The technomage was a menace to women. A major player. He got more women in bed than a mattress factory, and he'd clearly set his sights on Kayla.

Ray snarled. Not a fucking chance. Not if he had anything to do with it. A wave of territorial possessiveness swept over him, and his magic sparked in his veins in response.

Dammit. He breathed in and let it out slowly. He was a fucking moron. She was kryptonite. Being with her would fuck him up and turn him inside out. He wasn't going to let his dick lead him around like a puppy on a leash. Anyway, even if he did want to start something with her, she definitely had no interest in him.

He wandered closer to eavesdrop.

"Thanks for dinner," she said to Logan, smiling.

He grinned and slid a finger along the side of her cheek as if smoothing away a stray hair. Ray fought the urge to smash out every one of the technomage's teeth.

"My pleasure. Thanks for the goodies."

"Just remember you owe me."

"Only if you keep our dates." He scribbled on a pad of paper he took from the glovebox, tore it off, and handed it to her. "My number."

Kayla slid it into her pocket.

Ray decided enough was enough. Time to go. He stalked toward the cozy couple.

"I wouldn't mind seeing the coroner's report on those three from Keller Fountain," she told Logan.

He shook his head. "Won't be a coroner's report. Just the magical assessment."

"That's right. They aren't people." Her lip curled.

"One day things will change," he assured her, reaching out to take her hand. "They're already changing. People are adjusting to magic and figuring out how to get along with magical citizens."

"Are you coming?" Ray growled impatiently. "Runyon's likely to call for an airstrike if we don't clear out quick."

He glared at Logan who made *no effort* to let go of Kayla. Ray was about to break his fingers for him. Instead he said, "Get ahold of me as soon as you get any results from those samples. Call dispatch. They'll have my new number."

"New number?" Logan repeated curiously as Kayla finally slipped free of his grasp.

"I'm getting a new phone. Should have it later tonight."

"What happened your other one?"

Ray gave a slight shrug. "I slipped it to Landon. Let's go," he said before grabbing Kayla's pack and slinging one strap over his shoulder. He strode away without waiting for her to follow. He liked Logan, but at the moment, it was taking all his willpower not to kick him in the balls.

Kayla said something else to Zach and then jogged to catch up with Ray.

"Thank you," she said as she fell in beside him.

"For what?"

"Giving Landon a phone."

"Not doing any favors. I need him to have a way to contact me if he comes up with something else. Wouldn't trust the old man to call me if there was a ransom call."

That wasn't why, but he didn't need Kayla thinking he'd gone soft and wanted the kid to have a line to the rest of the world, and to Kayla especially.

"I'm still grateful," she said. "Leaving Landon here is just about the last thing I want to do. My father is going to lock him down."

"Lock him down?"

"It's pretty much prison with comfortable furniture."

"He did that to you?"

She made an affirmative sound.

A current of black fury jolted through him, and red flames curled around his fingers. He closed his fist and tamped them. Luckily Kayla stood slightly behind him and couldn't see. But the loss of control shook him. Being with Kayla shook him. Wanting her so badly he practically announced on a loudspeaker that he was a witch nearly brought him to his knees.

All because her father had locked her in her room years ago.

Ray was totally fucked up.

He'd damned well better figure out how to keep a lid on it, because they were going to be spending some quality time together. He wasn't about to let her investigate the kidnapping on her own, and he had zero doubts that's exactly what she would do. She'd end up in the middle of something dangerous without backup, and that was entirely unacceptable. On the other hand, he didn't have any illusions that his dick would lose interest in her anytime soon. Maybe he just needed to stuff some ice in his underwear.

Back at the squad car, he tossed the pack into the back seat and slid behind the wheel, adjusting himself before Kayla climbed into the passenger side and buckled up. As he touched his fingers to the ignition spell set into the dash, he felt something inside him uncoil at the rightness, the familiarity of the action. Having her beside him aligned his world back to right for the first time in years. Four years to be exact.

Don't get used to it, he told himself. *She's not a cop anymore, and she's got no interest in coming back to the force or you.* He'd be a whole lot better off if he didn't forget that particular fact. Still, an irritating voice in the back of his head wondered, *What if she just came back to you?* And now the image that flashed through his horny brain was her naked beneath him, calling out his name, not that fucker Logan's.

He nearly groaned at the ache that erupted in his groin at the thought of being inside her. Goddamn but he was out of his fucking mind. He turned the car around and headed for the main gate, praying that his dick didn't split at the seams. He reached for the microphone on his radio and called dispatch.

"This is Garza. I'm leaving the Runyon place. I need a new phone. My old one is out of service. Don't deactivate. I gave it to an informant."

A tinny voice acknowledged his report and told him a new phone would be waiting downtown. Ray told them to send out a station-wide notification of his new number and to make sure all incoming calls to his old phone got forwarded to the new before he signed off and hung the microphone back in its cradle.

They remained silent as he drove down the long drive and out through the main gate. A dozen questions danced on his tongue and vied for precedence. He decided to go with the one least likely to make her shut down.

"What did you say to your father there at the end?"

The question clearly startled her, as if she'd been braced for something else.

"I threatened him," she said after a moment.

"With what?"

"Death and torture, mostly."

Ray smiled. He'd missed that streak of righteous vengeance. "He's not going to take that threat well. I get the feeling he doesn't like to be challenged."

She snorted. "You noticed that, huh?"

"You should be careful. I peg him as vindictive and vicious." And if she wouldn't be careful, he'd be careful for her. He wasn't letting her out of his sight if he could help it.

Kayla gave a little laugh. "Stop telling me things I already know."

He started to maneuver her to the topic he really wanted to talk about. "How did you get him to let you join the force?"

She sighed and looked out the side window. "I held the family dirty witch laundry over his head. Plus, I found out about a couple of not-so-legal things he'd been doing. I helped him decide it was better to let me go and do my own thing under my mother's maiden name than risk I'd be believed. It helped that I had proof and I didn't give a fuck about his money."

"Must've hurt leaving Landon, not to mention your grandmother and aunt."

She didn't answer for a long minute. Just about the time Ray'd decided she wasn't going to and he needed to shift gears, she spoke again.

"It's the second hardest thing I've ever done. It about broke me to leave Landon, but Aunt Margaret is a good mom, and whatever else her faults are, Grandmother would rip my father a new one if he caused Landon physical harm. But I had to go. If I stayed, I'd have killed him."

She said the last quietly, without any force, which told him she really would have.

"Lucky he saw the light, then," Ray said in an effort to lighten the moment.

"It was. I had a couple of foolproof murder plans worked out."

"I take it he wasn't such a good dad?" Ray felt his anger rising again. He clenched his fingers on the wheel. "Did he hurt you?"

"You mean physically? Not really. He was more into psychological torture. He's good at it, too."

"*Not really* means he *did* hurt you," Ray said, the two words slamming into his brain with all the force of a baseball bat. "What exactly did he do?"

When she answered, he could tell she was choosing her words carefully. "He arranged for certain events. Only a few. I learned pretty quickly the lines I shouldn't cross."

"Events? Stop sugarcoating, Kayla, and just tell me straight."

He felt her eyes on him. He kept his fixed on the road. He didn't want her seeing the black rage that had erupted inside him.

"When I was twelve, I had this treehouse. Nobody but Landon and me went there. My father and I had gotten into a fight the night before. I'd been rude and loud at a dinner party and embarrassed him. I did it on purpose because he'd had my favorite teddy bear taken out to the firepit and burned. He made me watch. I can't remember why he did that."

Ray risked a glance at her. She was staring down into her lap, her forehead wrinkling as she tried to remember her crime. After a minute she shook away the effort and continued.

"I didn't notice when I climbed up that day that the windows had been covered with fine mesh. Next thing I know, bees start pouring in from a hole in the roof that hadn't been there before. I tried to get out, but the door was locked." She stared into space.

"The next thing I remember I'm in the hospital and everybody is crying. Everybody but my dad. He just looked at me, and I knew it had been his punishment."

"Jesus fuck," Ray muttered. "The man's a psychopath. He *didn't really* physically hurt you? The hell he didn't." His voice rose, and he felt power spinning through him like a hot cyclone. He clamped his lips together, gathering what calm he could.

"What else did he do?" he asked in a low voice when he'd found some semblance of control.

Kayla rubbed the back of one of her hands. "Doesn't really matter. The main thing is I got out and he can't touch me now."

"Why? Because of the history of witches in your family? If he's as vindictive as I think he is, he'll get you before you have a chance to leak the witch story."

"The news will still get out. I've made sure of it."

"He gets pissed enough, he won't care. He'll be after you regardless."

"Let him try," was her only response.

That brought Ray to his next burning question. "You say that like you've got an ace in the hole. Are you a witch, too? Like your aunt and grandmother?"

He felt her eyes on him.

"No. I never showed any signs of power, much to Grandmother's eternal disappointment."

Truth rang in her words. Ray digested them, a sick feeling beginning to churn in his stomach. He'd been certain she'd quit the force because she'd manifested witch powers. It had given him hope, not just that having her secret out in the open made it possible for them to be friends again, but that he'd finally have someone who understood what he was going through. He'd have someone he could confide in.

But she was hiding something else altogether.

He fell silent. He didn't know what to say to her. Anger started to build. It helped combat the ache of dying hope.

"My father won't let Landon keep the card you gave him," she said suddenly.

It took Ray a moment to get on the same page. "I gave him two. One to be confiscated and the other to keep."

"You always were two steps ahead of the game."

His lips bent in a bitter smile. "Not always. Not with you."

Neither spoke again until they neared the station. Ray figured he'd grab the new phone and take Kayla home.

As he pulled into the parking lot, Kayla spoke.

"I wish I could have done it differently," she said.

"Do what?"

"Quit. It's the hardest thing I've ever had to do."

She'd said leaving Landon behind when she'd joined the academy was the second hardest. Ray wasn't sure what to make of her statement, but he wouldn't ask why she'd left. Not right now. She wasn't ready to tell him, and he didn't think he could handle another one of her refusals to speak. Instead he focused on what she did say.

"*Had* to do?" he asked, fixing on the word. "No one forced you."

She sighed. "No. No one forced me."

Ray pulled into his parking spot and shut the car off. He unbuckled and turned in his seat to look at her. "Something happened to you at Magicfall," he said, the pieces falling into place again. Her anger over his dismissal of the witchkin's murders. Her quitting right after Magicfall. Her refusal to explain why.

But if she wasn't human anymore, what was she? And did he care?

"The world turned inside out that day. For everybody."

Another nonanswer. Disappointment washed through him. He swiveled away and thrust open his door.

"I'll be back. I'm getting my phone."

He didn't ask her to come inside. Neither did he tell her to wait. She would. She needed him. For now.

Bitterness flooded his mouth as he strode away and into the building, for once not aimed at Kayla. He had no right to be angry. Whatever had happened at Magicfall, he'd made it so she couldn't tell him. He should have put it together a long time ago. He should have sought her out and bulldogged her until he got the truth. How would the last four years have been if he hadn't had his head so far up his ass he couldn't pick up the obvious clues?

"Some detective I am," he muttered as he pushed the station doors open. He went directly to the property clerk where his new phone awaited pickup. He signed the paperwork and thanked the clerk, then headed straight back out. As sure as he was that Kayla would wait, he didn't want to give her too much time to decide to go it alone.

As he walked, he inserted the memory card he'd jacked from his old phone while Kayla was busy distracting Alastair, and made sure the pictures he'd taken at the Runyon estate were there. He sent a text to his old number, hoping Landon had managed to keep it from Kayla's father. He typed in his name and then hit send. The card he'd slipped the kid had the dispatch number on it, and his text gave Landon his new number.

Relief washed through him when he found Kayla still sitting in the squad car. He slid behind the wheel.

"Where do you live?"

The address she gave him took them to a neighborhood at the edge of Washington Park near the amphitheater. She lived in a quaint two-story brick house with several stained-glass windows and a pointed arch above the door.

Ray pulled into the driveway and parked. "I'm coming in," he said, not letting her argue. He grabbed her pack out of the back seat and followed her to the front door. Above the lintel were two beasts set in tile that looked like sea dragons. Above them protruded a ledge of brick covered with peeling white paint.

"How long have you lived here?"

"Two years. It was empty. Whoever owned it hadn't been here for quite a while."

The inside of her house was cozy, with a living room equipped with a comfortable-looking couch, several recliner chairs, and a wood fireplace. Kayla pointed to a spot in the mudroom for him to set her pack, then took off her boots. She stripped off her jacket, revealing a plum-colored long-sleeved shirt.

"Are you hungry?" she asked. "You haven't eaten since before I called, have you?"

She didn't wait for an answer but headed into the kitchen. Ray followed, sitting down on one of the two stools beside the breakfast bar. He watched as she pulled out the makings for an omelet, along with a slab of bacon and potatoes. She set to work in silence, pausing to put on coffee. When it was done, she poured him a cup.

"At least we didn't lose coffee with Magicfall," Ray said as he stirred in some sugar and sipped. Better to keep the conversation off heavy subjects for now.

"I've heard the Astoria coven of witches has it growing in greenhouses," she said.

They made small talk about changes in Portland and the rest of Oregon since Magicfall, carefully avoiding anything personal.

"That looks amazing," he said as she set a loaded plate in front of him. His stomach gnawing at his ribs, Ray plowed into the meal. Kayla ate hers more slowly, standing up on the opposite side of the bar. When they finished, she put on rubber gloves and rinsed the dishes and wiped down the counters. When she could find nothing else to do, she led the way back to the living room and sat down in the corner of the couch, her feet curled up beneath her.

Ray sat just in front of her on the coffee table. She waited warily for him to speak.

"If I'm going to let you investigate with me, I need some promises," he said. "First, you don't go off on your own. We'll do this together or not at all."

She nodded agreement.

"Second, you don't keep any secrets from me that bear on the case. That's non-negotiable."

Another nod.

He drew in a rough breath. Now for the tough part. "Kayla, I have to know what happened. I have some guesses, but I need your word that you'll tell me when this is all over. That we'll talk about it."

It wasn't a condition. He wouldn't make it one, because this is where she might draw the line and he wasn't going to drive her off. The fact that she hadn't trusted him hurt like a bitch still, and realizing he'd practically driven her off made it ten times worse.

Would you have told her you're a witch? The nasty little overly reasonable voice was back. Will *you tell her?*

Kayla was no longer looking at him. She stared at her knees and chewed her lower lip. One hand smoothed back a strand of hair. It trembled.

How bad could it be? It wasn't something obvious like becoming a troll or one of the harpies he'd heard had been hanging out near the massive Clatskanie Bay that now served as the estuary between the Columbia River and the ocean.

Finally, she looked at him, her dark eyes luminous with unshed tears. "When it's over. But—"

She broke off and swallowed hard, compressing her lips together and shaking her head and looking away.

That was all the answer he was going to get. It was better than he'd expected. At least she hadn't refused outright.

Ray decided to move on. "But first—for the record, I know I was an asshole. I made you think you couldn't trust me, and I can't tell you how much I regret that."

Her head snapped around, and her stunned gaze locked with his. "You what?"

He grimaced. "I apologize for the things I said to you back then. I should have tried to talk to you. I shouldn't have given up."

She gave a thin smile. "It wouldn't have mattered."

"But I should have tried."

She shifted uneasily, toying with the hem of her shirt. Before she could shut down on him, Ray changed the subject.

"The first thing we should do is get to Nuketown and see if we can find a witch who can tell us what these symbols are."

Kayla visibly relaxed as he switched gears. "They don't like cops."

"You're not going without me."

"They won't hurt me; they know me."

"How?" The question came out harsher than he wanted, but dammit, what was she doing hanging out in Nuketown? Didn't she know how crazy dangerous it was? A gun wasn't going to help her against witches and witchkin. Especially against the Sunspears and Shadowblades—warriors the more powerful witches created to guard their covens. They transformed humans into supernatural fighting machines with psychotic tendencies.

"I go there a lot," she said with a dismissive gesture. "Nessa—I sell my salvage to her shop—sets up a store there a couple times a month. I help her with it."

"Are you insane?"

Her cheeks flushed. "Why? Because they aren't human?"

His fist hit the arm of the chair. "Because they are fucking dangerous, Kayla. And unpredictable. Shit, you know what happened during the war, what sorts of atrocities they are capable of."

She gave a faint shake of her head. "From what I heard, most of the supernaturals who attacked humans in the war didn't want to. They were forced by the Guardians."

The Guardians were supernatural beings with god-like powers who had been responsible for Magicfall. They'd been angry at the way humans had covered the earth and forced the magical creatures into hiding, or driven them away entirely. Their plan had been to wipe out most of humanity and bring magic back into the world so that the magical denizens could thrive.

Fortunately for humanity, they hadn't expected the technology and architecture of the modern world to hinder their efforts. Nor had they expected the birth and power of the technomages. Not nearly as much humanity had died or changed as they'd planned. But a lot had. And many of those deaths had come at the hands of the magical armies led by witches.

Ray scratched his jaw, biting back the torrent of protective and angry words that threatened to spew out. Kayla was no helpless child. She was a grown woman with skills. The problem was that they sure as hell weren't enough to save her from a magical attack.

Unless they were. What the hell did he know? She'd managed four years living with witchkin and survived the Witchwar just fine on her own.

"We'll go together," he said with finality.

"I'll get more information on my own."

"Then we'll split up while we're there."

Not to mention Ray should spend more time in Nuketown and get acquainted with its denizens. The department tended to ignore arcane-on-arcane crimes. They didn't have enough manpower or the magic to deal with them, and who cared what Portland's magical denizens did to each other? But arcane-on-human crime was another kettle of fish, even though the city government refused to authorize all the resources they needed to investigate, especially since that would mean hiring non-humans onto the force. Not a popular idea. Making contacts in Nuketown could only help Ray do his job.

"When do you want to leave?"

Ray was exhausted and would have loved a few hours' sleep. He had a feeling he wasn't going to get them for quite a while. "When are we most likely to find what we're looking for?"

She glanced at the clock above the fireplace. It was coming up on one in the morning. It would take at least an hour to get there.

"No time like the present," she said and stood. "Let me get changed."

She ran up the stairs. Ray stood and paced, wishing he could grab a shower and a change of clothes. He'd stand out like a lighthouse beacon in his suit.

Ten minutes later Kayla reappeared. She'd brushed her hair and tied it back again, and she now wore heavy canvas Carhartt pants and a blue henley. Even in midsummer, the fog on the river and the late hour meant there'd be a chill in the air.

Over her arm, Kayla had slung a small pile of shirts. She handed them to Ray. "See if any of these fit."

Jealousy spiked and drove a rusty railroad tie into his gut. Had she found a lover? But of course she had. What man wouldn't want her? Well Ray would fucking well walk through fire before he wore her lover's clothes. He just barely resisted the urge to throw the clothing back in her face.

"I'll be fine."

She rolled her eyes. "You'll stick out like a bull in a chicken coop. One of those ought to fit. You're lucky I had them, though. Most clothes I find go to Nessa, but I haven't cleaned out all the stuff belonging to the former residents. If you want, you can check and see if any of the pants that got left behind will fit. Second bedroom on the right." She gestured toward the stairs.

Ray gave a short nod and went up the stairs, two at a time. He didn't trust himself to say anything else, his insane relief at knowing she hadn't given him hand-me-downs of one of her lovers crashing through him.

God but he had to get a handle on this jealousy and possessiveness. Now was not the time to go Neanderthal and start peeing on his territory. Kayla would definitely not appreciate that, and anyway, too much shit lay between them. Any relationship required trust, and until she came clean, he couldn't scrape up much for her. Just because his dick was raging to get inside her didn't mean his brain was willing to take the risk of getting fucked again. First he needed some truth from her. Then *maybe* there'd be a possibility for clawing back friendship going forward. After that? Well, that was wait and see.

He did find a pair of jeans that he could wear, though they fit a little tighter than he liked. He also found a green tee shirt with a silkscreened picture of a leprechaun drinking a beer on it. Over that he pulled a black wool sweater. Unfortunately, he couldn't fit his feet into the boots he found, which left him with his brown loafers.

Ray gathered up his rumpled suit and folded it, packing it into a gym bag he found on the floor of the closet and went downstairs. Kayla waited with a thermos of coffee and two full travel mugs.

He smiled appreciatively. One thing they both had in common was a deep love of coffee. He reached for one of the mugs.

"I forgot what you looked like in civvies," she said, looking him up and down. "You look—"

His brows rose as he waited for her to finish her sentence. "I look . . . ?"

"Fit," she said as she turned away. "We should go."

Ray nodded, uncertain whether "fit" could be read as a compliment or not. He didn't think that's what she'd originally meant to say.

He stashed the gym bag in the trunk and grimaced. He should update Crice.

The captain answered almost before the phone rang.

"What? Who is this?" Crice barked.

"Garza. I picked up a new phone."

"What've you got?"

"I located the crime scene. It looks like magic was involved in the abduction."

He found himself reluctant to report that Theresa Runyon and her daughter were witches, though he wasn't entirely sure why. Maybe because he didn't relish exposing their secret and ruining their lives.

His jaw clenched. Withholding information was not only stupid, it was a firing offense. Would he be so reluctant if he wasn't hiding the same damned secret? What did that say about his capacity to do his damned job? On the other hand, until he knew more, he couldn't know if being witches figured into the crime at all. He could report it later when he knew something for certain.

Yeah, right. On what planet? Their kidnapping had everything to do with being witches. Quit being a pussy, Garza. Suck it up, and tell him already. These aren't your secrets, and you can't compromise your investigation just because you're a fucking witch and you're terrified of exposure.

"Captain—" Before he could say more, Crice interrupted.

"What kind of magic?"

"Witch and something Logan couldn't identify. I'm headed to Nuketown to see if the witches might know what we're dealing with."

"Good. Update me as soon as you know something. Don't screw this up."

"There's just one—"

The call cut off.

Ray eyed his cell and shook his head. His confession would have to wait. His relief irritated him.

He tucked the phone in his pocket and slid behind the wheel. He used his radio to tell dispatch he was out of service and on his way to Nuketown.

A minute later, Kayla came out. She had a pack on her back—much smaller than the one she'd carried earlier. She set it on the back seat and then climbed in beside him.

"What's that?"

"Some things to soften up a witch's heart," she said. "Stuff they can't get all that easily. Tampons, for one."

"I could have lived without knowing that," Ray said, starting the car and backing out of the driveway.

"Men can be so squeamish."

"We could talk about ball sweat if you'd like," he offered.

She snickered. "Maybe not. Drink your coffee and drive."

Something in Ray's chest loosened like an overtightened rusty valve. He felt himself smile. This was the way things were supposed to be. He'd fight hard not to lose this again.

Chapter 13

Kayla

RAY YAWNED WIDELY as he backed out of the driveway. When he'd shifted into drive, he glanced at Kayla who stared through the windshield, her knees pulled up to her chin.

"'You okay?"

"Whoever took Grandmother and Aunt Margaret knew they were witches before he went after them. He probably went after them *because* they were witches," she said, voicing the thought that had been circling around in her skull.

"Agreed," Ray said, turning a corner.

"Why risk taking them at home? Why not wait until they were out shopping or something?"

"He might have had a deadline that couldn't wait."

Kayla hadn't wanted to arrive at that conclusion, but it was unavoidable. Which meant the kidnapper wasn't going to ask for ransom at all, and which also meant that whatever he wanted them for was happening soon, if it hadn't already.

"I hate him, but my father doesn't look good for it."

"He doesn't have much motive," Ray agreed. "He no doubt benefitted from their witchcraft. It's possible he needed them out of the way for some reason, but in that case, I doubt he'd have made such a public production out of it. Be easy enough to arrange an accident."

"I'm having a hard time believing they didn't know their kidnapper, either," Kayla said, twisting to lean against the door so she could look at Ray. "They couldn't possibly have been in a harder place for anyone to grab my grandmother and aunt. The kidnapper had to get on the grounds, in the house, and then down into the basement. Someone the family knew could have easily gained entry to the house. Question is, how did the guards and staff not see them?"

Ray nodded and glanced over at her. "Maybe one of the not-a-coven witches staging some kind of coup to take over and used magic to hide?"

"But wouldn't Zach have sensed their magic? Could they have covered their tracks so well he couldn't sniff them out? And what were those symbols? He seemed certain they weren't witchcraft related."

Suddenly Ray stiffened, his hands tightening on the wheel.

"What?" she asked.

He shook himself. "What do you mean, what?"

"You look like you just saw a ghost."

The corner of his mouth quirked in a humorless smile. "I did. Her name is Kayla."

"Funny." She twisted back around to face front.

The silence stretched. Then Ray let out an aggravated breath and touched her shoulder. "I'm sorry."

She swallowed, making an effort to sound careless. "For what? It's not like it's not true, and you've made it pretty clear you think I suck. I would too, in your shoes."

"I told you we could work together on this."

"You didn't say you'd be happy about it. Anyhow, no worries. I don't expect you to forgive and forget."

Kayla kept her eyes fixed on the passing scenery, emptying her voice of emotion. She'd so deeply missed the joy of working, of the give-and-take in hashing out a case with him, that she'd let herself forget that things weren't the way they'd used to be and she and he weren't friends. He'd flat out told her so at Keller Fountain.

He swore and punched the dash. That startled her enough to look at him.

"What did you do that for?"

Abruptly he twisted the wheel and hit the brakes, skidding to a stop on the side of the road. He jammed the shift into park and turned to look squarely at her. He looked as angry as he had that day she'd quit. She shrank back, bracing herself for his acrimony. Partners were closer than spouses, and by leaving without an explanation, she'd betrayed that soul-deep trust in a way that nobody should be expected to get over.

He noticed her movement, his lip curling as he jerked back. "I'm not going to hurt you."

Kayla lifted her chin. He would, but not physically, and not deliberately. He didn't think anything he said *could* hurt her. "I know."

"Do you? Because you're looking at me like you expect me to start throwing punches." His eyes glittered in the street lights.

She rubbed her fingers over her throbbing forehead, feeling drained and wishing herself just about anywhere else. "Look, I don't think you're going to hit me. I'm just tired, and this kidnapping and dealing with my father has thrown me. Let's just get going and get this all over with and then you won't have to see me again."

His face flushed. "You think that's what I want? To not see you? Goddammit, Kayla. I've missed the hell out of you every day since you quit. You were my best friend, the one person I thought I could trust with anything, and you left."

The ferocity of his tone stunned her as much as his words. She didn't know what to make of either. She didn't know how to make it right. He wasn't going to let this go, and Kayla realized she couldn't let him go on this way. She'd not wanted him to know because she'd been afraid of what he'd think of her. But maybe that's exactly what he needed to be free. It wasn't like it would make anything worse for her. He'd still be out of her life, only he'd stop torturing himself with wondering why. It had been cruel of her to put that on him.

"Can't you just *talk* to me? What the hell was so bad you'd dump your whole life in the toilet and me with it?"

"I don't—" She sighed and rubbed one of her eyes. Why not tell him? Because while he didn't know, she wouldn't have to see the disgust that she wasn't human. Wasn't a person. Then again, what difference would it make? Things couldn't get much worse between them. She snorted inwardly. *Never say never.*

"Let's just say that if I was murdered, I wouldn't qualify for an investigation."

He sucked in a quiet breath. "What are you?"

She searched for a description. Only one word came to mind. "A monster."

RAY PULLED INTO a dock just north of the hospital on the Willamette. He parked under a streetlight in a lot more full than it should have been at this time of night. Market night in Nuketown brought in a fair number of people from throughout Portland. The docks along this stretch of the river were reasonably safe, and a lot of boat taxis waited for fares.

It was getting late, even for the Nuketown Night Market, and more people were returning from the Island than were going. Most people willing to go to Nuketown tried to get to the Night Market right after dark. The witches who ran the market had elected to hold it at night because most everybody could be nocturnal but a few who needed the market couldn't stand the light of day. Plus, a lot of the witches preferred the ambience of night, especially since it made humans nervous.

Ray led the way down to the boat shed for the Metropolitan police. He hadn't said a word since her confession. A couple times it looked as though he wanted to speak but then thought the better of it.

He chose a patrol boat from one of the slips, holding a hand out to help Kayla get aboard when the boat rocked on the waves. Kayla cast off after stowing her pack in a waterproof box in the stern. Ray started the boat, and as with cars running on magic, it made little sound as he reversed out of the slip and turned upriver.

One of the things that had always struck Kayla as being strange and magical about the river even before Magicfall was the fact that it ran south to north rather than the reverse. Nuketown had developed on the south side of the metro area about ten miles east of Lake Oswego. The river had expanded into a vast lake with peninsulas and one giant island, which was actually the top of an underwater mountain. The lake started around where West Linn had been, swelling out to swallow Clackamas, Happy Valley, and Milwaukie before narrowing back down to river size again. Nuketown had grown up on the mountaintop island, imaginatively dubbed the Island.

The Island itself was five miles wide and shaped like a seven-legged spider. All the trading happened in Nuketown, situated where the two southernmost legs connected to the center. Quite a few magical people lived on the Island in little villages, family nests, and protected enclaves.

A six-foot-wide slatted bridge spanned the distance between the longest leg of the spider and the northeast side of the river. Magic held it in place. Other than that, the only way to get to the Island was by boat.

The separation by water from the rest of the city blunted the suppressive power on practicing magic that came with a mass of civilization like a city. That allowed the witches and other magic-wielding creatures better use of their talents. Their isolation also made them feel both more dangerous to humans and semi-contained. The contradiction didn't make any sense if you thought about it, but most humans tried not to think about it.

Getting to the Island by boat wasn't easy. The river had grown hazards after Magicfall, and most couldn't be seen. Kayla was fairly certain a few of those had been created by witches or other witchkin to help protect their island sanctuary.

Shortly after setting out on the water, they negotiated their way through the maze of giant, rippling coral that protruded out of the water in a dangerous ribbon forest. The colors ranged from cobalt blue, smoky purple, orange, yellow, to red as if a summer sunset had been captured, shattered, and planted into the river.

It took concentration and quick reflexes to get safely through them. Even with a magical motor, the boat had difficulty fighting the current that did everything in its power to dash passing boats to smithereens on the exposed reef. There was no way to go around except on the shore, but building docks on the other southern side wasn't feasible because of the waterspouts that would suddenly blow up out of nothing and wreak havoc on and off shore.

Ray maneuvered the boat with skill and ease that spoke of practice. In the meantime, Kayla hunched in her seat under the cabin cover that housed the steering console. She quietly prayed that no water would splash her. Tired as she was, and having already resisted transformation once, she doubted she could hold out more than a few seconds if she did get wet.

Most shifters tended to turn into something familiar like a lion or a wolf or an otter. Not Kayla. She didn't even know what the hell she turned into. She'd gone as far as she could go into the university libraries looking for a reference to something like her. Nothing. She'd gone to Powell's Books figuring there must be something in that huge variety. Again, a big fat nothing.

What would Ray think if he saw her? She didn't want to know. He'd crap his pants or run screaming. Maybe both. Her jaw tightened. It wouldn't happen. She wouldn't let it.

She braced herself as Ray swished them around a tight S-turn. Droplets of water splashed onto the windshield. She flinched.

The water on the other side of the coral forest was bizarrely calm, as if the water held its breath and waited for something. If she'd been alone, she'd have gone into the water and transformed to find out why.

They'd gone another half mile or so when Ray spoke. "Is there a less obvious place to tie up than the Night Market marina?"

"Why?"

He shrugged. "We're driving a patrol boat. I'm not sure it's the wisest choice for everybody to know there's a cop wandering around."

Kayla snorted. "Even dressed as a civilian, I'm not sure anybody's going to believe you're anything but a cop. Good thing you never wanted to go undercover. You'd have been made in seconds."

He gave her one of those looks that said he agreed but wasn't altogether bothered by that fact. "It's always worth a shot."

Kayla had explored the Island many times from under the water. The floor of Lake Sagalie was deep and craggy with one lone mountain sticking all the way up to the surface, the Island being its crown. The lake's name came from a Chinook shaman who showed up there as a cloud of rainbow light and declared the new lake would have that name. Wasn't a soul in all the city who didn't hear him. Even deaf people. After that, he vanished, but Kayla kept expecting him to show up any time someone forgot to call the lake the right name. Personally, she had a healthy enough respect for magic not to want to test the possibility. She had enough problems.

"There's a little cove where we can tie up the boat and pretty well be out of sight. From there it's only about a mile to Nuketown."

She'd wanted a private spot where her other self could bask unseen in the sunshine in the summer months, so one night when it was storming and nobody could see her, she'd dug out a bowl in the rocks and a trench to the river, piling rocks up on either side to screen her from sight.

"Where is it?"

"It's between the two hairpin legs."

Those two legs faced east and paralleled each other, with a small channel in between. It wasn't terribly deep and had a number of sunken boulders and outcroppings that made it difficult to navigate, not to mention a grove of underwater sawgrass that could literally cut through a boat's hull. Or at least the grove had been there, before Kayla had cleared most of it out to make herself a water road. Adding to the complication of getting in, the claws of the two legs curled toward each other, and on summer days when the water level dropped a little lower like it was now, a boat like this one would just barely get through.

Ray frowned at her. "You sure? I didn't even think anybody could get up in there with the boat."

Kayla gave a diffident shrug and looked out over the water. The fog had lifted, enough to see a few hundred yards ahead though everything still looked ghostly. "It's a little tricky, but you won't have any problem."

Ray turned the boat slightly toward the east, and Kayla thought she might have heard him say, "If you say so."

After the coral forest and the waterspout zone, the rest of the approach to the Island was usually pretty tame. But every so often a wandering whirlpool or three or four would pop up out of nowhere and pinball around the lake. They ranged from only a foot or two across to half a football field. Even the little ones were plenty dangerous. They could suck a boat down into the depths in nothing flat.

Ray had slowed to give them a better chance to see a whirlpool and react. They moved quick. In her other form Kayla had the ability to sense them, to feel them in the water, but in her human form she was blind. How stupid was she to risk the boat and Ray's life just because she was afraid to rip off the Band-Aid and show him? But no, stupid was too kind. She was a fucking coward.

A vortex swirled at them, dragging them in. Ray swore and gunned the magical motor, twisting the wheel sharply. Kayla grabbed on to the edge of her seat. He overshot and got the boat crosswise of the current. The wave of water shoved them, tilting them dangerously down on the driver's side. Any farther and they'd capsize. Panic exploded inside Kayla. This was it. This was how everything ended. Then Ray opened the motor all the way, swerving to get the push of the current behind them. The boat bucked slightly, hesitated, and then launched out of the whirlpool pull.

Once they were clear, Kayla sucked in shallow, panting breath, finding it difficult to slow her pounding heart. Until faced with the inevitability, she hadn't realized how much she didn't want Ray to know—to actually see— what she'd become.

Ray slowed the boat again and patted the dashboard. "Gotta love patrol boats. These babies are built for speed and endurance, and they can take a hell of a beating too." He frowned at her. "You okay?"

She nodded. "A little seasick." *As if.* But Ray seemed to accept that explanation for her short breaths and stiff posture.

Meanwhile, Ray had the expression of a kid who'd just gone down the best roller-coaster ride of his life, rather than narrowly avoiding certain death.

If he hadn't become a detective, she was willing to bet he'd be a waterdog, which is what the cops patrolling the river were called.

The tricky passage between the two claws and up to her cove seemed easy after escaping the whirlpool. Ray waded ashore and tied up to a tree. Kayla dug her pack out of the waterproof bin and slid it onto her shoulders before climbing up on the side of the patrol boat to jump to shore.

Her stomach dropped into her boots. *Too far.* No way to get around getting wet.

"Hold on." Ray waded back into the water and reached up for her. "Come on. I'll carry you. No sense both of us getting wet."

"My hero," she said with ridiculous relief. She reached down and braced herself on his shoulders as his arms circled her thighs. He turned and carried her to the bank.

"Thanks," she said, pulling out of his grasp, trying to ignore the electric sensations his touch evoked, hoping he didn't notice the hitch in her breath or the way her fingers lingered on his arms as he set her down.

She curled her hands into fists. She couldn't go there. And not just because he'd laugh in her face. If by some miracle he did respond positively to her, once he actually saw her, game over. Knowing how he felt about supernaturals, she knew he'd be repulsed. So many *humans* were.

Not that he'd ever be attracted to her. Just imagining it was an exercise in futility.

Focusing on the present reality, Kayla slipped a glow rock from her pocket. Made of amber, it contained a light spell that once activated, turned the rock into a fragment of sunshine.

She led the way to the narrow track she'd created over the years—in human form. She came here regularly to help Nessa and to renew her amulets. She had the one she'd drained at the fountain in her pocket and hoped she'd have a chance to get the drying spell refreshed.

The path wound through the trees and around stone outcroppings. In making her path she'd avoided getting too close to any of the inhabited trees, with the exception of a few that she couldn't get around. Mostly the dryads didn't mind her walking through, but she'd never brought a human with her before. She didn't know how they would feel about him.

Her first warning that something wasn't right came in the rustling leaves that sounded almost like a swarm of bees. No wind blew to disturb them.

"Stay close," she said over her shoulder to Ray. If anything went side-ways, she'd invoke the water amulet on her wrist, but dryads were generally peaceful unless somebody threatened their trees. Then they turned into a violent force of nature.

"What is it?" Ray's voice was a hushed rasp.

Kayla didn't answer. She didn't have time to answer. Massive tree roots burst up from the ground, weaving together and caging them in an upside-down wooden basket.

"What the hell?"

She was pleased to see that Ray had enough sense to keep his gun holstered despite their unexpected prison.

"Dryads," she said in a low voice. "They've never bothered me before. Something's going on." *Oh good, Kayla, way to state the obvious.*

The light from the amulet streamed through the little breaks in the cage, casting irregular shadows around them. Movement along the trunk of a big oak tree caught her attention. A ghostly form stepped out of the wood and grew solid. It appeared to be a man with long hair, wearing pants made of woven leaves and blackberry vines complete with thorns.

The dryad straightened and shook himself, his bare chest a grayish brown much like the bark of his tree. Two female dryads joined him though Kayla didn't see where they came from. As they walked forward and Kayla could see them better, she noticed their eyes were a vivid green the color of moss and matched the color of their hair.

They halted outside the cage. Though their expressions appeared serene, Kayla sensed a deep flow of anger and fear.

"Is there something we can help you with?" Kayla asked, putting a hand on Ray's forearm to keep him quiet. Dryads could be a touchy bunch and were sometimes easily offended. Using manners always paid off with them.

"We have need of you," said the male dryad.

"Us? For what?"

The dryad on the left shook her head. "Just you," she said, her gaze skewering Kayla.

Foreboding twisted in her stomach. She couldn't imagine that they wanted her to salvage something for them. The only reason they could possibly want her was for her other form. She hadn't been able to hide it from them when she dug the channel, nor when she sometimes swam here and emerged from the water to dry and transform. She'd known she couldn't conceal it from everyone, and this place seemed safe enough since the dryads didn't exactly talk to a lot of other people.

"For what?" Ray asked, his tone more than a little bit belligerent.

The female dryad on the right gave him a long look and then shifted back to Kayla. "Someone is killing us," she said, her announcement all the more chilling because she said it the same way Kayla might have said she wanted bacon for breakfast.

"Chopping your trees?" Kayla frowned. The witchkin on Spider Island protected each other. Anybody caught attacking a tree would be summarily killed. If not by the dryads themselves, then by the witches or any one of the hundred or more resident species living on the island.

"No," the male dryad said. "Come."

The roots in front of Kayla raveled apart and pulled her forward away from Ray while other roots reformed behind her encasing him once again. The roots let go of Kayla, and the dryads beckoned her to follow them.

"He comes with us," she said. If they knew what she was, if they wanted her *for* what she was, then they would know better than to argue. They didn't. Swiftly all the roots retracted into the ground leaving behind no evidence that they had ever erupted.

Ray said nothing as he joined Kayla, but grabbed her hand as she walked ahead of him, his skin hot on hers.

They turned east off the track Kayla had made. The bushes and under-growth pressed aside to give them a path. The leaves in the trees continued to rattle and shake, and an eerie chorus of low moans coiled around them as they walked. The hair on the back of Kayla's neck rose.

The three dryads led them into a large grove full of trees Kayla didn't recognize. They were taller and larger around than any trees she'd ever seen except for the sequoias in California. They blotted out the sky. A silvery glow emanated from ruffles of fungi and moss as well as trailing flowers, illuminating the grove with a mystical light. It was magical, like walking into a fairytale. Only this was a very grim fairytale.

Their three escorts stopped at the base of a silver-skinned tree. Its leaves had started to curl and dry, and its trunk zigzagged with cracks, a darkening stain spreading from them over the trunk. But that wasn't what caught Kayla's attention.

A male dryad had been pegged to the tree with steel spikes. His upper body showed no wounds, but the same couldn't be said for the lower half. One of his legs had been chopped off and taken. Greenish-black blood dripped into a puddle on the ground.

Who had done this? Why had they taken the leg? Possibly even more disturbing, how had the killer drawn the dryad out of his tree? Kayla could see no signs of chopping or cutting or fire. Those were the main threats to dryads because it harmed the armor of their trees. But while inside their trees, they were largely impervious.

Magic had to be involved. She couldn't see any other explanation for the scene.

"Do you have any witnesses?" She squatted down to look at the ground. Nothing disturbed the leaf meal. It didn't look as if anybody had been through the area in years.

"It was not seen," one of the female dryads said, her voice shaking.

Kayla frowned up at them and then glanced at the surrounding trees where other dryads surely lived. "How is that possible?"

"We do not know. All we remember is that all was right and then Nedir was like this." The other female dryad gestured toward the body with hooked fingers.

Kayla stood, trying to understand. "You're saying that everything was fine, including Nedir, and then like that"—Kayla snapped her fingers—"he was suddenly here on his tree, dead?"

"That is exactly so," said the male.

"And you saw no one come or go?" That was from Ray.

The dryads glanced at him warily. "We did not," the male said, directing his answer at Kayla.

"Did you sense anything?" The question was remarkably vague, but then Kayla had no idea what a dryad could see or feel when inside their trees. Did they sleep? Did they feel footsteps on the dirt near their trees? Could they smell?

"It was . . . as if we were not awake," said one of the females. "As if we were all in winter hibernation and all the world grew muffled around us." She hesitated and then added, "I dreamed of pain and fear, and I heard a voice chanting words of power in a language I did not understand."

The other two nodded. "For us as well," said the male dryad.

"For all of us in the grove," the other female said. "We could not wake. We could not feel our trees." She shuddered.

Kayla could only imagine what that might have been like, trapped and unable to move or speak. Like being paralyzed or buried alive.

"Then what happened?"

"The feeling left and we woke," said the male dryad. "We felt ill."

"What do you mean by ill?" Kayla asked.

"Burning and pain," spoke the male again. "Here and here." He touched a hand to his forehead and then his belly. The other two dryads nodded affirmation.

"How long did the pain and burning last?"

"It is still," said one of the female dryads. She shook her head in consternation and worry. "We do not know what has happened. We do not know if our trees are sick."

"Kayla, look at this."

Ray had gone around to the other side of the tree and pointed upward as she joined him. About six feet up, a hole had been bored through the tree. Curls of sawdust clung to the bark where they had fallen. Clear sap leaked out of the wound as if the tree bled. The three dryads made a high-pitched moaning sound, and the angry sound of leaves rattling increased.

She turned to the three dryads. "Why did you want me to see all this?"

They faced her, eyes full of rage and confusion. The male spoke first

"You are the Guardian of the River and the city. You are Justice. You are Vengeance. You are Law."

Kayla blinked at them. "Come again?"

She was what? She rubbed her temples with her fingertips and licked her dry lips. Clearly they referred to her other form, or at least she assumed so. She felt Ray's sharp gaze on her, but couldn't bring herself to look at him.

"You are the Guardian. You will find the killer," one of the females said, clearly bothered by her response.

"I'm not a cop anymore," Kayla said, knowing full well that the three didn't care. She was buying time until her brain could catch up.

"We do not need a human policeman," said the male reprovingly. "A human is not for witchkin. They do not understand us, nor do they wish to."

"Human police cannot stand against the one who did this," added one of the females.

But she could. Or so they thought. She wanted to deny that she was a guardian of anything or that she was any grandiose notion of justice or law or vengeance. The trouble was she couldn't possibly win that argument. The dryads had made up their minds and would not be talked out of it. She was still debating how to answer when one of the women spoke up again.

"There have been other killings in the city," she said. "Always witchkin, always brutal. Nobody hunts the killer who hunts us." The last sentence came with a wealth of accusation.

Other killings? Kayla's mind flashed to the three bodies pinned on the wall of the Keller Fountain. Had the same killer slaughtered them? Did it even matter?

Back at the fountain she had decided that she had to be the one to find that killer and the families of the victims and bring them the news of what had happened to their loved ones. It didn't bring much comfort, but it did end the unending cycle of hope, disappointment, and fear. It let families and loved ones move on instead of trapping them in the worst moments of their lives.

Someone had to get the answers. Someone had to get justice.

"What killings? How many?"

"Too many," said the same female who had last spoken, her eyes turbulent with emotion.

"I need to talk to anybody with information about these murders," Kayla said.

"Kayla —" The tone of Ray's voice indicated disapproval.

She looked at him. "Who else is going to do it?" And even though she tried to keep the accusation out of her voice, it ran through the words like a hot wire.

Ray scowled and folded his arms across his chest. "No matter what they say about you being a guardian—whatever the hell that means—you're not some kind of superhero. Going after this nut job is too dangerous. You don't have any backup, and you don't have the resources to investigate. You'll end up dead."

She smiled, not taking any offense. Truth was, if she were still human, he'd be right. "I'm all they've got," she said, then turned back to the dryads. "How do you know about the murders in the city?"

"The trees tell us," said the male. "And many come to this island for answers to their questions and to get help to protect themselves."

"Who helps?" Kayla asked. "The witches?"

The second female dryad nodded. "They seek protection spells. Speak to the witch known as Raven. She will tell you what is known."

"She's in town?"

A nod.

Ray had continued to quietly seethe throughout this conversation, but now he could no longer contain himself. "What the hell do you think you're doing, Kayla?" he said, grabbing her arm and turning her to face him. His eyes glinted, and his jaw flexed with knotted emotions. "First of all, you do remember your grandmother and aunt? They don't have a lot of time. We need to find the kidnapper."

Kayla resisted the urge to yank herself away from him. Not because she minded his hold on her, but because she didn't and because he was right, and because it didn't change the fact that she had to hunt down this killer before he killed again.

"I haven't forgotten," she said. "But this can't wait either." She gave a little shrug. "Sleep is overrated anyway, right?"

His hand on her arm tightened. "You can't—"

Kayla set her hand in the middle of his chest, stopping his words.

"Yes, I can. I have to. If I don't, nobody else will."

"You aren't a cop anymore, Kayla. This isn't your responsibility. You didn't *want* that responsibility. You *left*." Bitterness spun through the threads of concern.

"A girl can change her mind," she said lightly, cringing inwardly and expecting an instant tirade. She got it.

"Just like that?" He grabbed her other arm, his hands tightening as he pulled her closer. "You'll risk your actual family to take on a case that could get you killed?"

She tugged out of his grasp. "You heard them. A lot of witchkin have been killed. Who else is going to stop it? No one else is going to investigate. Only me. You've always said it—the strong have to protect the weak. That's not just what we do, that's who we are, whether we wear a uniform or not."

He thrust her away and raked his hands through his hair. "This guy's a psychotic killer with magical abilities. It's David against Goliath, and you don't have a sling or a stone. You'll be killed, or worse."

It was possible to kill her, she knew. In her human form she was as weak physically as any other human. So there was definitely risk, because she couldn't go running around in her alternate form without causing panic and mayhem. But she had the water amulet to help her turn in mere seconds, and Portland was full of water in the shape of creeks, lakes, ponds, rivers, and bathtubs. If she got into trouble, she'd be able to change quickly.

"I'll handle it."

Ray scraped his fingers through his hair, staring at her in disbelief. "Seriously? And just how the fuck are you going to *handle* this crazy motherfucker?"

"She is the Guardian of the River," repeated a female dryad, as if that explained everything.

"What the hell does that even mean?" Ray's eyes bored into Kayla's.

"I'm not entirely sure."

"Then why are you buying this bullshit?"

"I told you—nobody else will do it, and I am the most qualified and prepared."

"To deal with magic? Bullshit."

He shook his head and made a sound of exasperation, stomping away and then back again. Kayla watched in surprise. Ray was always so cool and so contained and why he should get so freaked out over what could happen to her after all she put him through these past years and the way she left, she didn't know. She got that he was worried about her—he was a good man, after all, and they'd been friends—but this seemed excessive. Not that she had time to think about it.

Before Ray could protest further, she turned back to the dryads. "I will stop this psycho."

The three accepted her promise with a solemn nod, and then turned and walked away, disappearing into the trees.

Kayla took a deep breath and let it out, then picked her pack up from where she'd dropped it and slid it on. "Maybe this Raven witch can tell us something about the symbols we found at Grandmother's house, too. Kill two birds with one stone."

"Christ Almighty, Kayla," Ray began again.

She cut him off before he could get started. "I promise, Ray, I'm not as helpless as you think. I'm not suicidal and I'm not stupid, so you don't have to worry about me."

She didn't wait for a response, but headed in the direction of the Night Market. Time was nobody's friend on the murders or kidnappings.

Irony swamped her, and she grimaced. She'd wanted a purpose after bobbling about like a loose boat on a turbulent sea, and now she had two—saving her grandmother and aunt, and stopping the witchkin murders.

Determination quickened her steps. She'd be damned if she'd fail either task, come hell or high water. She just hoped the universe didn't take that as a personal challenge.

Chapter 14

Ray

RAY BOILED INSIDE as he stalked after Kayla. His hands clenched and unclenched, and magic sluiced through him in a hot torrent. It built inside him like steam in a kettle. He couldn't let it blow. Normally when this happened, he found a way to discharge a bolt of the energy—into the ground or the river or somewhere it couldn't do harm.

But here? In his current mood? He'd be guaranteed to kill trees, and the dryads would most definitely take offense to that.

The myths that said the creatures were gentle beings lied. The best you'd get was live and let live. Fuck with them, and they'd come after you with a vengeance. He'd heard stories of them reaching out through uninhabited trees and plants and dragging people under the dirt and burying them alive. The rest of the time they fought dirty. Which in no way explained why they weren't going after the witchkin killer themselves instead of demanding help from Kayla.

He dragged in a deep breath, trying to make himself relax. An almost impossible task with Kayla in front of him. Running away from him. Again. Or at least it felt like it.

The neanderthal half of himself wanted to shove her up against a tree and kiss the living shit out of her. The other half wanted to throttle her. The fucking dryads knew more about her than he did.

He had no idea what to make of their claim that she had to hunt down the killer because she was the Guardian of the River. What did that mean? He didn't think she was suicidal, and yet she was acting like it, thinking she could go up against this killer alone.

Not that he'd let her.

A voice in Ray's head jeered at that. Like he could stop her. What was he going to do? Chain her up when he wasn't around? What about when he slept? He'd have to handcuff her to him so she wouldn't sneak away.

His entire body flushed hot as he imagined her curled up against him, his arms around her. How far gone was he that neither of them were naked in his little daydream? How far gone was he that just the idea of cuddling her made his dick hard?

God but he was fucked up. The last thing he wanted to do was start something up with any woman, but with Kayla least of all—even if she'd cooperate, which was laughable. Even if he did somehow manage to get her in bed, it couldn't end well and he'd lose her all over again.

Talk about a dose of frigid reality. The possibility drove icicles into his body and cooled his magic like it had been dipped in liquid nitrogen. Fear stalked across his soul. He wouldn't let it happen. Four years had taught him he could live without her, but it was a crap life. He had to fix things so he could have her back, no matter how much anger and hurt he had to swallow. He didn't need his pride; he needed her, and he needed to close the hole she'd left inside him.

Ray hurried to overtake Kayla, falling in beside her. She cast him a wary look, but didn't speak.

"You're thinking what happened here is related to the killings at Keller Fountain," he said, deciding to focus on solving the case—the one thing they always did well together.

"Murders," she corrected. "And yes, I do think they're related."

"Why?"

"The way they were pinned up and the missing body parts. Those similarities in the MO aren't likely coincidence. The timing's suspicious, too."

"The dryad didn't have any of those symbols around him," Ray pointed out. Not that he disagreed. Like most cops, he didn't put a lot of stock in coincidence.

"Maybe the murders had different purposes. Or maybe he didn't have time to do all he wanted," she said. "Hell, the dryad could just have been to get his rocks off."

"Okay, say that's true. What about these other witchkin murders? You think they're related?"

"Too soon to say, but it's possible."

Ray's gut had him leaning toward yes, but he'd let the evidence tell the story. And if they were related? A serial killer was loose in the city and nobody'd noticed. *He'd* not noticed, and that was going to eat at his conscience a long time. He should have done better.

They walked in silence for a minute, and then Kayla spoke again, musing aloud. "I wonder what the coroner's office will learn from the fountain bodies."

"They won't do an autopsy," Ray said. Before, that fact hadn't bothered him. He hadn't even thought about it. But now . . .

"I know, but Zach thought there might be some sort of clue on the bodies to tell him about the spell casting."

Ray managed not to say anything disparaging about the technomage. Iron-jawed, he pushed it away. Kayla's romantic life wasn't his business. He had to stay focused on solving the kidnapping and keeping her out of trouble. He had to remember he wanted her back in his life, and getting his cock in a knot over her and Logan wasn't going to help his cause.

They emerged from the grove into a broad meadow. On the other side, the lights of the Night Market twinkled in the darkness.

Ray hadn't been to the market in nearly a year. Set in a long oval, it had three entrances. Most of the stalls were made of wood beams with oiled canvas or corrugated steel roofs. Vendors frequently shared walls and were organized along crooked walkways. Clustered at the southern side were some permanent buildings housing a few shops, a café, two tiny restaurants, and a post office. A few island natives carried baskets and wandered through the crowd, peddling their wares.

It startled Ray to see so many shoppers at this time of the night. Or more accurately, morning. There had to be at least a few hundred.

"I've always figured it's because they have to wait to sneak out so nobody else will see them," Kayla said when he mentioned it. "Look at how many are wearing hoods and cloaks so they won't be recognized. I'd be willing to bet that a lot of them are either secret witches, secretly not human, or up to no good."

"No good?" Ray repeated, eyeing the crowd speculatively. His cop radar fired up.

"Humans are always out here looking for an advantage in their lives. You'll hear them ask for love potions, ways to spy on each other, attack spells, hexes, and whatever else they can dream up. Some salvagers even come looking for invisibility spells in order to bypass some of the magical dangers where they scavenge."

"Do they work?"

"Which?"

"The invisibility spells."

"They say they do, at least some of the time. I've never tried one."

Though Ray wanted to ask her why not, he didn't bother since he was certain it was tied to everything else she wasn't telling him.

They wandered into the market. Packed stalls crowded close, offering everything from salvaged goods to spell paraphernalia. An archway of vines had been trained over the top of the walkway. Silvery-white flowers gave off a slightly pungent perfume. Gold pollen mashed into the hard clay soil below.

They entered the enclosure and strolled through the throng. Ray eyed the sale stalls. Not for the first time did he wonder what he might be able to do with some of the supplies and a little training in witchcraft. He shook away the thought. *Never going to happen.*

Kayla paused at a booth selling herbs and a variety of amulets and other jewelry. A weedy-looking man with horn-rimmed glasses, receding brown hair, and ears that stuck out like the doors of an open taxi, negotiated with a pair of witchkin women wearing long white gowns made of a translucent gossamer material. Their bodies were slender to the point of near emaciation.

The first had green hair that fell past her waist and reminded Ray of pasture grass. The other appeared to be older, or maybe sick. Her hair hung yellow-brown and brittle. Her hands, when she reached out to pay for her purchase, were gnarled and curled with thick yellow nails sharpened into points.

Neither one of the witchkin women paid any attention to him or Kayla. All the same, Ray stayed close. His magic bubbled ready inside him. He could call it up and let a bolt of it go with little thought. It was a lesson he taught himself early on. Sometimes as a cop, he had to fight fire with fire, or in this case, magic with magic.

The two women collected their purchases and tucked them into the woven baskets they carried on their arms. After putting away their payments—not money but some sort of trade items—the seller turned to Kayla and Ray. His gaze settled heavily on Ray, examining him from head to toe. The man's lips tightened as he turned his attention to Kayla.

"May I help you?" he asked in a voice that said he had no interest in helping her at all, with a pinch of disapproval indicating he disliked her taste in companions.

"We are looking for Raven," said Kayla. "Do you know where we can find her stall?"

The man began sweeping up bits of leaves and stems that had escaped and now littered the counter.

"Why do you want her?"

"I would tell you," Kayla said, "but I've learned that witches aren't fond of others prying into their business. I have not met Raven, but I'd rather not start out on her bad side."

The man's mouth twitched into a thin smile of appreciation. Brown stains darkened the seams between his teeth. "It is true," he said as he finished cleaning off the table. "Witches can be a touchy bunch. Which is why I'd rather not send trouble to her door." He gave Ray a dark look. "We don't get a lot of cops here, and when we do they are never friendly."

"We're looking into the witchkin murders," Kayla said. "The dryads told us to talk to Raven."

At that bit of news, the man's brows rose and his face paled. "Go left, far end. It's the only stall that has a door."

He turned his back then, and Ray knew they weren't going to get any more from him.

"My name is Kayla. If you hear of anything you think I need to know, this is my number." She grabbed a paper bag and a pen and wrote her number out on it. "You might let others know," she added, pushing the bag toward him

The other man's lip curled. "Since when does anyone care what happens to witchkin? You humans hate us."

"You were our enemies in a war to kill most of us," Ray said.

The proprietor tensed as if to argue, and then slumped, giving a resigned nod. "We wanted our world back," he said. "We wanted to live free again. We wanted to stop being the monsters in your fairytales. We wanted to come and go as we chose. We wanted to live in a world of magic again. Perhaps we should have tried a different way."

Ray slid a hand around the back of his neck. In the years since Magicfall, he learned a lot about the way the world used to be before humans overran it and stamped out much of the magic. It wasn't a lot different from what the whites had done to the Native Americans when settling America. It was hard to blame the witchkin for their anger and for fighting back, but it was equally hard to forgive them for all the carnage and death.

But now they all had to live in the same world together, and they had to figure out how to treat each other with respect. As a cop, he should be leading the charge. His role was to protect and to serve people, and as Kayla had pointed out at the fountain square, just because they weren't human didn't make the witchkin any less entitled to the same rights as humans.

It was hard to accept. Ray had seen so much death, so much pain, but if he admitted the truth, he'd seen that same death, same pain on both sides. They all had to learn to forgive each other.

"You shouldn't have had to fight for it," he said, dragging his fingers through his hair.

The proprietor startled, his eyes widening. Ray was aware of Kayla looking up at him. Her fingers touched the back of his hand as if to say well done. Ray stiffened his arm to keep from lacing his fingers through hers.

"You should go," the man said gruffly. "Raven's been known to close up early."

Kayla nodded to him, and she and Ray began to walk away.

"I'm called Silas, by the way," the proprietor called. "I'm a Deva."

When Ray looked over his shoulder in surprise, Silas, the Deva, was looking right at him. Ray tipped his head.

"Ray Garza," he said with a nod.

"You did good," Kayla said as they cut across the central space.

"I didn't do anything."

"You treated him with respect."

"That shouldn't win me any prizes."

"Because you shouldn't have?"

He gave her a heavy look. "I guess I deserve that. But nobody deserves a prize for basic respect. It should be the rule, not the exception."

The corner of her mouth lifted in a crooked smile. "And lo, an old dog learns a new trick."

"You calling me old?"

"I'm calling you a dog."

Her grin widened, and he couldn't help but smile back. "I like dogs. Don't you?"

"As long as they don't bite."

If I ever get a chance to nibble on you, you're going to love it. Heat flashed through him, and his dick went hard. *Jesus.* He felt like a hormonal teenager on his first date. He told himself to cool off and hoped to hell Kayla didn't notice the log growing in his pants.

Raven's stall was more like a tiny cottage painted sea-blue with crisp white trim. Two small windows faced the commons area, and below each of them colorful flowers rioted in window boxes. The two of them stopped outside, and Kayla knocked on the door. It swung open silently.

Ray caught Kayla's shoulder and slid past her to enter first. Inside the place was cozy, looking more like a comfortable living room than anything else. A copper kettle sat on a petrified wood stump with curls of steam rolling out of its spout. Fairy lights danced along the ceiling. Overstuffed chairs filled the rest of the space along with bright hangings.

The witch sat in one corner. She wore a bohemian-style blouse and skirt with beaded bracelets on both wrists, and a host of rings on her fingers. She held a steaming cup low in her lap, her legs folded up under her.

"Welcome," she said in a husky voice as if she had a cold. "Please sit." She gestured toward the other chairs. Kayla sat opposite to her, and Ray chose a seat where he could watch them both.

"Would you like some tea?"

Raven didn't wait for an answer but turned to a small table beside her and set her cup aside as she poured tea for both Kayla and Ray. It smelled like cinnamon, cloves, and something Ray couldn't quite identify. She added cream and stirred and passed a cup to each of her guests. Picking up her own again, she leaned back in her chair.

"How can I help you today?" She sipped, watching Kayla over the rim of her cup. She ignored Ray altogether.

"You know who—what—I am," Kayla said.

Ray leaned forward, hoping she'd say more, but apparently that was enough. Raven tipped her head in agreement.

Kayla continued, "Then you know the dryads sent me."

The witch didn't waste any time small talk. "The killings started nearly three months ago," she said. "We knew right away that these were no ordinary murders."

"Ordinary murders?" Kayla asked.

"Humans don't like us, and they tell us so in blood in the backs of alleys. Their violence is filled with hate, but these killings have no emotion. They are calculated, clinically performed, and involve magic. Always the victims are missing bones."

"Bones? Any in particular?" Kayla asked, her brow furrowing.

"No. While the choice of bones taken from a victim doesn't seem arbitrary, neither have we seen any pattern. Sometimes the choice is repeated, but mostly all are different." A shudder ran through Raven, though neither her voice nor her expression revealed any emotion.

"How many victims are we talking about?" Ray asked. He pulled his notebook out.

Raven turned her head to look at him and then turned back to Kayla to answer the question. "There have been twenty so far."

"Jesus," he muttered, hand clenching on the notebook. This guy was a serial killer. Guilt coiled in his chest. He should have seen it. And if he had? What would he have done? He didn't like the answer.

The witch reached down beside her chair and lifted up a waterproof plastic food-storage box full of papers. "This contains all we know about the murders, including photographs of some of the scenes."

Kayla took the box and set it in her lap. "I'll find and stop the killer," she said, her voice thick with anger.

"*We* will," Ray added in a gravelly voice.

Raven looked at him again. "Your decision is admirable," she said in a tone so devoid of emotion it was clearly a condemnation. "But the Guardian is better equipped than humans. Witchkin will talk to *her*."

"What else can you tell us?" Kayla asked.

Raven tapped a finger against her lip, considering. Finally, she lowered her hand, decision made. "Everything about the murders is in there." She nudged her chin toward the box in Kayla's lap. "But there's something else, maybe connected. Maybe not."

Kayla's brows rose. "What's that?"

The witch glanced at Ray and then gave a little shrug of resignation, as if she didn't think he'd believe her.

"Something is . . . building, like a storm rolling in off the horizon. A big one. Like a hurricane, only bigger. When it hits—if it isn't stopped—disaster will fall upon the city. What is coming is the enemy of humans as much as it is the enemy of the witchkin."

"Is that a foreseeing?" Kayla asked.

Raven nodded. "One of my coven has had repeated visions, but they offer little detail. Just that a great storm is coming."

"And you believe it's a true seeing?"

"I do. Drea has never seen wrong."

"What makes you think it could be connected to the killings?" Ray asked.

He didn't doubt that Raven believed every word. Some witches had a gift for prophecy. He just didn't know how true the prophecy really was, or if they'd interpreted the vision correctly. All the same, doubting it seemed more than a little arrogant, given Magicfall and all that he'd witnessed since. It didn't pay to take magic lightly.

"The flow of energies," was Raven's not-so-helpful reply. She looked at Kayla. "If I'm reading things right, everything depends on you."

"What do you mean?"

"Whatever is coming, you can still stop it. Soon you won't be able to."

The witch held up her hand when Kayla started to ask more questions. "I've told you all I can. The visions aren't clear. I didn't even know you were the one from my foreseeing until you walked in the door. I've told you all I know. Now it's up to you. Start with finding who killed the witchkin and why."

Kayla dug her phone out of her pocket. It was an antiquated thing. Ray knew she was looking for pictures from the fountain square. He watched her fumble for a moment then drew out his own phone and called up his photo gallery. Thank goodness for cloud backup. Even if it was a technomagical cloud. He tapped one of the pictures from the fountain crime scene, enlarging it to better see some of the writing. He handed it to Raven.

"Do you recognize these?"

Kayla flicked a surprised glance at him before tucking her phone away and giving her attention to Raven.

The witch examined the photo for long moments. "What is this?"

"We found them at a murder scene earlier today," said Kayla, glancing at Ray again as if expecting him to challenge the designation of murder.

He just nodded.

"It certainly looks like ritual," said Raven, scrolling through several more pictures. "I don't recognize the language."

"Can you think of anybody who would?" asked Ray.

She handed him back his phone. "Perhaps a specialist in ancient languages."

"Ancient languages?" Kayla asked.

"The cartouches around the symbols suggest ancient Egypt," Raven said. "Though this writing is not Egyptian."

"How do you know?" Ray asked.

"Once upon a time I studied Egyptian archaeology."

The witch had an odd look on her face. It took Ray a moment to identify it as wry humor, as if she'd remembered a joke he and Kayla knew nothing about.

"Does the placement of the bodies or the location mean anything that you can tell?" Kayla asked.

Raven shook her head. "I would suspect the killer used blood magic," she said. "It is a powerful sort of magic, but requires suffering to invoke the strongest power."

"So the killer is some kind of sadist?" Ray asked.

Raven shook her head. "Blood witches gather power from people. Many of them have historically chosen to live near cities to tap that raw energy. But when a blood witch requires greater power for her spells, ritual sacrifice generates a strong rich flow, and symbols can help with the focus. Hex witches use symbols, but don't require blood. That said, it is impossible to know whether a witch cast the spell, a mage, or something else entirely."

"A mage is a magic practitioner who can command multiple witch magics, correct?" Kayla asked.

Ray had a feeling she'd asked the question more for his sake than because she needed to know. He had heard of mages. He hadn't heard of anyone running in to one, and doubted any sane person would want to. Of course, any sane person wouldn't be sitting in a witch's parlor either.

"That's right," Raven said.

"Do *you* think a witch could be behind these killings?" Kayla asked.

Raven didn't hesitate, giving a sharp shake of her head. "I know all the local witches. None of them could have done this."

Could have? Or would have? Ray wondered. Either way, *he* couldn't rule out witches because her conclusion was based on false information. She *didn't* know all the local witches. She didn't know about him. How many others still hid their power?

"What about witches from out of town?" Kayla asked.

Raven frowned. "I suppose it is possible, but the witch community has been keeping close watch. *I* have been keeping close watch," she said, a dangerous current running through her voice.

"Do you hold the local covenstead?" Ray asked. He didn't fully understand the covenstead system, or how a witch came to define one, but he did know that they tended to stake out covenstead territories, and within each, a center point witch ruled with the aid of the other coven witches.

"I have a coven here. But there is no local covenstead."

"I don't understand. Aren't they the same?"

"The covenstead is a territory. It has a heart and a spirit. A witch will connect to that covenstead and build a coven to protect and nurture it." The witch's gaze slid to Kayla. "Things work differently here. Someone else holds the heart of this place. My coven anchors to the well that flows from that heart. We serve by aiding the healing and nurturing of the land and the people who live here."

"You're saying I hold the heart," Kayla said with no little disbelief.

"You are the Guardian of the River."

"You say that like I should know what that means," Kayla said sourly.

"Don't you?" Then without missing a beat, Raven shifted back to the reason Ray and Kayla had searched her out. "The murders must stop. We must protect those who cannot protect themselves." This last pronouncement came paired with another pointed look at Kayla, who grimaced.

"Got it. You can quit beating that dead horse now."

A noise outside caught their attention. Shouts and screams shredded the night. Raven leaped to her feet and ran out the door with Kayla and Ray close on her heels.

The market enclosure churned as people scrambled in fear, pinballing off one another, their panic fed by being in Nuketown among witches and other witchkin.

Ignoring the humans, witchkin raced toward the thin screen of trees separating the market from the main dock. A roaring sound filled the air, along with the stench of dead fish and swamp mud.

Raven bolted toward the dock, thrusting aside anyone who got in her way. Her bare feet slapped the path. Kayla and Ray sprinted after her.

They burst between the trees to find that a whirlpool had entered the marina cove. The churning whirl drifted toward the docks, sending waves crashing over the wooden walkways. Boats jerked and jolted against their moorings. The turbulent water smashed them together. Several disappeared down the gullet of the whirlpool only to be thrust back up as confetti.

But that wasn't the worst of it.

A dozen or more boats on their way home to the city's mainland had been caught in its powerful current. Passengers screamed, and one or two dove off the sides hoping to swim to shore. Loud cracking sounded above the tornadic noise of the whirlpool. Wooden dock pilings and platform boards snapped like dry bones. A twenty-foot length of dock broke off and spun into the churn.

Several children carrying packages to departing boats for shoppers reeled at the edge. One boy fell, and another grabbed him, but then the broken piece of pier bucked and all three went tumbling into the water.

Kayla took off at a dead run before Ray even knew what was happening. He started after her but Raven snatched his arm.

"No. This is for her to do."

"Fuck that," he snapped, twisting out of her hold and dashing after Kayla.

She'd nearly reached the water and showed no signs of stopping. *What the fuck?* He raced toward her, lungs clutching in his chest, magic clawing through his veins.

He screamed Kayla's name as she leaped onto the buckling planks of the pier. She stumbled as the furthest edge rose sharply. She fell forward snatching at the lip still rising above her head. She climbed. As she neared the edge, the disintegrating mass dropped. She vanished from sight.

Ray screamed her name again, but his heart split in two when the planks ripped apart and swirled rapidly toward the sunken heart of the whirlpool.

Before he could leap in after her, inhuman hands caught him and yanked him back to the bank. His mind went numb.

She was gone.

Again.

Only this time she wasn't coming back. Nobody could come back from this watery hellhole.

He was barely aware when Raven came to stand near him. She watched the water as if waiting.

"She is the Guardian of the River," the witch said without looking at him. "The water can no more hurt her than flames can burn a salamander."

Ray's head jerked around, his gaze anchoring on her. "What the hell does that mean? What is a guardian of the river?"

"Not *a* guardian. *The* Guardian. You can ask Kayla when she returns."

Ray laughed, the ragged sound tearing from his throat. "Return? From that?" He gestured at the debris spinning across the surface of the muddy, brown water and emptying down into the throat of the pool before rising to the surface again. Bodies spun past, limbs twisted and bent. "You're insane. Nobody can survive that."

"You could be right," said the witch. "I hope not, because if she can't deal with something as minor as this, then there's no hope for any of us."

Minor? "Can't you help her?"

Raven gave a regretful shake of her head. "I haven't the power."

But Kayla did?

Before he could say another word, the churning in the water abruptly died and the surface went preternaturally still. Deathly silence fell, broken only by the cries of the frightened and the grieving.

Then forty feet away, the water bubbled and rippled. Ray couldn't look away, his body straining forward. Something was under the water. *Please God,* he prayed. *Let it be Kayla.*

It wasn't. What rose to the surface was a nightmare.

Chapter 15

Kayla

KAYLA HEARD RAY scream her name as the ragged edge of the wood cut into her hands. She muscled up the nearly perpendicular wood, ignoring the pain in her hands and the hot trickle of blood down her forearms. She still had time to save those kids. She had to *move.*

The dock dipped downward with gut-wrenching swiftness. The surface of the water came toward her. She let go of the dock and launched herself into it.

Her mind demanded the change, and her body, soaked to her skin, eagerly complied. She felt herself elongate, powerful ribbon muscles running down her neck and belly and over her back and down her tail. Her limbs lengthened and thickened, and massive claws erupted from her now-scaled fingers.

Cobalt scales covered her from nose to tail. Gold edged each one. The blue softened along her belly and beneath her tail. She shook herself, shaking away the feel of being human. She pricked up her razor-edged scales. They rose like short porcupine quills. Around her neck and down between her shoulder blades, the scales rose in a ruff, then smoothed silky flat as she lowered them.

The current of the whirlpool rolled over and around her. Whipping around, she darted like a torpedo through the water, her long thick tail and muscular body giving her speed.

She could see as clear as day. Even with the mud filling the water. Bits of broken debris pummeled her. Protected by her nearly impervious scales, she barely noticed. Her entire focus belonged to finding the three children and rescuing them. *Please God, let them still be alive.*

She couldn't find them near the surface. She dove. The water here was as deep as the underwater mountain was tall. She guessed it stood at least six or seven thousand feet. Underwater glaciers gleamed white along the ridges and down into the crevices, while lush forests grew beside them. The bore of the whirlpool extended no more than fifty feet. She found the children caught in its hungry throat as it devoured them and everything else in the cove.

Kayla's body cut like a knife through the raging current. She pierced the core of the whirlpool and snatched the bodies of the children. She held them against her chest as she thrust herself upward.

All three were limp. The first boy had been caught mid-shift, fur sprouting along his arms and face. His nose and mouth had begun to elongate, and the shape of his body was a disturbing cross between wolf and human. Another boy had completed the shift into wolf form, while the girl remained unchanged. A gash across her forehead explained why.

It was difficult to protect them from the debris that flew along the current like missiles. If she didn't do something, they'd be dead before she reached the surface.

What could she do? The whirlpool was a force of nature. Bitterness etched grooves in her heart. The dryads and Raven had called her the Guardian of the River as if that meant something. As if she ruled the river. Like hell. She couldn't even calm the stupid whirlpool, any more than she could shut off the sun.

Could she?

The idea was utterly ridiculous. But then again, what did she have to lose by trying?

Ignoring the fact that such questions usually ended badly, she drew in on herself, focusing everything she had on halting the spin of the pool. She almost peed herself when a glow suffused her body. A pearl aura wrapped around her while something inside her swelled, bright, hot, and ready. It pushed at her ribs, straining her muscles, and stretched her skin tight as a drumhead. Her tail thrashed, her body writhing with the pressure.

She clawed the water, mouth opening in silent protest against the pain. She drew a shallow breath from the water, but it wasn't enough. She pushed it outward. Power swept away from her like a shockwave from a bomb. It felt like sunshine on the water, like emerald moss on water-smoothed stone. Kayla could feel everything in the water.

She felt the stolid resistance of the mountain rocks, this soft push of mud, the rigid sway of the underwater forest, the bright spark of all who lived below, and closer, the broken bits caused by the whirlpool.

Power streamed out of her, saturating the water. Overcoming her shock, Kayla gave focus to it. Demanding calm, demanding obedience. The water fell still as glass. Kayla shot upward.

Her head broke the water's surface, and she rolled onto her back, holding the children protectively against her stomach. She swept her tail back and forth, pushing herself to shore. When she grounded herself, she flipped back over and crawled out to lay the children on the grass, all too aware of the hushed silence surrounding her.

For a moment all was still. Then Raven ran forward and dropped to her knees beside the small bodies. Her movement stirred everybody else into action.

All but Ray.

He stood like a stone statue, a bulwark against the rush of the children's parents and family who flung themselves forward in desperate worry. Kayla backed into the water to give them room, praying Raven could keep the children alive. A quick cheer and the sounds of coughing and retching made it clear that at least one was okay.

She should have been relieved. Instead dread filled her. It felt like being tied to the railroad tracks with a freight train barreling toward her. The outcome was inevitable.

She felt Ray's gaze heavy upon her. She didn't want to look at him. She didn't want to see the shock, the horror, and the disgust that she knew she would see. She didn't want to look, but she had to.

Slowly she turned her head, well aware of the dagger teeth protruding from her upper and lower jaws and fully exposed despite her closed mouth. Her nostrils flared, but she couldn't sort the smell of his reaction from the terror and joy from everyone else.

His face had gone pasty gray, his mouth gaping. He stared and slowly started shaking his head as if to reject the possibility that Kayla was a shifter, and not just any shifter, but a massive beast, an unholy cross between a Chinese water dragon, a lizard, and a crocodile. She clenched her claws into the mud. Then she couldn't stand it anymore. She whipped around and flung herself back beneath the surface, diving deep.

She streaked through the water as if she could outrun the fact that he'd seen the real her. Her throat and stomach clenched and burned. At the bottom of the river lake she tore boulders from the bed and flung them through the water. It did nothing to still the dreadful loss and humiliation that choked her.

Giving up, she streaked through the water in an effort to outdistance her feelings. All too soon she found herself at the turbulent junction of the Willamette River and the Columbia River. She headed out toward the ocean not knowing where she would go or what she would do.

It wasn't until she reached Newport, well down the western coast of Oregon, that she stopped herself.

Where was she going? The damage was done. Ray knew. Not just Ray but a hundred others. It wouldn't be long before word spread and everybody knew. But that didn't change the fact that someone was killing witchkin, or that her grandmother and aunt had been kidnapped.

Running away wouldn't solve anything. Besides Portland was her home.

She'd done without Ray before; she do without him again. At least this time she'd have a purpose, witchkin to help.

She turned back the way she'd come.

She swam more slowly on the return, but still made the journey in less than two hours. Before, she had been driven by a desperate need to escape; now she was driven by the need to do as she promised, to stop the killer and bring home her grandmother and aunt.

Now came the difficult part. In order to return to her human self, she had to dry completely. She didn't want anyone to see her leaving the river, nor did she want anyone witnessing her transformation. Of course the morning sun had chosen to shine bright, offering no shadows to hide in.

Her normal routine was to use the fog or darkness to disguise her movements as she crawled out the water and into an empty warehouse north of the Pearl District. That wasn't going to work today. She decided her best choice was to get out at Poet's Beach just north the Marquam Bridge pylons. They were all that was left of the bridge. A number of hotels and apartment buildings stood nearby. With any luck, nobody would be out this early and see her.

She swam just below the surface as she searched for what she was looking for among the hotels and condo towers. She decided on the brick-and-glass tower nearest the water. The bottom level contained a parking garage. A clock on the outside of the building to the left indicated it was just after seven o'clock.

The little marina—built after Magicfall—looked very much like the one she and Ray had embarked from earlier in the morning. A rack of kayaks and paddle boards, and another of canoes sat at one end in the little cemented area where people used to sit on benches and watch the river. The benches had disappeared some time ago. Kayla decided between the racks and the stand of trees to the right of them; they gave her the best cover she was going to get.

She swam closer until she felt rocks beneath her feet. She dug her claws in, coiling herself to spring. She pushed her head above the surface enough to expose her eyes and get a good look around. Several boats motored behind her, heading along the river in both directions. She heard several female voices from beyond the two racks. She waited, but they did not board a boat, nor did they continue along the path. All the while time ticked.

She couldn't wait any longer. Kayla launched herself up in an arcing leap, using her tail as well as the powerful muscles of her body. She landed on top of a rock wall designed to prevent flooding and erosion. Without hesitation she took off running for the base of the building. The women screamed, and several other people shouted. Kayla ignored them.

Once she reached the building, she dodged behind the cover of some trees, then turning, she dug her claws into the brick and climbed swiftly to the top.

She crawled onto the roof and curled up in a sunny spot, closing her eyes to wait. Her body felt heavy, and exhaustion netted her in its grip. She'd stopped a whirlpool. A fucking whirlpool. With magic. How the hell had she done that? Had Raven and the dryads known she could? Is that why they called her the Guardian of the River? Just what else did they know?

The warmth of the sun and roof, added to her exhaustion, soon put her to sleep. She woke to find herself back in her human body, her face pressed against the ground. She sat up, her stiff muscles protesting. She looked herself over, as always surprised that her clothing had returned with her. She checked her pocket for her cell phone. That was there, too. She flipped it open. The water hadn't destroyed it.

She eyed it a long moment before returning it to her pocket. She could call Ray, but she had no idea what to say to him, though she had a pretty decent idea of what he'd say to her. She could wait to hear that.

That is, if he still wanted to talk to her at all.

She clambered to her feet, not all that surprised when her stomach growled and pinched hungrily. She should have eaten while still in her other form. That body required a lot of calories, and in human form she could never eat enough to satisfy the monster's appetite.

Kayla ran her hands through her hair and made a face. First things first. She needed a shower—which she wasn't going to get since her bathroom couldn't contain her other self—and some caffeine. Then food. Maybe food first. After that, she'd have to call Ray. She was pretty sure that when everything calmed down on the Island, Raven would have made sure he took the box of information so that he could give it to Kayla. And even if the witch hadn't, there were still her grandmother and aunt to find.

As she'd hoped, Kayla found a door from the roof into the apartments. She quickly found the exit stairwell and descended, leaving through a side door to the street. Getting home was going to take her a while, though she supposed she could call a cab, or grab a Biketown bike. She stuck her hands in her pockets. She had no change, though she did find the emergency $20 bill she kept in the hidden zipper pocket inside her jacket.

A cab it was.

She hated the idea of spending money when her house was only five or so miles away, but she didn't have time to waste.

Pink Lady Cabs had set up shop at the old Avis car rental by the 3rd Avenue Max station. Kayla walked over trying to ignore the delicious scents wafting through the air from half a dozen food trucks parked in the parking lot.

She went up to the booth at the far end of the lot next to the bus stop. Inside the tiny glass building a slender witchkin woman dressed in hot pink stood on top of a barstool, with a headset over her hot-pink hat, and spoke into the microphone. She held up a finger telling Kayla to wait, and after a moment she turned and slid open the window.

"What can I do for you, hon?"

Her eyes looked like polished black marbles and short, gray, velvety fur covered her exposed skin. Her bright-pink fingernails curved into short talons. Pink Lady Cabs had a reputation for not discriminating against witchkin—either as passengers or employees.

"I need a ride," Kayla said, then gave her address.

"Sure thing." The dispatcher touched a finger to the side of her headset and rattled off a request for a cab. Dropping her hand, she looked at Kayla. "Be just a couple minutes."

"How much do you think that trip will run me? I've only got twenty bucks." Kayla couldn't help turning her head to eye the breakfast burrito truck.

"It'll run you about fifteen bucks plus tip," the witchkin said cheerfully.

"Terrific," Kayla said with a sigh. So much for filling the void in her stomach. She'd have to grab something at home. At the moment, time saved by taking the cab was more important than food.

"You look a little rough," said the other woman sympathetically. "Bad night?"

Kayla gave a wry smile and scratched behind her ear. "Something like that."

The other woman leaned forward, curiosity sparking in her dark eyes. "What happened to you?"

Kayla wondered what the woman would say if she told her the truth: *I discovered three people murdered in a ritual, then I called the partner I abandoned four years ago and hadn't seen since, went on a dinner date with a technomage, got called to the scene of a kidnapping, then a bunch of dryads and a witch told me I had to solve some murders before the end of the world, after which I transformed into a monster to save some shifter kids, and oh yeah I told a whirlpool to stop whirling and it did.*

"Shit hit the fan," she said, deciding that even she had a hard time believing all that had happened, and she'd been there.

The dispatcher nodded. "Been there, done that. Least you're on the right side of the dirt. That's all that counts."

"Ain't that the truth." Kayla and the witchkin woman shared a tired smile. Just then a bright-pink Toyota Highlander pulled up. Kayla said thank you to the dispatcher and climbed into the front seat. The driver—human looking—put the car in drive and headed out of the parking lot.

"Where to?"

Kayla gave her address and then slumped in the seat, eyes closed. She dozed, waking when the cab pulled up outside her house. Foreboding clutched in her stomach. Ray's blue-and-white was parked in the driveway. She was so not ready to see him.

As she got out of the cab, her front door opened. Ray filled the doorway, his face shadowed. The set of his shoulders looked tense. She closed the door, standing still until the cab drove away. It wasn't like she could put this off forever. With a resigned sigh she trudged up the walkway stopping at the bottom of the step and looking up at Ray.

"Hi." *That was good, Kayla.* Could she get anymore inane?

"You look like shit." He scanned her up and down, his face unreadable.

"Coincidentally I feel like shit," Kayla said with a halfhearted smile. Her stomach growled. She winced. "I seem to be a little hungry, too."

He didn't move for a moment then stepped aside.

"How did you get in?" She sat on the stairs to take off her boots and then hung her jacket over the railing. "I thought I locked up."

"I picked the back door lock," he said completely unrepentantly.

"When did you get back?" The words came out amidst a yawn.

He scowled. "Just after dawn. Where have you been? It's nearly noon."

Her brows rose. "Really?" She must have slept longer on the roof than she thought. Funny how she didn't feel rested.

"Really."

She wondered why he hadn't mentioned the whole transformation into a monster thing yet. Then again it wasn't the easiest subject to broach. What was he going to say? *Oh by the way, I happened to notice you turned into a giant water-snake-lizard-thing. What's that all about?*

"I fell asleep waiting to transform back to human," she said, picking at a loose thread in her pants.

When he didn't answer, she risked a glance. He just stood there looking down at her inscrutably, his hands jammed into his pockets. The silence between them stretched, growing uncomfortable. *More* uncomfortable, that is.

"Go get cleaned up. I'll get something going in the kitchen." Ray turned and walked away.

Kayla watched the empty space where he'd been, then gave a confused shake of her head. She grabbed the stair rail and pulled herself upright then climbed upstairs, legs feeling like lead. She stripped, all too aware of Ray being downstairs. She went into the bathroom and eyed the shower wistfully. Maybe one day she'd learn to control the transformation so that she could actually have a shower. Or soak in a bath. These days she had to settle for sponge baths or swims in the river. Neither did much for her hair.

She ran warm water in the sink, then took a quick sponge bath, drying each section of her body as she went to help keep herself from shifting. She turned the box fan sitting on the edge of the bathtub on high. The breeze across her skin raised goosebumps, but it helped her dry faster.

When she was reasonably clean, she combed out her hair and braided it. Later after she'd slept—whenever that happened—she'd try washing it. She'd reached the point where if she concentrated and dried it quickly, she could prevent her transformation about 70% of the time. One thing was for certain. She wasn't going to try it with Ray downstairs. She also wasn't going to try it in the tiny bathroom.

Usually she took a plastic tub of warm sudsy water outside, dipped her head in it, scrubbed, rinsed with the hose, then toweled her hair off and rubbed in some leave-in conditioner before grabbing the hairdryer she left on the back patio. It was always a race to see if she'd get dry before she transformed.

Once dressed, she went downstairs. The smell of cooking food wafting up to the second floor overwhelmed her urge to procrastinate.

Ray had found a couple of steaks she had stashed in the freezer, and was now searing them on the stove. She went to the refrigerator and poured herself a tall glass of orange juice, holding up the bottle to ask Ray if he wanted one. He nodded and she poured him a glass. Setting his on the counter beside the stove, she fished a handful of hazelnuts out of a canister and tossed a few in her mouth.

Neither spoke as Ray slid the steaks into the oven. He cut a cantaloupe he found in the fridge into wedges and arranged them on a plate with a sprinkling of blueberries. He set that on the counter in front of Kayla, then started butter melting in a pan. When it was ready, he cracked eggs into it, then popped some bread into the toaster. A few minutes later he pulled the steaks out, layered two sunny-side-up eggs on each, and added two slices of buttered toast before passing Kayla's plate to her.

They both dug in, Ray standing up by the counter opposite to her. Kayla practically inhaled the food.

"This is so good," she said, her mouth full. "I didn't know you could cook."

His lips flickered into a quick smile, and then it faded. "I guess we all have secrets."

His words froze Kayla to the core, turning her breakfast into a hard lump in her stomach. She carefully laid down her silverware and wiped her mouth with her napkin.

"I guess that means you want to talk about it," she said, pushing her plate away.

Ray scowled. "You only ate half of that. You should eat it while it's hot."

She took a breath. It caught in her lungs, and she blew it back out. "I don't think I can."

Ray set down his own knife and fork and gave her a steady look. "This happened to you at Magicfall? That's why you left?" His flat tone gave nothing away.

She nodded.

"You didn't think I'd be able to handle it?"

Still no inflection to tell her what he was thinking.

"How could you? I turn into Godzilla's fucked-up cousin. I'm a monster. You said it yourself—as far as the cops are concerned, I don't matter. I'm just another witchkin, just another enemy. I certainly am not police material." The last two words she said with air quotes.

At least Ray didn't try to convince her that she would have been welcome in her new form.

"I'd have dealt with it," he said tightly.

Kayla ran a finger back and forth along the edge of the plate. "It was chaos then," she said. "All these weird changes and people dying and then the war. Be honest. Anybody who looked at me would have seen a terrible threat to the city. You would have, too."

"I guess we'll never know since you didn't give me a fucking chance." Anger boiled in his voice.

"I did the only thing I could think of to do." Kayla wanted him to understand. "I couldn't control the transformation whatsoever back then. Hit me with a couple of raindrops and all of a sudden I'm the beast from the Black Lagoon. Even now I can't hold it off very long once I start getting wet. Dunk me completely under and I don't have a hope in hell of stopping the transformation. I can't turn back until I'm completely dry. It scared the shit out of me. By the time I got a little bit of a handle on it, there didn't seem to be any reason to tell you. You'd made your feelings clear. What difference would knowing have made?"

"Maybe I wouldn't have lost my best friend." Ray's jaw clenched and knotted. "Maybe I could decide for myself what I could handle?"

She looked away. "That last day when we got into that fight, you told me to stay the hell away, that you never wanted to see me again. That . . . hurt." Understatement of the century, but she didn't know how to tell him what his words had cost her. She gave a little shrug. "I figured once you got eyes on the new me, it would be worse. I couldn't face it," she confessed. "I was right, too. You should have seen yourself today when you got your first look at me. You looked like you wanted to throw up, maybe dig a hole, and pull in the dirt after you."

He grimaced and nodded slowly. "It was a shock," he admitted. He leaned his hands on the counter and bent toward her, his dark eyes piercing.

"Look at it from my point of view. You go diving into a killer whirlpool, and I think there's no way you could survive. Tore my guts out. Worse than four years ago, because at least then I had a chance to see you again. The next thing I know the whirlpool vanishes and a water dragon comes crawling out of the water. I wasn't even sure it was you. Then you vanish again, and I'm left wondering if you'll actually come home or disappear for good this time."

Kayla could only stare, her thoughts tumbling. *Tore his guts out?* He cared. Even after all these years, he cared. "After you saw me, there didn't seem to be much point in hiding."

"Thank fuck for that," he said heavily.

When he didn't say anything else, when he seemed to be waiting for her to say something profound or who the hell knew what, Kayla decided to ask the question burning on the tip of her tongue. "And now? How do you feel about me now?"

His mouth flattened. "The same as I did before we headed out to the Island." His lips snapped shut with a finality that said he didn't mean to say anything else.

Her stomach curled and sorrow weighted her bones. He didn't hate her more than before—just the same amount. It wasn't exactly good news.

"So now what?" she asked dully. Did he want to work with her still?

"Now we find your grandmother and your aunt, and we figure out who's killing witchkin and why," he said. He picked up his knife and fork again and gestured toward her plate with his chin. "Finish that. You don't want to let a good steak go to waste."

He ignored her as she just sat there and watched him. "Who the hell are you and what did you do with Ray?" she asked finally.

His brows rose. "What do you mean?"

"I mean the Ray that I knew would be asking me a billion questions right about now," she said. "He'd want to know what I was capable of, if I had any magical powers, how far can I swim, can I go into saltwater as well as fresh, how well do I do on land, and I don't know how many more things. You're like Stepford Ray."

He laughed at the last with genuine humor then sobered. He took another bite of steak and chewed thoughtfully as if preparing his answer. Kayla resisted the urge to tap her fingers impatiently. Instead she grabbed her knife and fork and cut her steak into little squares, then pushed it around into shapes. His confirmation that he continued to hate her had killed her hunger entirely.

"I have questions," he admitted. "But I'm not sure they're any of my business, and . . . I don't want to scare you off." The look he gave her bore through her. "This is a new world, and we aren't the same people we used to be, not by a long shot. But I've missed you. I want you in my life again."

Her mouth gaped. "But you just said you still hated me. Why would you want me hanging around?"

He frowned. "When did I say that?" He shook his head. "I said no such thing."

"Just a minute ago you said you felt the same way about me after seeing my shifter form as before, and if I recall correctly, you'd made it pretty clear you hated me."

He actually rolled his eyes. He never rolled his eyes. Kayla was affronted.

"I never hated you. I wanted to kill you a little bit and maybe shake the shit out of you, but I didn't hate you."

Kayla glared at him. "Then you did a damned good job of faking it."

He sighed. "I was pissed."

She snorted.

He had the grace to wince. "Okay, I was really, *really* pissed, and I said some pretty shitty things. But I never hated you. I couldn't if I wanted to," he added in a soft undertone as he reached for his orange juice.

Was he for real? Ray had never lied to her. He didn't have any reason to start now. He'd always had uncompromising integrity, courage, humor, and he never let her down. *She'd* been the one to let *him* down.

"You can ask," she said fixing her eyes on her plate and taking a bite, returning the subject to a marginally safer one.

If it gave him whiplash, he didn't show it. "You were beautiful," he said startling her.

Her head jerked up. "Say what?"

"Your other form. It's beautiful."

"Did you get hit on the head?"

He smiled. "Haven't you seen yourself?"

"Just reflected in the water. Sometimes a little bit in the windows facing the backyard."

"Then you know what I'm talking about."

"You have an extraordinarily strange idea of beauty," she said. "I'm a giant blue-and-gold water-lizard-snake-crocodile thing. With big sharp pointed teeth. I'm Water-Godzilla."

"On that, we'll have to agree to disagree," he said, then changed the subject before she could argue. "Raven gave me the box to bring to you. I left your pack of gifts there for her. She said she'd give it to your friend Nessa to bring back."

Kayla nodded grateful for the change of topic. Her shoulders relaxed a little. "Have you heard from Zach or the coroner's office?"

At hearing the technomage's name, Ray got an irritated look on his face. "Not yet, but I called a request in for a full autopsy. Should get it back in a few hours. I put a rush on it."

Kayla couldn't hide her surprise. He told Raven he wanted to get to the bottom of the killings, but this was going farther than she expected. This was getting into on-the-record investigation territory. He would get a lot of shit from the brass for this—wasting department resources on vermin.

"That could hurt you," she said reaching for their empty plates and taking them to the sink. "You could get reprimanded or busted down to foot patrol."

She put on her gloves and started washing the dishes, surprised when Ray grabbed a towel to dry them. The domesticity of the scene unnerved her for reasons she didn't care to examine.

"There's a serial killer in the city conducting magic rituals that a witch says will be very bad for us when he finishes whatever he's up to. That will keep them off my back."

For his sake, Kayla hoped so. Like Landon, he was a big boy and entitled to make his own choices.

"Where's the box?"

"In the dining room," Ray said.

Vintage houses often contained formal dining rooms, and hers was no exception. The previous owners had left behind a cabinet full of floral china and an ornate wood table with eight chairs around it. A crystal chandelier hung above it. Ray had sorted the papers on the table top. One, a handmade map of the current geography of the city, took up one end.

Kayla started with it. Red dots marked where bodies had been found. Most of the murders had occurred on the west side of the river, which wasn't all that surprising given the devastation on the northeast side from the fire. Two had occurred down south as far as Wilsonville, with three more on the east side of the lake. The rest were sprinkled over downtown into Tigard and Tualatin, out toward Beaverton, and around Lake Oswego.

She didn't notice an obvious pattern. Each of the murder sites was numbered and corresponded with a pile on the table. Some of the piles consisted of merely a single sheet of paper, while others contained pictures, witness statements, and even a few evaluations of the magic.

"Have you read this stuff?" Kayla asked Ray.

"I skimmed most of it."

"Anything helpful?"

"All the bodies were witchkin. Like Raven said, at least one bone had been taken from each, and none of the bones were the same."

"So is this guy taking trophies? Is he building his own skeleton a la Frankenstein? Or has he got another use for the parts? Something magical maybe."

"Could be any one of those, but I'm leaning toward the last one," Ray said. "Aside from the dryad, every single murder was accompanied by ritual symbols."

Kayla dug through one of the piles until she found some pictures. They were grainy. Either the camera or the printer hadn't been a particularly good quality, and the images were too small to make out details. "A magnifying glass might come in useful right about now," she said. "Give me a second. I'll see if I can find one."

After Magicfall, Kayla had continued to live in her apartment until she realized that she couldn't get out the windows when she transformed, and the place was very cramped for her other self. She could just barely get out through the door if she wriggled, but then she'd scare the ever-living shit out of those neighbors who remained.

She started searching for a new place to live, discovering this house not far from Washington Park and the amphitheater, the latter of which gave her a reasonably private place to hole up when she was waiting to return to her human body. No doubt the dryads of the trees surrounding the earthen bowl had also witnessed her transformations. She'd *thought* she'd kept a pretty good secret, but all this time, the magic community must have known about her.

This house had been abandoned and not yet looted or salvaged. She'd taken the tile serpents above the front door as a particular welcome, as if the house wanted her there. Despite living there almost four years, she hadn't bothered to rummage through the things the former owners had left behind.

She started her search for the magnifying glass in the laundry room which contained a folding counter/desk. She opened the drawers finding the usual collection of pens, pencils, paper clips, Post-it notes, electronic gadgets, computer records, and a variety of other household junk. In the middle drawer on the left, she found what she was looking for. A round, domed magnifying glass, the kind you could set on top of a paper in order to read it more easily. She would have preferred one with a handle, but this would work. She hoped.

She returned to the dining room and Ray. He'd spread out one of the piles on top of the map and stood poring over the documents.

"Find anything?"

He didn't look up. "Nothing so far. The statements do list the names of the witnesses and how to find them, so we can interview them ourselves."

They didn't have time for that. Kayla didn't say it. She didn't know it for sure, but tracking down witchkin and getting them to talk would take a week at least, probably longer. From the way Raven had spoken, Kayla didn't know if they had that kind of time.

She pulled aside one of the photographs and set the magnifying glass on top of it. Inside the four-inch-wide domed glass, images sharpened and grew big enough to see.

At first the familiarity of the symbols didn't register. After all, what could this serial killer of witchkin want with her grandmother and aunt? Her mind wasn't connecting the cases. Then the images sank in. Kayla snatched another picture. More of those symbols. She grabbed several other pictures. Still more of them.

"What is it? What are you seeing?" Ray asked.

"Have a look." Kayla thrust the glass and the picture she held at him, watching for his reaction.

He stiffened, and his eyes rose to meet hers. "Shit," he said.

"This guy has my grandmother and my aunt," Kayla said, horror lumping in her belly.

Ray read her mind. "That doesn't mean they're dead." He put a reassuring hand on her shoulder. "If he'd wanted to kill them, he could have done it right there. He had the time and the privacy. He's got to want them for something else."

It sounded believable, but it made Kayla feel only marginally better. Whatever the killer wanted, it couldn't be good. Sooner or later he'd be done with the two witches. She doubted he'd just let them go.

She bit the inside of her cheek to keep herself from saying something stupid. Like, *We have to find them* or something equally inane. That didn't stop the urgency from battering her. How much time did they have left?

Ray's hand tightened. "We will find them."

She believed him. She just didn't know if the two witches would still be alive when they did.

Wordlessly they went back to examining the evidence Raven had provided. Their conclusions didn't point in any particular direction, nor did the examination tell them anything new. The evidence clearly pointed to someone with a magical agenda and magical abilities. Neither cop nor ex-cop was ready to say it was a witch. Other beings had the ability to use magic. They couldn't rule them out, though witches were far more common. Nothing Kayla knew was helpful, but that wasn't surprising. What she didn't know about the magical community would fill the Library of Congress.

"What's weird is the symbols at Keller Fountain aren't the same," Kayla said, examining the images she'd taken on her phone. "Even though they have the same feel. But what are the odds there are two killers in the city butchering witchkin?"

"On the other hand, why would he suddenly change his M.O.?" Ray asked.

"New kind of spell, or escalation maybe."

"Possible. Or a copycat."

"I suppose," she said, but didn't believe it. Somehow the two had to be connected.

They didn't find a pattern for the location or the choice of victims. The number of victims in each particular instance seemed random, but only one person at any given scene had had bones removed. They concluded the others likely must have been innocent bystanders, or possibly witnesses the killer wanted to silence. The one thing those people had in common was that they had been beheaded. All except the Keller Fountain victims who were neither missing bones nor their heads.

"How medieval," Ray said thoughtfully. "Why beheading, though? That's got to be making a statement. There are a lot easier ways to kill someone. Cut looks clean. Like the killer only used one stroke. He's gotta be strong."

"Could be a she though," Kayla said. "A lot of witchkin have supernatural strength no matter their gender. But beheading does mean the killer has to be able to hold the blade, which means he or she has something that passes for hands. Probably not a shifter, since most don't tend to use weapons. They prefer teeth or claws."

Ray nodded. "Someone carrying a big blade like that would probably get noticed. These murders are messy. The killer's clothes would be covered in blood." He took a breath and blew it out. "There have to be witnesses who saw him coming or going from the scenes. We need to set up a tip line and get the word out."

"That's going to take a lot of manpower to check out," Kayla said. The department wasn't about to fund that. Not for witchkin. No way in hell.

Ray fished his phone out of his pocket. Kayla couldn't help her surprise that he'd even bother making the request. A fool's errand if there ever was one, and the request would earn him ridicule, if not a reprimand.

His choice, though. He didn't want or need advice from her.

She went back to examining the map and the pictures, only half listening to Ray's conversation. She felt as though there must be something there, something she could almost put her finger on. Or maybe she was rusty and was just hoping for a good clue to pop up out of nowhere. She couldn't trust her cop instincts. She wasn't sure they even existed anymore.

"Captain Crice? This is Garza. Got a couple leads. It looks like the Runyon/Valentine kidnapping could be connected to a series of witchkin murders in the city. Yes, sir. I'm sure. Found some ritual symbols at the Runyon house that match some symbols from the murder scenes.

"I want to set up a tip line and send uniforms to check out whatever seems likely. All I know right now is that we are looking for someone who's very strong. Killer could be male or female and has the ability to perform magic. They carry some sort of long blade—like a machete or sword or maybe even a bowie knife—that they use to decapitate victims. They may be covered in blood or possibly wearing some sort of overcoat or other covering. Yes, sir, that's right. I know that. Captain, but right now it's the best lead we have."

He paused a moment to listen.

"Thing is, sir, Theresa Runyon and Margaret Valentine are both witches."

Kayla's head jerked up, and she caught Ray watching her. Alistair would not appreciate his revealing the family secret. She'd have to warn Ray to watch his back, though he'd probably figured that one out already.

Ray stayed silent for a long minute. Kayla imagined his captain was chewing up the scenery. With her father's power and influence, letting a secret like family witches out of the bag could be a career killer. She expected Ray's boss knew that all too well. It spoke to Ray's integrity and honesty that he reported it at all, since shit rolls downhill and he'd be buried when Volcano Alistair Runyon went off.

Not that having witches in the family would ruin the Runyon name. More likely it would strike the fear of God into her father's enemies, of which there were many. On the other hand, maybe he'd be embarrassed he didn't have any witch talent. She'd always thought that chapped his ass.

"Yes, sir. Alistair Runyon confirmed it himself. No, sir, he isn't pleased. In fact, he kicked me and Zach Logan off the premises."

Another pause.

"No amount of diplomacy was going to soothe Runyon's temper," Ray said dryly, no doubt in response to the captain's criticism. "That doesn't matter at the moment. Chances are this killer has both women. We need to track him down quick before he kills them. For that we need that tip line. If we can retrieve them, Runyon's less likely to go nuclear on us. Especially if Theresa Runyon never gets wind that he decided family secrets outweighed her and her daughter's lives."

Another pause.

"Yes, sir. I understand. I will. Yes, sir."

Ray hung up his phone and pocketed it.

"So that went well," Kayla said.

"He didn't fire me," Ray replied. "Yet. He is setting up a tip line. And he's going to put together a press conference. He wants me there for it."

That didn't surprise Kayla. If any of this went sideways, Ray's captain would want a scapegoat. Ray on camera outlining what they knew of the suspect would make him the perfect choice.

"You see anything new?" Ray asked.

"No. But it feels like I'm missing something," she said, frowning at the pictures in her hand.

"Let's head to the lab," Ray said. "Maybe we'll get lucky and Logan will have found something. In the meantime, I'm gonna send some pictures of the symbols over to headquarters and get them started tracking down someone who can tell us what they are."

"I'll pack up the stuff. We should take it with us just in case."

Ray helped her gather and stack the papers back into the box. He didn't say anything, and his silence seemed ominous.

"Something wrong?"

"I should be sending teams out looking for witnesses, but witchkin aren't going to talk to human cops, and not a lot of cops are willing to talk to witchkin."

"They can suck it up. This is the job," Kayla said. "Besides there might be human witnesses too. If you want to solve this then you're going to have to crack the whip and get people out in the field."

He nodded. "Get together anything you might need," he said. "I'm going to give the captain a call back."

"Good luck," she said, taking the box with her as she left.

Kayla was tempted to eavesdrop on Ray's conversation again. Necessity beat out curiosity. She ran upstairs and found a crossbody bag. She packed it with a rain suit, waterproof gloves, rain boots, and an umbrella. She hoped it was overkill, but she couldn't take chances. Damn but she should have had Raven recharge the spell on her drying amulet.

She usually kept half a dozen or more on hand, but she'd let her supply dwindle, figuring since she still had one, she had time to get it done. Stupid mistake. She wondered if Zach could create something for her, but that would mean telling him why she needed it. Or maybe not. He seemed like he might be okay with 'don't ask, don't tell.' It was worth a try anyway.

She added a towel to the bag. From a cabinet in her closet she pulled out a .45 caliber automatic. She donned a nylon shoulder holster and put the gun in it, double checking that it was loaded and already had one in the chamber.

She tucked two extra magazines inside the storage pocket. She knelt and buckled a hunting knife around her right calf under her pants.

Straightening, she looked around, contemplating what else she might need. She grabbed a Leatherman tool from her nightstand and shoved it into her pants pocket. You never knew when you might need a handy-dandy multi-tool.

She made a pitstop in the bathroom before heading downstairs. She dropped her bag near the front door and returned to the kitchen. She could hear the rumble of Ray's voice in the other room, but couldn't make out any words. She rummaged in the cupboard for a couple of insulated cups and filled them both with coffee. She didn't expect to get sleep anytime soon. The more caffeine the better.

Ray remained on the phone another five minutes, during which time Kayla puttered around in the kitchen, putting their dishes away and cleaning the counters. Her body thrummed with nervousness and maybe even something like happiness. She wasn't sure. She couldn't remember the last time she'd been happy. But being with Ray again and working together made her blood fizz in her veins. Not only that, he knew what she'd become and hadn't run for the hills. Yet, anyway.

She couldn't help but wonder—*had* she done the right thing four years ago? If she'd told Ray then about her affliction, could she have stayed on the force? Could she have stayed his partner?

The thought made her nauseous. Back then she hadn't felt like she had any choice. Hell, in the wee dark hours of this morning she hadn't felt that she had any choice. Funny what a difference a few hours made.

"Ready?" Ray asked as he entered.

She studied him. He looked annoyed and yet faintly smug.

"What happened?"

"We'll need to stop at headquarters so I can map out the murder sites and assign canvassing zones."

Her brows rose. "Your captain agreed to that?" Then understanding dawned. "Of course he did. Anything for the Runyons, right?" She didn't wait for an answer. "Did you tell them about me?"

Ray scowled at her. "Of course not. Being a shifter is your secret."

"No, I meant did you tell him I was working with you? Did you tell him that Alastair Runyon is my father and Theresa Runyon is my grandmother?"

"Not yet. I figure it's need to know. Right now, I'm the only one who needs to know. If you're ready we should get going." He checked his watch. "It's already noon."

Ray drove them to police headquarters. As he shut down the car he turned to look at her.

"Coming in or staying here?"

"Staying here," Kayla said. "I could use a nap." Plus, she didn't relish seeing her old colleagues. They hadn't taken her leaving the force all that well, either.

Ray nodded as if he'd expected just that answer. "I shouldn't be too long."

After he was gone, taking the murder map with him, Kayla squirmed in her seat until she found a reasonably comfortable position and fell asleep.

The symbols from the crime scenes stomped across her dreamscape as if they had legs. They marched in intricate patterns, weaving in and out between each other, forming lines and patterns that made no sense.

She almost did a cartoon-cat-clinging-to-the-ceiling when Ray returned and jolted her awake. He slid into the seat while Kayla tried not to hyperventilate.

"You okay?"

"I fell asleep."

"Doesn't usually cause a person to have a seizure."

"I'm not used to waking up with company."

His lips curved in a smile. She glared at him.

"What's that smug smirk about? I *could* have had company if I wanted, you know."

His smiled widened. "I believe you."

"Then what's so funny?"

"Not a thing."

She folded her arms. "Right."

Ray ignored her irritation, starting the car and pulling out of the parking lot.

"We're going to see Zach now?"

His obnoxious smile faded at the mention of Zach. "Figure we'll have a talk with the coroner first. With any luck, they'll have preliminary results from the autopsies on the three Keller Fountain bodies."

"How did it go?" She gestured vaguely back toward the police station.

"First PSAs should start going out on the radio and TV within an hour," he said. "The captain gave me free rein to do whatever I have to do to get your grandmother and aunt back alive. I pulled in everyone I could get from every unit that could spare them. I sent detectives out to all the crime scenes, along with CSUs and uniforms for canvassing. With any luck we'll get a solid lead soon."

Unfortunately, tip lines were notoriously bad for pulling about a thousand times more garbage information than good. Every lead had to be checked out no matter how ridiculous it might seem. Hopefully the teams heading out to the crime scenes would find something that could help narrow the search area as well as help sift through the deluge of calls they were about to receive.

Ten minutes later, Ray pulled into the parking garage of the building housing the forensic labs where Zach worked and the morgue. They entered the building through the central spindle of the squat, X-shaped building. The central core held meeting rooms, lecture halls, offices, and controlled the visitor access to the other sections. With only one door in and one door out on each level, guards and magical wards kept unwanted visitors out.

Kayla and Ray entered through a door on the first floor. Beige industrial vinyl covered the floor. Its scuffed surface had definitely seen better days. The entrance to the morgue was blocked by guards monitoring body scanners the old TSA had only wished they'd had. After showing his I.D., Ray signed himself and Kayla into the visitors log for the morgue and they approached the scanners.

"Do you have any weapons or magical paraphernalia?" asked one of the guards in a musical Indian accent.

Ray pulled his holster and gun off his belt and set it on the table. He dug for a pocket knife and set that next to it. Flexing his fingers, he stepped into the scanner. A crosshatching of bars kept him from proceeding forward. The plate beneath his feet glowed green. Above him milky light poured out of the knob set in the center of the scanner's roof. It dripped down over his head, across his face, and down over his body until he was enveloped in what looked like a sarcophagus of Elmer's Glue.

Watching, Kayla shuddered. She wondered if the scanner was strong enough to see that she was not entirely human. And if it did? It wasn't illegal to be witchkin. Then again, they wouldn't want magic users inside the morgue or lab without permission. Evidence could be too easily tampered with.

The thick white light swirled over Ray and then drained downward into the green disc. When it completely vanished, the disc turned white and a bell chimed. The bars on the other side slid apart, and Ray passed through. He turned to wait for Kayla.

With a sigh she put her gun on the table followed by the knife from her calf. She drew off the silver bracelet. It stretched like elastic as she pulled it over her hand and then returned to normal. She set it on the table with the weapons. The drying amulet was exhausted, but she pulled it over her head anyway in case any magical residue clung to it and set off alarms. She drew out the light spell talisman and added it to the pile.

Glancing down at herself she took mental stock of what she carried. Nothing that should set off the scanner. Taking a breath and holding it, she stepped up inside.

As before, the green disc lit up. She shifted but her feet wouldn't move. The white milky magic poured down from above and wrapped around her. It felt wet and warmer than she expected and smelled faintly of cotton candy. It settled over her, then rippled and swirled as it had with Ray.

She waited for the alarms, but nothing went off. The magic ran down to the disk and turned it white, and the bars slid back. Kayla practically flung herself through it, stumbling as she did. Before she could face-plant on the floor, Ray caught her and pulled her upright. She caught his shoulders for balance.

"You okay?"

His dark eyes told her he'd worried about her scan as well.

Kayla nodded, trying not to notice the way the heat of his arms around her soaked through her clothes and sent her temperature rising. She also tried not to notice how good he smelled, or the hard swell of muscle under her fingers.

"I'm fine," she said, flushing and pushing out of his arms. But her blood raced through her veins, and her heart pounded. And it was wrong. All wrong. She could not be attracted to Ray. Could not and would not.

First, they weren't even real friends anymore. Second, he'd laugh like a hyena if he found out he turned her on. What was her damage? Sure, she hadn't had sex in years, since before Magicfall, and Ray was a beautiful man. But so were a lot of other men—like Zach. Anyhow, Ray would laugh his ass off if he had the slightest inkling she'd developed a crush on him. Kayla's cheeks heated. Definitely not something she needed to endure, thank you very much. Plus she turned into a lizard monster. He'd be insane to want to sleep with *that.*

Her body's entire reaction to him was ludicrous. It had to be her period. She was due to start it any day. This was all just hormones. That had to be it. There was no other explanation.

Relief flooded through her. She drew in a calming breath and let it out slowly.

Ray scowled at her and then turned away. She followed him as he stalked off. Her wrist felt odd without the silver band, but there was no way they were going to allow magic into the building, any more than they'd permit weapons.

Kayla caught up with him as he stopped in front of the morgue check station.

"State your business," said the short stout Hispanic woman with salt-and-pepper hair coiled up behind her head in a bun.

"I'm Detective Garza." Ray flashed his I.D. at her. "I'm here to check on a case that came in yesterday."

She noted his name down in her log and handed him a visitor pass. She eyed Kayla. "Who are you?"

"She's with me," Ray said. "A consultant on the case."

The guard frowned. "Only official personnel are allowed inside."

"She's official."

The guard's jaw jutted. "Then I'll need to see her I.D."

"*I'm* her I.D.," Ray growled. "She's a part of my case, and I need her inside with me."

"I appreciate your position, Detective, but I have my orders. Without official identification, nobody goes through." She waved at a set of uncomfortable-looking wood chairs against the wall. "She can wait there for you, if you like."

Kayla could practically hear Ray's teeth grinding together. Another man might have started bitching or throwing a mantrum. Not Ray's style. He leaned over the desk and snatched the phone receiver from its base and punched in a number.

The guard made a face as though she wanted to object, but her lips firmed and she remained silent. She glared at Kayla. Like it was her fault?

"Get me Angie Cordone," Ray snapped at whoever had picked up the other end of the phone.

He waited, tapping his knuckles on the desk blocking their way. Silence enveloped the three of them, and Kayla was all too aware that the guards on the other doors were watching them. What did they think she or Ray was going to do? They weren't armed, and she'd given them her magical artifacts for safekeeping. Sure, she could turn into a deadly beast, but they didn't know that. As far as they knew she was perfectly safe. Their scanner had said so. Maybe they knew it didn't work as well as it should.

Ray stiffened. "Angie, this is Ray Garza. I've got a situation. I need to get into the morgue wing. I've got Reese with me. She's helping on this case, but doesn't have an I.D. and can't past the guards."

He listened a moment and then returned the phone to its cradle. He looked at Kayla. "She's on her way."

If it bothered the guard that he'd called the head coroner and had addressed her by her first name, she didn't show it. Instead she continued to block their passage with obstinate determination.

It took about five minutes for Angie to arrive, which meant she'd dropped whatever she was working on. The door thrust open, and she strode through—a fireball of energy and sour irritation.

Kayla found herself tensing. Angie had been around since Kayla's rookie years. She was not known to suffer fools lightly. She had an acerbic disposition and a habit of speaking directly with no filters. Kayla had always liked her. In fact, they had become pretty good friends before Magicfall. But then Kayla had fallen off the radar. She expected Angie would be as annoyed with her as Ray was. Well maybe not as much as Ray, but not too happy all the same.

Angie's quick sharp gaze took in Ray and the guard and then skewered Kayla. She halted, hands on her hips.

"You're back. Civilian? Shouldn't you be over your midlife crisis by now?" She shook her head. "You're a little young for that yet. Insanity defense won't work either, not if you want your job back. Do you?"

Angie's dark eyes glittered at Kayla from behind black-rimmed cat-eye glasses. She had the look she customarily wore while testifying in court when she really despised either the prosecutor, the judge, or the defendant.

"I've missed the job," Kayla said, surprised at herself for admitting it out loud. In fact, she had a dead zone in her soul, as if a piece of her was missing. Or she had until yesterday when that part of her had come roaring back to life. Despite her exhaustion and her prickly relationship with Ray, she felt electrified and alive.

Angie rolled her eyes. "Of course you do. You're a born detective. I don't know what the hell you were thinking when you left. Now come on. You're wasting my time." She looked at the guard. "I'm vouching for her. Put her down as Kayla Reese."

Angie didn't wait for a reply but swept away like the force of nature she was. Ray's hand against the small of her back urged Kayla forward. She tried not to flinch from contact, but his touch sent strange jolts of electricity bouncing through her body. It took far too much self-control for her to not touch him back. The thought of that led instantly to a tumble of images that involved a shirtless Ray and a lot of petting.

Ugh! What the hell was this? She wasn't a teenager with her first crush. Of course, even having that thought suggested that she might be having a crush after all, which could absolutely not be true. She did not have a thing for Ray. No freaking way.

Unfortunately, the little voice inside her head just cackled at her. *Lie to yourself much?* it asked. *Or are you just delusional?*

Kayla shook her head to clear it. She was neither, she told herself and the voice firmly. She had just been without getting laid for too long, and now that Ray knew her secret, her mind thought he would be a safe bet to scratch her itch.

And you want that itch scratched hard, don't you? responded the little voice with irritating accuracy. *Better yet, you want* him *hard, isn't that so?*

More images tumbled through her mind, this time X-rated. She had a vivid imagination, and her knees went a little wobbly. Ray caught her by the elbow.

"You okay?"

Uh, no, particularly with him touching her and her brain going into overdrive about where else she wanted his hands.

"I could use some coffee," she said.

"I've got a pot in the office," Angie called over her shoulder. "You can have a cup and tell me what this whole thing is about."

Ray's hand fell away for which Kayla was infinitely grateful and equally regretful. God but she was a mess.

Angie's office was on the top floor, in a corner with a view to the east and south. Kayla barely noticed, her attention riveted by drops of rain on the window. It wasn't that she hadn't been expecting it—this was the Pacific Northwest, after all, and weather conditions had not changed all that much since Magicfall—but it was damned inconvenient.

Ray followed her gaze and then frowned at her. She ignored his concern and went to the table upon which perched the coffee pot and filled one of the ceramic cups beside it. She poured cups for each of them and then sat in one of the padded chairs in front of Angie's desk. Ray sat in the other while Angie perched on the edge of her desk and I eyed them both.

"What's going on?"

Ray explained about the kidnapping without revealing that Kayla was a Runyon. He explained that they had made a connection between it and the murders at Keller Square Fountain, and that they had come to the morgue for autopsy results.

"And why is Reese here?"

"She's helping me," Ray said, his tone discouraging more questions.

Angie set down her coffee and went around to her computer and typed some keys to bring up the report. "Hmmmm," she said as she read through it.

Neither Ray nor Kayla spoke, not wanting to interrupt. After a minute or two Angie hit the print button. She grabbed the pages as they came out and then stapled them together before handing the report to Ray. He held it so Kayla could see it as well.

It didn't say much, mostly describing the bodies. Ray twitched the papers in his fingers and scowled at Angie.

"Is this all? I ordered a full autopsy."

Angie smiled. "No, it's not all," she said. "There is a notation here for me to consult with the pathologist. He didn't want to file a report before talking to me. No time like the present." She stood and they were on their way again, this time taking the stairs down into the basement.

Putting the actual autopsy rooms in the basement seemed like a no-brainer. At the same time, Kayla had always thought it felt like dropping down into hell. Facing no windows and cold lighting, not to mention all the stainless-steel tables and instruments, she wondered how people could come to work every day without a whole lot of antidepressant medicine.

As they came through the fire door at the bottom of the stairs, they heard merry laughter echoing down the cavernous hallway.

"I know that this is a workplace and that people here are not ghouls, but laughter feels a whole lot like taunting the dead. I wonder if they ever worry about ghost revenge," Kayla said in a low voice more in keeping with their location.

"Squeamish?" Angie asked one eyebrow raised.

"Let's just say Magicfall has given me a new respect for the paranormal, fairytales, and things that go bump in the night."

"Well, we haven't had any hauntings yet," replied Angie with a dismissive wave.

"Yet," Ray added.

"Yet," Angie said in happy agreement. "It would certainly liven up the place, wouldn't it? No pun intended."

"Yes, it was," said Ray, shaking his head. "And a bad one at that."

"Just goes to show the dead have a better sense of humor than you do," she said.

Kayla chuckled despite herself.

"You're just encouraging her," Ray said.

"She doesn't need encouragement from me," Kayla said.

"Hmph."

"Very articulate of you," Kayla said.

"I forgot what a pain in the ass you are."

"See what my leaving did? It saved your ass from years of abuse."

As soon as she said the words, Kayla wished she could take them back. She and Ray were finally having an easy moment, and here she had to remind him that she'd walked out on him.

All the same she didn't expect his reaction. He grabbed her arm and swung her around to face him. They were practically nose-to-nose as he glared at her.

"There was nothing good about you leaving," he said, giving her a little shake to punctuate the word nothing. "These last four years have been hell because you left, so don't go pretending there's some sort of silver lining in this. There isn't. It's been one big black hole."

He released her arm and spun away, stomping down the hall to catch up with Angie.

Kayla stood watching him. Despite the anger in his words, she felt an odd thrill of hope. His words, the depth of his antagonism and anger—these told her more than anything else how much he had cared for her and maybe still did. Maybe they did have a chance to be friends again. Maybe there was a world in which she didn't have to exist alone.

Maybe.

Chapter 16

Ray

RAY SEETHED. KAYLA'S lighthearted jest had struck him hard. Especially after a moment when everything seemed like it used to be. Her joke had been a kick to his chest. Still, he shouldn't have grabbed her. If he wasn't careful he'd fuck up and chase her off again. That was the last thing in the world he wanted.

"What was that about?" Angie asked.

The woman had eyes in the back of her head. "Nothing you need to worry about." Which was as close as he could get to "none of your business" without being completely rude.

"I'm not worried," Angie said turning a corner down a side hallway. "But you've got a look like a bear with a sore foot. Maybe I can help you with the thorn in it. Or maybe I can help you take your head out of your ass if that's what your problem is."

Ray snorted. "I'd say my head is most definitely up my ass, but I don't think you're getting it out of there anytime soon."

"You know what they say, acknowledging you have a problem is your first step to solving it."

"My problem is Kayla," he muttered. "And I know how to solve it. I just have to keep from giving her any reason to leave."

Angie eyed him sideways. "You do realize you didn't make her leave?"

"Yes, I did," Ray said with rock-hard certainty. Sure, she'd become a shifter, but she hadn't felt she could trust him with what happened to her. She had thought he would tell her to fuck off. She'd thought he wouldn't want to have anything to do with her, so she'd left so that she wouldn't have to go through the hell of hearing it from his own lips. The worst part was he wasn't so sure she was wrong.

On the Island when she had risen up out of the water, at first he thought she was some kind of water dragon. She looked like she could tear a man in half with hardly a thought. When she brought the kids to shore, he realized who it must be and had been flooded with relief that she was still alive, fascination at her other form, and no small amount of horror. He'd quickly gotten over it, but not before she dove back into the water and disappeared, leaving him behind.

The Witchkin Murders

Again.

As soon as he could collect the box, he'd retrieved their boat and headed back to her house. And then he had waited.

Those hours until she reappeared again were the worst he could remember in a long time. Agonizing hours when he wondered if she'd come back at all. He'd been confronted by the realization that if he wanted her around, he was going to have to be careful how he dealt with her—if she came back.

And he did definitely want her around.

He didn't let himself think about the fact that he wanted her wrapped around him, and under him, and on top of him. He couldn't let her know that. If that cat escaped the bag, they'd never get back to their friendship, which he wanted above all else. If she knew how he felt, she'd avoid him, or God forbid, pity him. And even worse than that, she'd walk on eggshells around him, and he couldn't tolerate that.

They'd always shared a kind of brutal honesty with each other. He valued that, knowing that no matter what, she wouldn't lie to him. She never had, not even when the truth hurt or send him skyrocketing into rage. She hadn't even lied about becoming a shifter. She'd chosen to leave rather than tell him.

And now he was lying to her.

He'd had the perfect opening to tell her about becoming a witch when she'd come back to the house. But the words had caught in his throat and he couldn't bring himself to admit it. The stupidest part was that of everybody he knew, she was the least likely to shun him because of his power.

And yet he couldn't bring himself to confess it. He couldn't risk rocking the boat until he was sure that he and Kayla were back on even ground. His witch powers probably wouldn't drive her off, but he wasn't willing to chance their newly reborn relationship with yet another complication. He'd wait until things settled and they had time to really talk.

"Is this about your friendship? Or is there more to it?" Angie asked astutely.

Ray glanced back at Kayla who trailed behind, her brows furrowed as she watched him. He faced forward again.

When she had returned home, this morning, he'd managed not to strangle her or kiss her. He'd kept himself tightly under wraps, wanting to show that he accepted her other form.

All morning they'd found their old rhythm as they worked the case. It was almost as if those last four years without her had never passed. Had his outburst ruined that progress?

"That bad, huh?" Angie said when he didn't answer.

"Worse."

"You can always apologize."

"What makes you think I'm the one who needs to apologize?"

151

Angie's brows rose. "Aren't you?"

"Yes. But that doesn't explain why you think so."

She rolled her eyes. "Just because I work with dead people doesn't mean I'm blind to the living. Anyway, you and Reese made a good team. Try not to piss her off too much. Be nice to see her around more."

"I'm trying," he muttered. But one thing was damned sure—he needed to try harder.

THEY CAME TO A set of double doors at the end of the hallway. Angie waved her hand in front of a blue ceramic tile set into the wall. Its center lit with a stylized caduceus, with the two snakes wrapped around the stem of justice scales rather than a staff. The doors opened inward. Angie motioned for Ray to go inside, waiting until Kayla had also passed through the doors before she followed.

Ray had been to the new morgue more times than he could count. This would be Kayla's first visit to the facilities built after Magicfall. He looked around, trying to see the place with fresh eyes.

The room was rectangular with a wall of square doors stacked three high on one end. Storage for the bodies. Five wheeled stainless-steel gurneys marched down the middle, each with drains and catch basins attached. Each had a cart parked at its foot, with a scale hanging just above.

The floor was sealed cement, the walls covered in easy-to-clean fiberglass panels. Along the walls marched cabinets and drawers full of instruments beside two stainless-steel washing stations. A recording system dangled from the ceiling with hinged arms that could be pulled over any particular table.

A wash of antiseptic and death filled the air. Though many cops rubbed a little VapoRub under their noses before entering the dissection room, Ray believed he ought to feel some of the horror of the murders he was trying to solve. The smell was nothing compared to what the victims had suffered.

Three of the tables were occupied, with two pathologists bending shoulder to shoulder over the one closest. As the door opened, they turned, both looking relieved to see Angie.

"Dr. Cordone," the older one said, motioning eagerly with his hand. "Come look at this."

Angie tied on a mask and slid on a pair of nitrile gloves, then donned a pair of safety glasses. Ray and Kayla followed her as she went to stand on the opposite side of the table from the pathologists.

"What is it?"

This was the first time Ray had seen the bodies except for the pictures Kayla had taken with her phone. The first appeared to be a shifter killed partway through the shift. From the looks of it, he was some sort of big cat, maybe a cougar or a leopard. He'd been positioned on his back, but the contortion of the shift meant they'd had to strap him to the table to keep his body stable for the autopsy.

The pathologists had cut him open with a Y-shaped incision and folded back the skin of his chest. His organs had been removed.

"Look here inside," the older one said, pointing into the chest cavity. "Can you see it?"

Angie bent to peer closer.

"There's some sort of residue," she said. She looked up. "Did you test it, Dr. Martin?"

Dr. Martin shook his head. "I thought it might be evidence of a magic spell. I took pictures and sent them over to the magic lab. I didn't want to tamper with it in case they want to investigate it intact." He sounded worried that he'd not done the right thing.

Angie looked again. "You could be right. Good decision," she said. "Email me copies of the photos immediately. Is that why you wanted to see me?"

The younger of the two men, whose receding hair and skinny body made him look a lot like the corpses he worked on, shook his head.

"No. I mean yes, but there's more. Over here." He sounded practically giddy with excitement. As if he'd discovered the lost treasure of the Incas.

Ray wanted a look at the inside of the shifter corpse himself, but turned to follow the others. He'd take a look before they left.

This body was a nymph of some kind. Her green-black hair had been washed clean and coiled into a pillow beneath her head. She showed no signs of wounds, but for a giant hole in her forehead. Her stomach lumped grotesquely.

"Was she pregnant?" Kayla asked.

"That's what I thought, too," said the younger of the two pathologists. "But look." He switched on an x-ray lightbox, several films already in place.

"Definitely *not* pregnant," Angie said.

Even Ray could see that. The interior of the nymph's swollen stomach appeared to be a solid ball of white.

"What is that?"

"That's just the thing," said Dr. Martin. "We don't get anything off x-rays, ultrasound, a CT scan, or an MRI. We didn't want to risk contamination if cutting into the abdomen triggered some sort of malignant spell."

"It's fairly soft," said the other pathologist. He pressed on the top of her belly, and his mouth dropped open. "Wait—it's gone hard."

Angie reached over and felt all around it. "No indents that I can feel either, and it's certainly not pliable." Her brows drew together. "Let's get a technomage in," she said. "I think it would be a good idea to get a witch, as well. Dr. Aiken," she said addressing the younger pathologist. "Remove the other bodies immediately. Dr. Martin, send your reports and the photographs to me immediately and evacuate. I'll call in a technomage, and track down a witch. Dr. Aiken, hit the evacuation alarm on the way out. Dangerous magic protocol." She pointed at Ray and Kayla. "You two, out."

Before either of them could ask what the hell was going on, Angie picked up the wall phone and typed in a number. It connected after only a few seconds.

"Marta, this is Dr. Cordone. I'm down in lab seven. I need your best technomage stat. It can't wait." She paused a moment. "Good. We'll be here."

She hung up and immediately punched in another number. This time it took longer for an answer.

"This is Dr. Angie Cordone," she said in a clipped voice. "I'm the coroner. I have a couple of cases on my table that I need witch expertise as soon as possible. It's a level-two emergency situation. Can you send me someone?" She rattled off a telephone number and hung up.

"What are you two still doing here?" she demanded. "This is—" The phone rang. She grabbed it. "Cordone, here."

She listened and then nodded once. "Please do. I don't like the look of this."

Dr. Aiken and Dr. Martin had moved the two bodies to gurneys and were wheeling them out. Aiken paused by a row of colored tiles on the wall just outside the door, tapping the yellow one. Immediately a pulsing alarm started beeping. Angie made shooing gestures for Kayla and Ray to leave as a line of blue lights blinked along the center of the hallway floor. More flashed rapidly on the ceiling and then began a trailing pattern to guide people to the exit.

"What's going on?" Kayla asked over her shoulder.

"We've had incidents over the years where a spell has detonated in the labs. Given that blood sacrifice is involved in this case, combined with the change in the nymph's body, we can't take chances. Safer to evacuate and get experts in to handle it. Spell could go off and endanger everyone."

Kayla turned, putting her hands on her hips, a stubborn expression settling on her face. "We can't just leave you here."

Ray took her arm, willing to drag her out if he had to. "We'll only be in the way."

She dug her heels in. "I should stay in case they need me."

She meant in her other form. The idea of her staying made Ray's stomach turn, but he swallowed the completely rational and violent surge of fear and focused on logic. "What they need is a technomage and a witch, both of whom are on the way," he said. "We'll just be in the way." If she stayed, he stayed.

"I have no idea what you're talking about, but you can argue outside," Angie said, though she was too intelligent not to wonder why Kayla thought she could help with a magic situation. "Now move it."

A stream of employees walked quickly past toward the exit. Ray did his best not to throw Kayla over his shoulder neanderthal style and haul her ass to safety. She bit her upper lip, then finally gave a reluctant nod and allowed him to tug her along after the departing employees. Not bothering to hide his exhale of relief, Ray urged Kayla to go faster as they made their escape.

The exit into the parking garage was closed, with everybody leaving through two broad emergency doors on either side of the spindle. People hustled down the stairs and outside. Security personal directed them to keep moving toward Providence Park.

Ray pulled Kayla out of the line, ignoring the calls of the security guards. He took out his badge and flashed it over his shoulder and continued. They'd left the box of witchkin murder info in the car, and he wanted to get it in case the place went under extended quarantine. After showing the badge, nobody tried to stop them.

They went around to the entrance for the garage, which was now blocked by a series of four-foot-tall steel bollards. At the car, he grabbed the box while Kayla dug in her pack and donned a rain suit before shouldering her backpack. Ray slammed the door and snagged her hand again, breaking into a jog.

Once outside they headed in the direction of the park, joining the flow of people streaming out of the building. All four wings were being evacuated. Ray kept Kayla's hand clasped in his. The touch of her skin against his electrified him. Just from touching her hand. He told himself to let go. This was a road he couldn't go down. But then again, with all the people, they could get separated. Worse, she could turn around and return to the lab.

He firmed his hold on her hand, congratulating himself on the sensibility of his argument. Self-serving it might be, but also true.

Once they reached the park, they looked back in the direction they'd come. Ray wish to hell he'd stopped to retrieve his phone so that he could call Angie.

Kayla rubbed the wrist of her now free hand where she usually wore the silver band. She chewed her upper lip, lost in thought.

"Don't even think about it."

"I don't like this."

"Me, either, but we have to stay in our lane. Let the experts do what they do."

She sighed but didn't argue further.

A quarter of an hour ticked past, then half, then a whole. Still no signs of any problems from the lab. Kayla was growing impatient, as was the rest of the crowd. The drizzle had stopped and her hood had fallen back. She paced, tapping her fingers against her thighs. The same urgency to return punched at Ray's kidneys. He made himself stand still.

After an hour and a half, Kayla had had enough.

"I'm going back," she declared and headed back to the street.

Ray strode after her, dodging around clusters of nervous employees as they gossiped about what might be happening. He overtook her at the sidewalk.

Back at the lab building, security had extended the perimeter to the outskirts of the campus. The same guard who'd told them Kayla wasn't official stopped them.

"Can't go inside," she said, her dark eyes steely, her shoulders squared. "Best just turn around and go on about your business."

Kayla's only acknowledgment was a quick glance before she fixed her attention back on the lab building, leaving Ray to deal with the guard.

"I need to borrow your phone," he told the guard.

She got a look on her face that said he could kiss her ass. "No," was her flat response.

Ray fought the urge to tear her a new asshole. She was just doing her job, and anyway, he could catch more flies with honey.

"The evacuation is because of our case," he told her in a confidential voice, as if letting her in on a secret. "One of the bodies had something inside it, something magical. Dr. Cordone was calling in the technomage and a witch. It's imperative we find out if they are okay, and what was in the body. Lives depend upon it," he said.

Leveling a look at her, he went for the right hook. "You know how this is, Officer Zuniga," he said, reading her name from her name tag. "Cops like us don't get to run away from danger. Our job is to get in its way. Our job is to fight evil no matter what form it takes."

Even as a pride straightened her spine and swelled her chest, Ray couldn't help feeling disgusted at himself. Not for the words or for the way he used them to elicit her cooperation, but for the fact that by ignoring crimes against witchkin, he'd let evil thrive. He could do better. He *should* do better.

He'd won over Officer Zuniga. She took her phone out of a leather pouch on her belt and handed it to him.

Ray typed in the number for the morgue's switchboard, then tapped Angie's extension. It rang several times, and he began to think she wasn't going to pick up.

"Cordone," she said in a clipped voice.

"This is Ray. What's going on?"

"Wondered how long you'd wait. It's still not safe."

"I don't get paid to stay safe."

"Maybe not, but I get paid to make sure my employees don't end up dead because of the job."

"Good thing I'm not one of your employees then," Ray said. "We're coming back in. Tell Officer Zuniga we're cleared." He didn't wait for Angie's response, but passed the phone back.

"Zuniga here."

The security officer nodded a couple times, said "yes ma'am," and then hung up. She looked at Ray. "Follow me."

Much as he wanted to, Ray couldn't tell Zuniga to stay put. He had a pretty good feeling if she didn't go, he and Kayla weren't going either.

They started across the wide stretch of lawn and trees surrounding the building. Zuniga spoke into the microphone on her shoulder, notifying someone that she was escorting them in. When they entered the central spindle, Kayla halted.

"I need the stuff I left with security," she said, looking at Ray. "We'll be safer if I have my things," she added.

It didn't take much to put two and two together. Something in her belongings helped her to transform. She wanted that capability in case something went wrong. He looked at Zuniga who just shrugged and took them over to a set of wall bins, each marked with a picture. Ray found his and Kayla's pictures on the far-left side. They must've been taken when they came through the scanner.

They both collected their belongings and made their way down to the lab where they'd left Angie and the nymph.

She met them at the doors. "Come inside, but keep back."

Ray scanned the scene inside. Logan stood next to the nymph, staring down at her stomach which had tripled in size. The skin now stretched obscenely over whatever was inside. Lumpy knots moved beneath the surface. Beside Logan was a young blond woman—at least she appeared young. Witches didn't age past the point of age 21 or so. For all he knew, she could be an octogenarian or older. It occurred to him that Theresa Runyon was no spring chicken, and neither was her daughter. Illusion? He certainly hadn't grown younger since he'd turned into a witch.

He tucked the question away for later, and continued his examination. Like most witches, this one was slender to the point of being skinny. The hazard of the craft he'd heard. Magic required a lot of energy, and a lot of calories. Her sun-bleached hair hung to her shoulders. Magic swirled in the room thick and syrupy. It called to Ray, summoning his own to the surface.

The witch's eyes snapped up, and she stared at him. He stared back, expressionless. Most of the time he stayed far enough away from witches that they didn't recognize he was one of them. The rest of the time he kept his power tamped down. That seemed to keep them from noticing. Either that or it was general courtesy that witches didn't out one another.

After a moment, her gaze dropped back down to the corpse and she said something under her breath to Logan. The technomage shook his head. She rolled her eyes and then turned to face him, putting her hands on his shoulder and shoving hard. Caught off balance, Logan stumbled away. Instantly a silver shield rose up around the corpse and the witch, sealing them both inside.

Logan swore and slapped his hands against the shield. Power knocked him flying. He smashed against the cabinet and dropped to the floor like a sack of onions, leaving dents in the stainless steel. Kayla made a sound and sprinted over to him.

Hot jealousy boiled up inside Ray. He hauled back on it, but it bubbled up through whatever control he had. He snarled, unaware he'd made a sound until Angie put a hand on his arm.

"Down, boy," she said. She patted his arm, and then went to join Kayla.

Ray sucked in a couple of breaths, forcing himself to calm the fuck down, glaring at the technomage who now sat up. Angie examined his eyes, and Kayla held one hand and looked at the back of his head.

Ray tore his gaze away. No reason to torture himself by watching them together. Instead he watched the witch.

The stomach of the nymph continued to move. Magic coalesced around the witch's fingers, and she pressed them against the swollen, undulating flesh.

Light flared bright orange, and the witch screamed, the sound agonized.

Ray leaped forward, unable to see inside the shield, which had turned opaque. Magic leaped eagerly inside him, and without stopping to consider what had happened to Logan, he smashed his hands into the shield, releasing a bolt of energy.

The shield crumbled away, the released power whipping through the lab like frantic electric eels.

Ignoring the lashing pain, Ray dove toward the witch. She lay on the floor, bleeding profusely from a hash of gouges across her face and body. Standing on top of her and on either side were three creatures, vaguely dog like, but with armored bodies and clawed hands at the end of their serpentine tails. Blood dripped from their maws and ran down their chests. More coated their other four clawed paw-hands. As he watched, one chomped into the witch's shoulder with his teeth and yanked, twisting and clawing to get the flesh to separate.

She whimpered, clearly on the verge of unconsciousness. Ray clapped his hands around the beast's thickly armored neck and unleashed a bolt of energy. Red light flashed. The demon dog made a high-pitched sound and reared away, twisting out of Ray's grip. He kicked at the others to knock them away as he swung the wounded witch into his arms.

Robbed of their prey, the creatures leaped at Ray. Dagger-teeth knifed into his thighs and ass. He tried to shake them off, but they hung on. Suddenly an electric whip snapped, coiling around the one on his ass. The beast fell away, and the stench of burning fur filled his nose. Two more snaps and the other two fell off. One of the whips caught Ray on the calf, and fire seared through his leg. He dropped to his knees, the nerves in his legs giving out along with the muscles.

Kayla and Angie grabbed him and pulled him upright. They dragged him toward the door. Zuniga punched the automatic-open button. It didn't work. She kicked the seam of the doors, and they swung open a few inches.

Ray careened toward escape, holding the bleeding witch clutched against his chest. Blood bubbled from between her lips. Behind he could hear more screeches as Logan held off the ravenous beasts.

Zuniga shoved the doors wider and Ray burst through, followed quickly by Kayla and Angie and a moment later, Logan. The door slid shut, and Logan threw up a shield to keep the beasts inside. Three thuds hit the reinforced windows, shattering them. The beasts stood on their hind legs howling and snarling, unable to break through Logan's barrier. They'd grown to the size of Great Danes.

"Get out of here!" Logan yelled. "I don't know how long I can hold them!"

Ray staggered as fast as he could toward the exit, trying not to jostle the injured witch. If she didn't get help and quickly, she'd bleed out.

Angie ran beside him, her face gray, her lips pinched tight. Blood soaked through Ray's jeans where he'd been bitten. The wounds burned as if full of acid and sent streaks of fire to his toes and up through his chest.

He cursed himself for knowing so little magic that he couldn't perform even a basic healing spell. Hell, he didn't even know if a basic healing spell was even a thing. All he knew was he didn't know how to stop the witch's bleeding and he should. Goddamn, but he should know enough to be able to do some first aid! And not just for her, but himself.

But then he'd have to let people see what he was. What had Angie, Kayla, Zuniga, or Logan been able to see when he'd gone to help the witch? He'd been on the opposite side of the shield, so likely they hadn't seen him break through, but they could have seen his attack on the demon dog.

He didn't feel his leg give way, and only realized he was no longer standing when he hit the floor. The witch made a whimpering sound as they crashed down together. Ray rolled aside to get off her, but his brain seemed disconnected from his trunk, and he made a wheezing sound and barely moved.

"Shit! Get him up!"

Kayla and Officer Zuniga hooked hands under his armpits and tried to pull him erect. He tried to help get up, but had no feeling anymore in his legs. They let go of him.

Kayla swore. "Stand back," she ordered. "Zach! Get your ass down here! I'll handle the beasts. You take care of Ray and the witch."

She had gone for years without exposing her secret, and now she was not only going to transform, she was gonna do it in front of witnesses. Angie and Logan might keep her secret, but Zuniga was bound to shout it from the rooftops.

The fact that Kayla had already exposed herself on the Island didn't matter. No one but Raven and the dryads had known her in her human form.

He doubted anybody had gotten a good look at her before she'd plunged into the water, so her secret remained safe. If she shifted now, the entire city would likely know before sundown.

Ray told her to stop, not to do it. There had to be another way. Or at least he tried to. The words came out garbled. Then it was too late.

A burst of magic rolled over him followed by a sweep of damp air across his cheeks. Angie made a strangled sound, and Officer Zuniga yelped. Ray heard the sound of claws on the floor and the scrape of scales as Kayla ran back up the hall to the lab.

Then he was scooped up in a shroud of magic. The walls and overhead lights rushed past as Angie and Logan hauled him and the witch out at a run.

Ray wanted to demand that they stop, that they go back and help Kayla. Everything inside him howled in fear for her. The magic inside him roared, burning at the insides of his skin. Something in the bites from the creatures kept it contained.

The last thing he remembered was a shrill, unearthly shriek before he fell unconscious.

Chapter 17

Kayla

KAYLA ACTIVATED the silver band on her wrist. Water sluiced up from nowhere, drenching her in a spinning geyser. She summoned the shift, wanting it like she had never wanted it before. In the blink of an eye she turned, her body expanding and lengthening. Paying no attention to Angie or Officer Zuniga, she whirled, her body flowing in a serpentine back to the autopsy room.

Her claws gouged chunks in the concrete floor as she hurled herself down the corridor. Zach stood with his back to her, power rolling from his hands to create an electric barrier. The beasts inside flung themselves at the wall of energy, snarling and screeching with frustration and pain.

As she came abreast of the technomage, Kayla hooked her tail around his waist and thrust him back behind her. She crouched, her tail snaking back and forth as she prepared to attack. She heard Zach's footsteps as he ran in the opposite direction. Dear God, let him be able to save Ray. That was her last coherent thought before the predator inside took over.

The mage's energy wall thinned and turned to tatters and sparks. The creatures torpedoed through as if they'd been launched from a gun. They'd grown even larger, and each was now the size of a llama, with thick heavy jaws.

They pounced on Kayla, ripping and shredding with all five claws. Razor teeth pierced through her scales. Kayla crashed against the cinder block wall, knocking two creatures away. She picked one up and flung it back into the lab. It crashed into a table and let loose a shrill keening sound. She grabbed another in her teeth before it could reattach itself. She shook it viciously and then slammed it to the floor. It squalled and bounced back up on its feet. The one still attached to her back snapped and chomped at her spine, trying to break through her tough scales.

She flexed them, each ridge rippling upward into a carpet of diamond-sharp knives. The beast squealed, its grip loosening. She twisted and rolled her body, shaking the creature free. She whirled and smashed it with her tail. It flew across the lab and crashed into the cabinets above the sinks.

The other two leaped at her again, one fastening itself to her throat, the other diving at her eyes. She thrashed, crushing one between her skull and the wall while clawing away the other.

Fire burned where their teeth had pierced. Acid dripped into her veins. She shook herself and roared before rocketing into the lab. She forgot who she was. She remembered only the need to protect and kill. She snatched one of the creatures in her toothy maw, crunching down and flinging it against the wall.

It lay only a moment before springing back to its feet, its twisted limbs straightening, its wounds vanishing. Before she could do anything else, the creatures raced passed her, escaping down the hallway. She whirled to follow, leaping up over the gurneys.

She was fast, but they were faster. They streaked away, disappearing around a corner. By the time she got there, they had ripped apart the door leading into the main lobby, shredding the steel to confetti with their claws.

She chased them, but her body had grown sluggish and awkward. She staggered against the wall, then clawed her way through the door and into the spindle. She could see no sign of the creatures or her companions. She stopped, turning her head to search. The overwhelming scents of blood and the pungent odor of the three creatures smothered her senses.

She scuttled toward the nearest escape, pausing on the threshold to look outside. Far across the lawn she could see Angie, Zach, and Officer Zuniga. Zach kneeled beside Ray, while Angie worked on the witch.

As she watched, the ground began to shudder and tilt. Her insides felt as though they were turning to liquid. Cramps rolled down her body in fierce waves. Instinct told her to run, to find a safe place. She needed water.

She didn't try to hide. She lurched toward the river, following the most direct path. People screamed and ran, some leaping out of cars to get out of her way. She clambered over vehicles and bumbled through intersections with no heed for safety.

She just wanted—needed—water.

She hardly noticed when someone took potshots at her. The bullets ricocheted away. Dizziness made it difficult to see and stay upright. She staggered like a drunk, bouncing off buildings and trees. She tripped over a curb and fell onto her stomach. It took far more effort than it should have to lift herself up again. Her muscles had grown lethargic and stupid. She couldn't feel the bottoms of her feet or the end of her tail. The latter dragged behind her like a ratty rope.

The closer she drew to the river, the slower she went. Crowds of humans and witchkin gathered to watch her in breathless fear. Stupid. But then obviously she wasn't a particular threat. Her head swung side to side with ponderous effort as she dragged herself along. Her legs shook and violent shudders coruscated through her body.

In the dim recesses of her conscious mind Kayla knew she was dying. The creatures had poisoned her. So much for being a big bad monster. Pride goeth before the fall, and damned but she was falling hard.

Please God, let Ray be okay, she thought. It was the last coherent one she had before falling into the water.

She sank. The current pushed her against the bank as she tumbled deeper. A slight wiggle of her tail, a twitch of her legs, a twist of her body. She pushed herself further out into the current, sinking down and down until she lay on the stony bed of the river.

The current pushed at her, nudging her ahead of it. It cooled the burning flesh along her back in the bites along her limbs and throat, soothing where it touched but doing nothing for the acid chewing through her flesh and veins.

She drifted north into the confluence of the swift Willamette River and the mighty Columbia. The vortex of fast-running water tumbled and spun her. She fetched up against a reef of silvered-black glass coral. It stretched out craggy fingers into the water creating an intricate weaving of knotted glass and motion.

The current held her pinned. She could do nothing for herself. Her body refused to respond. She would die here, she realized vaguely.

After a time, she felt tiny presences darting through the water around her. The water told her they were water pixies mounted on tiny transparent seahorses. They swarmed like starlings, eventually daring to land. She heard the squeaks and chirps as they spoke to one another. Normally she understood them and could even speak to them. Not today. None of it made any sense. The sounds shattered apart and crashed back together like discordant nonsense.

Something prodded into a wound on her back. Her body spasmed in an uncontrolled reaction, shattering twigs of glass coral before dropping limp. The water pixies cried out and streamed away into the water. They halted in a cloud a dozen feet away. After a few minutes, they advanced again.

Once again a number of them settled down onto her back. Once again something prodded into her wound. This time her body didn't even twitch. She was entirely numb except for the throbbing in her wounds and the ribbons of acid running through her bloodstream.

Memories danced through her mind on a spiral of stars. She grabbed at one, but it melted through her mental fingers. Everything merged into a giant glob, and nothing made sense.

It seemed like forever had gone past, but in truth she had no idea. Something tugged. Far away she felt the vague pressure against her scales. Presences darted all around her, more now than just water pixies and their mounts. The taste of them flowed through her open mouth. Kelpies, mer-people, nayads, and more. They gathered around her in a dense cloud.

She felt herself moving against the current, up the Willamette. The flavors of the water changed as they went further inland. Here it was bitter with minerals, there it was sweet with lush greenery. She tasted life and death and the taint of pollution. A surge of witchkin shot away from the foot of the great underwater mountain. Kayla remembered them. Vodianoi. Warriors of the deep. They rode eels with mouths full of needle-sharp teeth that could strip flesh from bone in seconds.

They joined the collection of beings surrounding Kayla, pushing and pulling to draw her along. She had no idea where they were taking her. She couldn't find it in herself to care. She had harmed none, that much she knew. When she hunted, she ate only fish and often brought fat tuna and halibut from the ocean for others to feast upon.

That did not mean they were friends.

At the foot of the mountain, they turned upward. More creatures joined them, but Kayla could no longer tell who was who or what was what. The pain from the bites and poison in her blood increased. Her heart stuttered and fell off rhythm. She convulsed, contorting up into a tight knot. She thought she heard something crack. Bones perhaps.

The water began to turn around them. Buffeting Kayla and shoving her sideways. The current shifted and shifted again, spinning her around. She could no longer tell which way was up or down. The cloud of life around her loosened and then condensed, closing ranks as they maneuvered her through the currents.

She continued to tumble in the churning water. Her heart raced faster and faster, a metronome on crack. Fire bloomed in her chest, an ache so fierce she screamed. Or maybe she didn't. She couldn't tell.

Usually under the water, she could hear and smell and taste better than she could in her human form. Not now. Now she could see nothing. She heard only muffled tortured sounds, and the flavors had dulled to dust on her tongue.

The churning violence of the water stopped abruptly. The current around her died. Her body broke the surface of the water. The ground beneath her turned shallow.

Her body jolted up onto a shingle. Water washed beneath her hind end as rusty saws carved deep into her back. Air pumped feebly through her lungs and agony rippled after it. Her heart stuttered. Never in her life had she wanted to die before, but at the moment Kayla wished nothing more than to be put out of her misery. Even though she could feel nothing of her feet, legs, muscles, or face—pain scorched her nerves and drove knives through her brain.

A buzzing slur of noise cascaded into her skull. Something touched the wounds on her back. An explosion of pain. Then nothing.

Chapter 18

Ray

THE SMELL OF antiseptic filled Ray's nose and mouth when he woke up. For a moment he had no idea where he was or what had happened. Then memories flooded back.

Kayla.

Frantic urgency punched through his gut.

He thrashed, jerking himself upright. He wore a hospital gown. Needles punctured the backs of both his hands, and tubing ran to several bags of IVs, one of which contained blood. An oxygen tube thrust two prongs up into his nose, and a blood pressure cuff circled his right bicep. He started to yank it off and his arms tangled in his IV tubing and the cord of the oxygen monitor clipped to his finger. A machine whirred and air pumped through the cuff. Ray snarled annoyance and ripped it free. Shrill alarm beeps perforated the air.

He yanked off the oxygen tube and pushed it over his head, knocking the clip off his index finger. More beeping. He twisted and swung his feet over the edge of the bed. His knees turned to taffy and he sagged. Only his hold on the bed kept him upright.

Logan appeared in the doorway at that moment and swore. He rushed in, grabbing Ray under the arm. Angie followed just behind. After her came a tall, willowy woman with long brown hair.

"What the fuck do you think you're doing?" Logan demanded as he hoisted Ray upright and turned him around to sit back down on the bed.

It wasn't until then that he realized the wounds that the creatures had given him didn't hurt. He struggled against Logan's hold, but it quickly became obvious his feeble efforts had no chance against the other man. He felt weak as a newborn baby.

"What happened? Where's Kayla?"

"We don't know," Angie said from behind him.

Ray twisted to look at her. "What do you mean, you don't know?"

This time Logan answered. "Once we got clear, I called in an emergency. In less than ten minutes we had a dozen technomages on site. We went in, but the creatures had escaped and Kayla was nowhere to be found. Witnesses saw her—" he broke off, exchanging an uncomfortable look with Angie.

"Saw her?"

Logan's brows furrowed as he turned his attention back to Ray. "Do you remember anything?"

Ray wanted to say he remembered everything, but how the hell would he know what he remembered and didn't remember? But then he realized just what Logan was getting at. "I know about her," he said, meeting the techno-mage's gaze with defiant fury. "What of it?"

Logan looked surprised, but there was approval in his nod. "Witnesses saw her heading for the river. She was bleeding from wounds on her back and throat and legs. She seemed to be drunk—staggering and running into things. We traced her to the river where she jumped in, and no one has seen anything of her since."

Ray ignored the jackhammer driving into his heart. She wasn't dead. She couldn't be dead. Once again he struggled to stand up. Logan pushed him down with one hand on Ray's shoulder.

"How long?" he demanded. "How long has it been since she disappeared?"

"We brought you in about five hours ago," Angie said. "It was a close thing. You almost died. Thanks to Sarah here, you didn't." She gestured at the other woman. "She's a witch," Angie added, with a warning look at Ray that told him he'd better not act like a bigoted asshole with the witch, or Angie would rip his skin off.

He had no intention of it.

"Thank you," he said with deep gratitude.

"You're welcome," she said in a huskier voice than he expected. It reminded him of an alto sax—warm, rich, and mellow. She smiled surprise, as if she'd expected a much different reaction from him. Two days ago, she'd have gotten it, too.

Ray remembered the other witch, the one who'd thrown up the shield to protect them from the creatures in the morgue. "How is the other witch?" he asked, even as everything in him demanded that he get up off his ass and go searching for Kayla. "The one from the lab? Is she going to make it?"

"It was touch and go, but we got to her in time," said Logan with a grim look. "She'll be a little while recovering, though."

One small ray of good news, anyway. "Where are my clothes?" He was leaving whether they liked it or not. Kayla was out there and she needed help.

"You lost a lot of blood," Angie said. "The bite of those creatures is poisonous. Magic poison. Zach and Sarah were able to counter it before it caused too much damage. We're trying to get some blood into you, but even so, you'll be weak for a while."

"I can live with weak." *But he couldn't live without Kayla.* Four years had been too damned long, and a lifetime? His mind veered from the thought. Not going to happen.

Ray looked at Logan. "Who's looking for her? Divers? Search and rescue?"

Logan shook his head. "She's witchkin. You know policy. No wasting resources on the inhuman." His lip curled. Clearly he didn't think much of that policy.

Ray's own thinking had undergone a sea change. That policy was fucked up, and not just because of Kayla, but because the witchkin were citizens too, and deserved equal protection under the law. If having a war with somebody meant treating them like second-class citizens forever, then nobody in the US would be treated well, starting with people from the UK, Germans, Vietnamese, Italians, and pretty much everybody else.

"Witchkin are looking for her," Sarah volunteered.

Logan, Angie, and Ray all looked at her.

She gave a little shrug. "We look out for each other. Besides, we need her. So do you. We all thrive here because she's here."

"What do you mean?" Logan asked.

Sarah looked at each one of them as if debating whether or not she should speak.

Ray bit back his impatience, curling one hand into a fist around the sheet. "Please," he said.

The witch sighed. "She is of the divine," she said finally.

Her three listeners just stared.

"Divine?" Logan choked out. "Like God and angels and Jesus?"

Sarah smiled and shook her head and then shrugged again. "There are and have been many divine beings in this world. Some are small gods, some are powerful deities."

"And Kayla?" Ray asked, his mind reeling. Kayla was a god? She couldn't possibly know it. Could she? "The Guardian of the River," he said, the puzzle pieces clicking into place.

Sarah nodded. "We believe she is an aspect of a river god. Her very existence here lends fertility to the land, the water, the air, and all who live here. Because of her, this place thrives. The bites and poison from the creatures should not have hurt her." She frowned, clearly troubled. "Those creatures were summoned to kill a god. They can have no other purpose."

"Are you saying someone brought them here to kill Kayla?" Angie asked.

Ray could barely wrap his brain around it.

The witch shook her head. "If she were their prey, then they'd have stayed and fought until she was dead or they were."

"Kayla isn't the only god in town." The word sounded completely ridiculous coming from Ray's mouth, but Sarah's nod confirmed his logic.

"How many gods are in Portland?" Angie asked, startling to look unsettled.

Ray supposed it wasn't every day you found out you'd been hanging out with the divine.

"I couldn't say," Sarah said, and Ray wondered if she couldn't because she didn't know, or she couldn't because it would betray the magical community. "Witchkin of all stripes will be drawn here because of the River Guardian. Gods are no exception. Humans will come, too."

She frowned as if searching for words to explain and finding it difficult. "She's a protector. A being of justice and a preserver of life. She's like the sun or water. She is powerful in her way, but it's her existence that allows others to thrive and grow into power, rather than something she consciously does. Losing her would cripple this place, starve it of the light and life only she brings."

"You are saying that she can't do magic, is that right?" Logan asked.

She gave a little shrug. "Gods don't do magic in the way that witches or other creatures do. Theirs is a divine power and . . . it's different. We don't know a lot more than that. Most of what we know about her is from watching her."

Before she finished speaking, Ray slid off the bed, yanking the IVs out of his left hand and then his right. Blood dribbled down across his fingers and dripped on the floor. He ignored it, concentrating on keeping his feet. He didn't particularly care about the finer points of god magic versus witch magic, and he sure as hell didn't care what Kayla could or couldn't do. All that was important was that she had been attacked by creatures whose specific nature was the hunting of gods, and she needed help.

"I'm going to find her," he declared when Angie started to chastise him.

"You can't help her," Sarah said baldly. "You haven't the skills."

"I don't give a shit. She's alone and she's hurt, maybe dying," he said, the last word sticking in his throat, and squeezing his heart in a metal fist. "I'm not giving up on her. I made the mistake once of not following her when I should have. I won't do it again."

"You're an idiot," Angie said, grabbing a roll of gauze and medical tape and wrapping both his hands tightly to stanch the bleeding. "You can barely walk."

"Which is why I'm here," announced Sharon Dix from the doorway behind Sarah. She pushed in, her gaze running up and down Ray in his hospital gown. "I'm taking over the Runyon case," she said smugly.

"The hell you are," Ray snarled.

"Take it up with the captain. He wants me to take point until you're back on your feet."

"I am on my feet." For Kayla's sake and Landon's, Ray wanted this case. Dix wore blinders when it came to witchkin. Not that he could blame her. He'd just managed to get rid of his own blinders.

Anyway, she probably didn't even know all the facts. He doubted Crice had told her that Theresa Runyon and Margaret Valentine were witches. That was a secret Alistair Runyon would kill to keep a tight lid on, and Crice wouldn't want to be in the line of fire when Runyon decided to go on a rampage.

All the same, the captain had to be seen driving hard on the case if he wanted to keep his pension and his office. With Ray in the hospital, he needed another face to trot out in front of the news cameras and point to in order to demonstrate his commitment to solving the case. That and putting all the department's resources behind the investigation would play well on the news. So would Dix. Cameras liked her, and she had a decent record on solving cases. What she didn't have was enough experience, or gut instinct, and with magic and gods involved—she wouldn't get far.

"I came so you can bring me up to speed on the case," she said. "And I need your notes and files."

Like hell. Ray didn't have time to waste arguing with her. Kayla needed him, which meant getting out of here fast. A plan popped into his head and he instantly put it into play

Ray abruptly swayed, clutching Logan and the side of the bed before lurching forward to sprawl across the mattress and sliding to the floor like he could no longer stand.

"Shit!" Logan said as he dropped down beside Ray. "Follow me and sell it hard," he murmured with a wink. "We'll keep her busy."

A worried Angie squeezed in beside Logan, leaning down to check Ray's pulse.

"Is he going to make it?" Logan demanded, staring hard at Angie and waggling his eyebrows.

Her eyes widened as she caught on to the ruse. "He's going into tachycardia," she said urgently. "Get a nurse and a crash cart. Code blue! Go now!"

Zach leaped to his feet and hollered for help. Angie looked at Ray, rolled her eyes, and gave a fake shake of her head. "Drama queen," she mouthed.

The tiny room quickly filled as a nurse shoved in a crash cart and two others followed after. Zach and Sarah pushed Dix out into the corridor to make space in the hospital room.

"Help me get him onto the bed." Angie snapped out the order as she kicked the door shut.

The instant it closed, Ray sprang to his feet, much to the shock of the nurses.

"Get his gown off," Angie said loudly as she pointed Ray toward the bathroom, twirling her fingers at the nurses to tell them to keep up the charade.

They exchanged startled glances and then grinned as they started clattering around and shouting out orders to one another, and generally putting on a show for Dix.

In the meantime, Ray scooted around the bed and into the bathroom. It contained a sink, toilet, a large tiled shower stall, and most importantly a door into the hallway. Angie held up her hand for him to stand back, before cracking the door open. She peered out and then motioned for Ray to follow her as she slipped out into the hallway.

Luckily, the main door into the room was just around the corner, putting them well out of sight of Dix.

Angie pushed Ray through a staff-only doorway and led him down another hallway into a break room. Another doorway took them into a small locker room with bunk beds running along one wall. A cupboard at one end held stacks of clean scrubs. She pulled him down a pair of dark-purple pants and a purple shirt.

"You'll have to put these on," she said. "Your clothes and shoes went into the incinerator. Biohazard. I'll go fetch your personal belongings and see if I can find some shoes that will fit you."

Ray yanked off the hospital gown and donned the scrubs. Going commando was going to be a little awkward, but beggars couldn't be choosers.

He returned to the break room and grabbed a carton of yogurt from the refrigerator. He ate it quickly with a spoon he found in a drawer. He wasn't particularly hungry, but knew that after a healing and a blood transfusion, he needed the calories. He tossed the container and eyed a roast beef sandwich. With a silent apology to the owner, he ate that, too.

Angie returned a few minutes later carrying a plastic tote bag with his things. Inside he found his wallet, gun, badge, pocket knife, handcuffs, and a few other things.

"Shoes?"

She grimaced. "These are the best I could find on short notice."

She held out a pair of beat-up Birkenstocks, the soles worn thin. Ray slid his feet into them. His toes hung over the front and his heels sat on the back edge. Better than barefoot, he told himself.

"This way," Angie said. She guided him down to the employee-only elevators.

"Good luck," she said. "Find her. Don't get killed while doing it. Call me when you've got her and I'll come help."

He pulled her into a quick hug, startling them both. "Thanks, Angie. I owe you big."

"No, you don't," she said, waving away his thanks. "You're one of the good ones, and so is Reese."

He nodded grimly and stepped onto the elevator as it arrived. "Check the lab," he said before the doors closed. "Kayla had a backpack with a plastic box inside. I'm going to need that box."

"Technomages have everything under quarantine right now," Angie said. "I'll have Zach get a hold of it for you."

"Thanks. When this is over, I'll buy you dinner."

Raven's warning that Kayla had to stop whatever bad was coming echoed in his brain. Hopefully *when this is over* didn't mean the end of the world.

RAY'S FIRST ORDER of business had to be clothing. His place wasn't far, but he wasn't willing to waste time going out of his way. Instead, while following Kayla's trail to the river, he stopped at a little hole-in-the-wall salvage shop where he found jeans, a long-sleeved cotton shirt, socks, and a pair of boots a half-size too big. He paid the shriveled old man behind the counter, then changed in the tiny curtained fitting room, leaving the scrubs behind along with the now-empty bag.

Back on the street, he broke into a jog, but quickly found his body wasn't going to cooperate. He dropped to a walk, panting, cursing himself for his body's weakness.

He saw plenty of evidence of Kayla's passing. Broken bushes and windows, crumpled fenders and dented doors, deep gouges in the asphalt, and blood. A whole lot of blood.

Ray refused to contemplate how much blood Kayla might've lost, or how much she could afford to lose. He'd shunted his worry and fear into a separate box in his brain, throwing all his attention into the hunt. Losing his cool wouldn't help find her.

He also noticed the way plants and trees drooped as if starving for nutrients. The normally verdant foliage wrapping buildings and vines and thriving in parks and walkways was now spotted with black and yellow splotches. Even people looked washed out and tired.

Was that because of Kayla? Was this what Sarah had meant when she said the city thrived because of her presence here? The concept was hard to wrap his head around. That this one woman, his former partner and friend, could be the living heart of the city. What would happen if she died?

Just thinking of the possibility ripped open the box of his emotions and turned his chest inside out. *Let me find her. Let her be okay.*

When he got to the river, he found gouges in the grassy verge over-hanging the water, but no sign of Kayla. The bank dropped away in a sheer drop. Mounds of boulders piled up at the bottom to protect against erosion. Just below, the river eddied, the water muddy.

Ray scanned up and down the river for any signs of her. Nothing.

He needed a boat if he hoped to do a decent search. He wasn't far from a community dock. He broke into a jog again despite the tight constriction around his lungs. He must've been in really shitty shape if a witch's healing had left him this weak. Thank goodness for Sarah and her willingness to help when he'd been such an ass to her kind. To his kind. He had to start accepting the change in himself. He wasn't human anymore; he was a witch. For the first time ever, he didn't cringe away from the knowledge.

A quarter of a mile away, he staggered onto the busy dock. The sun had started to slide lower in the west, and people were tying up for the night.

He flashed his badge at a pair of women who'd just pulled into a slip. They piloted a twenty-six-foot Duckworth Offshore rig that had seen better days.

"I need your boat," Ray said. "Police business. It's an emergency."

The woman who jumped to the dock to tie up scowled at him. "Go to hell. You can't just take our boat."

"Actually, I can," Ray said, shoving his badge folder into his back pocket. The look he gave her made her step back. "And I am. If you ladies will just step off. Now."

"The hell we will," the driver said. She was older, probably in her sixties, with ropey muscles and short gray hair. Scars and callouses covered her hands as if she had been working with them a long time. "We aren't giving you our boat just for the asking. Go get yourself a court order."

Ray smiled in a not particularly friendly way. "Get off the damned boat," he said. "This is a matter of life and death for the whole city."

The woman on the dock folded her arms, her anger turning worried and curious. "What does that mean?"

"It means he's blowing smoke up our asses, Annette," said the driver. "Ignore him."

Ray couldn't see the driver's right hand. It had dropped out of sight. He was pretty sure she'd reached for a gun, or some sort of magical weapon.

He drew his .45, raising it to eye level and sighting in on the driver. "You want to keep breathing, let me see your hands," he ordered.

Both women blanched, and both lifted their hands up.

"Good. Now, step off."

"This tub is keyed to both of us and no one else," the older woman said defiantly. "You want to go somewhere, then we've got to take you."

Ray didn't know whether to believe her or not, but he didn't have time to care. "Fine. Let's go."

He jumped from the dock onto the boat. A canopy at the bow end housed two seats and the steering console. A bench ran across the stern, with the deck between loaded with cargo containers. The seals and the markings on the exteriors indicated that they carried fresh meat from one of the farms near Lincoln City and Newport. A lot of the area out there had become ranch land after Magicfall. Boats like this one made daily trips to haul meat back to feed the city.

Ray confiscated the shotgun the older woman had reached for, setting it on the stern bench. He waited until they'd cast off and Annette boarded before he holstered his gun again.

"Where we going?" asked the gray-haired driver.

"We're doing a search," Ray said. "Head downriver first."

She activated the boat's rotors and turned out into the current. "Who are we looking for?"

Ray hesitated, but three sets of eyes were better than one. "A kind of water dragon."

Both women whipped their heads around to look at him.

"A what?" Annette demanded.

She appeared to be about half the age of the driver. She wore her brown hair in a military-style buzz cut, a little longer on top than the sides. She stood taller than the driver, with broad shoulders and a narrow waist, her arms and face tanned, her nose peeling from a burn. She slipped on a pair of sunglasses.

"A water dragon," Ray repeated without batting an eyelash. "She's about thirty-five feet long nose to tail, and stands between five and six feet at the shoulder. She's got cobalt-blue scales edged in gold."

"You're serious," the older woman said, sounding as if she thought Ray had lost a few marbles.

"She's badly wounded," Ray added. "She needs medical attention, or she could very well die." He managed to get the last sentence out without his voice cracking.

"Why do you want to find a dragon?" asked Annette

Ray shook his head, turning to watch the banks rush past. "It's an ongoing investigation, but it's crucial we find her as soon as possible."

"How long since she went in the water?" the driver asked.

"In the neighborhood of four or five hours." In which time Kayla could easily have been washed out to sea. He might never find her. He squeezed his eyes shut for a moment against the deluge of emotion that slammed through him.

No. He would *not* let that happen. Ray opened his eyes, scrutinizing the shoreline.

"She dangerous?" asked the driver.

"Only to her enemies."

"How come you're the only cop out looking for her?"

Ray's mouth twisted into a bitter smile full of self-loathing. "Because if I told my boss what she is and what she means to the city, he'd have me locked up in a rubber room."

"What does she mean to the city?" Annette again.

"See those blackberry bushes there?" He pointed to an inlet where the bushes mounded up from the shore. "See how the leaves have gone yellow and crisp, like they've got some sort of fungus?"

"Sure," the driver said, sounding confused at his apparent change of subject.

"Before she got hurt, they were healthy and green. Same as those oaks." He pointed.

Both women stared at him as if he'd lost his ever-loving mind. Ray couldn't blame them. He sounded like a lunatic, and they had to wonder if he had gone insane. Except in a world of full of magic, everything he'd said was not only bizarrely logical if you knew the facts, but also entirely possible.

The two exchanged a look and then turned back to him.

"Are you high? Been drinking maybe?" asked Annette.

He could only wish. Then the beasts in the lab, the attack, and Kayla's disappearance might just be a bad drug trip. "Afraid not."

Ray kept his attention fixed on the water, scanning from the near bank across as far as he could see to the other side. He swept his gaze back and forth along an invisible grid, but could see nothing of Kayla or any hint that she'd passed by.

"That's a pretty tall tale," said the driver. "You really expect us to believe it?"

"I expect you to drive the boat. I don't give a fuck what you believe."

"What if you don't find her?"

Then the bottom fell out of his world. Again.

"I don't plan to find out. Put on some speed."

"What happened to her?" asked the younger one as the older woman increased their speed. The hull lifted slightly out of the water, and a small rooster tail rainbowed up behind them.

"We were attacked. She stayed behind while the rest of us escaped, but the creatures that attacked her poisoned her."

He shoved the words through gritted teeth, trying not to let his fear for her overwhelm him. He had to compartmentalize. It was a trick of the trade and one he was good at. But having Kayla's life on the line screwed his emotional control all to hell. All his walls, all his carefully cultivated perspective, had gone into the toilet.

"What kind of creatures?"

Clearly the unspoken question was whether she and Annette should be worried.

Ray thought about them. He had never seen anything like them before. A cross between a monkey, a wolf, a pangolin, and an alligator. They'd had wolf-shaped heads with stubby alligator jaws, monkey arms in place of legs and monkey hands in place of feet, each tipped with vicious claws. Pangolin armor wrapped their bodies, and as an added bonus, they'd had a fifth clawed monkey arm in place of a tail.

Sarah had called them god killers. Someone had summoned them to the city to hunt a god, and Kayla clearly wasn't their target. So, who was? Raven had talked about something bad coming. Hunting a god qualified. Hell, having an actual god living in town qualified. Two, if Kayla really was one, too. Or at least an aspect of one, according to Sarah. What the hell did that mean?

He didn't want to think about it. It didn't matter anyway. Nothing did but finding Kayla and getting her healed up.

"They were like armored wolves with clawed hands and an extra claw hand on their tails," he said finally, aware they were waiting for his answer.

Neither woman said anything, and Ray could hardly blame them. His response wasn't comforting.

Finally, Annette spoke. "Cops don't like witchkin," she said. "Fact is, most cops say the only good witchkin is a dead one."

Ray nodded grimly. The truth sucked. If he hadn't had a wake-up call, he'd still be ignoring every one of them he could, and killing the ones he couldn't.

"I had myself a come-to-Jesus moment," he said sardonically. They were getting close to St. Johns Bridge, or what was left of it. Only the uprights on either side remained standing. Between them, and spanning the broad width of the river, was a mass of greenery. Vines the width of tree trunks tangled together, their roots crawling over the uprights and digging deep into the soil on either side.

Most of the locals called it Snake Bridge anymore. And not because the vines looked like giant serpents, but because the damned canopy writhed with the things. They dropped into the river and slithered through the water, sometimes knotting together in giant wriggling masses. Most were poisonous and very unfriendly.

The older woman slowed the boat as they approached the bridge.

"Don't push it, Leslie," Annette said warningly. "Put up the shield. I don't want to give the screw-snakes a chance to burrow through the hull."

The driver—Leslie—activated something on the console, and magic prickled over Ray's skin. His own stirred in response. He clamped down on it.

The boat motored slowly through the masses of snakes. Overhead dozens dripped down from the canopy, some thirty or forty feet long. Many bore the normal colors Ray usually associated with them, but others were brightly colored and patterned. The screw-snakes looked more like lampreys, but with long snouts studded with flexible teeth. Those, combined with their natural twisting way they had of moving, let them burrow through stone, steel, and wood like nobody's business.

The snake venom from the magical snakes tended to have magical consequences, making their bites dangerous in whole new ways. Most people avoided the area, and those who traveled the river used magic shields to protect themselves.

As they passed through, snakes lunged at the boat, some launching up into the air almost as if they had wings. They struck viciously at the boat. Several landed on top of the boat shield, slithering in midair above and snapping their ire at the intruders. Ray couldn't help but watch them warily, even knowing they could not break through.

"Sometimes I wonder if they have their own witches," Annette said as she watched them slither and slide off the shield and drop back into the water. "If some of them can do spells."

"That's comforting," Ray said.

Just then, dizziness swept over him. He dropped down onto the bench straddling the stern of the boat. Black-and-gray splotches danced through his brain, reminding him of when he'd gotten clocked by a suspect with a beer bottle.

Annette grabbed his shoulder and pushed him back up as he started to slide sideways.

"What's wrong with you?"

Ray rubbed the heels of his hands into his eyes to clear the fuzziness. "I got attacked, too. I may have left the hospital a little earlier than I should have."

"Because this water dragon is in trouble and if you don't save her the city suffers," Leslie said.

Ray couldn't tell if she was mocking him or not. "That's right."

"How far out do you want to search?" she asked, not commenting on his sanity or lack of it. "She could have washed out to the ocean. If so, she could be just about anywhere by now."

That was Ray's second greatest fear, the first one being Kayla hadn't survived. "We'll turn around at the Columbia," he said. "We'll take the search upstream if we haven't found her by then."

"If she's as hurt as you say, she couldn't have swum upstream," Leslie pointed out with irritating logic.

He refused to concede that she might be right. Kayla wouldn't give up, and she would know that the only place she could get help was the Island. He gritted his teeth, wanting to slap himself for missing the obvious.

"The Island," he said urgently. "We need to go to the island. Now."

"Witch Island?" Annette said doubtfully using the slang name for Spider Island.

The two women exchanged doubtful looks.

"She'd go there for help if she could." And if she couldn't—he refused to allow it was a possibility.

"Suit yourself," Leslie said as she looped around and headed back through the squirming gauntlet of snakes.

Ray continued to monitor the banks and river for signs of Kayla. Annette dug a pair of binoculars out and handed them to him. He didn't know if he should be encouraged or discouraged when he didn't see her.

The return journey seemed to take forever. The passage to the Island frothed worse than the trip the night before. The whirlpools danced with waterspouts, the latter pinballing drunkenly across the water, and they seemed to have multiplied. Luckily Leslie was a helluva driver, swerving and dodging as she maneuvered them expertly through the chaos.

"Jesus Christ. What the hell happened?" Annette said as they approached the main cove of the Island.

Debris from the wrecked dock and boats floated in the water and collected along the shore. Ray didn't see any bodies, though a number of people had to have died.

"A whirlpool made it into the marina," he told his companions.

Leslie shook her head in mute shock, while Annette bit hard on her lower lip, her eyes wide, her cheeks pale.

Leslie reactivated the protective shield that she'd shut off when they'd left the snakes behind, nosing the boat through the debris field and up around the dog leg to where the marina used to be.

Ray wasn't sure what he'd expected to see. He'd been praying that he'd find Kayla alive and well. That the witches would have healed her and she'd be waiting impatiently for him.

But as they turned the bend and entered the little harbor, he saw nothing. Just the desolation of the marina's destruction. No witches and no Kayla. Nobody at all.

He dragged a shaking hand through his hair. His heart plummeted into his shoes. He'd been so damned sure she'd be here. So sure she'd come here for help.

Wire-thin pain drove into his chest, searing him with white-hot agony.

Where was she? How the hell was he going to find her?

Was she even alive?

Chapter 19

Kayla

WHEN SHE WOKE up, Kayla had returned to human form. She lay in a soft cozy bed. Where was she? What had happened?

Then the memories came crashing down. The lab, the creatures, fighting them, the pain, falling into the river, and being towed through the water.

She took stock of herself. She no longer hurt. She squinched her shoulders up and relaxed them. No pain. She touched her throat. No evidence of wounds, though her skin felt a little tender when she prodded.

She sat upright. She needed to get back. She had to find out what happened to Ray, Angie, and Zach.

Ray. Her throat tightened, remembering the wounds the creatures had inflicted upon him. Panic paralyzed her. Had he reached help in time?

It didn't seem possible. If the poison had hit her so hard in her other form, Ray's frail human body wouldn't have stood a chance.

An animal sound escaped her lips, and she kicked against the covers tangling her legs. She staggered to her feet, wobbling. She grabbed the bottom post of the bed to steady herself.

She stood in a small room containing a twin bed with a bookcase headboard, a closet, a small dresser, and a window between the latter two. An oval rag rug lay across the rough oak floor. A dim lamp on the headboard provided the light. But no, not a lamp. A witchlight.

A knock sounded on the door, and it swung open. A bright wedge of light fell into the room.

"You're awake," said Raven. "How do you feel?"

Kayla stared. She didn't know who she'd expected to see, but the witch hadn't made the list.

"Light of day," Raven said, and the witchlight brightened into morning bright. "How do you feel?"

"Better than I have a right to," Kayla said, scraping together what wits she could find and blinking against the sudden brilliance. "Pretty sure I should be dead. I take it I have you to thank for being alive?"

Raven nodded. "It was a close thing. Luckily the water folk brought you here and together we were able to siphon out the poison. The water helped you as well. It gave back what you've given it."

Kayla stared stupidly. "What *I've* given *it*?" She peed in the river occasionally, that was about all she gave it. "What are you talking about?" A frown creased her brows. "You know something about me. Who—no, *what* am I?" she asked finally.

Raven's eyes widened. "You don't know?"

"I know I'm a giant water-lizard-snake thing. But other than that, I don't know what else. I don't why you think I'm this Guardian of the River, whatever that means." Frustration made her voice rise.

Sympathy colored Raven's expression. "Maybe we should talk."

Kayla nodded, then shook her head. "I can't. I have to go. Ray was hurt. He could be—"

She couldn't put her fears into words. Her hands started to shake. God, what if he'd died?

The possibility rocked her, and it took everything she had to stay upright as her knees turned to gelatin. She caught the bedpost to steady herself again and frantically started searching for her shoes. She realized she was wearing blue cotton pajamas with little sheep roaming across them. "Where are my clothes?"

"In the dresser," Raven said, going to take them out of the top drawer. They'd been washed and folded. "But you don't have to worry. He survived his wounds."

Kayla stared blankly. "How could you possibly know?"

"Several witches work at the hospital. Sarah helped in his treatment and called me." She shrugged. "He's important to you, and therefore to all of us. Luckily the poison didn't affect him as severely as you."

Both revelations startled Kayla. She was important to all of whom? Because of the Guardian thing? But that wasn't as important as her other question. "He wasn't as affected? Why not?"

Raven hesitated. "We should talk. Get dressed and come downstairs. You need to eat. Calories will help you feel better. The injuries you sustained and the healing took a lot out of you. There's a bathroom across the hall. Shower if you like."

The witch didn't wait for an answer. She went out and vanished up the hall. Kayla stared blankly at the empty doorway. Ray was okay. Doubt gnawed at her. Wasn't he? She needed to see him for herself.

She flung off her borrowed pajamas and dressed, then went into the bathroom to pee. She splashed water on her face and quickly toweled it off. The fact that the shift magic didn't immediately surge in response to the wet had to be a testament to her exhaustion, or maybe it was because she'd just spent so many hours in her other form and was content for now. Not that she could remember much.

She leaned against the sink, her head hanging down as she closed her eyes. It had happened so fast. The eruption of the creatures out of the nymph's stomach like the *Alien* movie come to life, running to escape, and then her going back to fight the creatures. She hadn't had a choice. The urgency in Zach's voice as he told them to run had told her he couldn't hold them. They'd have killed him when his shield fell.

Whereas she'd been confident—no, she'd been totally certain—she could take them, sure that they couldn't really hurt her.

Stupid.

She'd been so, *so* very wrong.

Not that she'd do anything different if she had to choose again. Of all of them, she'd had the best chance to get out alive, and frankly the city needed Zach, Angie, and Ray a lot more than it needed her.

Ray.

It didn't make any sense that the poison affected her worse. Biologically, she had more mass in her other form, which meant that the poison should have worked faster on Ray.

She scrubbed her hands over her too-pale face, trying to wake her brain. He'd survived, Raven said, not that he was fine or whole, so that could still leave him paralyzed or a vegetable. Her stomach hollowed. He'd hate that. He'd hate anything that meant he couldn't be a cop. That was his entire life.

She swiped away the tear that escaped from the corner of one eye, swallowing the lump of rock in her throat. No. He had to be okay. Had to, that's all there was to it.

She opened the bathroom door and headed down the carpeted stairs. The only way to find out for sure was to ask for the details.

Kayla found Raven downstairs in the kitchen. The witch set two plates out on a dining room table big enough to seat a dozen people are more. The smell of brewing coffee wafted in the air, along with the scent of chicken soup.

"Sit," she said gesturing toward a seat at the end of the table.

"I can help."

"I've got it. You need rest."

Kayla did as told, thanking Raven when she poured her a cup of coffee. Kayla added cream from the little blue pitcher on the table.

"How long have I been out?"

"The water folk brought you here yesterday around six in the evening. It's now nine thirty."

"I was out twenty-seven hours?"

"And a half, plus however much time you were in the water."

"Probably five or six hours."

The lost time shook Kayla. Somehow it brought home how close she'd been to death. A chill ran through her, and she wrapped her hands around the warmth of her cup.

While Raven brought soup, bread, and butter to the table, Kayla sipped her coffee and examined her surroundings.

Next to her and running down the length of the wall were broad windows overlooking a deck. Two couches crowded in a small living area attached to the kitchen and dining room. Colorful pictures and textile art covered the walls, and thick rugs swathed the pine floors.

The kitchen looked pretty modern. Kayla didn't see any obvious signs of magic, though it was likely the whole place ran on it.

Witches could function around technology, but for most of them, their magic did better where there wasn't so much steel, which was ninety percent or more iron. The concentrated iron of the cities had kept the wild magic from mutating everything it came in contact with, though magic had found places to root all over Portland. Since then, Kayla couldn't escape the nagging impression that magic and technology were negotiating a kind of truce.

Raven ladled a bowl of soup and set it in front of Kayla and then served herself. Kayla immediately dug in to the food. Heaven in a bowl. For a while only the click and scrape of silverware broke the silence. Once the first bowl of soup took the edge off her hunger, Kayla slowed down and began to talk.

"So what exactly do you know about me? And *how* do you know about me?" she added, even though she expected the answer to the second question would be "magic," which was about as useful as saying water was wet. "But first tell me what's going on with Ray."

Raven set her spoon down and looked at Kayla. Kayla couldn't get over the combination of such a youthful face combined with old eyes, as if the witch had seen and done a whole lot that her body didn't reveal.

"How old are you anyway?" she blurted rudely.

Raven smiled. "I was born right around the end of the Great Depression," she said.

Kayla just blinked at her, trying to do the math in her head. "That makes you . . ."

"Right around 80," Raven said. "As for your friend, he left the hospital on his own feet and came here looking for you. He is resting now."

Resting? That didn't sound at all like Ray. She'd have expected him to be pacing up and down at the foot of her bed waiting for her to wake up. Or maybe not even waiting, but poking her with a sharp stick. She said so.

Raven shrugged. "He required rest for his own sake, and we required peace for your sake."

Kayla scowled. "What do you mean by *peace*?"

"Taking care of you needed concentration and quiet that he wasn't so inclined to give. He was very concerned for you and felt we weren't doing enough fast enough. He got a little agitated. So we put a sleep spell on him."

Worry clutched at Kayla's stomach. She couldn't say why. It wasn't that she doubted Ray was okay. Raven wouldn't lie about it, she didn't think. But amorphous anxiety urged her to check on him herself.

"I should go see him." Kayla started to stand. She couldn't get the memory of the creatures biting him and the blood soaking his jeans out of her head. Just thinking about it made her stomach ball up in an effort to eject the soup she'd just eaten.

"Of course, but first we must talk and you must finish eating. Your body needs to fuel."

"I won't take long. Where is he?"

"He's in another house, and is well cared for."

Kayla glared at the witch for a long moment. Raven stared back patiently. Clearly she had no intention of going anywhere until Kayla finished her meal and they talked. Kayla made an irritated sound and sank back into her chair. Pushing wouldn't get her anywhere, and would also be unforgivably rude. Raven had been nothing but helpful—above and beyond the call of duty.

That made her remember the early morning terror of the whirlpool and the drowning children. "What happened to the kids? Are they okay?"

Raven closed her eyes a moment as if in silent prayer. "Thanks to you, they will recover. Luckily they were shifter children. Humans wouldn't have survived."

"I may have got them out," Kayla said, "but you saved their lives, didn't you?"

The witch gave a dismissive little nod, clearly unwilling to accept credit. "Several of us were able to give them the healing they needed, just as we helped you."

"Thank you for that, and for helping Ray. I know witches aren't big fans of the cops."

Raven's smile was bleak with memory. "You'd be surprised. As for the healing—we try to make up for the war as best we can," she said. "Humans have little reason to trust us, and rightfully so. Even now, many of my kind continue to make war on humans."

"So we've got good witches and wicked witches?" Kayla asked with raised brows.

"Just don't call me Glinda," said Raven with a slight smile. "But right now we should talk about what happened."

"Okay, let's talk. Let's start with the Guardian of the River thing. I get the feeling you think there's more to me than there is."

Raven poured herself more coffee. "Actually, the truth is that I *know* there's more to you than *you* think there is."

"I'm listening."

"What happened? How did you become a shifter?"

"I thought you were going to tell me about myself."

"I am. Let's begin with how you changed."

Kayla lifted a brow, but decided to follow Raven down memory lane. She closed her eyes, thinking back. The day of Magicfall had been beautiful. Clear with an endless blue sky. And cold, as if there might even be snow. Mount Hood shined bright in the morning sun. She'd been the only one on the river. She'd been dressed head to toe in neoprene to keep herself warm. Everything had been perfect.

And then everything had *changed.*

Her body clenched at the memory, her heart starting to pound. The words tumbled out as she fell back into time.

"I'd gone kayaking. Just after sunrise. Everything was fine, and then the world exploded." Mount Hood erupted, as did Mount St. Helens and Mount Jefferson. All the Cascade volcanoes rumbled to life. Instead of ash and fire, they spewed fireworks that broke into sparks and floated through the air like blown dandelion seeds.

"It was gloriously beautiful. Like a rainbow had broken into a billion butterflies." Kayla shook her head. "I watched the show. I had no idea what was happening, but how could anything so beautiful be bad? Little did I know." She took a deep breath, trying to steady her racing heart.

"As they fell, they tended to bunch up. It almost seemed like they were alive. And then they started landing."

That's when the world had gone on an acid trip.

The ground had shaken and rumbled and bucked. The river had turned mad, not knowing which direction to flow. Kayla had been down past Oregon City and right in the middle of the first of the roller-coaster hills that rose in the river's bed and even now played havoc with boat travel. The river had stretched like taffy as the ground rose up under it and then dropped and risen, undulating like rope when you wiggle a length of it up and down. When it was done, the river had resembled a log ride with steep hills going up and down for an entire mile.

Kayla had paddled for her life, but had quickly been dumped into the water. It churned and twisted, dragging her under and spitting her up into the air. She had been driven against boulders and trees. Bones broke and if not for her neoprene suit, she'd have been fricasseed. She'd lost all sense of up or down. Occasionally she'd break into air and could breathe before the water drove her under again.

"I should have drowned."

"But you didn't. Why?"

She'd fetched up against a fallen western red cedar, its roots wedged between rocks on the bank. She'd started to slip down below it and had clung to a limb with what small might she had left.

That's when it found her. A ball of blue glitter the size of a hummingbird and zooming around about as fast. It came streaking down from the sky, dodging and zigging until it came hurtling toward Kayla. She didn't have time to think. She hung on the limb, panting and battered. The glitterball streaked straight at her and into her mouth, almost as if it had been searching for her.

It exploded. Quills of ice and fire punched through her flesh and bones. She didn't have a lot of memories after that. She transformed, that much she knew. She'd spent a long time in her other form. She remembered . . . eating . . . magic. Scooping it out of the air and water. She'd been there through the upheaval under the water as the ground dropped into a giant canyon filled now by the lake surrounding the Island. She'd watched the underwater mountain rise and sprout forests and glaciers and reefs.

Eventually, she'd crawled up on a bank to sun herself and when she'd dried, she learned she could turn back to human. After that, she'd had to figure out how to live. And she'd quit her job.

"You were chosen," Raven said when Kayla had finished.

"I always figured I'd won the crap lottery. Bad luck."

Raven shook her head. "No, from what you've said, it's clear that the power that came to you was searching."

"For me?" Kayla said doubtfully.

"Maybe." Raven shrugged. "There's no way to know why it picked you specifically, but it's likely it was drawn to you in particular."

Kayla didn't know if she bought that. "Maybe I was the only one close by."

"It had the whole city to choose from, not to mention all the surrounding cities. No, something about you fit its needs."

"Needs? You're making it sound like it's some kind of sentient being—or a parasite." The idea made the food in Kayla's stomach bubble alarmingly. Was something living inside her? Using her for its own ends?

"Not sentient, and not a parasite," Raven said, and then hesitated, clearly searching for words. "I don't know how to explain it."

"Just spit it out," Kayla said. It could hardly get worse.

Raven sighed. "You are aware that the gods of most of the religions of the world actually exist?"

Kayla frowned, not liking the direction this conversation was taking. "No."

"Well they do. Maybe not in the form that the worshippers believe, or with the powers, but they do exist. From Zeus to Jesus to Quetzalcoatl and everything in between. They all exist—those that aren't dead, that is."

"Gods can't be killed," Kayla protested, as if that made any sense at all, or was remotely important in this conversation.

"Jesus was killed, wasn't he?"

"He was raised from the dead."

"But that doesn't change the fact that he did, in fact, die."

"So you're saying he really does exist?"

"I presume so, though he's of the general collection of gods that doesn't interact with the real world much. At least, not anymore."

Kayla sat a moment, just staring as she processed the conversation.

"What does any of this have to do with me?"

"Little is really known about the divine in general. How they become gods—whether they are born or ascend to a state of divinity. However, one thing that we do know is that some gods will send off fragments of themselves. Or maybe they are more like seeds. Either way, they take a splinter of themselves and put it out in the world. The beings who absorb or are infected, if you prefer, with these splinters, become divine. They share the powers and abilities of the parent god."

Raven stopped and just looked at Kayla, waiting.

Kayla's lungs squeezed with something like panic "You're saying that the thing I swallowed was one of these god seeds." Saying the words out loud sounded so ridiculous, she started laughing. It was ludicrous. Impossible.

For a moment, her laughter took on an edge of hysteria. But then she looked at Raven's deadly serious expression and her laughter died. "How? How could you possibly know? You weren't there. I swallowed wild magic, that's all. I'm no god. I couldn't even save myself from some rabid dog-beasts. How is that godlike?"

The sympathy in Raven's expression made Kayla's teeth itch. Irritation dragged its fingernails across her bones. She folded her arms across her chest, glaring at the witch. She didn't have to prove she *wasn't* a god; Raven had to prove she *was*. And that was going to be impossible, because the witch was wrong. Dead wrong.

Raven reached for a carved wood box at the end of the table and pulled it toward her. She opened the lid, revealing a stone wand of silvery-white, translucent rock, about seven inches long and an inch in diameter. It lay on a bed of green velvet.

"This is selenite," she said, picking it up and turning the polished length in her fingers. "Named after a goddess of the moon—Selene. It's useful in healing and it holds other mystical properties." She offered it to Kayla. "Here, hold it."

This wasn't just a show and tell. Raven was proving her point. For a long moment, Kayla just stared at the rock without moving. *Stop being such a coward*, she told herself acidly. *If you're a god, then you're a god and you'll deal with whatever the fuck that means.* She just knew it couldn't be good.

She reluctantly took the stone wand from Raven. The moment her fingers touched the polished surface, it began to glow brilliant blue and gold—much the same colors as her scales in her other form.

She dropped the selenite wand onto the tablecloth, and its color faded back to white. "What happened?"

Raven picked up the wand and returned it to the box. "It confirms that you are indeed divine in nature."

Questions pounded against the inside of Kayla's skull. How the hell could she be a god? What kind of god? What was she supposed to do with that knowledge? She scraped her wits together. She'd been a detective—a puzzle solver at the job's most basic level. She could solve the mystery of her own self, starting with gathering all the facts that she could. "What made you think I was a god in the first place?"

"It took us a while," Raven admitted. "We knew that something or someone was having a positive effect on the river in the city."

"Positive effect? What does that mean?"

"Over the years, we began to see a kind of energy and vigor in the river and city that wasn't natural. At first we thought maybe a coven was responsible, or possibly a sorcerer or mage. The kind of power involved is substantial. We spoke to a spectrum of witches and covens from all over the world, but it soon became obvious that no witch, mage, or sorcerer could sustain that level of magic without us being able to track it. That left us looking at other options, and the only reasonable conclusion was that we were looking at some sort of divine intervention."

Though Kayla wanted to know more about the specifics, now wasn't the time. "So why me?"

"We started with a number of options. We believed that whoever was responsible had to live here. Then we simply watched, looking for anyone who might fit the bill."

"What sorts of things were you looking for?"

"A variety of things, but the main one we wanted to find was the epicenter. The magic had to extend outward from the source, like ripples in the water after you drop a rock in it. We were able to narrow it down to the general vicinity of the river in the downtown. Once we realized that the source had to be comfortable both in and out of the water, we realized you were the most likely possibility. You confused us, because when in human form, you read like a human. There is no evidence you are anything else.

"We were fairly certain we were right, but we continued to search for any other possibilities. Gradually we winnowed away the other options, until you were the only one left. The wand"—Raven motioned toward the box—"just confirms what we already know."

Kayla digested this information. "Okay, say I believe you. What's it mean? What do you want from me? What kind of god am I, anyway?"

"That," Raven said with a grimace, "is less clear. I was hoping you knew."

Kayla couldn't help but laugh. "So I'm the god of who knows what? How many gods can there possibly be?"

"Thousands. Tens of thousands."

"How is that even possible? How come we don't see more of them walking around turning wine in the water and walking on air?"

"Actually, they are walking around among us quite a bit. You are not the only god in town."

Kayla's mouth fell open. "How many are in Portland?"

Raven shrugged. "They don't advertise themselves, and I'm sure there are those who—like you—do not know what they are, but we know of twenty or thirty, and suspect the number is closer to a hundred."

"Just walking around and living their lives? Just like everybody else?"

"More or less. There seems to be a general agreement that they will share this territory and not fight. Though it's possible the peace is the consequence of your existence here."

"If I didn't know I'm a god, and I didn't know that they were gods, then how could I make them behave?"

"We think that one of the things you do as a god, is make wherever you are a fertile place, healthy, and generally content. We think that also extends to other gods. As I told you, you are a guardian. The river is your natural domain, but that includes the area around it. The longer you live here, the greater your influence extends. You, for lack of a better description, are both mother nature and mother justice. Life thrives anywhere you are. Your human and divine natures make you want to protect others."

Kayla rubbed her eyes. This was getting to feel like some sort of psychotherapy session. She had a crazy urge to lie down on the couch and talk about her mother. She snorted inwardly. Her mother was the least of her family problems. Her father was Tony Soprano and Sweeney Todd rolled up into one scary package. If she were to talk to a therapist about anybody, it would be him.

Thinking of him reminded her that her grandmother and aunt were missing, and that time was running out. Enough with the god shit. She could deal with that later. She needed to wake up Ray and get back to work solving the kidnapping and finding the witchkin murderer.

As if reading her mind, Raven's next words chilled Kayla to the bone.

"The creatures that attacked you nearly killed you because their poison specifically targets divine creatures. Ray's wounds were ugly and the poison did hurt him, but had very little effect compared to you. Left to your own devices, you would have been dead by now."

"But I wasn't their main target, was I? Otherwise they would have kept after me until I was dead." *Oh, fuck.* Those things were loose in the city somewhere. But the technomages would surely have gone after them.

Raven nodded. "They are here to hunt someone else, and given all the ritual killings, I'm afraid of what lengths they and their master will go to, to achieve their mission. Did that information I gave you lead you anywhere?"

"Not yet. Cops are canvassing and there's a tip line. Hoping to get some sense of where the killer is holing up." Kayla pushed back from the table. "I've got a bad feeling the clock is ticking down to zero and if we don't figure out what's going on pretty quick, I'm afraid it will be too late." She wasn't entirely sure what *too late* actually meant. Armageddon? Whatever it was, people were going to die. That much, she knew in every cell of her body. So she had to find the creatures and their masters and stop them. "Where's Ray?"

This time Raven didn't try to stop Kayla. "I'll take you."

Raven led her outside. The little house looked like one of those you'd find in fairytales. A little ramshackle and a little odd in its shape and proportions. Flowers grew in window boxes and down the front walkway. Roses climbed up the walls on either side of the door and crawled across the roof. The night was fragrant, and the sounds of crickets and night birds gave the impression of tranquility.

"So, what do you think is coming?" Kayla asked, not entirely sure she wanted to hear the answer.

"Now that we know someone is hunting a god, we think that the actual killing—or the battle between the god and his opponent—will cause great destruction to the city. There's a reason why gods don't spend a lot of their time fighting with each other. None of them like the scorched earth that generally results. Whatever reason the hunter has for killing this particular god, he thinks the consequent destruction is worth the price. He may also be a god, which means his powers may be stronger than we can imagine."

Kayla was now entirely certain she had *not* wanted to hear the answer. Unfortunately, she didn't have a head injury or amnesia, so forgetting wasn't an option.

Every muscle in her body had pulled tight in rejection of everything Raven had told her. Her brain shied from the idea of being a god. A *god*. She couldn't be one. She had *no idea* how to be divine, and more importantly, she didn't want that kind of responsibility. Gods messed with people's *lives*, for crap's sake. That sort of thing was the real God's job.

She didn't let herself think about that logic, or she might go insane. Which, at this point, was a better option than being divine.

"Tossing me into the mix could make things exponentially worse, couldn't it?" she asked. "I mean, if I'm a god, too. Three fighting is worse than two, right?" It was almost impossible to get her tongue around those bizarre syllables.

"Not *if*. You *are* a god," Raven said. "And yes, two could be worse than one, but if you can stop them from annihilating Portland, it's worth a shot, don't you think?"

Her tone had developed a vinegar tang, which Kayla interpreted as—*pull up your big girl panties already and deal with it*. But she needed a few more minutes to adjust, maybe a minute or two to scream and cry and throw a tantrum, and then she'd grab hold of her panties and hoist. Unfortunately, she wasn't up for a public tantrum, so she was going to have to skip it for the moment.

"Ray is going to shit a brick when he hears this," she muttered, her stomach dropping into her boots.

"He already knows," Raven said, guiding Kayla to a path through the surrounding trees.

Kayla stopped dead. "He does? How? What did he say?"

"We told him in the hospital. He immediately left and went searching for you on the river."

Which meant he hadn't run screaming into the night. In fact, he'd come looking her. That boded well. It didn't mean he wouldn't recover his sanity and go galloping off, but at least she didn't have to break the news.

Raven led her through the woods about half a mile to a clearing that contained three cottages. They all looked quaint, like something out of the English countryside. One even had a thatched roof. Lights illuminated the windows of the middle one—made of brick with Tudor accents.

Raven knocked on the door, and soon a slender young man in his early twenties appeared. His gaze went immediately to Kayla.

"You're looking much better," he said to Kayla, swinging the door wide for them to enter.

"Thanks. Did you help take care of me?"

He nodded. "Yep."

"Thanks for that, too. I'm looking after Ray." Kayla craned her neck looking for him, but the dining room and the kitchen through the archway looked empty.

"I sent Stanna and Evan to bed," the male witch explained to Raven. "They couldn't stay awake." He held his hand out to Kayla. "I'm Jerry Van Rine. Welcome."

She shook hands, appreciating his warm, firm grip. Nothing worse than a sweaty, fish-grip. "Where's Ray?"

He tilted his chin toward the hallway leading out of the small dining room. "Second one on the right, after the bathroom. You should be able to wake him up. The spell has about worn off."

Kayla nodded and practically sprinted down the hallway. Not that she was eager to talk to Ray about being a god. *Goddess?* Why two names? That was just sexist. Kayla mostly just wanted to see for herself that he was okay.

Ray lay in a queen bed. His exposed shoulders and upper chest were bare. His chest rose and fell in an even rhythm. His naturally tanned skin looked healthy. She moved to the side of the bed, lifting the covers to peer under.

He was naked, with no signs of bandages or scars. Just hard angles and curves wrapped in lickable tawny skin.

She should have put dropped the blankets, but she couldn't help admiring the scenery.

When he mumbled something, she let go of the blankets and jumped backward, her face flushing. He merely turned on his side.

That was close. She so didn't need him catching her ogling him.

Stepping forward, she put a hand on his shoulder. Hot satin over stone. She couldn't resist the urge to skim her fingers along his bicep up over his shoulder and along the taut span of his back.

Reminding herself that if he had been awake, he'd have slapped her questing hand away, she gripped his shoulder firmly and shook him.

"Hey, Ray. Wake up."

She wasn't prepared for his instant response. He snatched her arm, snake-quick, hauling her across him. He grabbed her neck and twisted, flipping her onto her back. He jammed a knee into her belly, still clutching her throat.

She lay stiff and gasping, too shocked to struggle. For a moment he was silent as his brain caught up with defensive instinct.

He frowned as awareness returned. "Kayla?"

She nodded slightly, his hand preventing any other movement.

"Fuck." He yanked his hands away. "What—?" He looked around the room and then down at himself.

Kayla barely had a moment to glimpse his very respectable man-parts before he jumped up and wrapped the sheet around himself.

"What the hell? Where did you come from? Where is this place?" Then memory hit. His eyes widened, and he went still. "You're okay. *Are* you okay? They got the poison out?"

He reached out to help her sit up, then pulled up her shirt so he could examine her back. He ran gentle fingers over her skin.

"Does it hurt?" he asked in a rough voice.

"No. I'm good."

He jerked her back around to face him. "Dammit! You could have died."

She could practically hear his teeth grinding together over the words. She managed a weak smile. "Just another day in paradise."

That had been their catchphrase for those seriously fucked-up days on the job, both well aware there was no other place they'd rather be.

"Shit, Kayla." He stared down at her with an intent expression she couldn't read, but it sent a horde of crickets jumping and popping around in her stomach.

Abruptly he pulled her against his chest, wrapping his arms tightly around her, his face pressing into the crook of her neck.

"You scared the ever-loving shit out of me."

"I'm sorry. I didn't know those creatures could hurt me that way. I didn't know I was—" She stumbled and made a face. "You know."

"A god?" He lifted his head to look at her but didn't loosen his grip on her.

She flushed and looked away. "Yeah." She started to push out of his grip.

His arms tightened. "Don't."

She went still, looking back at him. The ferocity of his gaze pinned her in place.

"I—"

Her voice faded to nothing. She had no idea what she wanted to say. Her tongue seemed to be paralyzed. All she could do was feel. And she felt glorious.

Being held by Ray sent little explosions of excitement and desire through her. She was all too aware of his bare skin beneath her hands. She fought the urge to fan her fingers over the ridges and valleys of his muscles and stroke down the elegant curve of his back.

Then she realized he was shaking. As in, emotional overload.

"I'm okay," she managed by way of reassurance.

He shook his head; she could see him putting walls around his emotions, shutting them down. "You're killing me, Smalls," he groaned.

"Did you just quote *The Sandlot* at me? That movie is older than dirt."

"It's a classic, and anyway, you've seen it plenty of times, too, so you can just keep your insults to yourself, Miss Kettle."

The intensity of his look had not diminished, though he clearly sought to lighten the mood.

"So, I've been wondering . . . how the hell could you let those beasts own you like that?" His mouth twisted in what might have been an attempt at a smile. Or it might have been a snarl. Hard to tell. "I mean—you're five times the size of them with knives at the ends of all your fingers. You should have wiped the floor with them. I thought you were better than that."

She pinched him. "If I'd known they could bite through my scales, I'd have fought differently. Nothing ever has bit through before."

"Rookie move, making assumptions." He shook his head in a show of sorrow. "You've lost your touch."

At a loss for a witty comeback, Kayla resorted to sticking her tongue out at him. His gaze dropped to her mouth, his arms tightening a fraction. Her heart lurched. Did he—? Was that—?

Before she could let herself go more than a few steps down that tempting and very forbidden trail of thought, Ray dropped his arms and backed away.

"Where are my clothes?"

"Try the dresser. That's where they stashed mine," Kayla suggested. "You been working out?" she asked, because the quiet was too much for her.

He glanced over his shoulder. "Maybe. See anything you like?" He swished his sheet-shrouded butt from side to side.

Kayla snorted and laughed. "In your dreams." And in hers, but that was a secret he really didn't need to know.

"You wound me. Now unless you want to see the rest of the goods, you'd best turn yourself around."

As much as she wouldn't have minded getting another good look, she turned, listening to the rustle of his clothes as he dressed.

"Have you been dating? Or maybe you got married?" Kayla asked suddenly. She hadn't seen a wedding ring, but that didn't mean anything. Ray wasn't exactly a jewelry kind of guy.

Why did the possibility deflate her completely?

"Not married, not dating anybody at the moment," Ray said after a moment. "I've kept pretty busy."

"What about—?" Kayla dug through her memory for the name of the woman he'd been seeing just before Magicfall. That one had been more serious than his normal pattern of short-term affairs. She'd been an ophthalmologist. She and Ray had been going out for a couple months at that point, which counted as a long relationship for him.

"Audrey?" he said, finishing her question. "She disappeared."

Like a lot of others who'd been transformed into something else or died during Magicfall or the war. "I'm sorry. That had to be rough." Wow. Impressive. Talk about the lamest offering of condolences ever.

She turned around when Ray didn't say anything. Dressed now, he leaned back against the dresser and eyed her broodingly.

"It pissed me off," he said finally, then shook his head. "Audrey and I had already figured out we weren't going anywhere romantically, but . . ." His mouth twisted. "I looked for her. She was a good woman—a good person. She deserved a lot better than to just . . . disappear." His jaw muscles flexed. "That damned magic hurt so many people."

From what Kayla understood, it had also returned life to a lot of magical beings as well. Beings who had been slowly suffocating in the human world. So, did they deserve to die so humans could own the world? Or did the humans who'd overrun their world deserve it?

She didn't have any good answers. She sighed and ran her hands over her head. "I'm sorry I wasn't there to help. I should have been." Should have found a way to be there for him. Should have figured out how to deal with shifting without abandoning him and her job. Should have just sucked it up and told him about herself and dealt with the fallout instead of running away.

His brows winged down and he straightened, taking two swift strides to stand in front of her. "Don't do that."

Kayla tried to smile and failed. She felt tired, as if she weighed a thousand pounds. "Don't do what?"

"Audrey wasn't your fault."

"Didn't say she was."

"Yeah, but you're thinking it."

"You read minds now? That's got to make getting women into bed easier." She started to turn away. This was not a conversation she wanted to have. "We should go."

Ray caught her wrist. "Dammit, Kayla. Hold still a minute, would you?"

"We don't have time—"

"We'll make time. Just listen to me for a minute."

She sighed. *Suck it up, Reese*, she told herself. *Whatever he has to say, just deal with it. Stop running, stop hiding.*

    "What's on your mind?" she asked, making herself meet his gaze.

    That intensity had returned. Her stomach tightened. This was not going to be good.

Chapter 20

Ray

NOW HE SHOULD tell her he was a witch. Tell her that she hadn't been the only one to undergo a transformation. The words stuck like chicken bones in his throat. What a hypocrite he was. Kayla clearly didn't have any issues with witches, but he'd made such an ass of himself over her not trusting him with her secret, how would she feel when she found out he'd done the same thing?

He'd been so damned angry after Magicfall. Angry at the magic, angry at becoming a witch, angry at the world going to hell. He dumped it all on Kayla when she left until all of it became the same thing and it was all her fault. Four years later he hadn't dealt with any of it. In fact, it had only gotten worse the more he thought about her, and the more he missed her.

If he didn't fix things with her soon, if he didn't tell her he was a witch, he could lose her again. And she'd be right to walk away. He'd made her the scapegoat of all that had happened to him, when he'd been the one to drive her away with his assholery.

She had a wary look like a dog expecting to get kicked and standing there bravely waiting for it to happen. He despised himself for putting that expression on her face. He despised himself for a whole lot of things. The past couple of days had gone a long way toward clarifying his priorities. No, these last days had revealed his priorities. Hell, he disobeyed his captain and ditched Dix, not because of the job, but because of Kayla.

Right now, she was the most important thing in his life. His job was a close second, but it definitely was second after her. That scared the shit out of him. He could control his job, but he couldn't control her. The one thing he knew for sure was that he couldn't afford to screw up with her again.

"I'm sorry," he said.

Her brows furrowed. "Come again?"

"Laying all the blame on you. If I hadn't been such an asshole, you might have told me what happened to you. Instead you had to do this all alone. I wanted you there for me, but I wasn't there for you."

About halfway through his speech she started shaking her head. "No, I was too afraid, and it was too new, too awful. I wouldn't have told you."

He could tell she was just trying to make him feel better which only pissed him off. Mostly because he deserved the opposite. She ought to be pissed as hell at him for acting like such a douche.

His hand on her arm tightened, and he forced himself to relax it, absently rubbing his thumb on the inside of her wrist. He felt her pulse jumping, and scowled. Was she scared of him? God but he'd fucked up more than he'd known.

His mind flashed to a few minutes earlier when he'd held her in his arms. It had taken every scrap of willpower he'd had not to kiss her and peel off her clothes. His dick had gone as hard as a crowbar. Luckily she hadn't noticed.

"Maybe," he said. "Maybe not. I acted like a spoiled brat. I made it impossible for you to talk to me." And did without her in his life for four years because of it. *Jackass.* No wonder none of his relationships worked. He'd been pining for Kayla. And if he wanted to keep her in his life, he'd keep on pining, he told himself firmly. *Do not fuck this second chance up.*

She started to say something else.

"Look, just let me finish, okay?" He had to tell her about being a witch.

Before he could say anything, Raven appeared in the doorway, looking grim. "There's news. You should come."

"It can't wait?" he asked Raven.

The witch shook her head.

Kayla looked almost relieved. "We'll make time later, okay? Tell me then."

Ray reluctantly let go of Kayla, and they followed Raven into the living room. He'd tell her later. As soon as he had another opening.

Waiting for them in the living room were two other witches. He recognized Jerry from the night before, but he didn't recall the woman. She was short, maybe 5'3" with broad shoulders and muscular arms, as if she lifted weights. Her red hair was shaved above the ears and spiked up a couple inches on her head. Her skin looked like it hadn't seen the sun her whole life, but what caught his attention was the odd clash of excitement and concern on her expression.

"You remember Jerry?" Raven asked.

Ray nodded and shook the witch's hand. "I take it I have you to thank for the nap?"

Jerry nodded unrepentantly. "You were getting underfoot."

"This is Laina Requa," Raven said, introducing the redheaded witch. "She's been doing some research for us."

"What kind of research?" Kayla asked.

"Come. Let's sit down." Raven gestured to the kitchen table, and they took seats around it.

Jerry poured coffee, and he'd already set out cream and sugar along with raspberry muffins and butter.

"What's going on?" Ray didn't like the worried looks on their faces, or the tense way Raven looked at Kayla as if she thought Kayla might drop dead at any second.

"In the course of healing you," Raven said to Kayla, "we drew some blood. Laina used to be a chemistry professor at Reed. She specializes now in potions and magical edibles."

"Edibles?" Ray knew there was a market for them. As with pot edibles, they came in all sorts of forms from brownies to gummy bears to suckers. The difference was that magical edibles had magical results. You didn't always know how skilled the witch who made them was, and you couldn't be sure you were getting what was promised. Nothing was regulated.

"We've all got to make a living," said Laina in a light, musical voice.

"We had her analyze your blood. We wanted to find out more about the poison. We took samples both before healing and after."

Raven looked at Laina and nodded for the other witch to take over the narrative.

"In the pre-healing sample, we extracted some of the poison to get a better sense of its properties and try to create an antidote," said the redheaded witch. "With the second sample we wanted to ascertain whether you had any residue in your system that might prove toxic."

"And?" Kayla prompted when Laina stopped.

"You've got a problem," the witch said bluntly.

She drew a small clear glass vial out of her pocket and set it on the table. Fine silvery-white dust coated the inside. Ray didn't have to ask to know that it was the dust from the Fountain Square murders.

"You know what this is?" Laina asked.

Kayla nodded, and then shook her head. "That stuff was everywhere when I found the bodies at Keller Fountain," she said. "Some of it absorbed into my skin. I take it that it's not as inert as I'd hoped it was?"

"Probably is for most people."

"But not for me?" Kayla grimaced.

"One of my specialties is figuring out what an unactivated spell will do," said Laina. "Particularly with edibles and other ingested things. A lot depends on what the edible is made from. Just like with anything else, if you mix this and that and a little more of this, you will get a predictable outcome. Edible magic is that way. If you've got a certain combination of herbs, minerals, and other enrichments, you'll most likely end up with certain kinds of spells. Most of the time I can refine my findings not only to a particular class of spells, but to the actual spell itself. Or at least I can usually make a good guess."

"So, what am I dealing with?" Kayla asked.

"Well, let's start with the bad first and move down the list to the worst. I have no idea what is. It's clearly meant to be inhaled or absorbed through the skin, but other than that, I have no idea."

Ray scowled, foreboding clutching his heart. "You said there is worse."

"I was able to extract the poison from the blood sample. It's really more of a venom. I mixed a little dust with it to see what would happen. Nothing. Then I mixed in a drop of your blood. Still nothing. Then I activated the powder."

Her expression was irritatingly sympathetic as she looked at Kayla. As though she was about to issue a death sentence, followed by a "nothing we can do," speech. Ray tensed, like he could somehow protect Kayla from whatever news was coming.

"Spit it out," Kayla said looking resigned.

"The powder makes the venom ten times as potent, maybe more. Together they would destroy all your red blood cells in under a minute. You're lucky it hadn't been activated or you wouldn't have made it fifty feet before you dropped dead."

Ray felt as if someone had kicked him in his solar plexus. He struggled to pull in a breath. "Can you get it out of her?"

"I'm afraid not," Laina said. "To do it we would have to put you on a bypass machine and run your blood through a filtering system. Even so, we probably wouldn't get it all. I'm pretty sure it's left deposits in your organs, as well as your brain and circulatory system. It's designed to stay in the body."

"What if we activated it now, when there's no venom in me anymore?" Kayla asked. "How long would it last before it used up all its strength?"

"We don't know," said Jerry. "Only the witch who cast the spell knows."

"This makes going after those creatures more interesting." Kayla drummed her fingers on the table as she thought.

"We can give you a shield spell," Raven said. "But there's no guarantee it will work against the creatures. Your best bet is to stay as far away from them as you can get."

"That's not an option," Ray said before Kayla could answer.

If he had his way he'd lock Kayla up in a deep mine somewhere until the bloodthirsty creatures were destroyed. But he wasn't going to get his way. He knew damned well she wasn't going to give up pursuing them. He wouldn't have in her shoes. So, if he couldn't stop her, he'd do his damnedest to help her and keep her safe

Raven nodded as if she'd expected nothing different. "It should only take an hour or two to build one that might protect you."

"Then you'll have to deliver it," Ray said. "If we can figure out their target, then we might be able to get the drop on them. I'd rather be the one setting the trap than the one walking into it."

"What do you plan to do?" asked Jerry.

"Find someone who can tell us what those symbols mean for starters," Kayla said. "I don't suppose any of you recognized the description of those creatures?"

"We have people researching both. A lot of our reference books were lost after Magicfall, and in books we do have, many of the descriptions of beasts and magical creatures don't match very well with reality. We hope to find something soon."

Raven looked at Jerry. "I'm going with them. You work with the others on a shield spell and bring it when it's done. Bring everybody with you. We'll need the help."

"I don't know if they'll come. I don't know if they'll want to risk themselves for humans."

Raven's lips flattened, her eyes narrowing. The air thickened and became hard to breathe. The hair on the back of Ray's neck stood up.

"They can come help, or they can leave the Island. Make it clear that I have no room for those who refuse to come," she said in an icy voice.

Jerry stiffened like she'd struck him. His eyes narrowed, but he just stood up and walked wordlessly out of the house.

"You'd better go with him," she said to Laina who looked a little shell-shocked. "They'll need you when creating the shield spell."

"I have a question," Kayla said, looking at Laina. "Am I susceptible to the powder in my human form?"

The redheaded witch frowned. Then shook her head. "I don't know. Why wouldn't you be?"

"I don't read as a god in this body. I'm pretty vanilla human until I transform."

"It's possible you wouldn't be affected, but I wouldn't bet the farm. I could draw more blood and test it if you want to come to my lab. Shouldn't take long."

Kayla gave Ray a questioning look.

He ran his tongue along sharp edges of his teeth and then shook his head. "Not a lot of point, is there? What are the odds you will face the creatures in your human form? They'd chop you to pieces, and you'd still end up dead. At least in the water dragon form you can fight, and maybe kill them before they bite you."

Kayla nodded agreement and then looked back at Raven. "I could use a charge on my amulet," she said pulling it out from under her collar and dragging it over her head. "It dries me out so I can transform back to human." She pulled the silver cuff off her wrist and set it down with the amulet. "This one too. It douses me in water so I can transform easily." Her cheeks flushed. "I don't have much control at this point in either direction."

Ray scowled. She was as bad as he was with his magic, though he was certain she'd at least tried to gain control. On the other hand, he'd learned as little as possible as if that would somehow cure what had happened. He'd never regretted it as much as he did now. He had a weapon that could help protect Kayla, and no idea how to use it.

He eyed Raven. He was pretty sure she'd teach him. All he had to do was ask. And he would. Just as soon as Kayla was safe and this case—cases—were closed.

"We should go," Raven said, picking up the amulets. "I can refresh these on our way."

"Who are you going to talk to?" asked Laina as she stood, tucking the powder vial back into her pocket.

"About the symbols?" Ray asked. "I figure the library is our best option."

"You know I had a couple of colleagues at Reed who specialize in ancient civilizations and languages. They might be able to point you in the right direction and narrow your search. Let me give you their names."

Laina grabbed a pad of paper and a pen from another one of her pockets. She jotted down the names and handed the paper to Ray. "I don't know where they live."

He glanced at the page. "We'll find them." He'd have to call in a request, which meant he'd have to deal with Crice. Or he could call Logan. The technomage could easily find out their addresses and numbers, and Ray could get an update on the lab results from two crime scenes and anything they'd learned about the creatures that had erupted from the nymph. On the other hand, he needed to see if the tip line had turned anything up yet, not to mention the canvassing of the scenes Raven had given them.

"Let's go," Raven said. "We'll have to make a quick stop at my place."

The three remained silent as they walked to her cottage. The night felt balmy with a hint of rain. Energy crackled in the air like the promise of a thunderstorm.

Kayla walked ahead of him, following Raven.

She didn't limp and showed no obvious signs of the attack. But her shoulders slumped with exhaustion she couldn't hide. Neither of them had had much rest in the past couple of days, and getting hurt hadn't helped. Not that she'd crack under pressure, but they already knew that the three beasts would be tough. Add in their master and the god it was hunting, and Ray didn't know if Kayla could withstand them. If she couldn't, then she'd be dead—only death would stop her—and Portland would be next into the toilet.

They needed help.

He brooded on the problem all the way to Raven's. He and Kayla waited in the kitchen while the witch went about her business. Kayla poured them both coffee.

"I need to tell you something," he said as she sank into a chair.

She stiffened, her hands closing around her mug tightly. She visibly braced herself as she gave him a wary look. "What's up?"

And then before he could say anything, she raced forward, words spilling out in a rapid torrent. "This is insane. I've no idea what I'm doing. I have no powers to counter these gods or those creatures. Plus, if I get bitten, I'll be useless. Tech kept Magicfall from totally destroying the city, but if I've been influencing things like Raven says I have, that means tech can't withstand divine magic, otherwise I wouldn't have had any influence on Portland. The devastation could be massive."

She swallowed hard. "Ray, people are going to die and they don't even know it's coming. We should do something—get word out. Warn people. Evacuate the city. Something."

"You know we can't. It would just create panic. The roads and river would be jammed up in no time. It would be gridlock. There'd be riots and fights. Plus, we have no idea where the epicenter of this god fight will be. We could send people into the heart of the fire."

"We can't just do nothing."

"We aren't doing nothing. Raven's going to help and so is her coven. I'll call Logan and get him to put the technomages on alert. Soon as we know anything, we'll call them in to help us."

"What if it's not enough?"

"It'll be enough."

She just stared at him.

"Look," he said, coming to crouch beside her, pulling one of her hands away from its death grip on the cup and holding it. Her fingers were ice cold. "We're doing all we can," he said, knowing it wouldn't help. But he couldn't lie and say everything would turn out okay. Even if he could lie well enough to sell it, she was too smart to buy it.

"It might not be enough."

"It'll have to be. We'll make it enough."

"I don't think it works that way," she said with wry look.

"Today it does."

"Cocky much?"

"It's not cocky if it's true." He reluctantly let go of her hand and stood. "Anyway, your logic is flawed. Just because tech hasn't suppressed your divine influence doesn't mean it can't suppress someone else's. One test sample doesn't make for a concrete conclusion."

She nodded, and he couldn't tell if she actually agreed or just didn't want to argue. "How do my grandmother and aunt fit into someone hunting a god?" she asked before he could return to confessing he'd become a witch. "How does that even make sense?"

"We can go," Raven said as she returned. She'd slung a backpack over her shoulders. "The boats in the marina were destroyed, so we'll have to hike a little to one of the private docks." She paused to look at Ray. "You're probably starving."

His stomach felt like the Grand Canyon. "Now that you mention it," he said.

"Let me grab something for you. We don't need you passing out. You've damaged yourself enough for one day."

She dropped her pack on the table and then scrounged sandwich fixings. She made three, piling them thick with roast beef, ham, and cheese. She handed one to Ray and another to Kayla, picking up the last for herself.

"We just had soup," Kayla protested.

"And you're already hungry, aren't you?"

Kayla nodded, looking a little surprised to be agreeing.

"Then eat."

Ray bolted his sandwich as they headed for the private dock. Despite his ravenous hunger, the food sat like stone in his stomach. Everything Kayla had said was true. Sitting on this news meant more people could die if they couldn't stop the coming violence. He was glad to know they had Raven's help. From the sounds of things, the coven carried a full roster of twenty-one witches to complete a witch circle, which meant together they could cast some powerful magic. Would it be enough? This was a David-versus-Goliath situation, or a ladybug versus Godzilla. Either way, the odds were bad.

And Kayla was going to be right in the middle of it.

Ray's jaw clenched. Not without him. She'd try. He could read that in the way her gaze slid away from his and the way she kept chewing her upper lip. That was her tell. Real nerves. Real fear. She would want to protect him and everybody else the way she'd tried to do in the lab.

He wasn't going to let her. Whatever had happened four years ago, they were partners again.

Ray brooded at her all the way to the boat. It was an Alumaweld with five seats protected by a canvas canopy. Once they were out on the river, Raven turned to Kayla.

"You should go in the water. Shifting will reinforce the healing, plus I know the water folk would be reassured if they saw you. I can dry you off when we get to the other side."

Kayla looked uncertain, glancing at Ray and then back to Raven. "I try not to change where people can see me," she said, her cheeks flagging red.

"It will help you, and anyway you can't hide who you are forever," Raven said.

Though she said it to Kayla, Ray had the distinct impression Raven was talking to him.

Finally, Kayla vaulted over the side and into the water. Ray stood and looked for her. She didn't break the surface.

"I think we should talk, don't you?" Raven said.

"I need to learn how to use my magic," Ray said bluntly, facing her. "I need you to teach me."

She eyed him, her brows raised. "You going to come out of the closet?"

The words were an accusation. "I'm a cop. There aren't any witch cops."

"Only you."

Ray shook his head. "Not if somebody on the force finds out."

"So, your solution is to fake that you're human. Why bother learning magic at all then?"

Ray's shoulders tightened. "One thing I've learned the past few days is that I've been stupid to ignore the powerful tool that I carry."

"You want to dabble."

"I want to be able to control it."

She didn't answer, and after a minute Ray got impatient.

"Will you teach me?"

"Not if you want to keep it a secret. Everybody knows everybody's business on the Island, and yours would soon be out. You're better off finding a solitary practitioner, though fair warning, many of those are self-taught and lack basic skills. Others are not alone out of choice—they've been shunned or banished from their covens. There are some solitaries who have chosen to walk alone for other reasons and are both trained and skilled. Though they are rare, you may be able to find one."

"So you're saying I either come out of the closet or I'm up shit creek?"

"I'm saying, make sure whoever you work with isn't a charlatan."

Ray turned back to watching the water. What would happen if it came out that he was a witch? There was no active policy against hiring witches but there didn't have to be to keep them off the force.

Could the department accept him? Then again, how much did it matter? The events at the lab pretty much guaranteed Kayla's secret was out, and Ray had no intention of letting her disappear from his life again. Associating with her would be just about as damning for him in the eyes of his colleagues as being a witch. Plus letting the world know he was a witch, too, might just help him convince Kayla he really didn't give a shit about her other form.

His brows furrowed together. Was that true? Did he truly not care?

That's when he realized how far he'd come since Magicfall. Back then the change had been new and terrifying. Creatures out of scary fairytales had started popping up everywhere. All the boogiemen turned out to be real. His initial reaction, like so many others, had been fear and hatred that the subsequent Witchwar had only aggravated. But he'd been learning a new truth the last few days—a truth he'd known but didn't want to acknowledge. That the world wasn't going back to the way it used to be. The city belonged as much to the witchkin as humans. The police should be protecting all of its citizens.

Maybe it was time to do something about it.

"She won't come up, you know," Raven said breaking into his thoughts.

He looked over his shoulder. "Why not?"

"A lot of those who turned different after Magicfall have this idea that if they don't make it too obvious, people will forget what they are."

Raven didn't point out that Kayla would just as soon everybody forget her other form. She didn't need to.

"You haven't told her you're a witch yet?"

"I started to," he said.

"You're good at suppressing your power. It means you're decently strong. What's your affinity?"

He turned his back on the water again. "What do you mean?"

"I'm an earth witch—I draw my power from there. There are hex witches and blood witches. A few others."

Ray shrugged. "I don't know."

"Have you cast any spells?"

"I've done a couple things. Not much."

"Hex witches use a lot of symbols and cast their spells as hexes. If you aren't doing some form of that, you can rule it out. Blood witches pull power from living beings. They pull from sacrifices as well as strong emotions and the general hum of life. They tend to accumulate near cities. You could be one of those."

"And earth witch is my other choice?" he asked, rejecting the idea that he could be a blood witch.

"There are others. Smoke witches are quite rare. Same with elemental witches, who draw strength from fire, wind, sun, and so forth. Then you have moon witches—also rare. My guess is that you are either earth or blood. Earth is most common."

"How do I know?"

"You figure it out pretty quick once you start casting regularly. A lot of new witches make the mistake of drawing on themselves. We're limited in what we can carry within us, so we channel from our affinities. Once you open that channel, you know where the power comes from.

"Mage power means you've got multiple affinities and can work with different varieties of magic, which can be initially confusing. But again, mages are rare."

"How do I open a channel?" If he could do that, he might have enough raw power to help Kayla out if it came to a fight. He could throw little grenades of magic, but they weren't particularly potent.

Her expression told him that she knew exactly what he was thinking.

"No point if you aren't willing," she said. "Truly willing, all the way down to your bones. You have to be ready to embrace what you are, otherwise, it doesn't work. And if you use magic without having an ability to channel, you can suck yourself dry enough to kill yourself. That's why working with a solitary practitioner might work. If you can keep your learning a secret, you're more likely to make a connection to your affinity. It won't happen with me. You'll be too afraid to get outed."

"Humor me. If I were to be willing, what would I do?"

"You reach for it, the same way you'd reach for the power you carry inside you. Only you'd reach farther, extending out past yourself." She shrugged. "It's not as New Agey as it sounds. When you reach, you're opening a channel of sorts. When you go beyond yourself, you're tapping into a larger magical well. To make the connection, you have to both be completely open to it, and you have to anchor yourself into that well.

"Once you do that, you'll be constantly connected, so you'll have to learn to put up stops to keep magic from overwhelming you. It's a balance that's pretty instinctual, but you have to be conscious of it at first. The other side of the coin is that the well will try to pull you into it—that's its nature—so having those stops will prevent that. Some witches can extend deeper into the current and are therefore more powerful."

"Sounds . . . vague," he said.

"It's not science, if that's what you're looking for. Mix chemical A with chemical B just so and get just this reaction. It's more like art than science."

At that point, she turned her attention fully to navigating the river, though it wasn't nearly so choppy and violent as it had been when Annette and Leslie had piloted him to the Island. Kayla's influence, maybe.

He sat down in one of the seats and started making phone calls, starting with Logan, who answered on the second ring.

"Zach Logan here."

"It's Ray."

"Kayla?" was the instant response.

Ray resisted the urge to tell the bastard to keep his damned hands to himself. "Alive. Healed up. Listen, we're going to be coming into the dock at Tom McCall Park. I need the plastic box that got left behind in the lab. Can you bring it?"

Ray would rather explain the god problem they had face-to-face.

"I can get down there in twenty minutes."

"Ten's better. Bring your lab results on the Keller Fountain murders with you."

"They're murders now?"

Ray grimaced. Trust Logan to pour alcohol in the wound. Not that he didn't deserve it. "They always were. I was just too stupid to know it. I've also got two names I need you to run down. I need home addresses and anything else that might be out there on them. Got a pen?"

He rattled off the two names Laina had given him, along with their academic titles.

"Who are they?" Logan asked.

"Hopefully the key to the unknown," Ray said sardonically. "Get your ass here as quick as you can. Oh, and one more thing. See if you can get any updates on the investigation. Just in case I get fired before you get here."

Though he might already have been for ditching Dix at the hospital.

He hung up before Logan could reply, and then hit the call button for Captain Crice.

When he answered, Crice sounded livid. His voice scraped hoarsely like he'd been yelling, which he recommenced as soon as he heard Ray's voice.

"Garza? What the fuck do you think you're doing? Do you have any idea what kind of shit storm is happening down here? What in the holy hell were you doing, blowing off Dix in the hospital? You'd better have a damned good explanation or your ass is canned."

Ray decided to go on the offense and shut Crice's tirade down before he really got wound up.

"Sir, there's a potentially catastrophic magical event going down soon somewhere in the city. I'm in the process of tracking down details, but I can tell you that there's at least one god involved. The Runyon case is directly tied to it, as is the attack in the lab."

To his credit, the Captain didn't bat an eyelash. In fact, he instantly calmed. "Did you say god? What kind of god?"

"Don't know, though I'm on my way to track down an expert on the subject."

"Dammit, Garza, why is this the first I'm hearing of this?"

"I only just found out myself. Have there been any leads from the tip line or the canvass?"

"Getting reports of a cluster of sightings down near Sherwood and Tualatin. Not a lot of detail, but everybody's seeing the same thing—a big guy wearing some kind of cloak or poncho and stained with blood. I sent extra teams out to follow up."

"Tell them to be on the lookout for those demon dogs from the lab. Wherever they are is where it's going down. Make sure everybody keeps their distance. Logan couldn't hold them on his own. Call me if they see anything. I recruited some reinforcements."

"Reinforcements? Who?"

"Some witches and one or two others," he said vaguely. Luckily Crice seemed content with that. Or maybe he didn't want to know.

"I'll put the word out. What about the Runyon women?"

"No leads, except a clear link between the cases. My bet is that we'll find them in the middle of this mess." Though Ray seriously doubted that they'd be alive.

"All right, Garza. I'm going to give you the rope you want, but I'll use it to hang you if this goes to hell."

"Captain, if this goes to hell, I'm probably going to be dead, so you won't have to worry about it."

"Goddamn, but I hate this supernatural crap!" Crice bellowed into the phone, and Ray could hear the sound of breaking glass, as if he'd thrown something. "They should keep their damned magic to themselves and leave the rest of us out of it."

"About that, sir," Ray said, the words popping out before he could think about the wisdom of what he was doing. "I'm a witch."

That announcement met with stony silence. Ray's jaw tightened as he waited for a response, but he wasn't sorry. At least, he wasn't completely sorry.

"You're a what?" Crice said, his voice slow and quiet.

"A witch. Happened at Magicfall."

"Garza, exactly why are you telling me this right now?"

Ray imagined Crice pinching the bridge of his nose.

"Word's going to get out."

"I have a don't ask, don't tell policy in this precinct, Garza. I do not want to know about your personal bullshit. I want the job done and without making me a target for the city council or rich assholes like Alistair Runyon."

Crice cut the call. Ray stared at his phone. That had not gone the way he'd expected.

"I take it you've decided to come out of the closet?" Raven asked drily.

"Seems like," he said. He wasn't sure how he felt about the confession. His heart pounded with adrenaline, but otherwise he felt . . . numb.

Raven nodded, but he could practically feel the skepticism rolling off her. It infuriated him for reasons he couldn't identify.

"What more do you want from me?" He fought the urge to punch the side of the boat as his temper snapped. All the stress and emotional upheaval from the last couple of days crushed down on him all at once, leaving him without patience and without any fucks to give.

"I've basically just torpedoed my career. If I'm willing to do that, then I'm willing to take this to the end."

"The end, Detective Garza? There is no end. This is life. This is truth. You want a pat on the head for admitting you're one of us? You can go to hell. So humans have to share their world. Big fucking deal. *We've* shared *our* world with humans since you crawled out of a swamp somewhere and decided you were the only ones who mattered. Everybody else was vermin.

"So congratulations. Have yourself a party. You told someone you're a witch. I don't give a shit how hard it was or that you might lose your precious job. You know what we've lost? The rest of us who've been out of the closet this whole time? We've lost our homes, our friends, respect, and most of all, we've lost most of our rights. We're no longer human, so we're no longer worth a damn. So no, you don't get any brownie points just because you finally owned up to who you really are."

The angry flow of words cut off with a sharp snap. Her spine was ramrod straight. Before Ray could formulate an answer, he became aware of movement along the side of the boat.

Kayla's cobalt-and-gold dragon head floated just above the water. Her large crystalline blue eyes stared at him. Through him.

She'd heard. *Son of a fuck!* This was not the way he'd wanted her to find out. He needed to explain.

"Wait! Kayla—"

He leaned over the side of the boat. She held his gaze another moment, and then dove out of sight.

He swore with a vehemence that surprised even him. God but what a fucked-up mess. He'd finally told her he was a witch, and he'd done it in the worst possible way.

He knew she'd come back, if only because of the case and her missing grandmother and aunt. What he didn't know is whether she'd let him explain. Not that he had a good explanation. Raven's searing condemnation had told him that.

He fell silent, clutching the rail along the side of the boat and searching the water for some sign of Kayla. Raven's voice broke quietly through his misery.

"I'm sorry. That was your secret to tell on your time."

"I should have already told her."

Her silence told him he wasn't wrong.

Chapter 21

Kayla

KAYLA DOVE DEEP into the river, down to the base of the underwater mountain, and then deeper, into a narrow canyon cutting south into the lake. Her mind whirled, and she didn't know what to feel.

Ray was a witch. A *witch*.

The bitter irony of it struck her first. That she left the force because she'd become a shifter, and he'd stayed despite the fact that he'd become a witch. She'd thrown away everything with him because he wouldn't have been able to accept her, only to find out he'd been changed too. She'd still have had to leave the force. Her inability to control the shift guaranteed that, but maybe they could have stayed friends.

Anger struck her next. Who the hell was he to bitch about her keeping secrets when he was just as bad? There he was yelling at her and getting all self-righteous.

Talk about the pot calling the kettle black.

She clawed a boulder from the underwater canyon wall and flung it.

And then once he learned the truth, he could've come clean. But apparently *he* was allowed to keep *his* secrets.

Jackass.

She dug out a couple more pickup-sized boulders and sent them careening. It was another fifteen minutes of thrashing and tantrumming before she calmed down enough to start seeing reason.

Ray didn't owe her anything. She hadn't even seen him in four years, and she walked away without any explanation at all. If not for the murders at Keller Fountain they still wouldn't be talking. He'd never been one to trust easily, and though he wore an impassive mask most of the time, she knew he felt things deeply.

She'd been at his side when his parents died in the car crash. To everybody else he'd taken it stoically, but then a few weeks later they had gone to a bar. Kayla helped him get good and drunk and listened as his pain came pouring out. Later she'd taken him home and they'd sat up most of the night talking and drinking coffee.

All-night-coffee-chats turned into one of their rituals when dealing with a hard case or tragedy, and then it turned into a regular thing. A way to wind down after a long week. They'd grown close. Closer than lovers, the way partners were supposed to be.

She missed those days and being able to talk to him.

She couldn't help but wonder if she'd just had the balls to tell him, what would've happened? Would he have understood?

The possibility made her feel physically sick. She sank down until she lay on the rocky floor of the canyon. She'd taken away his chance to decide what he wanted to do. She'd owed it to him to decide for himself. So now, four years later, what right did she have to blame him for not trusting her with his secret?

Besides, he turned into a witch not a sea monster. Not some kind of bizarro god from the Black Lagoon. Anyhow, he'd been trying to tell her something at Jerry's and at Raven's, and she'd put him off, afraid of what it might be. She really had to get over walking on eggshells with him if she wanted to have a real friendship again, which she did, more than anything.

So, what did she want to do now? Get over her damned self for starters. Put the past in the past and call this a clean slate. Hopefully Ray would agree.

Kayla rose through the water. A cluster of water pixies watched her pass, riding creatures that looked like a cross between a manta ray and a squid. Since jumping off the boat into the water, all kinds of water beings had come to see her. They kept their distance as if not entirely trusting her. She dipped her head to them, deciding that a smile would probably look more threatening than not

She broke the surface in the middle of the river. Raven and Ray had already tied up the boat. He paced along the dock talking on the phone and scanning the water. He looked worried. Probably wondered how she was going to take the news. Better put him out of his misery.

She swam to the dock and crawled up onto the wood decking, her claws gouging chunks out of the wood. Both Raven and Ray came to stand in front of her. Ray's face was stony, but his eyes were tortured.

"Give me a second, and I'll have you dry," Raven said.

She set one hand on Kayla's shoulder who made sure to keep her scales slicked down. It would be rude to slice off Raven's fingers.

The witch made a little humming sound and then hot power washed over Kayla, drying her. With Ray watching, Kayla's concentration was close to shot, so it took her a good minute to change back to human form. As soon as she did, Raven took a couple steps back.

"I'll give you two a few minutes," she said, walking down out of ready earshot.

Ray stepped forward, his hands coming up to hold Kayla's arms like he thought she might go running off. He caught himself before he touched her and dropped his hands back to his sides.

"Kayla, I was going to tell you—"

"Stop," she said, interrupting him. "You don't have to explain. I get it. I really do."

He scowled, the muscle in his jaw flexing. "Get what?"

"Why you didn't tell me, and it's fine. So, let's just forget it and move on. We've got work to do anyway."

Her words didn't seem to make him feel any better, a conclusion confirmed by the harsh anger of his tone when he spoke again. She just had no idea why he was so mad.

"Just how do I feel?"

"Well for starters, you're clearly pissed at me," she said.

He swallowed and shook his head as if to clear it. When he spoke again, his tone had evened out in a carefully controlled way, like when you try to reason with an insane person holding a gun. "Why aren't you mad I didn't tell you after I gave you such shit about not telling me? Why don't you care?"

Kayla drew back. "You don't think I care? Of course I care. But there's not a lot of point in holding a grudge. Sure, I was pissed. I had a grand hissy fit down in the water. When I got done tossing boulders, I decided I didn't have much right to get be all holier than thou, and I didn't feel like it either. I'd rather focus on today and tomorrow rather than yesterday. We're talking again. I don't want to fuck it up."

"I did try to tell you, but—"

"I know. I figured that out. It really is okay."

He shook his head, his dark eyes searching hers. "You sure you're not just saying that? You're letting me off way too easy."

"Oh, I plan to make you pay for it. Do you want me to call you Mr. Wizard? Mr. Oz? Maybe Gandalf? Merlin? Mr. Crowley? Or I know, Professor Snape. Glinda could work, too, if you want to go pink and fluffy."

He continued to stare at her in disbelief. "You're serious. You really aren't pissed."

"I figure you'll give me something else to get aggravated about before long. Why not just wait?" she said lightly, then sobered, chewing her bottom lip. One thing still ate at her. "Just—back at Keller Fountain, you said—"

She broke off. "Never mind. It's stupid."

"Tell me."

"You said we weren't friends. Is that still the way you see it?" Then quickly, "It's okay. I understand."

He winced. "I don't suppose you could forget that. I was an ass." He took a breath. "Look, I'll be honest. I don't know what the hell we are at this point, but if we aren't friends, I damned sure want to work to get back there, which means I need to apologize. I should have said something earlier about becoming a witch. I'm sorry I didn't."

"Why didn't you?"

"At first it was because I didn't want to scare you off."

"I'm a lizard-crocodile-snake-monster. A complete freak of nature. How could you being a witch scare me off?"

"I couldn't risk it," he said baldly, and it stunned her to see the raw vulnerability that touched his eyes. The intensity of earlier had returned as he looked at her. "I lost you once and it was pure hell. You were my closest friend. Practically family. The one person I could depend on no matter what happened. I want that back. I screwed the pooch last time. I made it impossible for you to talk to me, to trust me. I don't want to do that again."

"So to make me trust you, you didn't tell me you were a witch, which could easily make me not trust you. Is that man logic?"

"Stupid, right?"

"Pretty much."

"What can I say? I'm a man." The corner of his mouth kicked up in a half smile that didn't make it to his eyes.

"Okay, what was the other reason?"

"Other reason?"

"You said at first you didn't want to scare me off. What was second?"

He sighed. "I could barely admit it to myself. Telling someone else made it more real, more true, than I was willing to accept."

"And now?"

"I can't keep hiding from myself, and if you and I are going to be able to fix things, I can't keep lying to either one of us."

Kayla nodded. "Very adult of you." He looked as if he couldn't decide if she was teasing him or not. She decided to switch gears and ask more interesting questions. "So you're a witch. Are you any good?"

He drew back slightly. "I'd say I'm about as good at witchcraft as you are at being a god."

She snorted. "Wow, you really suck, don't you?"

That earned her a chuckle, and then he sobered. "I haven't exactly embraced the witch thing. Mostly I ignore it and pretend nothing ever happened to me."

"Sounds familiar. How's that working for you?"

"Better than for you." He put his hands on Kayla's shoulders and leaned in until his forehead rested against hers. Her hands drifted to settle on his waist. For balance. Nothing else. She had to concentrate to keep them from sliding around and investigating more of him. She didn't want to give him a reason to put up walls. More than anything else, she wanted his friendship back. His company. His laughter. His trust.

"I wish to God I'd pulled my head out of my ass years ago and learned how to use my magic. But don't even think about trying to leave me behind so I won't get hurt. There's no safety anywhere if we don't stop whatever's about to happen."

Kayla flashed to the creatures ripping at Ray in the morgue hallway, blood splattering the floor as he tried to get away. Her stomach clenched. She couldn't and wouldn't not try to protect him. Her jaw set and she didn't reply.

"Kayla," he said, voice harsh with warning.

"Ray."

"You know I'm right. I want you to promise me you won't get stupid and try to keep everyone else safe. None of us have that luxury. If you can't promise that, then I swear to God I'll find a way to lock you down until you do." He sounded like his throat had filled with jagged glass.

She leaned back, brows rising defiantly. "Think you can?"

His eyes hardened. "Do you want to find out? I'm not crazy about you being on the front lines of this mess, either, but that's what we do. So *you* don't try to keep *me* out of it."

She didn't speak for a moment, and then sighed. "If I say yes, then will you promise not to take any stupid risks, especially knowing what we're up against?"

"We don't know what we're up against."

"We know there's a god of unknown power involved and we know what those three creatures can do. What they have done."

He nodded as if she'd proven his point. Which she had, though she'd only meant to remind him of the wounds he'd taken, not her own near-death experience.

"Good. We're on the same page. I'll promise if you will."

"Agreed." Inwardly she congratulated herself. She technically hadn't promised. She wasn't about to let him or anybody else get hurt if she could help it. She'd do whatever she had to in order to prevent it. *And* keep Portland from getting destroyed.

Ray ran a finger down the side of her face and tucked a tendril of hair behind her ear. Kayla suppressed a shiver, knowing full well he was not flirting, and most definitely was *not* trying to send streaks of heat snapping all over her skin.

"Maybe we should work on your definition of what a stupid risk entails. I've got a feeling we're miles apart on that," he said.

"No time," she said, looking past him. Logan had parked in the lot above and now came jogging down the steps to the dock, followed closely by Angie. Raven went to meet them.

Ray followed her gaze and muttered something before facing back around. Her hands still rested on his waist, and he still held her by one shoulder, the hand that had toyed with her hair cupping her neck as she started to step back.

"For the record," he noted, "I'm well aware that you did not actually promise. Which means I didn't either. You want to try again?"

She bit her lower lip. Dammit. What was he, a detective? And a damned good one. She sighed. "Fine. I promise. No stupid risks." At least she got to decide what she figured stupid was. But then again, so did he. That didn't make her feel any better.

She sighed and he grinned as if reading her mind, his thumb making little circles on the back of her neck. "Sucks when you're stuck with the same rules as everybody else, doesn't it?"

She twisted out of his grip before she jumped him. "Don't be a dick."

"But I'm so good at it."

"Now that's a truth we can both agree on."

Kayla stepped around him and strode away, trying not to pay attention his rumbling laugh or the earthy-musky-masculine smell that was purely him.

Angie met her and pulled her into a tight hug. "Thank God you're okay."

Kayla hugged her back, startled. Or rather, gobsmacked. Angie and Logan had seen her other form. Why weren't they keeping their distance and carrying bazookas?

Angie pushed back and held Kayla at arm's length, scanning her up and down, looking for any evidence of injuries.

"The Island witches took care of me," Kayla said, flushing a little at the examination. "I'm fine. Ray, too," she said to distract Angie.

It worked. The other woman's attention jumped to him, and she went to wrap him in a hug.

"You should watch out for that Detective Dix," she said to him. "She's on the warpath and out for blood."

Ray shrugged. "I've got a bodyguard." He flicked a glance at Kayla. "At least, she's not going to let anybody kill me before she gets a chance to."

Angie snorted.

Kayla got distracted at that point by Zach, who pulled her into a hug and held her close against him.

"You know, we only just met. You could wait at least a week before you decide you can't live without me. In fact, you can have me if it will keep you alive," he said with a teasing grin.

"You wish." She hugged him back, and was surprised when she went to push out of his grip and he kept holding her.

"Just sit still. This pisses Ray off," he said in a low voice. "The idiot is jealous as hell. He's totally got it bad for you."

Kayla went stiff as a board. "Does not," she choked out.

"Looks like you're in denial, too." He loosened his grip and brushed a fast kiss across her lips, his eyes glinting wickedly. "Consider me your fairy godfather," he whispered and then mirrored Angie, stepping back to look her over.

"You look lovely as ever," he declared, and she flushed.

"You've got a strange idea of beauty," she said. "I look like a half-rotted corpse."

"Nonsense. You're beautiful, and I should know. I'm a connoisseur of beautiful women."

"Sort of like being a connoisseur of fast-food hamburgers? I bet you think rats are pretty, too."

"I'm sure there are very pretty rats," he declared loftily, and then pulled her back in for a hug. "Seriously, though, I'm glad you're okay. I would have missed you terribly."

Uh huh. "You barely know me."

"I know I like you."

A movement beside them caught her attention, and a hand clamped around her upper arm and pulled her away from Zach. Ray's expression was positively lethal.

"We're wasting time."

Zach darted an I-told-you-so glance at her. Kayla rolled her eyes and shook her head. Much as she'd like to think he was right about Ray, she knew that his intensity had nothing to do with anything romantic. She wasn't even his type. He liked professional women—doctors, lawyers, real estate agents. Women who wore skirts and heels and makeup, who didn't dribble food down their shirts, or do spit-takes when someone told a good joke. In other words, he liked purebreds, not mutts.

Kayla was most definitely a mutt, despite being a Runyon. Not that she couldn't play in the purebred leagues. Her father had made sure she knew how to act the part of wealth and education as deemed appropriate for Runyon spawn. She knew all the right forks and how to dance without treading on toes and how to choose a wine and how to make small talk. She knew how to dress and walk in ridiculous designer heels and put her hair into elegant up-dos. At least choosing a good wine was worth knowing. She hated the rest. But that sort of woman had always been a magnet for Ray.

The fundamental commonality shared by all his girlfriends was that they were always put-together, confident, independent, and well-grounded. On the other hand, Kayla was a cut-offs and old flannel sort of girl. She had a lot of daddy issues and a lot to prove when it came to being a cop. The disaster that was her parents' marriage had taught her to be suspicious of love and romance. Friendships were safer.

She'd made the job her entire world. Ray'd taught her that there really were good men out there. She'd been proud to be his partner, and proud of the work they'd done. Together they'd closed more cases than anybody else in the department. They worked together like a well-oiled machine. She'd made it a point to be worthy of his trust and friendship.

Whatever Zach said, whatever new feelings she seemed to have for Ray, she wasn't going to do anything to screw this up. Her cheeks flushed with embarrassment just thinking about telling him she was interested in him romantically. He'd laugh or be embarrassed or he'd pity her and try to let her down easy. Any which way she sliced it, the result would be deadly awkward-ness and a massive dose of humiliation.

She'd rather have the sure thing of a rekindled friendship. Besides, she could find someone else to have sex with, if she needed to scratch that itch, which wasn't likely. She'd practically been a nun before Magicfall, and after—

Well, she'd felt like such a freak, she'd pretty much kept everybody at arm's length.

"Logan's a tomcat," Ray said suddenly, breaking the flow of her thoughts.

Her brows crimped. "What?"

"Logan's a tomcat, and he swings both ways. You can't walk down a street without bumping into someone he's screwed or who's screwed him. He's put notches in so many bedposts they are practically whittled to matchsticks. You don't want to get involved with him."

She glanced over her shoulder at the man in question. He quirked his brows at her and winked.

Idiot.

"What makes you think I'm interested in him?"

"You had dinner with him. You looked pretty cozy together when you got to your family's estate, and that hug looked plenty romantic." He listed those off in the impassive way he went over crime details. "You don't—or didn't used to, anyhow—typically do anything with men unless you are getting romantically involved. Doesn't take a detective to see where the wind's blowing. Felt I should to give you all the facts."

"I hate to tell you, but your detecting skills need work. I like Zach, but I've got no plans to jump his bones."

He glanced at her and away. "All the same, you should know what he is."

She hated it when people pretended they knew her better than she knew herself. On the other hand, Ray had hit the nail on the head. He still knew her. Didn't make him any less of an asshole though. She smiled to herself. It felt unbelievably good to have someone watching out for her.

They gathered around Raven. Angie passed the plastic box to Kayla while Zach took a sheaf of papers out of the messenger bag he'd set down at the bottom of the steps. He jumped right in.

"We've got some preliminary reports. First, that white powder? Some kind of mineral, we think, but nothing we could pin down yet."

"It's a spell carrier," Raven said. "When activated and combined with the venom of those creatures, it becomes particularly deadly for divine creatures."

"And that's why Kayla got hit so hard?" Angie asked.

Raven shook her head. "The spell on the powder wasn't activated or else she wouldn't have survived long enough to get help. The creatures' venom naturally has a stronger effect on divine creatures than others. The powder ramps that up exponentially."

Zach's brows crimped together. "You're saying that if that powder gets activated and one of the creatures bites her, then her chances of surviving are—?"

"Zero. Even with several of my most powerful witches working on her, we nearly couldn't save her," the witch said baldly. "Add the powder and she's got no chance."

"Okay, so we keep her locked up tight until we can hunt these beasts and put them down," he said, looking at Ray whose expression had gone nuclear winter. "Right?"

"You and what army?" Kayla snapped. "Besides, the creatures are the least of our worries. I couldn't sit out of this fight even if I wanted to. So, get that shit right out of your pretty little head."

At the last, Angie gave a little snort. Ray's mouth twitched and then flattened again, and Zach looked like he'd eaten a live snake.

"You're a liability," he said.

"Only if you try to protect me. Otherwise, I'm just another soldier."

"Of course we're going to try to protect you," he said, the muscle in his jaw throbbing. "That's what we do. We watch each other's backs. Or have you been off the force so long you've forgotten that basic code?"

Kayla felt herself flushing, her teeth baring in a snarl as she jerked forward, poking her finger into his chest to punctuate her words.

"I'll tell you what I remember. Cops protect people. We walk into the line of fire and we bleed and we die and we keep going no matter who falls, because this is our city and we've sworn to protect it. And that's what I'm going to do. So, you can take your self-righteous crap and shove it up your ass sideways."

"You aren't a cop," he reminded her. "None of that applies to you. You're one of the civilians we"—he pointed to Ray and back to himself—"are sworn to protect."

Kayla's eyes narrowed to slits. A torrent of emotion spun inside her like a saw blade. Her fists had balled up, and it was taking all of her frayed control to not beat the crap out of the obnoxious technomage. She turned to Ray.

"You still backing me?"

She sounded deathly calm in that eye-of-the-storm kind of way.

"Nothing's changed for me."

She nodded. "Good. Then we're done discussing it." She glared at Zach. "Got anything useful to add? Because we don't have time for you to keep spewing shit out your mouth."

He started to say something. Angie cut him off. "Shut it down, Zach. You can decide for yourself, but she gets to choose what she's going to do."

"It's stupid. She'll get herself killed."

"Maybe, maybe not. But that's the way it is. Get over it. Now get on with what you've learned about the murders."

He made a *this-isn't-finished* sound in the back of his throat, but complied.

"We got a hit on some trace we picked up from the bodies. It was distill-ed from plants. We haven't identified all of them, but we found *ceiba pentandra*, also called the Silk Cotton tree. And *quararibea funebris*, which is also a tree. There are some hints of cayenne, cacao, and *salvia divinorum*, which is a psychoactive plant."

He looked up from the report. "All of those are native to South America. The last one is frequently used by shamans in vision quest sorts of ceremonies as well as sacred rituals."

"Sacred," Raven murmured. "That can't be a coincidence."

"We also found DNA. We won't get results back for at least a few days, and that's pushing the limits of the lab."

"Where did you find the plant residue?" Kayla asked. So far, the new information wasn't helping put the pieces of the mystery together. "Had the victims ingested it?"

He shook his head. "It was on their foreheads, eyes, lips, chests, and genitals."

"So definitely applied deliberately," Raven said.

"As part of a ritual, is my guess," Zach said. "The bodies were exsanguinated, but we didn't find any signs of blood in the pool or on the wall. We're not sure where they were killed, but not at the fountain, unless they used plastic tarps or some sort of magical trace collection."

"Not likely, given that the powder coated everything. If they'd taken anything away, it would have left a void," Kayla said.

"That begs the question, how did the doers get away without leaving a trail?" Angie asked.

"Maybe they flew," Ray said. "Or went through a different dimension. We're dealing with supernatural beings. Who knows what they can do?" Ray turned his attention back to Zach. "What else have you got?"

"Some long black hairs that we're hoping will tell us something about what we're dealing with. And we found this."

He pulled a photo from the sheaf of papers. On it was what appeared to be close-up images of the front and back of an earring—a beaten gold disk attached to a thick wire hook. An image of something that looked like a gargoyle peered out from one side of the disk, with a set of symbols on the back surrounded by a cartouche. They reminded Kayla of the ritual writing at the fountain murder scene.

"Where was it?" Kayla asked.

"It got caught in one of the drains where the water cycles back up to the top of the fountain."

"Did you get those addresses I asked for?" Ray asked.

Zach fished a lined piece of folded paper from his breast pocket and passed it to Ray who looked at it and nodded.

"Let's go," he said and trotted up the steps without another word.

Kayla dashed after him with the others close behind. Zach had driven a white SUV with a Portland city seal on the driver's door in black. Ray climbed behind the wheel without asking permission. Kayla jumped in beside him while their three companions squeezed into the back seat. Ray quickly pulled out of the parking lot heading west.

Over the years since Magicfall, a lot of the roads had been overgrown or the ground underneath had changed and made them impassable. Less of that had happened in Portland's downtown where there was a lot of tech.

Ray wound through streets heading north. Reed College had disappeared when the lake had formed with the underwater mountain. Determined to keep the college going, those who survived on the faculty and administration had moved into Portland's Linnfield campus and merged with it to become the new Reed College.

Ray drove past the college and turned west again, periodically checking the navigation map on the dashboard. Eventually he pulled up outside a two-story house painted red with white trim like an old timey-barn. Neatly trimmed bushes lined either side of the front walk, and a riot of flowers bloomed in the beds along the front porch.

Ray knocked loudly on the front door. This house belonged to Natalie Lyle, an expert in dead and barely breathing languages.

After a minute Ray pounded on the door again, hammering on it hard enough to make it rattle in the jamb. Lights went on upstairs and then down, and a voice came through the door.

"Who is it? Do you have any idea what time it is?"

Kayla didn't. It had to be close to one in the morning.

"Police business," Ray said holding his badge and I.D. up in front of the peephole.

A few seconds later the deadbolt slid back and then another one and then another one. The door swung open. A middle-aged woman stood there. Her graying brown hair hung loosely around her face in what was probably a sleek blunt cut. She had piercing blue eyes and a stubborn chin. Despite her small stature and the fuzzy green robe she'd wrapped around herself, she didn't look remotely cowed by having the police wake her up in the middle of the night. Mostly she looked irritated.

"Good morning, Professor Lyle," Ray said, adopting his professionally conciliatory tone. "We are sorry to bother you at this time of morning, but we have an emergency that requires your expertise. Lives are at stake, and time is of the essence."

The woman blinked and visibly shifted gears. She swung the door wider and motioned inside. "Better come in then."

She led them into a comfortable living room. Floor-to-ceiling bookshelves lined three of the walls with a wood fireplace dominating the last. The beige rug had seen better days, as had the well-worn couch, loveseat, and easy chair.

Two scarred wooden chairs bracketed the fireplace.

"Please sit," she said, settling into the easy chair. She waited until they'd arranged themselves on the couch and love seat. "How can I help you?" she asked.

Kayla dug in the box she brought in with her and spread the witchkin crime-scene pictures of the symbols out on the coffee table. Zach added pictures from the fountain murders and ones taken at the kidnapping site from the folder he carried. He added the earring photo last.

"We are hoping you can help us identify the language in these photos and what it says," Kayla said.

The professor's demeanor had shifted from irritated to interested as soon she saw the pictures. She scooted forward, leaning down to see them more closely. She picked them up one by one.

"Do you recognize anything?" Kayla asked.

"They bear a resemblance to some of the South American early civilization writings," the professor said. "But none used cartouches, and the symbols aren't anything I've seen before. But if I were going to place it in part of the world, I would definitely pick South America."

The others exchanged looks. That piece fit with the plant traces the lab had found.

"Is there any way to narrow this further?" Ray asked.

"I could ask some colleagues with expertise in South American languages and civilizations," the professor said. Then she frowned, tapping the side of her nose thoughtfully. She stood up. "Wait a minute."

She went to her bookshelves and started scanning the spines. At last she found what she was looking for on one of the bottom shelves. She pulled out a thin leather book. The cover was plain with no title and no author.

She opened it carefully, holding it in one hand and using the other hand to carefully turn pages. Her eyes scanned up and down the pages as she searched for something.

Kayla tapped her fingers on her thigh trying not to squirm in her seat. But she was too antsy. She glanced at the clock on the far wall. Nearly two. She stood and paced behind the couch.

"This might be something," the professor said at last. "This isn't my field, you understand," she said looking up. "This journal belonged to an associate of my wife. He gave it to Maggie shortly before he died back in the late eighties."

She looked down at the open book again and then came to sit back down.

"This was long before Magicfall you understand, and most everyone considered his theories ludicrous. Prestigious journals wouldn't even consider publishing him. His theories went counter to the generally accepted account of history."

"What did he say?" Zach asked.

"He was certain that the early Egyptians—Pharaohs—had communicated with the Olmecs and Zapotecs—even visited them. In fact, he posited that the Egyptians may have strongly influenced the Olmecs in the building of their civilization. Among other proofs, he argued that the pyramid constructions were too similar to have evolved separately. But what cemented his conclusions were some writings he discovered in a lost pyramid he found between Oaxaca and Veracruz.

"He said that the writing showed that Egyptians really *had* visited and look—" She turned the journal to show them.

Inscribed on the yellowed pages were lines of text very similar to what they'd discovered at the crime scenes, including cartouches.

"So, our killers are what? Egyptian? Olmec? Zapotec?" Kayla asked. And how did that help?

"Did he translate any of this?"

She shook her head. "He died in a fire, which destroyed most of his research. He'd given the journals to Maggie for her to read, hoping that she'd help him find funding to continue, which is why they survived. But because his work wasn't believed, no one kept track of the pyramid after he died. It was lost again. When Magicfall happened, it became clear that his theory was more feasible than previously believed. The Egyptians may well have had the magical capability to travel to South America. Certainly we can't rule it out, but there's been no research on that subject since Hima died."

"Would your wife know what these could mean?" Ray asked.

"Maybe, but—" The professor sighed. "She's been sick and I gave her something to sleep. Even your pounding on the door didn't wake her up. She's down for the count."

"Would you try?" Ray said, and it came out more like the order it was than a request. "We don't have much time. Lives are at stake."

Professor Lyle hesitated and then nodded. "I'll see what I can do."

"If you're willing, I could help," Raven said. "I'm a witch. I have healing skills."

The professor's face went from pinched concern to sudden hope. "Would you? She's not been well for months, and the doctors don't know what's wrong. Nothing we've tried has helped."

"Show me," Raven said as she stood.

The two women disappeared up the stairs on the other side of the entry.

"So how does all this help us?" Kayla wondered, turning pages in the journal. "We know our bad guys are probably from South America, and they use a language that has been found in precisely one place in the world, and may be a combination of Ancient Egyptian and Olmec or . . . what was the other one?"

"Zapotec," Ray said.

"Right. We still don't know anything about who they are hunting and why, except that it's likely a god of some kind." She pushed the journal away in disgust. "It's not written in English. Or Spanish. I don't even know what sort of language or code the archaeologist used."

"Professor Lyle said that he gave the journals to her wife to read. Presumably that means she can read them," Ray said.

More waiting.

Frustration sent Kayla pacing again. They were fast arriving at the point she hated most in any murder case—waiting for the next body and hoping it pointed them to the killer. Only with this case, the next murder could very well bring on the Portland Apocalypse.

"We've got to be missing something," she muttered. She stopped and looked at Zach. "Can't you do anything? With your magic? Track them in some way?"

"Afraid not."

"What good is magic if it can't do the stuff that can't be done normally?" she complained.

"It can do that stuff. Just not for every practitioner," Zach said with annoying reason. "Maybe Raven can, though I expect if she could have, she would have."

"But I bet it can give a guy a hard-on for days on end," she muttered as she resumed pacing.

Tension boiled and tumbled inside her, and the beast part of her clawed to get out. Thunder pounded against her skull and skin, sending shockwaves rippling through her bones. A rush of darkness surged into relentless momentum, dragging at her like heavy gravity. Every fiber of her being warned her something bad was about to happen, and she needed to stop it. *Needed* to, on a level she couldn't understand. It was biological, down in the nucleus of every cell. It wasn't just her job; it was an imperative rooted in her very being.

She didn't realize she'd made a sound until Ray's voice cut through the tornado of razor wire whipping through her brain.

"What?"

"I asked if you're okay."

"Don't I look okay?"

His jaw hardened. "No."

She tried to rein back the firestorm growing hotter inside her even as her pacing became frenetic, her movements jerky. Something began to tear inside her, a slow separation, ripping apart with fiery agony. Her breath caught in her chest, and her heart thumped like a jackhammer.

"How do I look?" Her words came out sharper than she intended, but she couldn't seem to care.

"Feverish. Wired for sound," Ray shot back.

She fought to calm herself. "I'm antsy. I feel like we're out of time." She shook her head. "It's probably too little sleep. I'll go splash some water on my face."

She fled out into the foyer as the pressure inside her ballooned and pain tore at her insides. No, deeper than that. Down in a place beyond the physical.

She staggered along the hallway into the back of the house where she found a bathroom just off the kitchen. She locked the door behind her and leaned against it, gasping for breath. The pain had eased slightly. Or maybe she was just adjusting to it. At least it wasn't getting worse.

She straightened and went to look in the mirror. She'd told Ray she was going to splash water on her face. She snorted. *As if.* The way she was feeling, a couple drops would trigger a shift. She glanced around the small half bath, barely four feet across. If she transformed, she'd have to tear her way out.

Her gaze caught on the window above the toilet. She started moving before she knew what she was doing. Kayla pried up the window, then crawled through, landing in a hydrangea bush. It caught her and set her gently upright.

She turned to look at it. "Thank you." The purple-blue flowers bobbed in the moonlight as if to say, "You're welcome." The leaves started rustling, traveling down the bushes running the length of the wall. They urged her to hurry.

Kayla turned and ran back to the front of the house, down the driveway and up the street. Far off in the back corner of her mind, guilt scraped at her. She shouldn't be going alone. But they needed to wait for the information, and the rest of her had gone on autopilot as she raced into the night, pulled by some inexplicable beacon.

Her skin was alive with movement, as if the city had imprinted itself on her flesh. She could feel cars running down her sides, cats climbing up her arms, the breath and heartbeat of every living soul tapping against her heart. But in the middle of it, a poisonous boil swelled and strained like a volcano racing toward eruption. Inside it bubbled death. She had to stop it.

Her territory, her city, her *people*, were under attack.

Anger exploded. Brutal savagery peeled the humanity from her soul, leaving behind only single-minded resolve.

Whatever it took, she would protect them or die trying.

Chapter 22

Ray

"SHE'LL BE OKAY," Logan said to Ray as Kayla disappeared. "She's been off the force a while. Plus, this whole business is pretty strange. She's probably just jittery."

Ray stood behind a chair, gripping the top to keep himself from going after her.

"She doesn't get jittery," he said. "Kayla's always had nerves of stone."

"Well, like she said, she hasn't been getting a lot of sleep and all that's been happening has to be pretty hard to take. She's got to be overwhelmed, not to mention still recovering from the attack. I mean, there's that, plus her grandmother and aunt getting kidnapped, seeing you again, and finding out you're a witch—" He broke off, cocking his head at Ray. "That's a hell of a secret you've been keeping."

Ray had stopped paying attention to the technomage. Professor Lyle and her wife descended the stairs, followed by Raven. Lyle had her arm around her wife, who blinked and stared around owlishly, as if not completely awake.

Lyle settled her wife on the couch, pulling a brown-and-pink knit throw over her legs.

"I'd better make coffee," Lyle said, and disappeared.

Raven leaned in the doorway while Ray went to sit on the coffee table facing Maggie. "Ma'am," he said. "We've got some questions we need you to answer."

She gave him a distant look and nodded slowly. "Natalie told me," she said, her words slow and a little slurred. She frowned and gave her head a little shake. "I'm sorry. I'm very tired. I can't seem to wake up."

Ray darted a questioning glance at Raven.

"They used a potion," she said in a low voice. "A good one. I countered what I could, but she'll have to work her way through the rest. She's in rough shape. Whatever disease she has, it's eating her alive."

Shit. Ray examined Maggie. She was taller than her wife, with curly brown hair and a round face that appeared gaunt. Her brown eyes appeared glassy. She sat slumped as if she carried a heavy burden. Purple circles surrounded her eyes, and her wrist bones jutted beneath her skin. She looked as though she'd lost substantial weight and very quickly.

He flicked another look at Raven. She shrugged.

"We'll try to help her. She's very weak. Even if we can cure her, we may not be in time."

Ray nodded and turned his attention back to Maggie, who sat with her thin hands clasped in her lap as she listed slightly to the side.

"Professor Lyle said you might be able to understand what these mean," he said, holding up a picture of some of the symbols. He let her get a good look, and then held up another.

"Do they seem familiar to you? Can you tell me what they say?"

She opened her mouth and yawned. Ray clamped his teeth together, forcing himself to be patient. Getting testy with her wouldn't help, and he didn't want to do anything to shut her down or divert her attention from the task at hand.

Maggie reached for one of the pictures, and he let her take it. She held it on her lap and stared. Seconds ticked passed. Ray's leg bounced as he waited.

"It's familiar," she said at last, speaking slowly. "My colleague—Hima Mubarak. A brilliant man, but his ideas were on the fringe. He showed me writings like these. And his journals. You'll want to read those. He explains."

She spoke in short, disjointed sentences.

"We can't read them. Could you tell us what's inside? Perhaps translate these symbols?"

She blinked at him as she sorted through his questions.

"I don't know how good at them I am. After Hima died, I read the journals and studied them—it got to be a sort of game. Relaxing, you know? But it's been quite a while, and the truth is that few agree on how to translate Olmec writing. Whether to read it right to left or vertically even."

Ray was glad to see that she was scraping her wits together a little and becoming coherent, even though she didn't offer a lot of hope for translation.

Just then, Professor Lyle returned and handed her wife a mug of milky coffee.

"It's single serve," she said apologetically to Ray and his companions. "I've started another cup."

"Thank you," Zach said.

Maggie sipped the hot liquid, and it helped clear some of the glassiness from her expression. She focused back on the photograph.

"These are definitely similar to those in Hima's journals," she said.

Ray tamped down his impatience and kept his voice calm. "Do you have any idea what they say?"

"The cartouche says the images are meant to be read together," she murmured as if to herself. "But generally those are used with pictograph and hieroglyph types of languages. The symbols here are representational already in a more advanced way of language, beyond hieroglyphs, and obviously Olmec in nature. Now these"—she pointed to several—"group together symbols for strength—the kind that bends and burrows and conquers—and one for connection or binding together, and another for digging a well, or maybe a spring."

She tapped her fingers against her lips, and Ray had to clamp his teeth together to make himself wait.

"I just can't say with any kind of certainty what these symbols might mean together, particularly without more context."

"Guess," Ray said.

She narrowed her eyes in disapproval, but acquiesced. "If I'm just guessing, then I would say that together they are a kind of command to tie two things together, possibly against their natures, or against their wills."

"And the others?"

Before she could answer, Ray's phone rang. He contemplated ignoring it, but it could be an update on the search.

"Garza," he barked, standing and moving off to the side in an attempt at privacy. He gave Zach a sharp look as the technomage's phone rang.

"We've got a bloodbath," said Captain Crice with no preamble. "Down in Sherwood-Tualatin. The Mound. Hundreds killed and—what?" he demanded, obviously not talking to Ray, who heard a rumble of voices, and then Crice returned. "We've got a magical event underway. Sending for tactical teams of technomages now, and evacuating around the area. Get your ass down there with your *reinforcements* and shut this down. Now."

The line cut off. Ray stared at his phone. Shut it down? How? They still didn't know what the hell they were up against.

"You heard?" he asked Logan as the technomage pocketed his cell.

Logan nodded, his expression thunderous and cold. An expression Ray knew was mirrored on his own face. They'd both worn it often during the war.

"Get Kayla. I'll meet you at the car. You, too," he told Raven.

Ray looked at Angie as they disappeared. "Stay here and see if you can get anything more from the professor or her wife. Any details may give us something to go on. See if they know anything about the creatures or the plants. Call me the minute you learn anything."

"She's gone!" Logan appeared in the doorway, face turned to granite. "Out the window. Kayla. She's gone."

"Son of a fuck!"

Ray launched himself into the hallway, Logan at his heels. He stormed to the bathroom and looked out the window. A waste of time. He ran back up the hall and outside, jumping into the car. Logan slid into the seat beside him. Raven climbed in the back. Ray didn't wait for Angie. With any luck, she'd keep digging into the meaning of the symbols. In seconds they squealed out on the roadway, flying down it as fast as Ray could drive.

"What was she thinking?" he demanded, pounding the dash with his fist. "What the fuck is *wrong* with her?"

She'd left without him. Again. This time running into a danger that would more than likely kill her. A danger she *could not* handle alone, and she knew it.

"She may not have had a choice," Raven said from the back seat.

Ray twisted to look at her over his shoulder and swerved. He faced back around and hung a tight corner, tires screeching. "What do you mean?"

"It's possible that her divine aspect took control."

Ray lifted his gaze to watch her in the rearview. He definitely did not like the sound of that. "What does that mean?"

"We all have instinctual behaviors that come out of our DNA. The most basic parts of our natures. Because of her divine nature, she's connected to the city. It could be that whatever has happened summoned her in some primal way. You said it yourself—she knows she can't handle this alone, but if her other self took over, then it's running the show and unless she can assert her human side, she's sitting in the back seat for the ride."

"Fuck." He took another corner and stomped the gas to the floor as they straightened out. Magic tightened inside him, taut, like an arrow knocked to a bow, ready to spring. Crimson and blue flames danced over his fingertips, and he felt the steering wheel soften in his grip.

"Easy now," Logan said. "She doesn't have much of a lead on us. We'll get there in time."

Logically, Ray knew the other man was right. But magic didn't answer to logic, and who knew what Kayla was really capable of? She might have transported herself in some way. Or jumped in the river and swam. He had a feeling she was more than fast in the water.

"Or just go ahead and speed like a bat out of hell," Logan said when Ray didn't respond, buckling his seat belt. "But do try to keep your magic under control, would you? I'd hate for us to go shooting off into the sky like a comet."

"If I knew how to control it, I would," Ray said through clenched teeth.

"You know how," Raven said with a noticeable note of disgust. "You've been doing it for years. *You're* out of control, so *it's* out of control."

She didn't bother waiting for his reply, but pulled out her cell phone and typed in a number. She held it up to her ear. "It's happening," she said. "We're headed for Sherwood-Tualatin. The Mound. Yes. Get there as soon as you can. Don't bother finishing the shield amulet. We're too late for that."

Too late. The words echoed in Ray's skull on endless repeat.

He jumped on the freeway, pegging at a hundred miles an hour, which was as high as the speedometer would go. They went faster.

His cell phone rang again, and he put it on speaker.

"Garza."

"It's Angie. Natalie—Professor Lyle—recognized the description of the creatures. She said they're Mayan, though some archaeologists believe their origins go back possibly to before the Olmecs. They are called Tahuizotls. They typically serve the gods and guard the temple pyramids. The myths say they are very smart."

"Any idea how to fight them?" Logan asked, getting right to the point.

"Not really. They seem immune to fire, and they are supposedly good swimmers. They eat humans, but only the eyes, fingers, teeth, and toes. The rest they leave."

"What about the plants?" Ray asked.

"Those don't help us much," Angie said. "They were used in a great many rituals. Maggie thinks that one of the symbols is different from the rest."

"Different how?"

"There's one symbol that shows up at almost all the crime scenes except the one at Keller Fountain."

"I remember the one," Ray said. It had looked more primitive than the others, and more bold. It had been geometric, with a spiral in the center. "What about it?"

"Maggie texted a couple pictures of the symbols to a colleague in Texas specializing in ancient South American studies. He told her that most of the symbols have a feminine quality to them, but that this one is clearly masculine—thicker lines, fewer curves, sharp points. The arrow points suggest a hunter. He thinks that it's possible that it's an amalgam of several symbols. The eight lines radiating from the center spiral could signify a spider, while the zig-zag line could signify a snake. He says they look Olmec, but that the Olmecs didn't have writing like this. Neither did the Mayans."

"Does he have any idea what it could represent?"

"If it does translate as a hunter, or multiple hunters, then it could be related to a ritual for finding someone."

Of course it was. Why hadn't he seen it? *Multiple hunters.*

That piece clicked into the puzzle, and suddenly Ray had a picture of what could have happened. Bad Guy 1 had conducted the rituals where he took bones from his victims. Bad Guy 2 was hunting Bad Guy 1 and had performed the ritual at Keller Fountain. He'd spread the white powder on the wind to infect his prey, and then summoned the three demon dogs— Tahuizotls—to either kill him, or keep him treed until Bad Guy 2 could arrive on the scene and take him down.

"Plausible," Logan said when Ray explained. "Sure wish we knew why, though."

"Does it matter? The two are fighting, and Portland is their battle ground."

"Why here? Why not have this fight somewhere down south of the border? Why Portland?"

"Because of Kayla," Raven said, not looking up as she tapped rapidly on her phone screen. "Her presence here lets things flourish. Encourages them.

But it also settles the magic. In most other places it's still really unstable. Think of the ghost storms in the east and midwest, or the changeling fogs in the south, or the warp fires in California, Arizona, New Mexico, Nevada, and Texas. Even just north of here they get the dread rains. Magic is still changing things, still knotted up and twisted and trying to find a natural flow in the world. But not here. Not where Kayla's influence extends.

"Chances are the first bad guy came here because the magic's stable and he can cast whatever spells he needs to without worrying about weird interference in the flow of magic." She frowned and looked up. "Which means he's probably not got a lot of experience. He may have come into his power at Magicfall, or he's just not strong enough to deal with the turmoil on the magical plane."

"Or what he's doing is too important to him to take unnecessary risks," Logan said.

She nodded and shrugged. "That, too."

"Shouldn't a god be more powerful than that?" Ray asked.

"It could be a smaller god, or perhaps one who's not yet mastered his power."

Made sense, and might offer a sliver of hope. If he hadn't come into his power, then maybe they could beat him. Another thought occurred to Ray, one that sent ice down his spine. "Could he know about Kayla? Could that be why he took her grandmother and aunt? Maybe this is all a lure to bring her to him." Ray's hands tightened on the wheel, and magic flames ran up his forearms. The temperature inside the car increased, and Logan rolled his window down.

"It's possible," Raven said quietly

Ray's jaw tightened, and his teeth audibly ground together. Too damned few answers and too damned little time to find them.

"Anything else?" he asked, remembering Angie remained on the phone. "No."

"Stay there. Keep at it. Call if you get anything else." Ray swiped to hang up and the phone scrunched, the screen popping audibly. Green and black smoke poured from it while red energy snapped over its surface.

"Christ!" Logan grabbed the phone and tossed it out his window.

"Get a hold of yourself," Raven said, leaning forward to slap Ray's shoulder. "This is how witches like you get dead."

Logan checked his fingers for burns. "Dammit, Ray. You're lucky I can protect myself," he said, blowing on his fingertips.

"Like me?" Ray asked Raven, trying to divert his brain and calm himself.

"In denial. Deliberately untrained. Suicidally stupid."

"What she said," Logan added.

Ray tossed him an aggravated look, but didn't try to argue. They were right. Something he was determined to correct once they took care of this situation and Kayla was safe.

Thinking of her made the storm inside him surge. He fought to contain his emotions. How the hell had he denied his feelings for her for so long? How the hell had he not recognized them? Denial. Stupidity. Just like with his magic.

It's not over, he told himself. *You're going to have time to get this straight.*

He chanted the words over and over, refusing to contemplate that he might not have time. That Kayla could already be dead.

DESPITE THE EARLY hour—just before three a.m.—by the time they reached the Tualatin exit, the local area was lit up like a Christmas tree with dozens of emergency vehicles with lights flashing and three miniature magical suns bobbing in the sky.

Ray pulled off the freeway, eyeing the chaos. A command center had been erected under tents in the Cabela's parking lot. A horde of emergency personnel and vehicles crammed in around it. He didn't bother to stop, heading instead for the barriers blocking the road just past Boone's Ferry Road.

He rolled down his window as he approached. He'd managed to get control of his magic. For now, anyway. A young uniformed officer stepped up to the door, looking pale but resolute. He had his hand on the butt of his gun. Not that it would help him much in a magical attack. Ray didn't say so. He flashed his credentials.

"We're headed to The Mound," he said.

"Orders are to keep everybody back."

The kid's voice cracked. Ray tried not to wince. He couldn't be more than ten years older than the young officer, but it might as well have been a century. The kid had probably still been in high school during Magicfall.

"Civilians, kid. Not us. We're the cavalry."

The young officer looked doubtful. "I'd better check in," he said, and then turned away, talking into the microphone on his shoulder.

Ray held tight to his patience—what was left of it.

"What?" The kid's voice rose. "Yes, ma'am. Yes. I will."

He turned back around and gestured for the gates to be moved aside.

"Just so you know, Detective, there's been a sighting of a big monster up there."

"Monster? Any details?"

"Witnesses say it looks something like a dragon. Blue and gold." The kid stuttered over *dragon*.

"Thanks," Ray said and then pulled past the barrier before speeding up the road.

"How the hell did she beat us?" he muttered, veering around other emergency vehicles and civilians evacuating, hitting his siren to help clear the road.

"The lake hits the Tualatin River and she's fast in the water. She probably came down the river, through the lake, and up the Tualatin and then overland to The Mound," Raven said.

"Raven. Is that your real name?" Logan asked out of nowhere.

Ray flashed a scowl at him. So not the time.

"For now," Raven said and nothing else.

The Mound occupied what once had been a sand and gravel pit. After Magicfall and during the war, it had become a mass gravesite when bodies had begun to pile up and there was nowhere and no time to bury them properly. Witchkin and humans alike had been dumped into the pits and buried, and eventually the place turned into a massive burial mound.

Most people claimed it was haunted. A group of Native American shamans had attempted to cleanse the place in a grand smoke ceremony a few months ago. It hadn't worked. They'd all come away shell-shocked and glassy-eyed, whispering things in what they later said was the language of the dead. Many had not yet recovered.

Luckily not many people chose to live nearby. A lot of that had to do with the creeping slime molds and fungi that piled and grew in turgid columns and monstrous shapes, some as large as a Greyhound bus. They overran trees and houses alike for a mile radius around The Mound. Some people claimed if you stood there long enough it would cover you, too.

Ray slowed as they reached the outskirts of the rotting zone where a smaller command center was being established. He pulled over, and the three of them got out. Several cops stood nearby including Dix. She turned and saw him and stomped over to block his way, hands on her hips.

"What the fuck is your problem, Garza? Did you get a sudden aneurysm or something? Because if you didn't then I'll see your ass fired. You don't get to pick which orders to follow. We don't need a rogue cop on the force." She spat the words like bullets. She didn't wait for an answer, her gaze shooting first to Logan and then to Raven. "Who the fuck is she? Civilians shouldn't be here."

"She's a witch. She's working with us," Logan said.

She turned her ire on the technomage. "A witch? Are you shitting me? You can't trust them. They are probably behind this clusterfuck." Her voice rose until she was actually yelling.

"Exactly what's going on?" Ray asked in a calm tone guaranteed to piss her off. She didn't disappoint.

"Oh, now you want me to share information with you?" Dix demanded belligerently. "That street goes both ways, asshole. Maybe you should step up to the plate first, because the way I see it, you owe me, big time."

"We don't have time for your PMS, Dix. I need an update and I need it *now*."

She took a breath as though she was going to start harping again, but then restrained herself, her lips pressing tightly together. That's when Ray noticed her skin had gone pale and clammy, and she looked like she was walking a tight wire.

"Blood sacrifice," she said abruptly, her voice knife-edged. "Hundred people, maybe more, all women and children." Her lips snapped close, and she swallowed hard before continuing. "Hearts cut out. While they were alive. Fingers, toes, and eyes missing, too."

Ray's stomach churned, and bile burned on his throat and tongue. Angry tremors ran up through his legs and filled his chest before running down to his fingers. Energy crackled over his skin as he swore in the filthiest language he knew.

"What the fuck?" Dix exclaimed, jumping back and eyeing him as if he'd grown a second head. "You're—"

"A witch," Raven supplied acerbically. "A severely untrained one at that."

"A witch?" Dix echoed, turning a slack-jawed look on Ray. Fast as a snake-strike, she recovered. She leaped forward. "You asshole!" She punched him in the chest and ribs, her strikes full of muscle and fury.

Ray's breath exploded from his lungs, and he grabbed her, twisting her around and holding her against his chest, her arms crossed in front of her. She made a guttural sound and stomped his foot while simultaneously smashing her head back. He turned so that she hit his jaw and pain exploded up the side of his face.

He flung her away, not wanting to hurt her. She whipped around and launched herself back at him, only to get caught in mid-stride by a coil of technomage magic.

"Enough," Logan said. "You two can sort your issues later. Right now, we've got bigger problems." He looked at Dix. "You can be part of the solution or you can get the hell out. Choose now."

His voice had gone toneless. The less emotion he showed, the more he felt. Ray had seen it often enough in the war. Logan turned into a machine, shutting down everything soft inside him. Ray had always been grateful to be on the same side as Robot Logan. Robot Logan was relentless, merciless, deadly, and utterly terrifying.

Dix fought the containment, and then stilled, hatred and fury contouring her expression. "Fine. We'll do this your way."

The coil of magic unwound. Logan's gaze skewered her. "Good. Here's what you need to know. We've got at least two gods about to have a fight. Don't know anything about them, except that one is probably from South America and was around during the Olmec period. Those creatures from the lab—you heard about those?"

"Wait. Are you serious? Gods? Two?"

"As a heart attack and at least two."

Dix eyed Logan as if expecting a punchline.

"You heard about the creatures that escaped the lab?" he prompted.

Dix nodded slowly, looking grim as he explained.

"They're called Tahuizotls, and they answer to one of these gods. They're dangerous as hell, and I couldn't hold them very long with my magic. There are tactical technomage squads on the way. You'll need to coordinate them for me. Tell them what's going on and try to get them in position to help. I'll need an earpiece to communicate with you."

"My coven will be arriving as well," Raven said with a cool look at Dix, whose lip curled as the witch spoke, but she kept her cool. "You'll need to let them through to me."

"And where will you be?"

"I expect I'll be in the middle of a fight," the witch said dryly. "I'm sure they won't have trouble finding me once the fireworks start."

Dix eyed the three of them. "You all are going to stop a battle between gods. How exactly do you think you're going to manage that?"

"Any way we can," Ray muttered.

Logan just shrugged as if the question didn't bear consideration. Maybe it didn't. Ray had no idea how they were going to do stop this battle from happening, but he damned well meant to do it.

"Where are the bodies?" he asked Dix.

She jerked her chin toward her shoulder. "They're in a circle on the top of the big mound."

"Who found them?"

"Uniforms. Once the canvassing began in the area, people started figuring out a bunch of the women and children were missing, front doors left open like they'd walked out on their own. By the time our guys tracked them here, it was over." Her nostrils flared as she sucked in a tight breath. "Killers worked fast. Couldn't have had more than a couple hours max to kill everybody."

Even with people standing still to be slaughtered, Ray had a hard time picturing one or even two people getting it all done in that time frame. Hearts, eyes, fingers, and toes. Though he suspected the Tahuizotls had eaten the missing parts, all but the hearts. Angie hadn't mentioned they liked those. He shook his head, trying to wrap his brain around the level of carnage. He'd seen that sort of thing a couple times during the war. But not this bad, and not since. He'd thought those days were long behind him.

"All right. We'd better go in."

Dix went to her squad car and popped the trunk. She pulled an earpiece from within and turned to handed it to Logan. She held out her hand to give one to Ray and Raven.

The witch shook her head. "No thanks."

Dix shrugged and held one out to Ray. He took it.

"No point," Raven told him. "You'll burn it up soon as you start using magic."

He handed it back to Dix who eyed him with a mix of disgust and hate. "All this time—" She broke off and looked at Logan. "You knew?"

"Sorry," Logan drawled, as he finished inserting his earpiece and tapped it to activate. "I don't have any fucks to give right now."

Her lips compressed into a white line, and her eyes narrowed to slits, but Dix said nothing more. Not that she wouldn't have things to say later. If there was a later.

Ray fished a tactical vest out of the trunk. Squad cars were always kept fully stocked. He added a dozen magazines for his .45 and then grabbed one of the shotguns. A dozen shells already filled the loops on the front of his vest. Also attached to the vest were four flash bombs and four tear-gas canisters. He didn't know if any human weapons would work on gods, but he was willing to use whatever he had.

"Let's go," he said when he was ready, and then headed into the rot zone.

It was slow going. Though the ground appeared fairly level, the mold and fungus hid a rocky, uneven terrain. Ray set his feet carefully, trying not to slip on the slick rocks hidden under the foul rot or step off into a hole.

The entire area smelled like dead bodies and a garbage dump on a hot day. Breathing through his mouth only made Ray taste it. Spitting did nothing to clear it.

Some of the stuff grew in wet, turgid clumps, while other molds grew in feathery gray swells, like cotton candy made from spider webs. Clouds of it grew in odd-shaped towers, bobbing and weaving on the breeze, parts of the puffs collapsing into themselves, leaving black holes in the rotting mantle like mouths.

Logan slipped and fell to one knee, swearing in a low voice as he caught himself on one hand, sinking elbow deep into the sludge. He flung himself upright, and little splots of crud flew through the air, landing with soft plops.

Ray glanced at him to be sure he was all right, and then kept moving.

"Better stop," Raven said after they'd gone about fifty feet.

Ray and Logan instantly obeyed.

"What's the matter?" Ray asked.

She came up beside him. "I'm not sure, but that looks like it's moving." She pointed to an area just ahead that looked exactly like the rest of the godforsaken terrain, but as Ray concentrated, he realized she was right. The ground undulated slowly.

"What the fuck?"

"Water, maybe," the witch said. "There used to be a lot of catch basins and trenches. Could have filled up and been grown over."

Before Ray could respond, a noise pierced the air. It knifed through his head and his gut and drove needles through the marrow of his bones. He clasped his hands over his ears, but it didn't help.

He wasn't the only one. Raven's and Logan's faces were scrunched tight against the onslaught, even as they also covered their ears.

Abruptly the sound dropped below hearing, but now it scraped against his bones like nails on a blackboard. He shuddered.

"What's that?"

A roar sounded. A bellow of rage and challenge echoing up to the stars. That sound he recognized.

"That's Kayla," he said, jerking forward.

Logan caught his arm even as the roar was answered by another gut-chilling scream. A second one joined it. Ray wrenched to free himself, straining forward. The battle was beginning. He had to get to Kayla. *Now.*

"Take it slow," Logan commanded. "We're no good to her with busted legs."

Ray twisted free, snarling, but he made himself take careful, deliberate steps. He wished for a stick or something to test the ground with.

"Can't one of you give us a path?" he demanded.

Raven and Logan exchanged a look.

"If we do, it will warn them we're coming," Logan said.

"Won't matter if we don't get our asses up there to help Kayla fight. If they pick her off, we're not going to be able to do much until backup comes, and who knows when they'll show up?"

He spoke as if the thought of someone *picking Kayla off* didn't shove a knife into his gut.

"True enough."

"Me or you?" Raven asked Logan.

"I'll do it."

Logan didn't use anything like finesse. Orange ropes of electric magic flew from his fingers. He swept them in front of him, burning away the mold and sludge. Oily acrid smoke billowed up and engulfed them. Ray pulled his shirt up over his nose and mouth, his eyes watering. A dull keening sound reverberated through the sludge all around, making his joints ache.

The flames died revealing a thirty-yard strip of scorched earth. Ray didn't wait, he jogged down it, carefully avoiding piles of bones that seemed almost artistically arranged in little cairn towers.

Smoke made it difficult to see. He stopped when he reached the end of the strip, looking back impatiently for Logan who repeated his performance.

They were forced to twice go around murky ponds. The thick oily water moved as if something beneath had been disturbed.

The Mound loomed ahead, a broad, squat hill, steep sided and surrounded by ghostly trees with pale trunks and gray leaves that rustled with a sandpapery sound. The dry noise mixed with the ongoing keening sound in a discordant harmony. What worried Ray was the lack of noise from The Mound since the initial roar and shrieks.

As they approached, Ray caught a glimpse of movement among the trees. Tall shadows stretched too thin walked between the trunks. They didn't appear to have any facial features. Their long, spidery fingers brushed the ground.

"What are they?" Logan asked Raven.

She shook her head. "I don't know."

"Can we fight them?" He'd no intention of letting these things keep him from getting to Kayla.

"Why do you think we need to?" Scorn dripped from Raven's words. "Magical creatures are not inherently evil, any more than humans are. We must talk to them."

"We don't have time." It irritated Ray that he had made that quick judgement about the creatures. Whatever they were, they were also citizens of his city. A city he'd taken an oath to serve. They deserved the same consideration and respect of any human.

"We'll have to make time," Raven replied tartly.

She paused on the path as more of the beings appeared. They stood inside the tree line, ominous specters in the gloom.

"No time like the present," Logan said.

He fell in beside Ray as they approached the trees. Raven stepped up beside him on the other side.

Ray felt like a powder keg about to blow sky high. Magic ran over his skin like electricity, standing every hair on end. It boiled inside him, the pressure rising. He had no way to ease it and no real desire to. He wanted it to build so he'd be able to release it like a missile. Maybe he could be of some actual use. But if he didn't do something to let the pressure off soon, he was going to split apart at the seams. Literally.

They came to a halt just beyond the tree line. Up close and personal, the tree creatures appeared no more solid than the shadows they had seemed to be from a distance. Their heads were shaped like the top of a bowling pin, and the rest were taffy-shadows pulled long.

"You bring war," one of them said, and Ray detected a faint movement, as if of a mouth.

"We're hoping to stop one, actually," he said. "We need to pass through."

"Death," another of the ghost-tree dwellers said, and an involuntary shudder ran down Ray's spine. The word thrust inside him, ice filling his body and shriveling his dick.

Logan shifted and Raven shivered. Apparently Ray wasn't the only one getting a cold burst.

He didn't know how to respond to the one word. Was it a question? An accusation? Maybe a warning?

"Troubling," said the first voice, and the leaves of the surrounding trees rustled louder as if in agreement.

"We need to go find out what's happening," Ray said, pointing to The Mound.

"Wounds," the first voice said and up and down the tree line, arms lifted like shadowy claws, pointing behind the three visitors.

Ray looked back at the path Logan had burned through the mold and sludge. The dull keening that had started up when Logan first began continued, setting his teeth on edge. He took a breath and faced back around. This time he was pretty sure the word was an accusation. Maybe condemnation. But it was done and no way to fix it.

In the meantime, the silence on The Mound shattered. Snarls erupted, and then the frenzied sounds of enraged fighting.

Reason jettisoned out the window. Battle mode took over.

Ray plunged through the ghostly beings and trees. He was aware of surprise when the tree creatures proved to be solid. They didn't try to stop him. He knocked through them, slipping and sliding on the thick mold as he scrambled up the steep sides of The Mound. Somewhere a road spiraled up to the top, though he couldn't have said where. It had been the access during the burials.

He plunged his hands under the sludge looking for handholds as he made the climb. He pushed magic down to his hands and it burned through the mold, helping him to scale upward more quickly, but even so, the going was far too slow.

Screeches and snarls and growls poured over the edge of The Mound, punctuated by small pauses of quiet broken only by the rasps of breathing.

Ray had nearly reached the top when he encountered the ring of corpses. The bodies lay on their backs, legs hanging over the edge. Each person was barefoot, a meaty gash where their toes had been.

The coppery scent of blood overrode the stench of the mold. Ray's gorge rose. The fence of legs circled the top of The Mound in what had to be some perverted sort of spell circle.

He clawed up between a middle-aged woman and a boy maybe twelve years old. Rigor hadn't yet set in. Both stared upward, faces twisted in a rictus of pain and horror, minus their eyes. Their hands had been flung wide, the fingers also gone. Their chests had been sliced open from throat to pubis, their ribs ripped wide, their hearts torn free. Similarly, mutilated bodies lay as far as Ray could see in either direction.

He had only an instant to notice any of this. His attention was yanked to the center of The Mound where Kayla faced off against the three Tahuizotls, each the size of a Shetland pony. Behind her stood a pyramid made of stair-stepped retaining-wall stones, the top point constructed from what appeared to be sheets of beaten gold or brass. A ten-foot-by-ten-foot opening on the side provided the only entrance or window. Just within, Ray caught a glimpse of a woman.

Further out toward the middle of The Mound, a giant of a man crouched. He had to be near seven feet tall with long blond hair, some of it braided with beads. His beard was likewise long and braided. He knelt inside an intricate pebble pattern that had been laid out on a cleared space. The lines appeared to be made of obsidian, with crushed white stone in between. The shapes were a mix of jagged and curved. Eight pieces of two-foot-high obsidian stood at equal intervals around the pattern, flames burning blue on top.

In the center of the pattern, the man kneeled beside a glowing hole that bubbled with what appeared to be lava. He held a long stick of some kind in his hands and was chanting. What startled Ray was the woman just outside of the pattern. She wore dirt-stained witch robes with her brown hair caught up behind her head in a draggled bun. Her eyes were closed, and her mouth moved as she held her hands out before her. A flickering barrier of lavender circled away from her to seal itself in a dome protecting the chanting man.

She appeared to be in her early twenties, yet Ray was certain she had to be Theresa Runyon. But why would she be protecting the giant?

A flash of red smashed into the barrier, sending angry ripples through the lavender walls and exploding the ground just outside. Theresa Runyon staggered back a step, then straightened and seemed to pour more energy into the magic shield. Her hands shook with the effort.

More flashes. The source was two massive creatures on the opposite side of the dome. Their size would have put The Hulk to shame. Even the giant man in the middle of the pattern looked like a mere toddler next to them.

They must have stood twenty feet tall, their beefy shoulders rolling with muscle. Their hands were the size of dinner platters, each finger oddly squared off. Their faces were round and thick. Black mohawks sprouted from the middle of their otherwise bald heads, ending in thick tails that hung to their thighs, both decorated with bright feathers and bone beads. One wore two heavy gold earrings, the other had one. Both wore loincloths, arm bands, bracelets, and anklets. Ritual scars covered their chests and legs, appearing white against the elephant-gray skin, except where blood had dried dark red.

Most unsettling of all were their eyes. They glowed red, like the inside of a blast furnace. One of them turned and said something to the three Tahuizotls in a guttural, harsh language Ray didn't understand. Instantly the animals leaped at Kayla.

Ray's focus narrowed to them, their shining teeth, the poison that could kill Kayla in seconds if the dust in her blood had been activated.

Sound died. All he could hear was his own desperate breathing. He thrust out his hands. Slow. Too slow. Every move felt as if he were running into a hard wind. He shoved every ounce of magic his body held into his hands—raw, blistering, wild. The bolt launched like a comet, streaking across The Mound and smashing into the head of the third beast and the hindquarters of the second.

They both went flying. The first one crunched into the pyramid and dropped to the ground in a broken heap. The other spun in the air like a frisbee, then crashed to the ground. It lay still a moment, then rolled over and stood, shaking itself before launching again at Kayla, just behind the last of the three.

Her scales had lifted into razor petals. Her tail lashed as she batted aside the first Tahuizotl. It hit the ground and sprang back. She reared up on her hind legs and grabbed it in her claws, flattening it to the ground. She held it there, head raised as she searched for the other two.

The second one grappled her neck with its hand-like claws, then fell away, yelping. She shook herself, her crystalline eyes flashing brilliantly.

One of the hulks heard the wounded cry of the second beast and turned. It flung out a hand. A streamer of red magic rolled from his hand.

Ray heard himself yell a warning. He pulled up all the magic inside him. It wasn't enough. He reached for more. It came in a geyser, pouring into him from everywhere and nowhere. He released it at the massive attacker, unaware of the heat blackening his clothing and searing his skin. He heard sounds vaguely, as if from very far away, or deep underwater. He saw his attack strike the colossal horror.

It moved faster than something its size should have been able to. It swung its arm and directed its attack at Ray. Their two magics collided.

The world exploded.

Chapter 23

Kayla

MAGIC SLAMMED RAY. His body arced high in the air before plunging over the side of The Mound.

Kayla's brain went white.

She'd come to this place, driven by a protective instinct that overwhelmed everything else. She'd hardly known when she transformed or how she got to The Mound.

She'd arrived in time to see the two goliaths finishing their blood ceremony. They'd stood on either side of a pile of warm human hearts, chanting guttural words in a language she didn't recognize. A cloud of red rolled up out of nowhere, enveloping them and the hearts. It flared and then vanished along with the hearts. Only now, the two giant creatures' eyes had begun to glow blood-red.

They still hadn't noticed her, but they turned toward an intricate pattern of stones where a blond man knelt. He was big, but more NBA to their Fee-Fi-Fo-Fum. He held a long object over a pool of molten rock and chanted, though Kayla couldn't make out what he said.

At that moment, Kayla saw her grandmother. Theresa Runyon stood inside a magical barrier surrounding the rock spell pattern. Kayla had never seen her without an aging glamour. Though her face was pale and her eyes sunken and bruised looking, she appeared near the same age as Landon. She stood with her shoulders square, her mouth flat and resolute as she fed power into a lavender shield protecting her and the giant from the two goliaths.

Kayla swung her head back and forth. Where was Aunt Margaret?

The pyramid caught her attention. She could smell sickness emanating from it, and a perfume she recognized. No, not a perfume. Sage, rosemary, lavender, cedar, sweetgrass. They overlayed the stench of illness, but didn't eradicate it.

Movement inside the doorway. Aunt Margaret. Like Grandmother, she'd dropped her glamour and now looked like her mother's sister. She gazed out at where Kayla's grandmother poured energy into the barrier.

Suddenly the two goliaths marched toward the pyramid, ignoring Grandmother and the chanting man. A note of desperation colored his words, turning them ragged and short as he watched the mammoth men stomp across the packed dirt.

The three creatures from the lab—she tried to remember what they were called. She couldn't. Demon dogs. Hellspawn. Either worked. They trotted toward the pyramid ahead of their enormous masters, who should have moved ponderously, but instead walked with liquid grace.

Whatever they wanted inside, Kayla couldn't allow them to get there. Not just for her aunt. Fury over the slaughter they'd committed on so many innocents boiled her blood. Her talons clutched deep in the ground. This was *her* city; these were *her* people. These fuckers needed to learn they couldn't waltz in and hurt whomever they wanted. There would be consequences. She bared her teeth, making a low growling sound in her throat. Deadly consequences.

She slunk forward, her long elegant body undulating back and forth. She carried her tail out behind her. Every scale on her body lifted in preparation for battle. She'd neglected that when she first fought the three devil dogs. She wouldn't underestimate them this time. They wouldn't be able to bite through the scales easily, and not without cutting the fuck out of their mouths.

Malice glittered icy cold in her heart. Time for justice.

She roared, announcing her presence before lunging to stand between the intruders and the pyramid. One of the goliaths gave a harsh command. The three devil dogs leaped at her.

Instinct took over. She whirled, lashing one of the beasts with her tail, sending it bowling. She snatched another in her teeth and shook it viciously, then threw it at one of the goliaths. The last jumped on her back, but screeched in fury and pain before dropping off. She remained in position, guarding the pyramid entrance.

The animals regrouped, and their masters lost immediate interest, turning instead to launch an attack on Grandmother and the chanting man.

The three hellhounds came at Kayla again. Before they could reach her, a bolt of energy came from nowhere. It slammed the second and third demon dogs. She knocked aside the first one. It hit the ground and launched at her again. She rose on her hind legs, grabbing it in her claws and slamming it to the ground. She held it there while it squirmed and moaned with pain.

One of the others leaped at her again. It grabbed at her neck with its clawed hands, then screamed in pain and fell away. Kayla snarled triumph. They'd thought her easy prey. In the lab, she had been, her human mind holding her back, but not now. Now she was fury and justice and vengeance rolled into one.

Now she'd make them pay.

One of the goliaths turned at the sound of the demon dog's cry. It stretched out a giant hand and magic unraveled from it. In that moment, she heard Ray's yell, and then a blast of magic hit the goliath.

It turned and fired back. The two streams of magic met, and the world exploded. Kayla clutched her claws into the ground as it shook and shuddered.

She saw the blast wave strike Ray. She saw him flung up into the air. She saw him falling. Saw him disappear off the edge of The Mound.

Her mind collapsed to a single point of unbearable pain. She roared, unable to contain it all. She zeroed in on the goliath who'd killed Ray. He couldn't have survived the fall, much less the blast.

Her world narrowed. Every cell, every nerve in her body burned with unimaginable pain. It exploded from her in a scream that tore her throat. She'd make the creature pay. Show this *thing* exactly what pain meant. This creature who'd invaded her home and killed the person who meant most to her in the whole world. It was all she had left.

Sensation ran through her. She shuddered as something moved within, a feeling like a dozen different-sized gears sliding together and turning in a complicated pattern. Her human self swelled, flowing outward and melding with her transformed self. No longer was her mind and being divided. They'd joined together, sharing rage, burning loss, a need for vengeance, and the unrelenting compulsion to protect her territory and people.

She stalked forward, head lowered, body tensed, her tail slowly winding back and forth.

The goliath watched her come, its red eyes somehow vacant and shrewd at the same time. It spoke sharp-edged words she didn't understand. A warning or maybe a curse. Invisible *somethings* hit hard on her chest and sides. Her breath whooshed out of her. She didn't stop. The goliath lifted its hand again.

She leaped, thrusting herself like a comet. She crashed into the massive creature. It felt like hitting a stone wall. Its hand slapped her head. Magic jolted through her, electrifying her insides. She staggered to the side, her body shaking as the power washed through her.

She collected herself and leaped again, clawing at its stomach as she snapped her jaws tight on its arm. She dug runnels into its skin, and her teeth pierced its flesh and ground against rock-hard bone. It tasted of dry leaves and gravel.

The goliath made a hollow sound and punched its other fist into her chest. This time the jolt of energy seemed to liquefy her flesh. She dropped to the ground, fire searing through every cell of her being.

The snarls and growls of the demon dogs coming for her broke through her pain. She rolled to her feet, scrambling hastily back to the pyramid. Her body shook with continuing reaction. To her frustration, the goliath barely looked the worse for wear.

As luck would have it, both of the hulking monsters decided to lavish their attention on her as the two remaining demon dogs closed in.

What could she do? What the hell use was it being a god if she didn't have any power to *do* anything?

No. She rejected that. She must have some ability she could use against them. She'd quieted the damned whirlpool and that was a force of nature. If she could do that, there *had* to be more to her than brute strength and teeth and claws.

Unfortunately, nothing came to mind. No last-minute saving grace. No sudden bolt from the blue.

So be it.

Kayla crouched, tensing herself, her tail winding slowly back and forth as she watched them come.

A piercing scream ripped open the night. Kayla felt the agony of it in the air, in her veins. She leaped forward in answer, though she had no idea what she was answering.

Then everything stopped.

The lavender barrier protecting the blond giant had disappeared. He now stood in front of Kayla's grandmother. Several inches of bloody sword stuck out through her back. With little ceremony, the giant pushed her grandmother's body to the ground, unsheathing the sword from her body as he did.

A cloud of gauzy magic clung to the weapon, roiling and twisting, and slowly sank inward to disappear along with the blood coating the blade. The sword gleamed brilliant white, a tooth of ivory.

The giant of a man swung the blade back and forth as if testing it, then set his sights on the closest goliath. His not-particularly-handsome face twisted with hate. He let out a war cry and lunged.

To Kayla's amazement, the goliath jerked away from the sword and lobbed a bolt of magic at the giant, who slashed the sword through it. The magic exploded into sparks. Kayla rocked backward as the shockwave hit her.

Now the other goliath joined the fight. In the meantime, the devil dogs slunk closer to her, clearly undecided about what they should be doing. Blood coated the jowls of one, though the cuts it had taken from her razor scales seemed to have closed. The other limped, leaving blood prints on the ground.

She snapped at them, and they groveled on the ground, whining.

Deciding to press her advantage, Kayla charged. Both sprang away, retreating a good twenty feet. She charged again and they retreated again. She pulled back too, having come too close to the ménage-à-trois fight.

Both goliaths flung bolts of magic at the giant who parried and danced aside, but continued to push toward them. Clearly the sword could hurt the goliaths, and all three of them knew it.

She could have let them fight it out and then attacked the winner, but she knew for sure she couldn't beat just one of the goliaths. The blond giant was still unknown. Better to help him defeat the mammoth monsters than risk them winning.

Kayla sprang at the closest hulk, landing on his shoulders and digging her talons deep. She raked at him with her back claws as her weight and momentum knocked him to the ground. She clawed at its spine, raking the flesh from its back.

It barely seemed to notice. It pushed up from the ground and Kayla jumped off it, grabbing its foot in her teeth and shaking it viciously as she threw her weight back. It fell again.

A bolt of green magic came from off to the side, spreading over the creature and weaving into a net. It dug runners into the ground, rooting itself. Another bolt of electric lightning smashed into the second goliath. That distraction gave the blond giant an entry. He lunged and drove the sword into the creature's chest. It slid in easily, as if the goliath was made of mist.

The giant yanked the sword free and backed up, watching. Kayla did the same, hypnotized. The goliath's body turned shiny black, and cracks zig-zagged wildly across every inch of it. A glow built inside where the sword had gone in. Fiery red liquid oozed out and ran down to the ground.

Red power leaked out of the eyes, coalescing into a vaguely man-shaped cloud with what might have been wings.

"You may win today," it told the giant in a deep, raspy voice. "If my brother fails, we will come again for her. We will bring her back and send her soul to Tipolihuican forever. Then I will travel to Tamoanchan and destroy your mate and spawn. This I vow. I will never allow such vermin to rest safely beside the fountain of the misty skies."

Before Kayla could really register that she understood the words though they had not been spoken in any tongue she knew—the ghostly creature whipped downward, swiping all-too-solid claws at the blond man who swung the sword to deflect. Too late. Streaks of black rose on his face. His shirt shredded, and more putrid black streaked his chest and arm.

His eyes rolled up into his head, and he collapsed.

The second goliath seemed to take this as an invitation. It pushed against the magic net holding it to the ground. Red flared around its body, and the net melted away with the not-at-all-pleasant smell of cooked cabbage.

Kayla raced forward, getting to the prone giant first and snatching the hilt of the sword in her mouth before racing to the other side of The Mound, avoiding the rock pattern and the crumpled body of her grandmother. The goliath lumbered after her, moving quicker than she expected.

Now what should she do? Could she hold the weapon in her mouth well enough to attack?

"Kayla!"

Zach and Raven raced toward her, flinging magic bombs at her attacker as they sped across the ground.

The creature turned and launched a sweeping attack of its own. Magic poured from its hands, coiling around the two and reeling them toward it. Both fought back, but it was clear they couldn't overwhelm the goliath's power. God's power, Kayla reminded herself with no small bitterness. Why didn't she have some useful tool of her own?

Another battery of magic struck the goliath. This time from the cave. Her Aunt Margaret had come out and sent a swarm of spinning gold stars at the creature. They whirled and cut at it, but the thing hardly seemed to notice.

Kayla had to get close enough to it to use the sword. In beast form, she couldn't do that. Not with any degree of certainty, and she had a feeling she'd only get one chance. Anyway, to wield the sword she needed hands. That meant transforming, which meant she'd be as vulnerable as the slaughtered people sprawled around the edge of The Mound.

The goliath kept attacking Zach and Raven. The air crackled, and the night lit on disco fire as their magics collided. The air shuddered and bulled into Kayla, knocking her around.

Now was her chance.

Kayla concentrated on transforming. She wasn't wet. Hadn't been for a while, but she'd also embraced her shifter form, wanting its power and speed. That had let her stay in that form. Now she felt a *give* inside her, a twist like a key in a rusty lock, and then her flesh melted and reformed into her own ordinary self.

The sword dropped to the ground. Keeping one eye on the goliath, Kayla bent to pick it up. The moment she touched it, she wanted to vomit.

Souls and death clung to the weapon. She looked at it. It was formed from bone, or rather, bones. A 3-D puzzle of many. Two and two clicked together and she realized that they must be the missing bones of the murder victims. She undoubtedly held in her hand the bone from the dryad and many others.

Use us, a tart voice said inside her head, sharp among the feathery whispers of multiple voices chorusing with it. *We are what we are, and we are dead because of these bastards. We cannot kill what possesses them, but we can make it impossible to stay.*

Kayla almost dropped the sword. "Grandmother? But how? He didn't take any of your bones."

She almost rolled her eyes at herself. Because of course she knew so much about magic and the blond giant and the spell he'd cast.

He wanted my blood not my bones. Now don't waste time. They will kill Margaret and you, and my sacrifice will be meaningless. We can talk later.

Damned right they'd talk. Kayla had a shitload of questions for her grandmother.

Kayla firmed her grip on the sword. Long and slim, the blade didn't look particularly sharp, except for the point. Symbols and words etched its length.

This is necessary, Grandmother said, and something sharp cut deep across Kayla's palm. Blood welled between her fingers and ran in streamers down the blade. It filled the etchings. As blood covered the last one, power exploded. It burned through Kayla like a Nebraska lightning bolt. Her entire body went incandescent.

The power flashed outward, driving out along invisible filaments connecting her like a spider web to everything around her. She felt the uneasy stir of roots in the ground, the haze of pain mantling the ground surrounding The Mound, the army of dead piled deep and wide, the many heartbeats of the living pattering away in an ocean rhythm, and so much more. Her entire body lit with sensation, signals coming at her in a sonic hail storm.

She dropped to her knees, head reeling, trying to make sense of the inundation, or at least keep from being overwhelmed. But more kept rolling in, and she didn't know how to understand it or sort through it.

Stop your whining. You're a god. Be one and hurry up about it, her grandmother's voice said in that no-nonsense vinegar tone Kayla remembered so well. *You can't fail.*

The hell she couldn't. But Kayla wasn't going to take up the challenge. The cost would be high. Too high. It was already too high. She squeezed her eyes shut, determined not to think of Ray.

"I don't know how to be a god. I don't even know what it means."

We can feel your connection to us, to this land. Grutte Pier and the Butterfly don't know it, but the weapon will do far more in your hands than anybody else's. Your land and people will give you strength.

"Grutte Pier? The Butterfly?"

Focus. Claim your power. We're almost out of time.

Grandmother and the other voices fell into expectant silence.

At first Kayla had no idea what to do. She ran over the conversation with her grandmother again. Connections. All the connections to the sword and the city and that she was the center of the web.

Taking a slow breath, she made herself relax and opened herself to the connections. At first she tried to sort through them, but couldn't. There were too many, and they came bulleting at her too fast. Instead she let herself float in the swarm of sensations, letting them stitch and harpoon into her without paying attention to the individual strikes. She'd let her subconscious deal with sorting them out and try to stay sane in the meantime.

She had no sense of time. It could have taken days or minutes or seconds. She had to hope that Raven, Aunt Margaret, and Zach would keep the goliath and demon beasts occupied.

When she finally felt the deluge slowing, she brought herself back to alertness, holding herself carefully as she adjusted to her new awareness. It was like having a sixth or seventh sense, a dimension of feeling that anchored into her being and buzzed through her with a not-too-unpleasant electricity and let her touch and have an awareness far beyond herself.

Good. We can start. The sword will want to drink him, but you mustn't let it. We are not enough to overwhelm him. Do you understand?

Not even a little bit. "Don't let the sword drink him," Kayla repeated as she pushed herself to her feet, leaning heavily on the sword.

Take him down, came the imperious order. Winding around her grand-mother's voice were other voices, surging angrily. A call for vengeance, for justice.

Their call woke an answering resolution deep in the core of Kayla's being—a raw and wild instinct to protect her domain, her people, and if not protect them, give them reckoning.

She rolled her shoulders, lifting the sword. It gleamed silvery white, like the light-embroidered edge of a cloud, the symbols flickering with burnished fire.

The goliath stood forty feet away. She approached quietly. Zach and Raven saw her and stepped up their attacks to distract him. So did Aunt Margaret. The night strobed with brilliant light. Kayla skirted the rock pattern. At the center, the small pool of lava heated the air, making her sweat.

The next seconds slowed. She lifted the sword, holding it overhand like a giant knife. She reached the goliath and drove it into its back. It went in with nearly no resistance, as if its flesh was no more substantial than honey.

It stiffened and arched backward, then staggered and dropped forward. The sword twisted and so did Kayla's arms, wrenching her off her feet. She tried to let go. She couldn't. Her hands were glued to the hilt.

She fell on top of the goliath. It rolled to dislodge the sword, making dry chuffing noises. Kayla managed to swing herself aside, but her legs still ended up underneath the massive creature who was, in fact, very substantial. Her body torqued so hard she thought her spine might pop apart.

Kayla wrenched at her hands, fruitlessly. The sword neither moved from the goliath's back, nor did it allow her to let go of it.

It drinks. Stop it.

Her grandmother sounded distracted and wavery.

How was she supposed to stop it? But then, the sword had forged a connection to her using her blood. The sword and the souls and bones of those who'd died to create it. Her people, for better or worse.

But how to use that bond? How to stop the sword from doing what it was apparently designed to do? Why hadn't it swallowed the first one? She had no idea and no time to consider it.

She concentrated on the sword and her hands and tried to find the binding that connected them. Her attention roamed over the dense jungle of filaments spreading out from her in every direction. She zeroed in on a tumultuous brilliance. She slid inside it, discovering a metaphysical battle raging within.

The goliath's soul—or really the demon inhabiting it—appeared as a de-vouring red cloud, much like the first one. The spirits fighting against it were shining shards of jewels, slashing at the cloud. The sword pulsed white and drew the cloud to it.

And if it did take that soul in? Kayla would be connected to it as well. Fun times.

The damned knife needed an off switch. Or a time-out. Maybe a swat on the snout with a rolled-up newspaper. *If only.*

Her grandmother had said she could control it. Maybe she was overthinking. Maybe she shouldn't think of it as separate from her, but as a piece of her. A hand, an eye. And if it was part of her, then she ought to be able to simply make it do what she wanted, the way she'd tap her foot or clap her hands.

She closed her inner eyes and opened herself fully to the connection. For a moment it was too much. A deluge of information coming in from every single capillary tying her to the land and people of Portland. She shrank away despite herself, but it kept pouring in. She made herself relax and accept. Much to her surprise, after a minute, she adjusted. She let that all go fuzzy, like ignoring an itch. Or a billion bee stings. Little by little, she pushed them out to where she was aware of them, but focused on nothing in particular. Now she concentrated on the sword. It throbbed and hungered. It wanted to dominate, to control, to take.

It was like one of those terrible nighttime cravings for barbecue or ice cream, one that required you to get out of bed and go get what you hungered for as fast as possible.

But Kayla had no intention of giving into this craving. Barbecue, sure, but god-chow? No thanks.

She had a sense that the sword was both the bones and the souls bound to it, and something separate. Maybe the spell that had created it. It had a purpose. A desire. A hunger. She understood them all, but those things needed tempering. Hysterical laughter bubbled in Kayla's chest. Tempering. Sword. Funny.

She let her awareness flow down into the sword, feeling its pull. But it couldn't eat her. It *was* her, at least in part. It trying to eat her was like a snake snacking on its own tail. Couldn't be done. But it *was* enough to keep it busy so that it couldn't suck up the enemy god like a strawberry milkshake.

Kayla felt the release when the sucking stopped and the other god wrenched free of the sword's summons.

Freeing herself was like swimming up a waterfall. By the time she came back to awareness, sweat drenched her body and her heart thundered like a dozen stampeding elephants. She ached, and cramps invaded her muscles.

"Little god," came a husky voice, oddly accented.

She opened her eyes. She'd somehow let go of the sword, and it had fallen free onto the ground a few inches from her hand. Crouching on top of the goliath and facing her was a figure similar to the being that had come out of the first goliath. Its insubstantial body shifted and blurred like red smoke, or maybe a cloud of tiny red birds, all swooping and moving in a pulsing rhythm. A shadowy pair of partially folded wings rose from his back. Watching him—or it—was mesmerizing.

"Who are you? *What* are you?" Kayla asked, blinking to break the hypnotic draw. She was too tired to dig up any fear for herself. Mostly she hoped he wouldn't turn on everybody else.

He made a liquid-sounding answer that sounded maybe like, "Nietzchecheese."

"That's a stupid name." She sounded far more belligerent than she should, lying on the ground with the sword just out of reach and a giant dead thing flopped on top of her, but she didn't have any fucks left. "Or maybe that's your species. Which one is it?"

Mr. Plague of Red Death smiled indulgently as if she was some sort of child to be humored. "You cannot protect her, little god," he crooned.

"Protect who?"

That seemed to startle him. He straightened slightly as if affronted. "The Obsidian Butterfly. Itzpapalotl. She who betrayed her people, her sisters and brothers, and tainted the place she no longer holds sacred."

Kayla shook her head. "Sorry. Don't know who you're talking about. Don't care, either. Just want you to get the hell out of my city."

He contemplated her a long moment. "You will banish her as well?"

Banish? Could she do that? If not, he didn't need to know that.

"What I do is none of your damned business."

"Then you give her refuge."

She sighed and rolled her eyes, so done with this fight, and done with the whole mess. She was exhausted beyond measure. She wanted nothing more than to go home, bolt the doors, climb into bed, and grieve for Ray.

The thought sent a burrowing ache deep into her body. She couldn't breathe. Couldn't move. It saturated her, growing and pushing, and she had nowhere to put it. Tears leaked from the corners of her eyes as she stared straight up at the sky, her body rigid.

Since she'd met him, Ray had been her anchor, the nucleus of her entire world. He'd been the only one in the world she could trust. The only one in the world who cared about her for her. The only one in the world who understood her, who believed in her, who'd be right there beside her no questions asked.

And then came Magicfall.

How fucked up was it that she'd found her way back to him, and this god, this demon from the bowels of hell, had taken him away from her? Taken the gravity of her world, and she was coming apart and floating away in pieces.

The feelings frothed up and overflowed, pouring out along the bonds tying her to the city. She didn't try to pull it back. Every feeling she'd held locked inside her for the last four years had ruptured free, and she couldn't have stopped the deluge if she'd wanted to.

Hate rose to the surface as she stared at the smug god sitting just in front of her. But at the moment, she couldn't kill him the way he deserved. But she didn't have to do anything to make him happy.

"I don't know who this Obsidian Butterfly is," she said through clenched teeth, "but I'd gladly keep her safe from a dick like *you*."

Her words seemed to have a physical impact. The gauzy red outline of his body jerked and twitched.

"You cannot stop us. We *will* come for her, and we *will* punish her sins."

"Then do it now," Kayla dared him. "Right now. Take her." Her lips curled. "If you can." Let him try. She'd stop him, even if she had to let the sword drink him up. She laid her hand on the hilt of the sword. Instantly voices swelled in her mind, and with them came a hail of emotion, hitting her like meteors. Her mind wavered, and it took all she had to keep herself focused on Nietzsche-cheese. They skewered her, and she could hardly breathe.

He gathered himself, raising himself up haughtily. "Careful, little god. Challenge me at your own risk."

"So, you can't do it." She broke into a choked laughter. "That's got to chap your ass. I may be just a flea of a god, but I'm strong enough to cockblock you."

He swooped down so she practically had to go cross-eyed to look in his face. She could see his features now. A beak of a nose, predator eyes, high flat cheekbones, thin flat lips.

"You are *nothing*," he hissed. "A mere pebble."

"Yeah? For want of a nail the battle was lost. If I'm such a termite, why don't you crush me and get on with your evil plans?" Surreptitiously she lifted her hand so it no longer touched the sword. The relief of separation was nearly unbearable.

"Because of *her*. Because of the sword *she* gave him the knowledge and power to create. Without it you would be on your knees. I would tear your beating heart from your chest and I would eat it while you watched."

"Just like I said: you lose. So take your sorry ass back to wherever you came from. Better yet, why don't you just go straight to hell, don't pass go, don't collect two hundred dollars."

Something seared up from inside her. A cocktail of hate, loss, pain, and defiance. She felt it explode from her, ramming into him like a comet. It struck him, whooshing him off into the sky like something from a Roadrunner cartoon.

Kayla watched in awe and no little triumph. Her body convulsed. Her head snapped back against the ground, her back arching, her arms flopping. Brightness bloomed behind her eyes and swelled and shattered.

Chapter 24

Kayla

SHE CAME TO herself with Zach and Raven kneeling over her, arguing. Or maybe just discussing with intensity. Kayla didn't pay attention to them, instead taking stock of herself. They'd pulled her out from under the goliath. That was about all she could say for certain, besides the fact that she was alive. She felt hollow and spent. She just wanted to crawl into a hole and pull the dirt over her.

You can't always get what you want. The line of the Rolling Stones song ran through her head on an endless loop. Story of her life.

She made a sound and struggled to sit up. Zach helped her, putting an arm around her shoulder to support her.

"Easy now," he said. "You've been out of it for a while." He sounded strained.

"I told you she'd be okay," the witch said. She pressed her palm to Kayla's forehead and hummed. Warmth sluiced through Kayla, along with a gentle fizz of energy.

She looked at Raven. "I don't know what that was, but thanks."

"Call it caffeine for the soul. Won't last long."

"Better than chicken soup, any day of the week."

"I don't know. I make a fabulous chicken and wild rice soup."

"Really? We're going to shoot the shit over food?" Zach demanded. "Hello! God fight. Near death experience. Wild demon dogs, not to mention a massacre. Don't you think we've got more important things to deal with than chicken soup?"

"He's a little high-strung, isn't he?" Kayla said to Raven.

"Men tend to get emotional in tough situations," the witch agreed.

"Okay, how about this? When the cavalry arrives, they're going to want to know why you're here and what happened. They're more likely to blame you than thank you for saving the city. You need to get out of here," Zach said.

His words motivated Kayla to stand. Her legs shook with tremors, and she felt about as steady as a newborn colt. Zach caught her around the waist to steady her.

"What happened?"

Raven and Zach exchanged a concerned look.

"I don't have amnesia. I mean, what happened after I passed out?"

Zach gave a little nod. "You went into convulsions. We got you out from under that massive carcass and got you stable. Took you a while to wake up, though." He cast a dark look at Raven.

"I've done a lot of healing," she said in a tone that said she'd explained this before and more than once. "Sometimes you've got to have a little patience and let the body and mind recover."

He said something under his breath that didn't sound particularly nice. Kayla didn't ask for clarity. Her gaze roved over the top of The Mound to settle on her crumpled grandmother.

Kayla wasn't sure what she felt about her death. Certainly, she didn't feel anything like the pain of losing Ray.

At the thought of him, feelings surged up again. She slammed the lid on them, refusing to let them out again. Not until she could go home and fall apart without an audience.

Her grandmother wasn't really gone anyway. Not that they'd been all that close. She'd been totally against Kayla joining the police academy, though she hadn't been the asswipe about it that Alistair had been. Anyway, Grandmother remained in the sword.

Kayla frowned and looked for it. The weapon lay near goliath. She staggered toward it.

"Where are you going?" Zach asked.

"The sword. Nobody else should touch it." Though the blond giant— Grutte Pier, according to Grandmother—hadn't seemed to have much of a problem, Kayla didn't want to subject anybody else to it, nor did she want the Obsidian Butterfly, whoever she was, to get a hold of it.

"It's fine. We need to get you out of here before the cavalry moves in. They'll take you into custody until they sort out what happened, and even then they might not let you out."

"I'd like to see them try," she muttered, but he was right. Mostly because she didn't want to have to deal with the bigoted bullshit, and she definitely didn't want to have to fight her way clear. "That stupid sword is *not* fine. It's dangerous, and I don't want anybody else handling it."

"Fine, but then we get you out. They're already on their way up."

"What about my Aunt Margaret?"

She followed his glance to her grandmother's body. Her aunt knelt beside her, crying as she stroked her mother's face. Both still wore the robes they'd been wearing when they were kidnapped.

"She should put her age glamour back on if she doesn't want everyone to figure out she's a witch. And I should call Landon," Kayla said. "Tell him his mom's okay." Not that Alistair would let him get on the phone or pass along the message. Asshole.

"When you're somewhere safe, you can do it. Or I can, if you want," Zach said.

"I'll help your aunt with the glamour. And your grandmother," Raven added.

"There's someone else. Nietzche-cheese called her the Obsidian Butterfly. She had another name, but I can't remember it," Kayla said, the numbness she'd been feeling starting to wear off. Her body hurt like someone had used her for a punching bag.

"Nietzche-cheese?" Zach gave her confused look.

"The second god-critter. That's what his name sounded like."

"Right. No worries on the woman. We've got her contained. She's pretty sick so she's not much of a threat right now."

"She's a woman? What's with the Obsidian Butterfly stuff?"

Raven answered. "Since they were hunting her, likely she is also divine. Perhaps she also takes another form."

Made sense. "What's going to happen to her?"

"I don't know," Zach said. "I don't know how long we can contain her, and how much does she deserve it? If she's a victim and hasn't committed a crime . . ." He trailed off, looking at Raven.

"We can take her to the Island," she said slowly. "But when she regains strength, if she proves to be malevolent, we may not be able to handle her."

"She needs to come home with me," Kayla said with a sigh.

"Go home with you?" Zach echoed. "You're nuts."

"I've got the sword, and I'm betting it can at least hurt her. Plus Nietzche-cheese and his buddy said they'll come looking for her again. I don't want them showing up on anybody else's doorstep. They'll kill first and ask questions later. This is *my* damned town, and I'm not letting them kill anybody here again."

"And if she's a psycho-murderer just like them?"

"Then I'll deal with her."

"Jesus," Zach said, sliding his fingers through his hair. "If I let you do this, you know Ray will skin me alive, right?"

Kayla froze. "Ray will—?" she whispered, hope flaring painfully. She shook her head. "They killed him. Hit him with magic and blew him off The Mound."

"No. Well, maybe that happened. He was definitely not looking good when he dropped out of the sky. But we caught him—" He motioned to Raven and himself. "Before he hit the ground. Raven applied a healing spell, and I called the paramedics. He's at the hospital by now."

Kayla barely heard anything more than Ray was still alive. *Alive.*

"If we hadn't been there, he *would* have been killed," Raven said. "He has no idea how to use his magic." She shook her head. "Any witch with even the least bit of training would know how to anchor themselves and deal with the energy from an attack like that."

"He really is alive?" Kayla asked, her voice cracking

"If nothing ate him while we've been up here," Zach said with gallows humor, and then seemed to realize just how distraught Kayla was. He put an arm around her. "He's really going to be okay."

"I want to see him." Kayla turned blindly and started in the direction of where he'd been blasted from The Mound.

Zach caught her arm and pulled her back. "You can. But you'll have to wait. You can't be seen. There will be too many questions that you're not going to want to answer. You need to hide until we're done, and then we can take you out of here."

"I don't—"

"Have a choice," Zach finished for her. "It's what Ray would want. He isn't going to want to wake up to find you're being held in a containment facility while the bureaucrats figure out what part you played in all this and if you're a threat to the city."

Her lip curled. "I'd like to see them try."

"I'll remind you that you're in pretty shitty shape right now, and you'd have to take on cops and technomages. You'd certainly end up killing someone, and I know you don't want that. Anyhow, you'll see Ray faster if you do as I say."

Kayla hated that he was right. She didn't want to wait, but she didn't have much choice. The last thing she wanted to do was start another fight, especially with the good guys.

"Okay," she said not particularly coherently. Her brain vibrated like she'd been smashed between two giant cymbals. It was all she could do to keep standing up. "He's really okay?"

"He'll need more healing," Raven said "but he's fine. Now you must go. They've got technomages clearing the road up The Mound."

Kayla became aware of sirens and flashing lights.

"We'll be swarmed in a few minutes." Raven frowned. "You'd be better transforming. That would help your natural healing process, and you'd be more comfortable while you wait for us."

"I don't know if I can," Kayla said. Her gaze drifted to her Aunt Margaret. "I should talk to her."

"Later," Zach said. "We'll be putting her in an ambulance. You can see her when you see Ray."

"I don't . . ." Leaving seemed wrong. Shouldn't she stay and make sure Nietzche-cheese and his buddy didn't come back? Make sure this Obsidian Butterfly didn't suddenly bring on the apocalypse?

"We'll handle things," Zach said, exchanging a quick nod with Raven when Kayla asked. "We've got it covered. We cut a path you can follow and we're not far from the main road. There's a little grocery store in an old gas station about a quarter mile up. You can wait for us there."

Though she could hear the sirens coming closer, Kayla still resisted. "What about those dog creatures?"

"They ran off when the second of those gods went down. We'll hunt them down later, if they didn't go back where they came from. Are you done now? Will you please leave?"

Kayla reluctantly nodded.

Despite trying several times, she couldn't transform without the help of water. She'd embraced her other self in her fight, but exhaustion played havoc with her concentration. She couldn't sort out how to shift. The water spell in her bracelet had gone wonky, probably because of the fight or her initial bonding with the sword, Raven said. Since there was no time to fix it or create a new one, Kayla opted to climb down The Mound.

But leaving had its own challenges. For one, she had to take the sword. Picking it up sent her brain on another roller-coaster ride. It took a couple minutes until she found equilibrium and could get her legs to start working again. At the edge of The Mound, she was confronted with the bodies of the people the goliaths had sacrificed. They'd begun to smell already, and some had begun to sink into the dirt as if The Mound was claiming them.

It took all the control she could scrape together to not heave up her stomach contents. The sword flashed incandescent white in her hand as anger and hate at the murders, at the wanton carelessness for life, surged inside her. The red lettering unwound and slithered around the blade in undulating strands.

She stopped just within the ring of bodies. Once again driven by instinct, she kneeled down and laid the sword across her thighs. She lowered her hands to the ground and dug her fingers in deeply, curling them around fistfuls of soil.

She pushed downward and out, feeling the grit of minerals on her skin, the damp of the dirt, the many bones of the dead buried beneath, and something else. A pulsing of something that wasn't life, but gave the impression of sanctuary. Haven. A somber welcoming and a protectiveness, as though the souls buried here mourned the newly dead and offered them comfort.

Kayla touched that ethereal coalescence, felt it recognize and welcome her. Their Guardian. She *pushed* out of herself. As had happened with the whirlpool, power flowed out of her, digging roots into The Mound. Those roots rose out of the ground, wrapping each of the dead, pulling them under. Not wanting them to be forgotten, any of them—those who'd died before or now—Kayla invited flowers to grow across the entire Mound. Lilies, roses, lupin, poppies, dahlias—every flower she could remember seeing, some that grew from her imagination.

In no time at all, the top of The Mound became a lush garden of ever-blooming flowers. Sweet and spicy floral scent pushed away the stench of rot, mold, and death. Beauty in the heart of horror.

With nothing else she could do, Kayla slowly drew back into herself. She picked up the sword again and stood.

"I'll go now."

But getting down was a lot easier said than done. The steep hillside was close to vertical and slippery as hell. In the end, she sat on her butt and half slid, half scooted down.

By the time she hit the bottom, Kayla was pretty sure her ass was purple with bruises. She'd torn three fingernails completely off and dislocated two fingers when she'd tried to catch herself on a particularly out-of-control part of the descent. Her body ached and throbbed.

She lay there, too exhausted and sore to even care that she'd landed nearly a foot deep in stinky mold and fungus. She could rest here. Nobody would find her.

The idea was far more inviting than it should have been. But after a few minutes, the stench and the gooey damp got to her. She wrinkled her nose in disgust. *Ew.*

Rolling onto her stomach, she awkwardly pushed herself upright and picked up the sword. It remained pristine and clean. Stupid magic sword.

She took the trail Zach had mentioned and limped along it, using the sword as a cane.

She passed through a copse of white-skinned trees. Amorphous dark figures drifted near, collecting around her. They towered, thin gnarled fingers scraping the ground

Kayla stopped as they surrounded her. She didn't feel any malice from them. Instead, they seemed curious and maybe a little apprehensive.

"Hi," she said. "Can I help you?"

Funny how that question had become more weighty since she'd found out she was a god, a guardian for these creatures and everybody else in Portland. Now the concept of help meant a lot more. Required a lot more.

"Is over?"

A ruffling in the darkness of one of the figures told her who spoke.

"The fighting? Yes."

"All leave? Peace again?"

"Soon. They are cleaning up the scene, and then everybody will go."

"The scar?"

Kayla frowned. "Scar?"

Fingers like spidery moon-shadows cast by tree branches pointed at the trail burned in the rot where she stood. They had stayed off it, Kayla realized.

"I can fix it." Instinctively she touched a place within herself, a series of dark strands connecting her to the trail. A visible tremor ran through the darkness of each of the figures in response.

"Now?" It was more plea than question.

It would make getting out a lot more difficult, but the touch to the strands had told her they suffered. She couldn't refuse.

She just hoped she could actually do it.

Hunkering down, she laid the sword aside and dug her hands into the soil as she had up on The Mound. This time, instead of an outward push of power, she stroked inner fingers over the darkened strands connecting her to the place, calling them to heal.

Violent tremors rolled through the figures, and they made a moaning sound. It didn't sound particularly happy.

She stopped. She could grow flowers like she had on The Mound, but doubted that's what these guys were looking for.

Kayla leaned over and scooped up a handful of moldy sludge-rot from beside the path. Maybe she could clone it somehow. Concentrating, she searched inside her again. It took her a while, but she finally found a microscopic thread connecting her to the handful in her hand. Actually, it was more like several dozen, so thin and fine that they almost weren't there.

She uprooted them from their anchorage and twined them around the dark threads, then *pushed* at them. The threads merged and hummed, then the darkness developed a tangible shine, if that was a thing. Kayla couldn't see it, but she could *feel* it.

Letting go, she opened her eyes. The trail was covered in a layer of plant sludge. It breathed and bubbled, growing as she watched. *Yuck.*

She dropped the slimy handful of gunk and wiped her hand on her pants as she stood.

The dark creatures swayed and echoed the hum from the merged threads.

Well, then. A good deed done. Kayla gave a lethargic smile through the dragging net of exhaustion that flung itself over her. Two good deeds, if she counted the flowers. Maybe being a god wasn't so bad.

The creatures didn't seem to be interested in talking anymore, so she slipped past them.

The slog back to the road was harder than she'd expected. The mold and rot covered the ground, giving it a deceptively even look. She'd gone maybe a half mile when she stepped into a hole and fell into a shallow pond. She went under. Slime coated her skin and she swallowed water that tasted like sewage.

She didn't even think about transformation. It came over her in seconds, and she welcomed the armor of her scales. Thrashing, she clawed her way up the gooey clay-mud bank. The sword had vanished with her clothing. Hopefully it would come back when she transformed again. She was too tired to worry about it, and continued on her way, her other self unfazed by the uneven terrain or the heaped rot and mold.

At the road, she simply kept going. No point waiting for Zach and Raven. They didn't need her, and she didn't need a ride home.

She found a creek and followed it back to the river, swimming up to

Poet's Beach. The water refreshed her, and when she climbed out around eight a.m., she wasn't quite as tired. She ignored the pedestrians and morning boat traffic, and started toward home. She didn't have time to bother with avoiding notice. Besides, her race to the river the day before guaranteed her secret was out.

That didn't stop her from trying to transform back to human. She was three quarters up SW Harrison when she dried enough to summon the shift. She staggered against a bas-relief of trees carved in a brick wall, catching herself before she whacked her head. She wasn't sure whether she was happy or not to see that the sword had returned with the rest of her belongings.

From there, she caught a Pink Lady cab home. On the way, she couldn't stop thinking of Ray, of the battle with the gods, of this Obsidian Butterfly person, and the question of what she'd do next.

Scavenge? It made her a living and she enjoyed it. But after working a case again—no matter how informally—she realized how much she'd missed it, and how much the witchkin needed her. Not that she could go back to the force. They weren't going to have her, and she wasn't going to be able to follow their "humans are the only people" policy.

She could be a private investigator. That would let her help people, and she wouldn't have to charge clients much if they didn't have much. She could keep scavenging on the side. It wasn't like she needed a lot of money. In her other form, she could live entirely off fish if necessary. That just left buying coffee and a few other necessities that she couldn't scavenge, and those weren't many.

Definitely a possibility worth thinking about.

She wondered how Ray's captain would treat him now, knowing he was a witch. Would he lose his job? But then again, Ray'd helped stop a major magical threat, and Zach would probably get the technomages to rally behind him. He might catch a lot of flak from his fellow cops, but he'd keep his job, though whether it would be worth keeping with all the shit that was going to be running downhill to bury him was another question entirely.

Once at home, she put the sword in the umbrella stand and went straight to the kitchen to put on coffee. She grabbed some wheat bread and spread it liberally with butter and honey and wolfed it down. It barely put a dent in her hunger. She made another, considering whether or not she should try to shower.

She was filthy, and her hair felt both greasy and crunchy. The idea of a cold shower made her shudder, which is what she'd get using the camp-shower setup in the backyard. Did she want to risk transforming in her bathroom?

Screw it.

Resolutely she went upstairs. In the bathroom she started the hot water and then stripped. She kicked her clothes aside. Steam already filmed the mirror when she stepped under the spray.

Deciding she was not only going to get her hair cleaned and conditioned before she transformed, but she was also going to enjoy the lovely hot spray, Kayla squirted shampoo into her hand and went about lathering her hair.

She felt the beast inside her rising and pushing at her thin control. *You just swam in the river. Give me a freaking break*, she muttered to it as she rinsed her hair. Deciding it needed another scrub, she lathered up again, then took a scrubby and washed the rest of herself. The urge to transform had steadied, and though it pushed, she continued to hold it off.

With building confidence, Kayla rinsed her hair and applied conditioner. Since the beast seemed inclined to let her stay in human form for once, she decided she'd shave her legs. Not that anybody would see them. Not that she'd be wrapping them around anybody any time soon—

Her mind flashed to Ray when she'd lifted the covers to check on him after her near-death experience. The memory of his sculpted body, the rippling planes of muscle, the deliciously lickable tawny skin.

Her entire body went hot, and aches kicked up in places that had no business aching when it came to him. She drew a breath and turned the shower to cold, letting the chilly water cool her imagination and her body's fevered response.

After her shower, she dried off and blew out her hair. No sense playing with fire.

She considered her wardrobe, which mostly consisted of jeans. She didn't have a lot of cause to dress up these days, but it would be nice to not look ratty when she went to see Ray.

She couldn't remember the last time she'd worn a dress. Or heels. Or makeup. Or done anything more than put her hair in a ponytail or braid. She wasn't the girly-girl type, but when had she turned into a frump?

When she had decided she'd rather be invisible. Only now she wanted to be noticed. Or at least, not cause people to wince when they saw her. They. Who was she fooling? Ray. She wanted Ray to notice her. Wanted him to find her attractive.

God but she was an idiot.

In the end, she pulled on a pair of jeans, a pale-blue blouse, and a pair of strappy sandals, and then pulled her hair up into a messy bun. She called a cab to take her to the hospital, drinking coffee while she waited.

As they wound up the hill between the children's hospital and the big lower parking garage on their way to the main hospital campus, Kayla smiled at the reaching vines of the watchful roses that had grown up over the parking garage and across the skybridge. The flowers were nosey and protective of patients and staff. They made for great security.

The cab dropped her at the main entrance of OHSU. Just inside, Kayla stopped at the reception desk. It was surrounded by bulletproof glass layered with wards. All the entrances into the hospital required staff to open the doors for you. During the Witchwar, there'd been a lot of attacks here, trying to get at wounded technomages when they were down.

She stood in line behind a gray-haired man with a quality beer gut and a young couple holding hands. Ten minutes later it was her turn.

"Can I help you?" The receptionist eyed Kayla with cool assessment, the kind snipers use before choosing a target.

"I'm here to see Ray Garza. He was brought in early this morning."

"Name?"

"Kayla Reese."

The receptionist's fingers flew over the keyboard, and then she looked back up at Kayla.

"I'm sorry. I can't help you."

Worry clutched Kayla's stomach. "Why? Is something wrong? Is Ray okay?"

"I'm sorry. I can't help you," the woman repeated, her eyes narrowing slightly. "I must ask you to leave now."

Kayla stepped forward, putting her hands on the glass. "What's going on? Why can't I see him?"

"Ma'am. I'll ask again. Please exit the premises or I'll have to ask security to escort you."

The receptionist flicked a meaningful glance at several burly men and women in black pants and white shirts sporting sidearms. They stood watching the exchange, eager for the invitation to intervene.

"Fine," Kayla said, backing away. "I'm going."

She retreated outside and crossed the street to a bench where she sank down, confusion and concern rolling through her. Was Ray not here? Was she simply not allowed to see him? Maybe he didn't want to see her? Or had Raven and Zach been wrong? Had his injuries overcome him?

Her heart clenched, and her throat closed. No. No no no. She refused to accept the possibility. She probably just didn't have the security clearance to see him. Or maybe he was in a ward where only family was allowed.

She didn't have Zach's number to call and find out. She tried Angie, hoping to track down Zach's number, but ended up getting voice mail.

Well then, she'd wait. Sooner or later Zach would show up. She didn't let herself consider that he might use a different entrance. All she knew for sure was she couldn't go home.

Around two in the afternoon, she lost that choice. Thunder grumbled in the near distance and the wind kicked up, blowing in the scent of rain. She looked up and around. There was no place for her to take shelter. The parking lots were guarded, and she'd watched hospital security roust several people loitering around the bus stop.

Still she waited. Droplets plopped down on the bench and dotted her head. She held in a sigh. She could either transform and stay, or she could go home and wait it out and hope Angie got back to her. Eyeing the sky, she could tell the storm wouldn't be a quick one, and she didn't relish getting hit by lightning.

Home it was.

She just barely made it before the sky opened and dropped a deluge. She'd run the last mile, regretting her choice of footwear with every step.

With the door shut, she contemplated what to do next. Exhaustion fell on top of her like a tree trunk. She'd been awake the better part of the last sixty hours. Stir in all the emotional angst, nearly dying, and the fight with Nietzche-cheese and his buddy and she was surprised she was still upright.

Going upstairs to her bed took far too much energy, so she collapsed on the couch, pulling a fuzzy blanked over her. Within seconds she fell asleep.

Chapter 25

Ray

GIVEN HIS LAST memories before blacking out, Ray was mighty pleased to wake up at all. Once again, he was reclining in a hospital bed with tubes running into both arms and an oxygen tube up his nose. A clip on his finger monitored his pulse and oxygen levels, an automatic blood pressure cuff circled his left bicep, and this time, bandages wrapped his arms and chest. Arcane witch markings written with a Sharpie covered them. A dusting of herbs and something else layered his chest in a light blanket. It smelled of rosemary and things he couldn't identify.

He looked around. Through the window on the door he could see the back of a uniformed officer. Interesting. Was he supposed to keep enemies out or keep Ray in?

He took an inventory of himself. He had aches as if he'd worked out too hard, but no real pain. *Scratch that.* A thin, needle-sharp spike of pain stabbed through his lungs and traveled down his spine to his heels. It hurt so badly he could hardly breathe. Nausea burned his stomach and boiled up his throat.

After a few seconds, the pain passed, leaving Ray panting. Sweat beaded on his forehead, and he clutched the sheet with white-knuckled hands.

What in the holy fuck was that?

It had to do with magic, he was pretty sure. His clash with the giant beast.

He jerked upright. *Kayla!*

For the second time in a couple of days, he tore out his IVs, shoving off the oxygen tube and the pulse monitor. He swore when he fumbled at the blood pressure cuff and finally tore it free. By this time, loud alarms beeped frantically from several machines.

Swinging his legs over the side of the bed, Ray stood up, bracing himself against the bed. No dizziness, no weakness. *Hells to the yeah.*

Except for his bandages, he was naked.

The door swung open and a doctor came in. With her pixie hair and tiny figure, she looked about twelve years old.

She cocked a brow at him, letting the door close behind her. "Just where do you think you're going, Mr. Garza?"

"Out of here," he said grimly, refusing to be embarrassed by her scrutiny. Where was Kayla? Had she survived?

Horror struck him in the gut and he bent over, bracing his hands on his knees. Tears burned in his eyes. He gritted his teeth. He wasn't going to mourn her. Not yet. Not until he saw her body,

The doctor's brow arched again. "You think you're well enough for that?"

"Right now, Doc, I don't really give a fuck."

She nodded, a tiny smile quirking the corner of her lips. "I've got several people waiting to talk to you. Cops," she clarified as his head jerked up in hope.

"I don't have time for that shit," he said.

She pursed her lips and then shrugged. "Not for me to say one way or another. However, I do want to bandage those holes in your arms."

She gathered tape, gauze, and sanitary wipes, cleaning the blood running from his IV sites.

"You're going to want to talk to a witch about your metaphysical wounds," the doc said matter-of-factly. "They were the real danger to you, aside from serious dehydration and iron depletion. I'd leave the bandages on until someone with skill can take them off. If you don't, you might do more than suffer a little bleeding."

"I will," he agreed impatiently.

"You're checking out AMA," she said, "so you'll need to sign forms."

"Fuck that. I don't have time."

Again, that tiny smile. "Yes, you do." She produced a clipboard from a drawer and held it out with a pen. "I had a feeling," she said when he scrawled his signature. "I read your chart from your previous visit. Getting out of here without being stopped, however, is your problem."

She smiled, this time with a wicked glint in her eye. She held out a hand to shake his. "Good luck."

"Thanks, Doctor—?"

"Andrews. Samantha Andrews."

"Thanks, Dr. Andrews. Where are my clothes?"

"They didn't survive. You took significant burns on your torso. Your lower body didn't take quite as much damage, but you're lucky you came away with your genitals intact."

Ray tried to hide his gulp, but that quirk of her mouth told him she'd read him like a book.

"Now if you'll excuse me, I have my rounds," she said and left, stopping to speak a moment to the guard.

He nodded as she walked away, then glanced through the window in the door. The guard's mouth fell open, and he grabbed his radio, talking into it rapidly.

Goddammit!

But there was little Ray could do.

Within a minute Captain Crice came storming through the door. By this time Ray had managed to find a hospital gown and cover himself.

"Garza!" Crice barked. "Just what the hell do you think you're doing out of bed?"

"What happened?" Ray shot back.

"What happened? Damned near the apocalypse if the technomages are right."

Ray clenched his teeth in order to keep from swearing at his captain. "What happened?" he repeated. He didn't want to mention Kayla if Crice didn't already know she'd been there.

"Lucky for you, Logan and that witch you found managed to stop those three fuckers before they wreaked havoc. Theresa Runyon was killed, and Margaret Valentine is being treated. She'll be fine."

Ray dragged his fingers through his hair, trying to put the pieces together. He wished to God that Logan was here so he could get the real truth. He didn't want the whitewashed version the technomage had given to Crice.

"Apparently those two giant muscle-heads were vessels for two Aztec gods. They were after that big blond guy. Name is Grutte Pier. From Denmark or Finland or something. Born a few centuries back. Anyhow, he'd been harvesting bones from witchkin to build a magic sword to kill those things. He killed Theresa Runyon to complete the spell and then killed the two vessels. The gods themselves escaped along with two of the beasts they summoned. Technomages are hunting them now."

Ray blinked, his mind tumbling. Where was Kayla in all this? Surely Logan wouldn't have kept her out of the story if she'd died. What would be the point?

"Craziest thing was the witches. They cast some kind of spell to bury all the bodies and grow a garden on top of The Mound." Crice shook his head. "Lotta people not happy about that. They wanted a chance to bury them proper."

He looked at Ray. "You need to be debriefed, and then I have to decide what to do about you."

"*Do* about me?" Ray's chin jutted slightly, his brows rising.

"You're a fucking witch."

"Yeah, and I've been one since Magicfall. You haven't had a problem with me in all that time."

"Maybe not, but now everybody knows, and it isn't sitting well."

"Then fire me."

Crice practically growled at him. "You're my best detective. You going to quit?"

"Not a chance. It's time we got over the witchkin bias and started protecting everybody, not to mention taking advantage of their talents and skills. Some shifters on the force wouldn't be a bad idea to start with. Neither would more witches."

His captain smiled with a smug triumph that made Ray more than a little nervous.

"Glad to hear you say so. I'm planning to start a new investigative division investigating magical crimes and hiring witchkin. Pitching it to the brass next week. You're going to head it up, though don't think it's going to be administrative. You're going to lead from the field."

Ray stared. He had *not* seen this coming.

"You know that's going to go over like a lead balloon?"

Crice shrugged. "People are going to have to deal. World's changed, and we've got to change with it. This business last night cut it too close. We can't have that sort of thing again. We might have headed it off if we'd been paying attention to the witchkin deaths and if we had more witchkin on our side."

Murders. Ray didn't correct him. Crice had made strides. No point in antagonizing him by pointing out his bias. It wasn't like Ray didn't have a long way to go himself.

A grumble of thunder called his attention to the window. Droplets spattered the glass. Hopefully the storm would keep Kayla home until he got there, which couldn't happen fast enough. *If* she was home. But first he had to get rid of his boss.

"What about staff? Hiring? I get free rein?"

Crice gave a ready nod. "Within reason. I'll need to sign off."

"I want Logan assigned to the team. Permanently."

"I can do that."

"I don't want to be the redheaded stepchild. If I do this, we'd better be funded with adequate manpower and financial resources."

"You'll have it." Crice gave a terrifying little smile. "You'll have plenty. He doesn't know it yet, but Alistair Runyon is going to start a memorial fund in his mother's name to get the division going and make sure it never runs short."

Ray couldn't help his answering grin. Crice was a lot of things, but being devious might be his best quality. He didn't doubt that his boss would make it happen, either. Runyon didn't want it out that witchcraft ran in his family. He'd pay a lot to keep it a secret.

"Now, I want to hear what happened, starting with what you found at the Runyon house," Crice said, settling into an uncomfortable-looking chair.

Ray hesitated.

"Faster you talk, faster you get out of here. But to be clear—you aren't leaving until I say you can. Unless you want to quit?"

He was tempted to just to be able to go check on Kayla, but instead Ray started talking in quick, terse sentences, leaving out any references to Kayla's identity, calling her his confidential informant.

"Who is that?" Crice asked.

"Can't say."

"Gotta register all CIs with the department."

"Not this one." His jaw jutted.

The captain eyed him from beneath lowered brows. Apparently he realized that it wasn't negotiable. Ray'd quit before he gave up Kayla.

Crice nodded. "Okay. What next?"

Ray continued all the way up to when he got blasted by one of the Aztec gods, again without mentioning Kayla's role.

"Then I woke up here."

"Why do I get the feeling you aren't telling the whole story?" Crice asked, rubbing his hand over his jaw.

"Because you aren't stupid," Ray said without missing a beat. "But if you want to keep me around, then you won't push it."

The captain eyed him for several long moments. "All right. Two things. I don't want to find out shit from the papers. If it goes public, I'd better know first. And second, this better not come back and bite me in the ass or I *will* bury you."

He leaned forward, pointing a blunt finger. "I mean it, Garza. I'm giving you rope here, but I'd better not end up with my head in a noose. I'll make sure you regret it if it's the last thing I do."

Despite the captain's gruff threats, Ray felt gratified Crice trusted him enough not to force the issue. Or maybe it was a case of don't ask, don't tell. Either way, he'd take it.

"Is that all?"

"Where you going in such an all-fired hurry?"

"See my girl." The words slipped out before Ray knew he was going to say them, but he did know he meant them. Now he just had to bring Kayla around to the idea.

Crice's brows rose in mocking disbelief. "Didn't think you were the relationship type."

"Wasn't."

"But you are now? Maybe you should stay in the hospital. Looks like you've got a head injury." Crice snickered.

"My head's just fine. In fact, it's finally on straight. So, if we're done here, I'll be on my way."

"Wearing that?"

Ray looked down at himself. The hospital gown hadn't miraculously turned into street clothes. "Shit."

"Well, guess I'll get out of your way." Crice stood. "Take a couple days off. Stay off the radar, and stay the hell out of the papers. Email your report by tonight, and Garza, don't do anything stupid."

He stomped out leaving Ray wondering what stupidity Crice thought he'd be committing.

He managed to collect clothes from the lost and found. A Ducks sweatshirt and a pair of khaki trousers. He borrowed a pair of flipflops from an orderly, as his shoes had been considered a bio-hazard after his tromp to The Mound.

Tempted as he was to head straight for Kayla's, he wanted to clean up first. Right now he looked like a hobo. Better to look cool and collected if he was going to tempt her into a relationship.

Sure, Garza, he mocked himself. *Get a grip. You'd better show up looking like Chris Hemsworth if you want to* tempt *her. Better to figure out how to bribe her into going out with you, or plan on getting her seriously drunk.*

He didn't know when he'd decided he was done pretending he could stick to just friendship with Kayla. Or maybe he'd decided to stop being a coward and take a chance on being happy. Of coming home to her every night, fixing breakfast for her every morning, and having her in his bed.

The last birthed a flurry of erotic ideas. All the things he'd like to do to her; all the ways he'd touch her, pleasure her. He squeezed is eyes shut. *Jesus Christ Almighty.* He'd never been so hard in his entire life. His dick throbbed, and walking had become an exercise in torture. Maybe the rain would chill his fever.

When he reached his apartment, he tore off his borrowed clothes, swearing as he remembered the bandages. Much as he wanted to tear them off, he knew better. Digging in his kitchen drawers, he found a roll of plastic wrap. He rolled it around his chest tightly, covering the bandages. Hopefully water wouldn't get underneath.

After his shower, he dressed in black jeans, boots, and a soft blue shirt that hugged his torso. He snorted as he checked himself in the mirror. You'd think he was sixteen on his first date. But damn if it didn't feel just like that. Nerves made him smooth his hair.

When he arrived at Kayla's, he knocked. The rain had lightened, pattering lightly on his rain jacket. His stomach took a dive when she didn't answer. *Fuck.* Where was she?

He tested the door, startled when it opened. He reached for his gun on his hip, holding it ready as he stepped inside. When he saw Kayla asleep on the couch, the relief nearly put him on the floor. He holstered his gun and went to sit beside her on the coffee table.

She lay under a blanket with her shoulders and arms exposed. Small bruises, red marks, and scratches ran over her exposed skin. She had a bruise on her left cheek and dark circles beneath her eyes. Her face was too pale and too thin.

Ray reached out a finger and lightly brushed her hair from her eyes, smoothing back over her ear. "Kayla?"

Her eyes opened. Her head turned, and she saw him. Her brow furrowed. "Ray? What are you doing here?"

"I was worried about you."

"But—you were in the hospital."

His brows rose. That stung. And punctured his balloon of hope. She knew he was in the hospital and hadn't come to check how he was? She'd chosen to take a nap? *Shit.*

She scrutinized him. "You're really okay? I came to the hospital, and they made me leave. I didn't have Zach's number and had to leave a message for Angie. I waited outside, but then it started raining and I had to come home."

She touched his hand as if to reassure herself that he was really there. He caught it and rubbed her palm with his thumb.

"I'm fine. A little sore, but nothing serious. I woke up, and Crice insisted on a debriefing or I'd have been here sooner." She *had* come to the hospital. He let out a breath.

"I got the sanitized version of the story, but what happened?"

She let go of his hand to scoot up and cross her legs, sliding her tongue over her dry lips as she did. The small gesture sent blood rushing to his dick. Why did that turn him on so much? But then if he was honest, everything about her turned him on. Always had. But he'd ignored the awareness, convincing himself his feelings for her were limited to friendship. It's why he'd taken her leaving so badly. He could've accepted her quitting the force, but not leaving him. That wound had continued to bleed and fester.

It was time to face it and deal with it.

Eyes shadowed, Kayla told him all that had happened. She kept her voice emotionless, but her hands knotted on the blanket, giving away her anxiety.

"Your grandmother is inside the sword?" he asked when she'd finished.

Her mouth twisted down. "She and the others who . . . contributed . . . to the sword's creation."

Ray leaned forward, taking her hand again. "God, Kayla. I'm sorry."

"We weren't close."

But her expression belied her words. She obviously cared more than she was willing to say. Ray didn't press her. She was too raw and still coming to terms with all that had happened in the last few days. He wasn't about to make it worse.

"You're not hurt?" he asked.

She shrugged. "Sore. Tired. A little dented."

Strained silence fell between them. Ray knew he needed to talk about the two of them, but how to start?

"Crice wants me to head up a new division," he said finally. "Supernatural crime. Wants to hire witchkin. Says we have to start paying more attention to those crimes."

"About time. I guess having a couple gods throw down in the middle of the city makes an impact," she said wryly. "But I'm glad. Congratulations. You totally deserve this," she said and reached out to hug him.

He held her loosely, fighting the urge to pull her in tight and kiss her.

Reluctantly, he let her pull away, but he retained hold of her hand. An uneasy frown creased her brow as she glanced down.

Now or never. "I have something I need to ask you," he said.

Understanding dawned on her face. "I can't."

It kicked him in the gut. His expression tightened and he pulled away. "That's it? Just . . . can't? You won't give me a chance at all?"

"It's not about you," she said, scooting forward and sliding her feet to the floor, her legs between his as they faced each other. "I can't even think about being a cop again until I figure out what this guardian-god thing means. If not for that, I'd be there so fast your head would spin."

Ray's head was already spinning. He felt as if he were a ping-pong ball, bouncing back and forth between hope and despair. "I wasn't going to ask you to come back."

Kayla jerked back, her cheeks flushing. "Why the hell not? I'm not a good enough cop for you?"

He ran his hands through his hair. "You're one of the best I've known. I'm not asking you to come back because I'd be your boss and I don't want to be."

Her brows drew together. "Why not?"

"Because."

"Because? Just because? That's all? How old are you? Twelve? What's so wrong with being my boss?"

Ray opened his mouth, but the words wouldn't come. The moment stretched. He needed to say something. *Do* something.

Before he could think about the wisdom of just going for it, he kissed her.

Chapter 26

Kayla

KAYLA STIFFENED as Ray's lips pressed against hers. He was *kissing* her? Why?

She didn't care. A whirlwind of sparks swept through her, and she gave a little gasp. Ray took advantage, pulling her closer and sliding his tongue between her lips. Kayla went up in flames. She curled her arms around his neck and made a purring sound in her throat. He deepened the kiss, and a wild explosion of aches and pleasure detonated inside her like fireworks.

Abruptly he pulled her to her feet, turned her around, and sat on the couch, pulling her down to straddle him, her dress riding up her thighs. His hands caressed her back. An arm came around her hips and pulled her tight against him. She felt his hardness against her and couldn't help but rock her hips in response.

That seemed to flip a switch, and his kiss turned hungry and desperate. He slid a hand up her thigh and ribs and cupped her breast, lightly thumbing her nipple. She'd been so long without being touched she nearly broke apart right there. She made a little whimpering sound and pressed into him.

His hands swept over her, urging her closer, as if that were even possible. He pulled away, dropping hot kisses along her neck, pulling aside the strap of her dress to string them along her shoulder. She tilted her head to give him better access, her heart pounding as if she'd run five miles uphill.

He pushed his hands up along her ribs and brushed his thumbs across both nipples. Kayla nearly jumped out of her skin like he'd hit her with a thousand watts of electricity. Heat streaked through her, and the needy ache low in her belly intensified, becoming nearly unbearable. He gave a smug chuckle and this time circled her nipples. She moaned and squeezed her legs against his and rocked her hips forward in silent demand.

Ray sucked in a sharp breath and locked both arms around hers, yanking her against him and grinding into her.

Kayla clutched him as her brain went nova. The pleasure was beyond anything she could remember. Sex with the few men she'd been with had been nice, but hardly mind-blowing. Never as good as this, and there were still layers of clothing between them. What would it be like to be skin on skin with Ray? Have his mouth on her breasts? Have him buried inside her?

The only thing she knew for sure is she wanted to know. *Now.*

She slid her hands down and pushed up his shirt, her fingers gliding over the hard ripples of muscle. She delighted in the way he tensed, his heart thudding rapidly under her hand as she stroked the flat plane of his pecs.

Then sudden panic made her brace her hands and push back from him. His brows winged down over his dark eyes. He held her hips tight so that she couldn't climb off him.

"What's wrong?" he growled.

"What's going on? I don't—" She bit her lips and shook her head, words evaporating.

He spoke slowly as if choosing his words, his voice gravelly with emotion. "I'm explaining why I don't want you working for me."

"I—help me out here. What does that have to do with kissing me?"

He grimaced. "I can't date a subordinate. Against policy."

It took Kayla a few seconds to register what he was saying. "Date? Us? Me? Why?"

A tense smile turned up the corners of his mouth. "I like kissing you, for one."

"I like kissing you."

His smile softened, and his eyes flamed. "I noticed."

"You don't want to go out with me," Kayla said though her heart had begun to gallop with wishful hope.

The scowl returned. "Why not?" He shook his head. "No, don't answer that. I don't care that you're witchkin or that you're a god. I don't care that you turn into a water dragon, though you are beautiful in that form as well as your human one. I don't care that you scavenge for a living, especially since I know you're a walking weapon. I'm over what happened four years ago. I'm beyond sorry for making it impossible for you to trust me. Does that cover it? If you've got any other reasons I don't want to be with you, put them on the table now so I can tell you how much I don't give a shit about them."

He waited for her to speak, but Kayla could only stare. He was serious about this. Really, really serious.

"Oh, and I also don't give a shit about your father. I'll bury him if he tries to hurt you or us."

Us.

"What happens when we break up?" she asked, throat dry.

He flinched back, his face closing up, eyes cold and bleak as an arctic winter. "*When* we break up?" he asked harshly.

"Okay, *if*," she said. "What happens if we break up?"

He glared at her a long moment. "Let me be clear. I'm in this for the long haul. I'm in love with you, and I don't plan to walk away. So, if or when we break up is entirely up to you."

It was her turn to stare, her brain scrambling to digest his declaration.

"You love me? Since when?" Her voice, when she found it, sounded angry.

"Christ, Kayla." He dug his fingers through his hair and then ran them up her arms. "You have no idea how much I wanted to gut Logan just for taking you to dinner, and then you showed up at your father's mansion together and I almost broke his arm for touching you."

He pulled her closer to him. "We can do this. If you want to. Do you?"

His entire body tensed, and his jaw knotted as he waited for her answer. He dug his fingers into her hips and she could feel his arms shaking. He really meant it. He loved her. She'd never had anyone say that to her before. No one single person ever. Not even her father. If her mother had, it was before Kayla could remember.

"Kayla?"

She swallowed. "I'm sorry. I just—" She rubbed her hands over her face. "God this is humiliating."

He tugged her hands down, wrapping them in his warm grip. He looked confused. "What's humiliating?"

She averted her gaze, her cheeks flushing hot. "Nobody has ever told me they loved me before. Wow. That's not only humiliating, it's pathetic."

"It's fucking criminal. But then again, given your family, I guess not surprising. What about your mom?"

"They divorced when I was young. Alistair had money and lawyers, though he told me she was delighted to take a payoff and leave. I never looked for her. As long as I didn't know, I could imagine she loved and wanted me and that Alistair had lied. And yet another pathetic point to me."

"Don't do that. It's not pathetic. Your family failed you, and that's on them, not you. Now, I don't suppose you could get back to the question. I'm dying here. Do you want me?"

"Yes."

"Yes?"

She nodded.

The tension didn't leave his body. "Why?"

"That's not enough?"

"No. I need more."

Saying the words was harder than she imagined. Just as she'd never had them said to her, she'd never said them to anyone else. Her mouth went dry, and her tongue seemed to stick to the roof of her mouth. All the same, she wanted to say them.

She leaned her forehead against his. "Because I could live without you, but I wouldn't want to. I've done that for four years, and I wasn't doing much more than existing. Walking away from you nearly broke me. I never dreamed you could accept what I've become, much less love it. Love *me*. But you'd better be sure this is really what you want because if we stop this now and stay friends, I'll survive, but leave me in a week or a month or a year and I won't."

The words poured out in a flood. Tears stung her eyes, and emotion knotted her throat.

His answer was to drag her down, twisting so that she lay beneath him on the couch. He kissed as if like he'd never get enough.

"Whoa! Sorry to interrupt you teenagers. I *did* knock."

Ray jerked his head up and swore. Kayla couldn't have agreed more.

"Go away," she groaned.

"Love to, but you should probably meet your new roommate first," Zach said.

"Roommate?" Ray pushed up to his feet, pulling his shirt down. He didn't seem in the least bit embarrassed to be caught making out on the couch like two teenagers. That made one of them.

Kayla stood as well. She touched her fingers to her swollen lips, her cheeks flushing hotter. She sidled away from Ray, but he snatched her hand and tugged her back, slipping his arm around her shoulders.

It was a statement.

She slid her arm around his waist, a shiver running through her. Not because of the contact, though touching him dumped gas on the fire doused by her uninvited guests. It was because she *could* touch him, something that had been so taboo before that it felt like she was getting away with something. Deciding she wanted more, she slid her fingers up under his shirt to explore the warm smooth skin just above his belt. His muscles jumped, and his arm tightened around her shoulders. Her cheeks heated with her daring. Who'd have ever thought she'd be allowed?

Zach stood just inside the door, grinning at them like an idiot. He gave her a smug *I told you so* look, and she resisted the urge to flip him off. Behind him stood Raven and a slender woman with long black hair. She looked emaciated and gaunt. Her coppery skin had an ashen cast, and she had scarecrow arms and hair that was dull and crisp like straw. Black tattoos flowed along the edges of her hairline.

When Kayla met her black gaze, ancient knowing and defiance stared back. Despite looking as though she was halfway to becoming a zombie or vampire, she resonated power. She had to be the Obsidian Butterfly that Nietzche-cheese had talked about.

Her roommate. *Crap.* Ray wasn't going to like this one bit.

"What's going on?" Ray demanded. "Who is she? What do you mean—roommate?" He'd gone into cop mode, targeting the heart of the issue with sniper-like precision.

"This is Itzpapalotl," Raven said. "Also known as the Obsidian Butterfly. The one the other gods were hunting."

"Why?" Kayla let go of Ray and came around the coffee table, stopping just in front of the other goddess. Finally, some answers. "What makes you so important to them? Why did you come here?"

She felt Ray come up behind her.

"I made them angry," she said in a husky voice that sounded a lot stronger than the rest of her looked.

"No shit. How?"

"I did not obey their rules."

"So they want to kill you?"

Izta-pops-a-lot, or whatever her name was, nodded. "It is so."

"What rules in particular?" Kayla didn't let her annoyance at having to dig for the information get away from her. She had too much experience interviewing uncooperative witnesses and suspects to lose her cool.

"I rule Tamoanchan. *I* rule Tamoanchan," Itza repeated with bitter emphasis on the *I*. "*They* do not tell *me* who may enter or who must leave. *They* do not tell *me* who is worthy and who is not. I am a Tzitzimitl—hunter from the stars, vengeance in the darkness, defender of the weak."

"If you think that answered the question, it didn't," Kayla said. "Try again. What rules didn't you obey?"

"I allowed the spirits of Grutte Pier's wife and children into Tamoanchan, though they are not of the People."

Grutte Pier, the blond giant. "Tamoanchan?"

"It is the land *Between*, after death and before birth, an oasis of rest and hope. His wife and children were hunted, and I gave them refuge. My act angered the others. They decreed outsiders did not belong in Tamoanchan and demanded I expel them. I do *not* take orders."

"So they decided to kill you?"

A shake of her head. "No. Epizotal—a Tzitzimitl sister—declared me unfit to guard Tamoanchan. She wishes to steal it from me. But I must be taken to her altar and then the ritual performed. Then she would take it and I would die."

Kayla considered that information. "She sent two hench-gods to bring you back?"

"Nitziquiza and Zepatiloa," she clarified. "They have long hated me and were willing to do her bidding."

Her explanation didn't fit the events—the spreading of the white powder and the unleashing of the three creatures, designed to kill a god, not capture her. "Then why would they actually try to kill you if their boss needs you alive for this ritual?"

"They vent their anger. They are tired of the hunt, of being bound to my sister. They would take me back for the reward she offers them if they could, but are willing to kill me rather than continue the hunt. I die and they are free. Since I am not, Epizotal will send them for me again."

Kayla frowned. That the two red gods would be free if they didn't actually complete their mission seemed stupid. Plus, the bastards had seemed a whole lot of determined to return and take Itza-pop down. So, either the goddess was lying, or she didn't know what she was talking about.

"And your buddy, Grutte Pier? He killed a lot of innocent people to make this." Kayla gestured to the sword she'd stashed in the umbrella bucket. She was going to have to find someplace a lot more secure to put it. "The crimson twins said you gave him the recipe. That he couldn't have done it without you and that makes you just as responsible in my book."

"This was the pact. He protects me so I can protect his family. The sword was the only weapon he could use to succeed."

Classic ends justify the means.

Kayla didn't care that the goddess or whatever she was had been trying to save herself from certain death. Her life wasn't more valuable than those her henchman had killed to make the sword. Not that Kayla could entirely fault either of them. She'd investigated too many domestic violence cases not to know that people did horrendous things out of desperation. It was human. And apparently divine. If it were her? If Ray's life was on the line? Would she have killed innocent souls for him?

She didn't think so. She hoped not, but she couldn't say for sure.

"So, what should I do with you now? They'll come back for you." Kayla frowned. "Why are you so sick? What happened to you?"

"I am bound to Tamoanchan. They attacked it to weaken me. Otherwise Epizotal could not best me."

Kayla didn't want to ask, but the drive to protect the weak and innocent drove the question. "What will it take for you to get well?"

The other woman leveled a searching look at Kayla. "Time and welcome in this place," she said finally.

"That's it? Rest and recuperation?"

"Not just anywhere. Here. In your domain."

Kayla's forehead wrinkled in confusion. "I don't get it. What's so great about here?"

"What is planted here thrives, but especially those tied to the Ba of Iteru."

"The what?"

Itzpapalotl stared. "You do not know?"

"Would I ask if I did?"

"Iteru, the great river."

"The Amazon?"

A shake of her head. "The great river of life, the river of the desert. They call it The Nile now. Ba is divine spirit."

Kayla was reminded of the oddly Egyptian appearance of cartouches in the writings they'd discovered and the theory the one archeologist had come up with that Egyptians had traveled to South America. "Why would people tied to the Ba of Iteru find my territory particularly beneficial?" Her territory. That concept was becoming easier to wrap her mind around and accept. Not just accept, but claim. *Her* territory. *Her* people. *Her* responsibility.

"Because you are Sobek," Itzpapalotl said, as if that explained anything.

"I'm what?"

"Sobek," she repeated because repetition always makes things clearer.

"What's a Sobek?"

"You are. That is your nature, your Ba."

This conversation was growing no less confusing, but it seemed Kayla finally had someone who had a few answers about her nature, answers that she could explore. But first she had to figure out what to do with Itza. She was Kayla's problem because Nietzche-cheese and his buddy Zappy would come for her again, and Kayla had the only weapon that could stop them. A weapon she wasn't going to turn over to anybody else. It was too dangerous. Then again, having this Itza stay in Portland was dangerous.

Life was dangerous.

"What happens when you recover?"

"I will hunt and kill Epizotal."

"And her two goons?"

"They as well."

"What's to stop them from attacking this Tamoanchan place again to hurt you?"

"You."

"Say what?"

"Your protection of me will extend to Tamoanchan. If I am welcome here, they can no longer hurt me that way."

Well, hell. That pretty much sealed it. Kayla couldn't see sending her out of Portland in such bad condition. She'd be a sitting duck, and her death would be on Kayla's head. Add in the fact that the Itza-pop's sole chance at healing lay here in Portland, she couldn't say no.

She sighed. "You can take the room upstairs at the end of the hall," she said finally. "I can help you clear it out later. But just to be clear, if you start any trouble or hurt anybody, you won't be welcome here anymore."

The god nodded. "I will not."

"Kayla? Can I talk to you? In private?" Ray didn't wait for an answer, grabbing her elbow and drawing her away into the dining room.

Oh great. Their first fight as a couple. That didn't take long. Kayla braced herself for the argument.

Ray pulled her around to face him. "I know you have to do this and I get why, but I'm not letting you live here alone with her. She lives here, so do I."

His brows rose, waiting for her to protest. Like that was going to happen. Have him with her every night? Sounded like Christmas morning to her.

"Are you going to wrap yourself in a bow, too?"

"What?"

"That's what you do with presents, right?"

His slow smile made her stomach flutter. "If you want me in a bow, you've got it."

"We may need a bigger bed. I'm not sure we'll both fit in mine."

He put his hands on her hips and pulled her against him. "I'm okay with tight quarters."

She put her arms around him. "Come to think of it, so am I. But I still want a bow. You can leave off the other wrapping."

His grin widened. "Why, Kayla Reese, I like the way you think."

"But there is one thing I need you to do," she said soberly.

His smile faded. "What's that?"

"I need you to train with your magic. Raven said if you had some, you wouldn't have been hurt like you were."

"The past few days have convinced me I need to get my shit together and do it."

"Really?"

"Really, but you've got to do something for me, too."

"Anything."

He brushed his knuckles along her cheek. "No more hiding in the shadows. No more keeping secrets from me, no matter how bad you think they are. There's never going to be anything bad enough to make me walk away."

"You two going to take all day?" Zach asked from the doorway.

Ray glared. "Do you not know the meaning of privacy?"

"Sure. But I also know it's rude to leave guests standing around without any refreshments. I'm hungry. Came to tell you I rifled the fridge and I'm going to fix us all something to eat." He glanced at a nonexistent watch on his wrist. "That gives you kids forty-five minutes to do . . . whatever." He grinned. "But take it upstairs, will you? I don't know how thin the walls are, and the last thing I need is to be scarred for life by hearing you two getting down and dirty."

Ray flipped him off. Zach laughed and headed into the kitchen. Ray looked back at Kayla.

"Much as I'd like to carry you upstairs, I'm not going to rush through our first time like teenagers in the back of a car, and I'm sure as hell not going to have Logan hanging around."

Kayla's cheeks flushed. "Your way or the highway?"

His lips curved, and he slid his hands under her shirt and pulled her tight against him. His lips brushed hers. "Our first time is going to be private, and we may not leave the bed for days."

Shivers ran over her skin where he touched. "We might get hungry."

"Sometimes you have to make sacrifices."

"Talk about sacrifices . . ." Kayla pulled away reluctantly. "I'd better put that sword some place safe."

He kept hold of her hand. "You're really going to be okay with me moving in? If this is going too fast for you, we can take this slower. I can move into another bedroom. We can spend time getting to know each other again."

Her head cocked. "Is that what you want?"

"I want you to not have any regrets."

Kayla smiled, reaching up to smooth the furrow between his brows. "I have regrets, but being with you isn't going to be one of them."

His fingers tightened, his eyes searching hers. "You're sure?"

She nodded. "I want this."

"Good."

He pulled her tight against him and kissed her. It was raw with need, yet tender. He explored her, his lips and tongue asking and giving at the same time. His hands roved over her, his body quaking with the force of his emotions. Everything about his touch promised things Kayla never thought she could have. Not with him, not with anyone. A connection so deep and sweeping she didn't know if she could contain it.

Kayla held tight to Ray, her body melting into his as heat scorched through her. Her mind spun, and she couldn't manage a coherent thought. It was like riding fireworks into space, going higher and higher, racing for the explosion of color and light. She wanted him to know just how much she wanted him, how much she trusted and loved him. She pressed closer, trying to show him all she felt. One of his arms clenched around her lower back while the other hand twisted into her hair and held her as though he never meant to let her go.

She didn't know how long the kiss went on before he pulled back, his dark gaze boring into hers, his breath warm against her lips.

"Holy shit." It sounded like a prayer.

He brushed his lips against hers again as if he couldn't stop himself. She made a little annoyed sound when he pulled away again, her fingers digging into his hips as she tried to keep him from moving away. He smiled with satisfaction, his gaze dropping to her mouth.

"We don't stop now, I'm not sure I won't have you naked on the table in the next minute or two," he said roughly.

She caught her breath, his words sending ropes of electricity zinging through her. Goosebumps ran down to her heels, and desire tightened in her belly. She couldn't help glancing at the table, imagining what it would be like to have Ray inside her as she lay back on it.

"I wouldn't complain." Her own voice came out low and hoarse.

"Don't fucking tempt me. I'm holding on with my fingernails here."

"You're the one who suggested it."

"It wasn't a suggestion."

"Could have fooled me."

He groaned and wrenched himself away, taking a step back. He ran his fingers down the side of her face as if he couldn't resist touching her. "Help me out here, Kayla. I really don't need Logan offering his critique of my performance."

She giggled. "He would, too." She raised her hands in defeat. All right. I'll behave. But just for the record, you're the one who started it."

From the kitchen came laughter. Three days ago she'd never have imagined she'd have guests—friends—in her house. Three days ago she'd never have dreamed she'd talk to Ray again, much less be moving in together. Loving each other. Three days ago she'd almost skulked off into the fog and given up on herself again.

Not anymore.

Ray held out his hand, and she took it, walking with him into the kitchen. Izta sat beside Raven at the breakfast bar while Zach chopped vegetables.

"A cop, a witch, a technomage, and two gods walk into bar . . ." Kayla murmured. It sounded like the beginning of a joke. But it wasn't a joke. It was her life. And dammit, she liked it.

The End

Acknowledgments

When I was a kid, I had a shirt that said, "I'm too lazy to work and too nervous to steal." I think of that from time to time when I'm writing. Sometimes it feels almost lazy (in fact decadently so) to be a writer because I love the job so much. Sometimes it's painfully hard work, too, but I try not to dwell on that. The point is, I couldn't do this amazing job without readers like you who buy my books and recommend them to libraries and tell your friends and write reviews. You are truly the best readers in the world. I thank you so very much.

Writing in my house doesn't happen without the support of my family. They pick up the slack when I am deep in the work zone, and they bring me food and tea when I imprison myself in my office. I am so lucky to have such wonderful children and an amazing husband.

With all my books, I send a draft out to my beta readers who will read and give me honest feedback. With this book, I struggled with some of the elements and desperately needed that feedback. Thanks to Christy Keyes, Donald Kirby, Adrienne Middleton, Theresa Johnson Miller, and Heather Osborne.

Every good book needs an editor, and mine is fabulous. Deb Dixon is generous, understanding, and helpful, but on top of that, she's an amazing editor. She understands what I'm going for and helps me get there. Thank you for always being such a great support, Deb!

A lot of work in books goes on behind the scenes. Though I do the heavy lifting of writing, others help me focus, help me stay on task, talk out plot threads with me, and so many other things. Devon Monk, you are the best writing partner ever! The Word Warriors so helped motivate me. R.J. Blaine bribed and coerced me, and I love her for it. Lucienne Diver helped make this book possible.

I want to also thank all the staff at Bell Bridge, who do so much for me. I love you.

I know I've missed thanking some people, and I apologize for that. I sometimes have the memory of a steel sieve. Know that I appreciate everything you've done and continue to do for me. I'm so blessed to have so many good people supporting me. You're the best.

About the Author

DIANA PHARAOH FRANCIS is the acclaimed author of more than a dozen novels of fantasy and urban fantasy. Her books have been nominated for the Mary Roberts Rinehart Award and RT Magazine's Best Urban Fantasy. Find out more about her at dianapfrancis.com.

CPSIA information can be obtained
at www.ICGtesting.com
Printed in the USA
LVHW092056220820
663870LV00006B/483